"PASSION SMOLDERS...
KRENTZ IS A MASTER...
The characters are the heart of the
book and the reason why she has
sold more than 23 million
copies of her novels."
—*The Seattle Times*

"SPARKS FLY."
—*Publishers Weekly*

From the New York [...] *Found comes a new* [...] *and riveting passio* [...] *house full of secrets—and danger . . .*

A con artist and seductress, Meredith Spooner lived fast—and died young. But her final scam—embezzling more than a million dollars from a college endowment fund—is coming back to haunt Leonora Hutton. The tainted money is stashed away in an offshore account for Leonora. And while she wants nothing to do with the cash, she discovers two other items in the safe-deposit box: a book about Mirror House—the place where Meredith engineered her final deception—and a set of newspaper stories about an unsolved murder that occurred there thirty years ago.

Now Leonora has an offer for Thomas Walker, another victim of Meredith's scams and seductions. She'll hand over the money—if he helps her figure out what's going on. Meredith had described Thomas as "a man you can trust." But in a fun house–mirror world of illusion and distortion, Leonora may be out of her league . . .

"Quick and witty and the romance sizzles . . . What else could you want?"
                                          —*The Columbia (SC) State*

continued . . .

SF

SMOKE IN
MIRRORS

Jayne Ann Krentz

JOVE BOOKS, NEW YORK

SMOKE IN MIRRORS

A Jove Book / published by arrangement with
G. P. Putnam's Sons

PRINTING HISTORY
G. P. Putnam's Sons hardcover edition / January 2002
Jove edition / November 2002

Visit our website at
www.penguinputnam.com

ISBN: 0-515-13399-X

A JOVE BOOK®
Jove Books are published by The Berkley Publishing Group,
a division of Penguin Putnam Inc.,
375 Hudson Street, New York, New York 10014.
JOVE and the "J" design
are trademarks belonging to Penguin Putnam Inc.

PRINTED IN THE UNITED STATES OF AMERICA

10 9 8 7 6 5 4 3 2 1

For Alberta Castle,
mom and role model,
with love

Prologue

The hallucinations were worsening rapidly.

She halted at the top of the staircase and tried to steady herself. The hall of dark mirrors stretched away into infinity, a treacherous fun house filled with night and shifting shadows. She had to forge a path through this disorienting landscape before she lost her grip on the last remnants of her sanity.

The planes and angles of the shadowed corridor were melting and flowing into bizarre shapes that reminded her of Möbius strips. Endless loops with no beginning and no end. She did not know how much longer she could hold together the disintegrating fragments of her awareness. She longed for sleep but she could not give in to the nearly overwhelming urge. Not yet. There was something she had to do first.

The electricity had flickered out of existence a moment ago. Weak starlight seeped in through the narrow windows at either end of the endless corridor. She gazed down the length of the writhing passage and saw a sharp sliver of silver. She knew it marked the entrance to the library. Fourth door on the left.

A desperate urgency swept through her. If she could get to that shard of light she could leave her message.

"Bethany?" The killer's voice came from shadows at the foot of the stairs. "Where are you? Let me help you. You must be very sleepy by now."

A bolt of icy panic gave her the energy required to overcome the drug's effects for a moment. She tightened her grip on the strap of her purse, staggered a few steps down the hall and came to a stop again. She fought to remember what it was that she had to do. It had been so clear there at the bottom of the stairs. But now it kept slipping away.

She stared into the nearest of the dozens of black mirrors that lined the walls. In the gloom she could just barely make out the heavily gilded and scrolled frame of the eighteenth-century looking glass. She searched the bottomless pool behind the glass for wisps of her memory.

There was something she had to do before she went to sleep.

"I can help you, Bethany."

She thought she saw a shifting of the shadows in the old looking glass. An image gelled there for an instant. She struggled to make sense of it. The library. She had to get to the library. Yes. That was it. She had to go there before the killer found her.

A number swirled up out of the depths of her disappearing memory.

Four.

The entrance to the library was the fourth door on the left.

She clung gratefully to the number. It steadied her as

nothing else could have done. She was at home in the universe of mathematics; comfortable and serenely content in a way she had never been in the world where human emotions made things complicated and illogical.

Four doors down on the left.

Getting there meant running the gauntlet of mirrors. The enormity of the challenge almost paralyzed her.

"There's no need to hide from me, Bethany. I only want to help you."

She had to do this. Deke would need answers. He would not be able to rest until he got them. And Thomas would help him because Deke was his brother and the Walker brothers stuck together. She had never fully understood the depths of that kind of bond, but her logical mind accepted the strength of the link that existed between Deke and Thomas. It was as real as any mathematical relationship.

Summoning every ounce of will she possessed, she made her way toward the shard of light that marked the library door.

The hallucinations intensified. Strange creatures pulsed behind the reflective surfaces of the antique looking glasses that surrounded her. They beckoned her to join them.

Not yet.

She set her teeth and concentrated on putting one foot in front of the other.

She dared not look directly into any of the old, dark mirrors for fear that she would be sucked into the world on the other side. It was not that she was afraid to go there, it was just that she knew she had to stay in this universe for a few more minutes. She owed that much to Deke and Thomas.

"Bethany? You're ill, Bethany. Let me help you."

The killer was in the hallway behind her.

"Not much longer now, Bethany. The hallucinations must be terrible. But soon you'll sleep and then it will all be over."

She focused intently on the triangle of moonlight. The glowing lines drew her and calmed her. The mathematical purity of the moonlit angles was a strong, if temporary, antidote to the hallucinations.

She reached the fourth door, went through it and paused in the middle of an aisle of books, trying to think. There was a small office in here somewhere. And inside the office there was a book. She had been looking at it just this afternoon. It was a very important book because it contained a picture of her killer. She had to mark the picture for Deke and Thomas.

The shelves of books around her curved and warped themselves into a maze. Gathering her waning strength, she staggered through the twisting corridors to the office.

The little book was lying on the desk, just as she remembered. She got it open and stared helplessly at the first page. The picture was here somewhere. She had to find it quickly. The killer was halfway down the hall.

She turned pages, taking refuge once more in the comfort of numbers.

Seventy-nine.

Eighty.

Eighty-one. There it was. A picture of the killer.

There was a pen next to the book. After three attempts she finally managed to pick it up. She was beyond being able to write a name but she had enough eye-hand coordination left to draw a shaky circle around the picture on page eighty-one.

She paused when she finished, concentrating hard.

There was something else she wanted to do just to make sure Deke and Thomas understood.

The envelope, please.

She smiled with satisfaction as the memory blazed clearly in the fog of her thoughts.

The envelope was in the purse draped over her shoulder. She got it out. Managed to slip it inside the book.

Now what?

Hide the book and the envelope. She could not risk having the killer discover them.

"I know where you are, Bethany. Did you think you could hide in the library?"

She looked around, searching for a place in which to conceal the book and the envelope.

The large, old-fashioned wooden card catalog stood against one wall, the rows of little drawers neatly organized in lovely straight lines.

Perfect.

"Mirror, mirror on the wall," the killer chanted from the door of the library. *"Who is the smartest one of all? Not you, Bethany. Not Sebastian Eubanks, either. I'm the smartest one of all, Bethany."*

She ignored the taunting and wedged the book with the envelope inside into the hiding place. Deke and Thomas would find it sooner or later.

It was done. A sense of peace flowed through her. She had completed the task. She could sleep now. She turned around, clutching the desk for support.

The killer came to stand silhouetted in the office doorway.

"I'm the smartest one of all, Bethany."

Bethany Walker did not respond. She closed her eyes and slipped into a peaceful world on the other side of the looking glass, where the laws of mathematics reigned supreme and everything made sense.

Chapter One

A shifting of the light reflected in the mirror above the dresser was the only warning she had that she was not alone in the dead woman's apartment. Her hands went cold. The fine hair on the nape of her neck stirred as if she had been zapped with an electrical charge.

Leonora straightened swiftly from the drawer she had been searching and spun around, a soft, pale pink cashmere sweater in her hands.

Two junkyard dogs stood in the doorway of the bedroom.

One of them was human.

His broad shoulders filled a lot of the available space and cut off the view of the hall behind him. There was about him the deceptively relaxed, totally centered grace of the natural-born predator. Not an impulsive young hunter overeager to take down the first of the prey that bolts from cover, rather a jaded pro who prefers to pick and choose his targets. He had the face of a man who had done a lot of things in life the hard way and he also had the cold gray eyes to match.

The ghost-gray beast at his heels had a lot in common with his companion. Not real big, but very solid. One of his ears was permanently bent, the result of a fight, no doubt. It was difficult to imagine this creature springing playfully in pursuit of a Frisbee. Probably tear the thing to shreds and eat the plastic raw.

Both of the intruders looked dangerous but her intuition told her to keep her eyes on the man. She could not see his hands. They were thrust casually into the deep pockets of a charcoal-colored windbreaker. He wore the lightweight jacket open over a button-down denim shirt and a pair of khaki trousers. His feet were shod in leather work boots. The boots looked large.

Both man and beast were damp from the rain that misted this stretch of the southern California coast today. Each gave the impression that going for her throat would be no big deal. All in a morning's work.

"Were you a friend of hers or did you just happen to hear that she was dead and decide to drop in to see if there was anything worth stealing?" the human junkyard dog asked.

His voice suited him. A low, dark, very soft growl.

She got a grip on her hyperactive imagination. "Who are you?"

"I asked you first. Which is it, friend or casual opportunist? Either way, I figure you're a thief so maybe the answer is moot."

"How dare you?" Outrage incinerated some of the alarm that had quickened her pulse. "I am not a thief. I'm a librarian." Damn, that sounded dumb. Well, no one could say that she couldn't hold her own when it came to snappy repartee, she thought.

"No kidding." His mouth curved into a mockery of a smile. "Looking for overdue books? You should have known better than to give Meredith Spooner a library card. Doubt if she ever returned anything she stole in her entire life."

"Your sense of humor leaves a lot to be desired."

"I'm not auditioning for a late-night comedy show."

One had to be forceful in situations such as this, Leonora thought. Take the initiative. Take charge. Gain the upper hand with a show of confidence and authority. It wasn't as though she had not had some experience with difficult people. In the course of her career as an academic librarian she was occasionally obliged to deal with a variety of obnoxious patrons, from egotistical, demanding faculty members to boorish frat boys.

She went deliberately toward the door, praying that the stranger and his dog would step back in that automatic way most creatures did when you made it clear that you wanted to move past them.

"As a matter of fact I have every right to be here, which is probably a good deal more than you can say." She gave man and dog a steely smile. "I suggest we discuss this with the apartment manager."

"The manager's busy. Something about a plumbing emergency down on the third floor. I have a feeling we'd both rather deal with this privately, anyway. Got a name?"

It became glaringly apparent that neither he nor the dog was going to get out of her way. She was forced to halt in the middle of the room.

"Of course I've got a name," she said crisply. "But I don't see any reason why I should give it to you."

"Let me take a wild guess. Leonora Hutton?"

She froze. "How did you know?"

He shrugged. The easy movement drew her attention once again to the impressive width of his shoulders. The fact that they fascinated her was worrisome. Normally she was not the least bit attracted to male muscle. She preferred the intellectual type.

"Meredith didn't have a long list of friends," he said. "Mostly she just had marks, from what I can tell."

"Marks."

"Marks. Targets. Victims. Dupes. Whatever you call the people she used, conned or fleeced in the course of her scams. But unlike most of the people in her email address book, you and she went back a ways from what I can tell." He paused a beat. "Assuming you're Leonora Hutton, that is."

She set her teeth together. "Yes, all right, I'm Leonora Hutton. Now, who are you?"

"Walker. Thomas Walker." He glanced down at the dog. "This is Wrench."

Wrench tilted his broad head and grinned in response to the sound of his name.

She looked at Wrench's impressive array of teeth. "Does he bite?"

"Nah." Thomas was apparently amused by the question. "Wrench is a real sweetheart. Very nonconfrontational. Probably a miniature poodle in his former life."

She did not believe that for one moment. If Wrench had had a former life he had no doubt lived it as a giant medieval hunting mastiff. But she decided not to make an issue of it.

"We've been waiting for you to show up, Miss Hutton," Thomas said.

She was aghast. *"Waiting* for me?"

"Three days now. Spent most of the time in that coffee shop across the street." He angled his jaw toward the window and the partial view of a block of small shops. "You were the one who claimed the body and made the burial arrangements last week. Figured you'd come to clean out her apartment sooner or later."

"You seem to know a great deal about me."

He smiled. It was the kind of smile that made her want to take a couple of steps back, turn and run for her life. But that would be the worst thing she could do, she told herself. She knew enough about animal behavior to know that predators only got more excited by fleeing prey.

"Not nearly as much as I'd like to know about you, Miss Hutton."

There was nowhere to run, anyway. He had her cornered in this small, barren room. She stood her ground.

"How did you get hold of Meredith's email address book?" she asked.

"That was easy," Thomas said. "I came here and helped myself to her laptop just as soon as I heard the news about the crash."

The casual admission left her speechless for a few seconds.

"You *stole* her computer?" she finally managed to ask.

"Let's just say I borrowed it." He gave her another one of his chilling, humorless smiles. "In the same spirit that she *borrowed* one-point-five million bucks from the Bethany Walker Endowment Fund."

Oh, damn. This was bad. This was very, very bad. Embezzlement had been one of Meredith's favorite sports but her preferred victims had been other cons and scam artists who had not been in a position to complain too loudly. And to the best of Leonora's knowledge, she had never gone after a score of this magnitude. Trust Meredith to go out with a bang, not a whimper.

And trust her to leave me with the mess to clean up.

"Are you a cop?" she asked warily.

"No."

"Private investigator?"

He shook his head. "No."

Not the law. She didn't know if that was good news or bad news.

She cleared her throat. "Did you know Meredith personally?"

"Oh, yeah, I knew her," he said. "Of course, like a lot of folks who had that privilege, I wish I had never met her, but hindsight is always twenty-twenty, isn't it?"

Understanding descended with the inevitability of a shroud.

"I see. You were one of her—" She broke off, searching for a diplomatic turn of phrase. "The two of you were, uh, acquainted socially?"

His mouth was a flat line. "Not for long."

He had been one of Meredith's lovers, then. For some reason that news was oddly depressing. Why should she care whether or not this man had had an affair with Meredith? He certainly wouldn't have been the first. It occurred to her that he might have had the distinction of being the last, however.

"I'm surprised," she said, without stopping to think. "You're not her usual type."

Oh, jeez. What in the world had made her say that?

It was the truth, though. Meredith had had a long-standing policy of sticking to men she could manipulate. Something about Thomas Walker sent a message that he wouldn't play the puppet-on-a-string game for long, not even for a woman as savvy and sexy and as skilled in manipulative techniques as Meredith.

If she could see that stark truth, Leonora thought, Meredith, who'd had preternaturally acute instincts where the male of the species was concerned, had almost certainly seen it also. Maybe that was why the relationship hadn't lasted long.

"Meredith had a type?" Thomas looked mildly surprised by that information. Then he nodded in a thoughtful way. "Well, hell, I guess you're right. She did have some distinct preferences when it came to her social life, didn't she? Far as I can tell she only dated men she figured could help her further her own agenda."

Leonora wondered if the real problem here was that Thomas had been badly hurt when Meredith's true nature was revealed. A broken heart could generate a lot of pain, and pain could produce anger. Maybe he was grieving in his own macho, masculine fashion.

She offered a sympathetic smile.

"I'm sorry," she said very gently.

"Yeah, me, too. More than sorry. When I found out that she had embezzled the one-point-five mil I was kind of pissed off, if you want to know the truth."

Okay, he wasn't exactly prostrate with grief. He was mad.

"Uh—" Inspiration failed her.

"What about you?" Thomas asked much too pleasantly. "Any fond memories of the deceased? How far back did you two go?"

"We met in college. We've kept in touch all these years, but—" She swallowed and tried again. "I didn't see much of her in the past few months."

Not since I found her in bed with my fiancé, she added silently, but she saw no reason to bring up that dismal subject.

"You should probably consider yourself fortunate," Thomas said. "Meredith Spooner was bad news. But, then, I'll bet you already know that."

Old habits were hard to break. The instinct to cover up, defend and make excuses for Meredith kicked in, just as it always did when crunch time hit.

She raised her chin. "Are you absolutely certain Meredith embezzled that money?"

"Positive."

"How did she manage that?"

"Easy. Took a job as an alumni endowment fund development officer at Eubanks College. As the person in charge of the money on a day-to-day basis, she had access to all the accounts and to a lot of wealthy alumni. Add in the fact that she had the morals of a con artist and great computer skills and you have the recipe for embezzlement."

"If what you say is true, why are you here? With that kind of money involved, I would have thought you'd have gone to the police."

"I'm trying to avoid the cops."

"When there's more than a million dollars missing?" She saw a chance to go on the offensive and grabbed it. "That sounds very suspicious to me. It certainly casts some doubts on your story, Mr. Walker."

"I want to avoid the cops because that kind of bad publicity can really hurt an endowment fund. Undermines the faith of potential donors. Makes them question the integrity of the folks entrusted with the responsibility for managing the money, know what I mean?"

She'd had enough experience with the delicate politics of academic endowment fund-raising to realize that he had a point. But that was no reason to let him off the hook. Besides, he didn't look at all like the kind of person who got involved in college endowments. That business was run by suave, cultured types who wore good suits and who knew how to make nice with wealthy alumni.

She gave him her most polished smile. "I think I'm getting the picture here. My turn to take a wild guess. Could it be that you haven't reported the missing money to the authorities, Mr. Walker, because for some reason you think you might be a prime suspect?"

His dark brows rose in silent appreciation of the direct hit. "Close, Miss Hutton. Not quite on target, but very, very close."

"I knew it."

"Meredith left a trail that would point to my brother, Deke, if the embezzlement is exposed."

"Your brother." She digested that slowly. "Where exactly is the headquarters of this Bethany Walker Fund?"

"It's part of the alumni endowment of Eubanks College. It was set up to support research and teaching in the field of mathematics."

"Eubanks?" She frowned. "I'm not familiar with that institution."

"It's a small college in a little town called Wing Cove. About an hour and a half's drive north of Seattle."

"I see."

"The fund is named for Deke's wife, Bethany, a brilliant mathematician. She died last year. Deke is the head of the board that oversees the fund's operations and investments. In three months there will be an audit. If that money turns up missing, he will look like the guy responsible for making it disappear, thanks to sweet Meredith."

A typical Meredith operation, Leonora thought. Make sure the victim of the scam won't call the cops.

"I realize how upsetting this must be for you and your brother, Mr. Walker. But I must say, for a man who wants to keep the situation low profile, you seem to be quite chatty on the subject."

"That's because I have a strong interest in recovering the money. I want it back in the fund's account before that damned audit."

"I understand," she said. "But why are you talking to me about this?"

"Simple. You're my best lead."

She stared. "I beg your pardon?"

"Let me put it this way, you're my *only* lead."

Panic shot through her. "But I don't know anything about that missing money."

"Yeah?" He looked unconvinced. "Let's say for the sake of argument that you're telling me the truth—"

"I *am* telling you the truth."

"Even if that is the case, you're still my only lead."

"Why?"

"Because you knew Meredith better than anyone else, as far as I can tell. I'm really hoping that you can help me out here, Miss Hutton."

In your dreams, Leonora thought. "I just told you, I didn't have much contact with her this past year. I wasn't even aware that she had a job at Eubanks College. I didn't know she was living here in this apartment until the authorities contacted me after the accident."

"No kidding. According to the manager, she used your name on the rental application."

Leonora said nothing. It wasn't the first time Meredith had borrowed her good name and credit references.

"I doubt that she intended to stay here long." Thomas surveyed the room with its bare-bones furnishings and uninspiring view. "Probably just needed a staging area and an address she could use while she set up her next scam."

"Look, I really don't know what to say. I can't help you, Mr. Walker. I'm only here to pack up Meredith's belongings. I intend to donate most of her stuff to a local thrift shop. When that job is done, I'm going straight home. I have reservations on an evening flight. I'm supposed to be at work in the morning."

"Home is Melba Creek, right? Outside of San Diego?"

She tried to ignore the unsettling sensation that trickled through her. "Okay, so you know where I live. Is that supposed to scare me?"

"I'm not trying to scare you, Miss Hutton. I'm trying to work with you."

"Uh huh."

"I've got a business proposition for you."

"Give me one good reason why I should listen to it."

"I'll give you a couple. The first is that if you cooperate with me and help me locate the money, I'll see to it that you get a finder's fee."

"Let me get this straight. You'll bribe me to return the money?"

"Beats going to prison for embezzlement, doesn't it?"

"Prison?" She did take a reflexive step back at that. Wrench shifted a little in response and looked interested. She froze. "Why would I be arrested? You said your brother was the one who would appear guilty if that money isn't found."

"I don't intend for my brother to take the fall for Meredith's embezzlement scam," Thomas said softly. "If that money isn't back in the account before the next audit, I'm going to make sure the cops look real hard at you."

"How?"

"Deke is a wizard when it comes to computers. I'm pretty good on the financial side. Shouldn't be too difficult to create a trail from Meredith to you."

"Me?" She was dumbfounded. "But I had nothing to do with Meredith's embezzlement."

"Who knows? Maybe you'll even be able to prove that in the end. But I can arrange to make life damn miserable for you in the meantime. Tell me, how do you think your employer would react if it got out that you were being investigated for embezzlement?"

"How dare you threaten to drag me into this mess!"

He took one hand out of his pocket. It was a very large, powerful, competent-looking hand, the hand of a man who worked with tools or climbed rocks. Not the soft, manicured hand of a businessman.

He spread his fingers in a fait-accompli gesture.

"In case you haven't noticed, Miss Hutton, you're already in this mess. Right up to your very nice ears."

"How can you say that?"

"You're the closest thing to a friend that Meredith had, as far as I can tell. In my book that makes you the closest thing she had to a partner."

"I wasn't her partner."

"The two of you have a history. You're the only person she kept in touch with through thick and through thin. I'm pretty sure that with a little help from Deke, I can make you look like her accomplice."

"My God, you're serious, aren't you?"

"With one-and-a-half million, plus my brother's reputation on the line? Yeah, Miss Hutton, I'm damned serious. Cooperate with me. Help me find the money and we can both walk away from this without anyone having to hire a lawyer."

"Just where do you think I would stash that kind of cash?"

"At this point, all I know for sure is that it's not in your personal bank account."

She felt her jaw drop. "You checked?"

"First thing after I found your name in Meredith's email address book."

"How?"

"I told you, my brother is good with computers."

"That kind of invasion of privacy is illegal. I could have you arrested."

"No shit. I'll have to remember that for future reference."

She glared. "And you have the nerve to accuse me of criminal behavior."

"Go figure."

"I don't believe this." She felt dazed. "It's beyond bizarre."

He looked almost amused. "Be grateful. You've got the easy part. All you have to do is help me find the money."

She watched him warily. "What's the hard part? Getting it back into the endowment fund?"

"No. That will be simple. The hard part is going to be convincing my brother that Meredith Spooner wasn't murdered."

She felt the air leave her lungs in a rush. Stunned, she gazed at him, her mind a complete blank for about three full seconds.

"The police didn't say anything about murder," she finally got out.

"That's because they didn't find any evidence to indicate the crash was anything other than an accident," he said. "Probably because there wasn't any."

She got the feeling he'd had this conversation a number of times in recent days.

"But your brother takes another view of the situation?" she asked.

"Deke is—" He broke off, apparently searching for the right word. "Some people think he's a little obsessed with his theory that his wife, Bethany, was murdered a year ago. When he heard about Meredith's accident he leaped to the conclusion that the killer had struck again."

"Good grief. What do *you* think?"

Thomas was silent for a time. Wrench leaned heavily against his leg, as though offering support.

She thought that Thomas might brush off the question with all its horrifying implications. But to her amazement he just shook his head.

"I don't know," he said eventually.

"You don't *know*? What is that supposed to mean? We're talking about murder, here."

"Look, all I can tell you is that a year ago when Bethany died, I didn't think there was any question about what had happened. The official verdict was suicide. Unfortunately, it seemed to fit the circumstances and there was no evidence of violence."

"Was there a note?"

"No. But that's not as unusual as people think."

"Suicide is always so difficult for those who knew the victim. No wonder your brother is looking for other answers. But what is it about Meredith's death that makes him think there's a connection?"

"Not much," Thomas admitted. "Meredith didn't arrive in Wing Cove until six months after Bethany died. The two never even met. But Deke is trying to see patterns where none exist. The only thing Meredith and Bethany had in common as far as I know was that each of them spent a lot of time at Mirror House."

"What is Mirror House?"

"The headquarters of the Eubanks College Alumni Association."

"That's it? They worked in the same place? That's the only connection you've got?"

He hesitated briefly. "The only solid one."

"No offense to your brother, but that's extremely weak."

"I'm aware of that, Miss Hutton." Thomas's voice was grim. "Like I said, Deke has had a difficult time coming to terms with Bethany's death. I've done my best to discourage his conspiracy theories. I thought I was making progress in the past few months. He seemed to be coming out of his depression, at least. But Meredith's death has set him off again."

She replayed his earlier comment in her head. "Wait a second. You said the fact that Bethany and Meredith worked in the same place was the only solid link between the two deaths. Are there other, less substantial connections?"

"Maybe," he said slowly. "One possibility, at any rate."

His obvious reluctance told her that he was not buying into his brother's conspiracy theory completely, but that he felt obligated to give it some credence. A family loyalty thing, probably. She knew only too well how that worked.

"What?" she asked when he offered no further details.

"After the funeral, there were rumors."

"Rumors?"

"Some local gossip that Bethany may have been experimenting with drugs at the time of the suicide," he said reluctantly. "Deke and I agree that would have been completely out of character. She never did drugs so far as we know."

"Were any drug tests run at the time of her death?"

"There were some routine things done, but there was no reason to go looking for anything exotic that would have required a lot of unique and expensive testing. Small-town law enforcement and medical examiner budgets don't allow for extensive tests unless there's a serious question about the cause of death. She had no history of drug use. Deke had questions about the suicide, but they didn't revolve around drugs. And there's no going back now. Bethany was cremated according to the stipulations in her will."

"Meredith's death was ruled an accident. There was no indication of drugs or alcohol involvement. How do the rumors about Bethany Walker link to her death?"

"After the news of the crash reached us in Wing Cove, there was some gossip that Meredith had been doing drugs while she lived there."

"No," Leonora said flatly.

He narrowed his eyes. "No? You're sure of that?"

"Oh, yes. Very sure. Lord knows, Meredith had her faults, but doing drugs was not one of them. Her mother killed herself with them, you see."

"Huh."

Thomas said nothing more. Just looked thoughtful. Wrench looked bored.

"Traffic accidents happen all the time." She wondered if she was trying to convince him or herself. "And there's no motive for murder."

"I wouldn't say that. One-point-five mil is a lot of money. Let's assume for the sake of argument that Meredith did have a partner. Someone who didn't want to split the profits."

She felt as if she was falling down the rabbit hole. This was getting worse and worse.

"For the last time, I wasn't Meredith's partner," she said tightly. "I knew nothing about this scam you claim she was running at Eubanks College."

"Prove it. Help me find the money she embezzled."

"You're threatening me. I really hate that."

"I've also offered a hefty finder's fee," he reminded her. "Think of it as the carrot-and-stick approach."

"If you don't mind," she said icily, "I've got to finish packing up Meredith's things."

"Which reminds me. I've got a question about that."

"What question?"

"Why are you the one who came here today? Why is it your job to clean out the apartment and deal with the final details of Meredith Spooner's life?"

Leonora looked around at the unadorned walls and the impersonal furnishings. It was difficult to imagine Meredith, always so vivid and exciting, spending the last few days of her life in this plain, dull space.

A great sadness welled up inside Leonora. Meredith had been complicated and frequently maddening. Whenever she had appeared, trouble had followed. But the world would certainly be a less colorful place without her.

"There was no one else to do it," Leonora said.

Chapter Two

Perpetual night infused the interior of Deke's house. The curtains were drawn closed on all the windows even though the low, gray clouds of the cold November afternoon offered no real threat of sunlight. The gloom was relieved only by the eerie glow of the computer screen. It reflected off the lenses of Deke's gold-rimmed glasses and bathed his face and untrimmed beard in an unhealthy light.

Thomas sat in the leather armchair on the other side of the desk, a cup of coffee beside him, Wrench sprawled at his feet, and felt depressed. Whatever progress he had made in the struggle to drag Deke out of the netherworld inside his computer had been lost when the news of Meredith Spooner's death had reached them. Deke had immediately plunged back through the looking glass, searching for connections and patterns to support his theory that Bethany had been murdered.

"Leonora Hutton showed up at the apartment?" Deke

asked. His eagerness was so painfully obvious that it hurt to look at him. "Just like you thought she would?"

"She showed. Said she'd come to pack up Meredith's things."

"Well? What happened? Will she help us?"

"I don't know," Thomas said.

"What do you mean? You told me that she was our only real lead."

"I know." He hesitated. "But she's not quite what I expected."

"How's that?"

Thomas thought about his impressions of Leonora. He was still trying to sort them out. He'd spent most of the time on the trip back to Wing Cove yesterday and a lot of last night on the task, but he hadn't made much headway. No matter how he approached the problem she refused to be stuffed into a neat category.

"She's nothing like Meredith," he said. "Complete opposites, in fact. Reverse images. Day and night."

If Meredith, with a voice that hinted of honey and Texas, golden blond hair and eyes the color of a summer sky, had been the day, Leonora was the night.

"Good twin, bad twin?" Deke suggested.

"Trust me, those two were never twins."

A memory of that first glimpse of Leonora yesterday when she had turned away from the dresser to confront him hovered in his head. The image haunted him like the remnants of a dream he could not shake.

He saw her again now in his mind and tried to employ a measure of objectivity. She had been dressed in a pair of dark green trousers and a green pullover. Her dark hair had been caught up in a French twist. Stylish, black-rimmed glasses emphasized her green eyes and the striking planes and angles of an intelligent face that had fascinated him for some inexplicable reason. So much so that he had had to make an effort to look away, even for a few seconds. She had worn little if any detectable makeup. Not a woman who traded on her looks the way Meredith had, he thought.

Within five seconds of meeting her he had known that Leonora was a lot like him in one respect. She was accustomed to going after what she wanted. Probably didn't give up easily, either, once she had set herself a goal.

"What did she say about the finder's fee?" Deke asked.

"Called it a bribe. Then I sort of implied that if the police got involved they might look in her direction to find the money, what with her being such a good friend of Meredith's and all."

Deke was startled. "How did that go over?"

"I don't think she liked being threatened."

"No big surprise there, I guess." Deke gazed into the oracle that was his glowing computer screen. "I've been thinking about the money."

"What about it?"

"In a way, it's the least of our problems."

"Got news for you, Deke, when the audit turns up more than a million missing from the fund we're going to have a big problem."

"I'll replace the money before the audit. No one will ever know it disappeared."

"Replace it? Just where do you plan to get that kind of cash?"

"I'll liquidate some accounts."

"The hell you will," Thomas said softly. "I'm your investment manager, remember? Damned if I'll let you take that kind of a bath."

"I can replace it. Take a few consulting assignments."

"Forget it. Meredith Spooner stole that money. We're going to get it back."

Deke smiled slightly.

"What?" Thomas said.

"Nothing. Just that when it comes to finding that missing money you're starting to sound as obsessed as I am about figuring out who murdered Bethany."

"It's the principle of the thing, damn it."

"Yeah," Deke said. "Gotta love those principle things."

Thomas slumped deeper into the chair. "We're getting a reputation around here, you know. They're calling us the 'crazy Walker brothers.'"

"I heard."

They sat together in the gloom for a while. Wrench stretched, changed position slightly and went back to sleep.

"We need to find the money," Thomas said eventually, "because it's our only shot at figuring out whether or not you're right about Bethany and Meredith being murdered."

"What's this? You mean you're starting to buy into my conspiracy theory?"

"Let's just say that my conversation with Leonora raised some questions I'd like to see answered."

"What questions?"

"You know that stuff about the drugs?"

Deke's hand clenched fiercely around a pen. "What about it? Bethany didn't do drugs."

Thomas reached down to scratch Wrench's ears. "Leonora Hutton swears Meredith didn't use them, either."

"No shit?" Deke put down the pen, sat back and combed his fingers through his untidy beard. "And yet the same rumors are circulating. Now that is interesting."

"Yeah."

"You knew Meredith pretty well there for a while," Deke said. "What do you think about those drug rumors we heard?"

Thomas hesitated. It was a little weird to realize that you could sleep with a woman a few times and not know something as fundamental as whether or not she used illicit chemicals. All he could truthfully say was that she hadn't used them when she was with him and he'd never seen any indication that she had been under the influence.

"I can't be sure, but if I had to guess, I'd say Meredith Spooner was too focused on her scams to risk messing herself up with drugs," he said finally.

"Just as Bethany was too focused on her work to fool around with them. It's another link, admit it."

"Okay." Thomas sighed. "We've got two links. Maybe. Both women spent a lot of time at Mirror House and both women are rumored to have used drugs even though there was no evidence they had done any at the time of death and everyone who knew them well claims they wouldn't have used them at all."

There was a short silence.

"Not much to go on, is it?" Deke asked wearily.

"No."

"Maybe Leonora Hutton will turn out to be the key," Deke said.

Thomas did not respond. He wasn't sure whether or not he wanted Leonora Hutton to be the key to this thing.

The rain had stopped by the time Thomas and Wrench left Deke's house but the damp chill bit deep. The clouds hung low and heavy, obscuring what little light was left in the short day. The fir trees dripped and the grass at the edge of the path was muddy. The surface of the bone-chilling water in the cove was agitated and choppy, as though some monstrous denizen of the deep was roaming about down below in search of prey.

Thomas snapped on Wrench's leash and together they headed for the footpath that would take them home. Wrench didn't need a leash, but people got nervous if they saw him without one. Thomas empathized. People sometimes got the wrong impression about him, too. Maybe that's why he and Wrench had hit it off right from the start, he thought. They were both innocent victims of their genetic inheritances.

The paved path followed the outline of the cove. At this time of day the traffic was fairly heavy. Joggers, runners and power walkers jockeyed for position. Those, including Wrench and himself, who moved at a more leisurely pace were expected to give way to others who took their fitness seriously.

Several dogs bobbed at the ends of leashes. Wrench acknowledged a chocolate Lab and a retriever as equals and politely ignored a fluffy little white powder puff that wanted desperately to be best buddies.

Wing Cove was tucked into a densely forested stretch of landscape that bordered Puget Sound. Under other circumstances, Thomas thought, he would have liked the place a lot better, in spite of the fact that it was heavily oriented toward the academic crowd. The cove itself was aptly named. It roughly resembled the shape of a gull's wing in flight. The widest section was at the entrance where it connected with the Sound. The town was located at the far tip of the wing. A sprinkling of houses and cottages was scattered on the wooded hillsides that rose up from the water's edge.

Wrench led the way to the narrow footbridge that crossed the cove at midwing. The wooden bridge provided a shortcut to the opposite side. The route saved less enthusiastic exercisers from having to go through town or all the way to the cove's entrance to use the highway bridge.

When they ambled off the footbridge at the far side Thomas saw a white SUV bearing the blue-and-gold logo of the Wing Cove Police Department parked near the edge of the path.

He recognized Ed Stovall, the chief of police, behind
the wheel and raised a hand in casual greeting. Ed rolled
down the window and nodded brusquely.

"Evening," Ed said. There was an edge to the greeting.

He was a small, compact man with thinning hair and
no discernible sense of humor. Ed always seemed a little
too rigid as far as Thomas was concerned. He figured the
guy for a frustrated military commando wanna-be or an
ex-Marine.

Then again, he and Deke were biased against Stovall.
They had locked horns with him more than once during
the months following Bethany's death.

Ed had handled the investigation. When he had called
it a suicide and everyone else, including the medical examiner, had gone along, Deke had protested. Loudly. Stovall had not been real happy when Deke had insisted that
there was an unidentified killer running around tiny Wing
Cove.

The college administration hadn't been particularly
thrilled with Deke's conspiracy theory, either. Wing Cove
was a company town and Eubanks College, the community's largest employer, was the company that made the
rules. The trustees and the alumni were a conservative
bunch. In Thomas's opinion, the college administration
was obsessed with the reputation of the institution. But
he had to admit that he could see their point on the subject of campus safety. A campus that acquired a reputation for violence made parents nervous. Nervous parents
sent their offspring elsewhere for higher ed. Every tuition
fee counted at a small institution like Eubanks.

Although he understood where Stovall and the campus
authorities were coming from, Thomas had had no choice
but to back Deke's request for a more thorough investigation of Bethany's death. Push come to shove, the Walker

brothers stood together even when one of them was privately convinced that the other had gone off the deep end.

"Hello, Ed." Thomas came to a halt beside the SUV's front window. Wrench sniffed at a tire. "Keeping an eye out for speeding joggers?"

Ed did not smile. Thomas had never seen him smile.

"Had a few minutes," Ed said in his serious Ed tone. "Got a cup of coffee. Came down here to drink it. Nice here this time of day."

Thomas realized Ed was not looking at him. He was watching the crowd on the footpath. Thomas followed his gaze. It appeared to be focused on a woman in pale sweats, walking briskly and determinedly at the edge of the path. She looked to be in her late thirties, attractive in a serious sort of way. There was something very focused about the way she moved. He got the feeling she was working off some heavy stress.

He glanced back at Ed and recognized the expression. Any male would have understood it. Ed had it bad for the lady in the light-colored sweats. For a couple of seconds he even felt a twinge of sympathy. Then he reminded himself that this was Stovall, who thought Deke was crazy.

"Friend of yours?" Thomas asked.

"We've met a few times," Ed said. Very offhand. "We both spend a lot of time at the Hidden Cove."

The Hidden Cove was one of the town's two bookstores. Thomas was mildly surprised to discover that Ed read. Police procedural mysteries and high-tech military thrillers, no doubt.

Thomas watched the woman. "Who is she?"

"Elissa Kern. Professor Kern's daughter."

"Didn't know he had one."

"Elissa told me that her parents were divorced when

she was five. She and her mother moved away. Didn't see much of her dad for a long time. Elissa got divorced, herself, last year. Came back here to get to know her father." Ed took a swallow of coffee and lowered the cup. "Don't think it's working out. Kern's got a problem with the bottle. Only reason he hasn't been fired is because he's got tenure."

"I heard."

Everyone in town knew that Dr. Osmond J. Kern, distinguished professor of mathematics, was slowly drinking himself to death. Bethany had been a great admirer of Kern's and had always spoken highly of him. The professor had made his name and reputation nearly thirty years ago with his work on an algorithm that had won prestigious prizes in mathematics and had proved enormously important to the computer industry. He hadn't done anything else of note before or since as far as Thomas knew. But, then, Kern hadn't needed to do much more than show up occasionally for classes and seminars. As Ed had just pointed out, Kern's work on the algorithm had been his ticket to academic nirvana: tenure.

Elissa Kern was almost directly in front of the SUV now. Ed watched her with a tight, stoic expression. She noticed the vehicle parked in the deepening shadows. Thomas thought her tense expression lightened a little. She did not pause but she raised her hand in greeting.

Ed responded by lifting his own hand six whole inches.

Seething passion, Ed Stovall style.

But who was he to judge? Thomas thought. Not like he was getting any seething passion, himself, these days.

"Hey, Ed, you hear those rumors about Meredith Spooner doing drugs?"

Ed's gaze followed Elissa as she moved off down the footpath. "I heard."

"Yesterday I met someone who knew her pretty well.

She said that Meredith had a thing about drugs. Claimed she wouldn't have used them. That strike you as familiar?"

Ed sighed and pulled his attention away from Elissa's disappearing backside. "We've been over this ground before, Walker."

"Just thought I'd mention it."

"Sounds like your brother is working on a new conspiracy theory. Tell him not to waste his time. The investigation into Bethany Walker's death is closed and it will stay that way unless you've got some solid evidence to show me."

"Sure, Ed. Always good to know you're keeping an open mind."

"Best thing you could do for your brother is get him to a shrink." Ed switched on the SUV's ignition. "Might not be a bad idea if you had a chat with one, yourself. You're starting to sound like you're buying into Deke's fantasy."

Wrench chose that moment to lift his leg beside the front tire of the SUV.

Fortunately, Ed did not notice the canine insult. He was too busy looking back over his shoulder to check for traffic behind the SUV. He put the vehicle in gear and drove away down a narrow lane.

Wrench came to stand quietly beside Thomas.

"That was very passive-aggressive of you, Wrench."

Wrench grinned.

"Okay, maybe I am getting as bad as Deke," Thomas said. "But at least I'm not parking in the trees down here near the footpath to watch a woman do her daily exercise routine. A man's gotta be desperate to do that."

Wrench looked up at him.

"All right, so we hung around that apartment down in L.A. for a while waiting for Leonora Hutton to show up. Different matter entirely. That was business."

He and Wrench continued along the footpath at their own easy pace, ignoring the thundering herd. A short while later they turned off the path to follow a lane up the wooded hillside to the house in the trees.

Thomas paused on the porch to dig out his key and open the door. Inside the small foyer he unleashed Wrench. He removed his jacket and hung it in the closet. Wrench went into the kitchen to find his water bowl.

There was a chill in the house. Thomas paused in the front room to light the fire. When the blaze was crackling properly he rose and walked between the two large recliners positioned in front of the hearth to the counter that divided the kitchen and living areas.

Virtually every surface gleamed in these rooms. Ditto the bathroom and front hall. It had taken him several months to complete the tile project. Sometimes he wondered if he'd gone a little overboard.

He checked the phone for messages. There were none. Leonora Hutton had not called.

He opened a cupboard, took a doggie treat out of a large bag and tossed it to Wrench. Wrench crunched happily away on the fake bone.

"Supposed to be good for your teeth," Thomas said.

Wrench did not appear to be concerned about his teeth.

It was hard to explain good oral hygiene to a dog that had been blessed with excellent teeth. Thomas abandoned the attempt, opened the door beside the refrigerator and went into his favorite room in the house, his workshop.

He switched on the light. Ranks of gleaming tools were neatly arranged on the walls. Pliers, screwdrivers, wrenches, all were organized according to size and type. Storage chests with clear plastic windows on the drawers held precisely sorted nails and screws. A sack of grout left over from the recent marathon tile project stood in the corner.

He walked to the large wooden table in the center of the room and lounged against it next to the drill press. He did his best thinking in this room and right now he wanted to think about Leonora Hutton.

Night and day. Reverse images in a mirror.

He'd been so damn sure what to expect from the woman he assumed had been Meredith's partner. But Leonora baffled him. She hadn't even tried to seduce him. He told himself he shouldn't take it personally. Still, he had a feeling it would have been an interesting experience. A lot more interesting than it had been with Meredith.

Sex had been a precision tool for Meredith. She had wielded it with professional competence. As far as he had been able to tell, she hadn't taken any real pleasure in the work itself, though. All she had cared about was the end result which, as he had learned the hard way, had nothing to do with an orgasm. But like any good craftsman, she had taken care of her equipment and kept it clean.

That had been enough for him for a short time. For her part, Meredith had not asked him to pretend a depth of feeling that they both knew did not exist. Looking back, he knew now that she had been content to terminate the relationship as soon as she had realized that he wasn't going to give her anything she could use to further her embezzlement scam.

Meredith had been a con artist, a professional liar and a thief. But when you got right down to it, she was not a mystery. He was pretty sure he understood what had made her tick.

Leonora, on the other hand, was a mystery.

He thought about the mysterious Leonora and wondered if he'd used the right tools to get the job done.

"*He actually threatened* you?" Gloria Webster demanded.

Leonora looked at her grandmother who sat across from her on the other side of the restaurant table.

Her grandparents had raised her from the age of three following the death of her parents in an airline disaster. Her grandfather Calvin had died six years ago.

Gloria was eighty-something. She kept her helmet of permanently waved curls tinted a bright, brassy blond and she never went out of her apartment without a fresh application of her favorite crimson red lipstick. She favored polyester pantsuits with tunic style tops designed with little stand-up collars to hide neck wrinkles. Tonight's ensemble was in a shade of green that matched her eyes. There were a number of gold bracelets on her wrists and several rings glittered on her hands. None were very valuable but Gloria liked a lot of sparkle.

Leonora considered Gloria a role model. She planned to dress just like her when she got to be eighty-something. She had decided years ago that she would never go too far wrong if she patterned her own life after her grandmother's. At the very least, she would never be bored.

"That's how it sounded to me," Leonora said. "He more or less indicated that if I don't help him find the money, he'll see to it that I'm implicated in the embezzlement."

"Think he meant it?"

Leonora ate a shrimp while she contemplated the question.

"Yes, I think he meant it," she said. "Thomas Walker certainly didn't look like he was bluffing."

"Sounds like a desperate man."

The comment startled Leonora. "Desperate? I don't think that's quite the right word. *Determined* would be more accurate. Think of an ocean liner. Very hard to turn around."

Gloria's eyes brightened. "Oh, my. Is he a big man, your Mr. Walker?"

"More like unstoppable."

"Dumb as a brick?"

"Unfortunately, no."

"Hmm." Gloria took a sip of her pink zinfandel and put down her glass. "Doesn't sound like Meredith's type."

"I got the same impression. I doubt if the affair lasted long. She no doubt tried to use him to further her scam, and dropped him fast when she realized she couldn't manipulate him."

"You don't think she was able to control Thomas Walker?"

"I don't think anyone could control Thomas Walker except Thomas Walker."

There was a short silence. Leonora occupied herself with her baked potato.

"Well, well, well," Gloria said very softly.

Leonora looked up sharply from the potato. "What's that supposed to mean?"

"Nothing," Gloria said with a suspiciously airy tone.

"Stop." Leonora aimed the fork at her. "Stop right there. I know that look and it is entirely inappropriate in this situation. Don't get any ideas, Grandma."

"No, dear."

Leonora was not satisfied with that soothing response. She knew her grandmother too well. Gloria wanted her married. Ever since the engagement to Kyle had ended, she had taken an almost obsessive interest in Leonora's love life. Gloria had adopted a now-or-never attitude toward the project that was downright scary at times.

"Do you think Meredith really embezzled that money?" Gloria asked.

"Probably. She was a con artist."

"Sad but true."

"The thing is," Leonora said slowly, "I'm not sure about Thomas Walker's goal in this thing."

"You said yourself that he wants to find the missing funds."

"Yes, but maybe he doesn't intend to put the money back into the endowment account."

"Aha." Gloria arched her carefully drawn brows. "You think he's after it because he wants to steal it himself?"

"As he so succinctly pointed out, a million and a half dollars is a very motivating amount of cash."

"My, this is complicated, isn't it?"

"There's more." Leonora paused. "Brace yourself. He implied that there's a very remote possibility that Meredith was murdered."

Gloria had just taken another sip of the wine. She coughed, sputtered a bit and took another sip to fortify herself.

"Murdered?" Gloria looked momentarily blank. *"Murdered?"*

"Walker suggested that an accomplice might have been responsible for the accident. I think he suspects that she might have had a partner."

"Who would that have been?"

"Me."

"You? Utter nonsense. You and Meredith had nothing in common."

"Thomas Walker doesn't know me as well as you do, Grandma."

"Well, I suppose that's true." Gloria pursed her lips. "Perhaps Mr. Walker invented the murder theory to terrorize you into cooperating with him."

"Who knows? That's the whole problem here. I don't know what is going on or what to believe."

"This is all so typical of Meredith, isn't it?" Gloria

said. "Create a mess and let someone else pick up the pieces."

Leonora drove Gloria back to Melba Creek Gardens after dinner. She parked in the visitors' lot, got out and hauled the sleek, wheeled walker out of the trunk.

Gloria had the passenger door open by the time Leonora got the walker unfolded and in position. Together they made their way into the elegantly appointed lobby of the retirement community. The receptionist nodded in greeting as they went past.

They got into a glass elevator that overlooked the lushly landscaped grounds and rode it to the third floor. Leonora got out and waited for Gloria to get the walker aimed in the right direction.

A number of apartments opened off of the carpeted hall. Next to each door was a small wooden shelf, just large enough to hold a vase of flowers, personal knick-knacks or a holiday decoration. It was understood that each resident was expected to do something creative with his or her shelf. Leonora was always amused to note that none of the shelves had been left unadorned. Peer pressure was a powerful force at any age.

Halfway down the carpeted hall the door of one of the apartments opened. A man stuck his head out into the corridor. What little was left of his hair was very white. He eyed them over a pair of reading glasses.

"Hello, Herb," Leonora said.

"Evening, Leonora. Thought I saw your car downstairs in the parking lot. You two have a nice time?"

"We had a lovely meal," Gloria said. "I'll probably pay for it later, but who cares? Got a cabinet full of antacid."

"You look real nice, Gloria," Herb said. "I like that green on you. Matches your eyes."

"Skip the compliments, Herb. They won't get you anywhere. Finish your column?"

"Hell, yes," Herb said. "I don't miss my deadlines, unlike some people I know."

"Now, now, you know Irma had a good excuse last week. Her nephew was visiting from Denver."

"So what? My niece came to see me two weeks back. I still managed to get my column done."

"Irma turned in a great travel article this time," Gloria assured him. "A detailed list of Las Vegas hotels that have handgrips in the bathrooms and wheelchair-accessible gaming tables. I'm following up with a hard-hitting editorial that asks the tough questions."

Leonora looked at her. "What are the tough questions?"

"Why is it that fancy hotels always locate the rooms that are supposed to be accessible to folks in wheelchairs and walkers at the end of the hall as far from the elevators as possible? And why is it those rooms are always the ones with the worst views?"

"Good questions, all right," Leonora said.

Gloria's Gazette, the online e-zine that Gloria had founded a few months before, after taking a series of computer classes for seniors, had proved to be a resounding success. The subscription list grew daily as more and more seniors got on the Net.

"So, Herb, what's the major issue in the 'Ask Henrietta' column this week?" Leonora questioned.

"Millicent in Portland emailed to tell me that her family is pushing her to give up her car keys. She says she's not sure she's ready to stop driving, but the pressure from the relatives is getting to her. Also, one of her friends had an accident recently. Made her nervous."

"That's a difficult problem," Leonora said.

"Nope," Herb said. "Not difficult at all. I reminded her how much money she'll save if she gives up her car.

Costs a lot of dough to keep one in the garage, what with insurance and gas and all. Told her she can apply that amount to cab fares and have a lot left over."

"You're good, Herb," Leonora said admiringly. "You're really good."

"I know," Herb said. He looked pointedly at Gloria.

"Don't get any ideas," Gloria said.

"You know what I want."

"Not yet, Herb. I'm still thinking about it."

"Damn it, I deserve to have my name on the advice column," Herb said. "I'm sick and tired of folks emailing 'Ask Henrietta.' They oughta be writing to 'Ask Herb.'"

"Hasn't got the same ring," Gloria said.

"Who cares about the ring? This is a matter of journalistic principle."

"I told you, I'm thinking about it." Gloria put the walker in gear and moved off down the hall. "Let's go, dear," she said to Leonora. "It's late. Herb needs his sleep."

"The hell I do," Herb called after her. "I haven't had a good night's sleep in twenty years. Sleep's got nothing to do with this. I want my name on that damned column."

"Good night, Herb." Gloria did not look back.

They turned the corner in the hall and stopped in front of another door. Leonora waited while Gloria got her key out of her purse.

"You know, I think Herb is kind of sweet on you, Grandma."

"Hah. Columnists are all alike. They'll do anything for a byline."

Leonora drove home through the balmy southern California night. Melba Creek was a comfortable town on the fringes of the San Diego suburbs. She had moved here a

few years ago when she had been offered the position in
the reference department at nearby Piercy College, a
small liberal arts school. Gloria had followed after Calvin
died.

For a time Leonora and Gloria had lived in neighboring apartments in the same building. But after two fright-
ening falls that had left her lying helpless for hours on the
floor of her living room, Gloria had opted for the security
of the Melba Creek Gardens retirement community with
its emergency pull cords in every room, handgrip-
equipped bathrooms and twenty-four-hour staff. Not to
mention the nonstop activities that included everything
from daily bridge to swim aerobics and computer classes.

Gloria claimed she had made the move because it
suited her to do so, but Leonora knew her grandmother
had done it for her granddaughter's sake. There was no
denying that it was a huge relief to be able to go to work
or leave town for a few days without having to worry
about Gloria taking another bad fall or getting sick with
no one around to help her.

Leonora noticed the blinking light on the phone as
soon as she walked in the door. Her first thought was that
Thomas Walker had called to see how well his carrot-
stick thing was working. Adrenaline flowed, leaving her
with an odd, tingling sensation.

She would be delighted to tell him that the carrot-stick
thing wasn't working one damn bit. Looking forward to
it, in fact. Couldn't wait.

She had been right, she thought. He had caved first.
Triumph blazed through her.

She stopped tingling as soon as she heard the familiar
voice of her ex-fiancé.

*"...Leo? It's Kyle. Honey, I'm starting to get the
feeling that you're avoiding my calls..."*

"Very perceptive."

"... We need to talk, Leo. This is important. I've got
a good shot at getting on the tenure track here in
the English Department this year. There's just one
teeny little glitch. Your friend Helena Talbot is on
the committee. You know how she feels toward me
because of what happened last year. But I think we
could clear things up if you would give her a call
and let her know that I wasn't responsible and that
you don't blame me in the least..."

Leonora hit the erase button. There were no other
messages.

Thomas Walker had not called to apply pressure. She
had no business feeling so...so deflated. This was a
game of brinksmanship, not seduction, for heaven's sake.

Damn. Now she was thinking about sex. What had
made her think about sex?

Sex should be the last thing on her mind tonight. But it
wasn't.

Thomas did not call the following evening, either. Instead
of being relieved, she grew increasingly uneasy. Something told her he was not the type to just give up. He was
still playing the waiting game, letting the suspense work
on her nerves.

She would not be the one who blinked first.

Two days later she awoke from a restless sleep feeling
groggy and out of sorts. She didn't fire up her laptop to
check her email until after she had made a strong pot of
Dragon Well green tea.

There was only one message.

It was from Meredith.

The message line read *"From beyond the grave..."*

She could almost hear Meredith going *heh, heh, heh* as she wrote the words.

> *Leo:*
> *If you're reading this, I'm dead. Bummer. I set this message up to send to you only if I wasn't around to cancel it. Creepy thought, isn't it? What really bothers me the most is that it means your grandmother was right when she said that I was going to come to a bad end. Hope I went out in a blaze of glory.*
>
> *I'll cut to the chase here. I hereby bequeath to you all my worldly possessions. There are about a million and a half of them. Not bad, for a small-time operator like me, hmm? My biggest score ever.*
>
> *You'll find your inheritance in an offshore account in the Caribbean. Given that email is not exactly the most secure form of communication I won't write out the magic number that you'll need to access the account. There's a safe-deposit key on its way to you. In addition to the number of the account there are a couple of other items in the box.*
>
> *A word of advice. There are some folks out there who will be a tad upset when they find out what I've been up to lately. (What else is new?) If anyone comes around asking about me, just say you haven't seen me since I wrecked your engagement. By the way, I still think that I did you a huge favor. By now Kyle would have cheated on you with someone else. Trust me, I know men.*
>
> *One more thing, if for any reason things turn nasty call a man named Thomas Walker. You can*

*reach him at the number below. He and I were an
item for a while and if he figures out what I did
he'll be really pissed off. Some men have no sense
of humor, you know? Nevertheless, he's one of a
rare breed: a man you can trust.*

*Here's hoping you'll miss me once in a while. I
know I caused some trouble but we had some good
times, too, didn't we? Sorry we didn't get a chance
to say good-bye.*

Love, Meredith

Leonora gazed at the email message for a long time.
She was still staring at it when the doorbell chimed.

The overnight delivery person handed her an envelope.
She signed for it, took it into the front room and opened
it. There was a safe-deposit key inside and the address of
a San Diego bank.

She was at the door of the bank when it opened.

An hour later she dialed Thomas Walker's number.

He answered on the second ring.

"Walker here."

"We need to talk," Leonora said.

Chapter Three

She had called.

About time.

Relief mingled with a roaring exhilaration. The suspense of wondering if he had miscalculated had kept him awake again last night. Thomas wasn't sure he could have played the waiting game much longer.

But Leonora Hutton had lost her nerve and called first. He had won.

He leaned back in the swivel chair, phone to his ear, and gazed unseeingly at the details of the bond account he had called up on his computer. He had just sat down to earn his daily bread when the phone had rung.

Remodeling houses was his passion, but it was a tough way to make a decent living, especially when you put as much into the craftsmanship and materials end of the business as he liked to do. He had a good eye for the architectural bones of a house and he stuck to the three fundamental laws of real estate—location,

location, location—when he bought his fixer-uppers. Nevertheless, he rarely made a killing when he sold. He was lucky to clear expenses and make a few thousand on the plus side of the column.

When it came to earning real money, he did it the easy way, at least the way that was easy for him: He invested.

His first major investment had occurred when he had sold one of his remodeled houses and used all of the profits as venture capital to fuel Deke's fledging little software company. Two years later the firm had been bought out by one of the major players in a bid to acquire Deke's revolutionary security program.

Thomas and Deke had both come out of the deal with a whole new perspective on life, the perspective of young men who could afford to retire before they reached thirty.

Thomas had chosen to study the markets in an effort to ensure their newfound financial security did not dissipate. Deke had gone back to school, gotten some fancy degrees and accepted a position as a professor in the computer science department at Eubanks College.

Deke said Thomas had a near-paranormal talent for making money in stocks and bonds. He didn't know about the paranormal part. All he knew was that he was good at seeing trends before they took hold. With the aid of some software that Deke had designed to meet his specifications, he had gotten even better at it. These days he only had to spend a couple of hours a day at the computer to keep the investment portfolio tuned up and humming along.

The rest of the time he was free to fool around with his tools.

"I'm glad you've decided to cooperate," he said to Leonora. He was careful to keep all signs of the satisfaction he was feeling out of his voice. "Mind if I ask what made you decide to get in touch?"

Stretched out on the floor beside the desk, Wrench abruptly raised his head and looked very intently at him. Maybe he hadn't managed to keep all emotion out of his words, after all.

"It's a long story," Leonora said. "The bottom line is that Meredith says I can trust you."

He went cold. "Meredith's dead."

Wrench hauled himself to his feet and put his head on Thomas's knee. Absently, Thomas reached down to scratch him behind the ears.

"I got what you might call a time-release last will and testament note in my email this morning," Leonora said. "She wrote it before she died and arranged to have it sent in the event anything happened to her."

That stopped him for the count of two. "Did she imply that she was in danger?"

"No. I think she was just taking precautions. Taking care of details. Meredith was very good at details." Silence hummed gently on the line for a few seconds. "But she may have had some qualms."

"What makes you say that?"

"In her message, she said that if things turned nasty I'm supposed to call you."

"Huh. Wonder why she did that?"

"Meredith was very intuitive."

"Yeah?" He stroked the muscles behind Wrench's bent ear. "I'll take your word for it. I didn't know her very well."

"You slept with her."

"Like I said, I didn't know her very well."

"Do you sleep with a lot of women you don't know well?"

"No." He let it go at that. Unlike Meredith, apparently, he was not real intuitive. But it was obvious, even to him, that this particular conversational direction would lead to a dead end.

There was a short, tense silence.

"I think I know where your one-point-five million is," Leonora said after a while.

He was on his feet without being aware of having come up out of the chair. Wrench sat back on his haunches, head cocked attentively.

"Where is it?" Thomas asked.

"In an offshore account in the Caribbean."

"That figures. She was a very sophisticated scam artist, wasn't she?"

"I'm afraid so, yes." Leonora hesitated briefly. "I'm sorry. Meredith had a long history of, uh, pilfering funds from other people."

"When the amount involved is one and a half million, the term *pilfering* doesn't seem adequate."

"No, I guess not."

"Can you access that offshore account?"

"Yes, I think so. She gave me the number of the account."

He went to stand at the window that overlooked the cove. "If you've got the number, I should be able to transfer the funds back into the endowment account without anyone being the wiser."

"Yes, well, that's something I feel we should discuss in more detail."

Damn. He had known it wouldn't be that easy. Meredith had been a thief. He had to remember that. Thieves hung out with other thieves, or, at the very least, they probably favored friends whose own moral and ethical standards tended toward the low end of the spectrum.

"If you're worried about your finder's fee," he said, "relax. I'll make sure that you get the money."

Leonora cleared her throat. He got the feeling she was working up her nerve for whatever it was she intended to say next.

"That's not quite what I had in mind," she said.

He braced one hand around the wooden window frame and prepared to negotiate.

"How does fifty thousand sound?" he said evenly. "Together with a guarantee that your name will not be brought up in any conversation related to the scam in the event that someone, say a cop or a lawyer, for instance, gets wind of it in the future?"

"No."

Her refusal came swiftly. Too swiftly. There was no hesitation whatsoever in her voice. That worried him. She made her living as an academic librarian and he knew for a fact that there was no serious money in the family. He'd checked her out online. All she had was a grandmother who survived on social security, a tiny pension and the income of some small investments. Fifty grand had to sound like a very nice chunk of change to anyone in Leonora's position. Of course, it wasn't exactly one and a half million.

She was playing hardball.

"It's a good offer," he said. "The best you're going to get. Meredith told you to trust me, remember? Take my advice, Miss Hutton. You do not want to try to hang on to the money in that numbered account."

"I don't?" She sounded almost amused.

"No."

"Why not?"

"Because I will hound you to the ends of the earth. I promise I will make life very difficult for you."

"I believe you," she said dryly.

"Good."

"Look, this isn't about the money, Mr. Walker."

"Sure it is. It's always about the money."

"If you actually believe that, you've led a very limited and extremely barren life."

The lecturing tone annoyed him.

"Okay," he said. "If it's not about the money, what is it about?"

"You said that your brother believes that his wife, Bethany, was murdered and that he sees some possible links to Meredith's death."

"Let's leave Deke out of this. His theories about Bethany's death have nothing to do with our negotiations."

"I'm not so sure about that," she said quietly.

"What?"

"In addition to the number and location of the offshore account, I found two other items in Meredith's safe-deposit box," Leonora said quietly.

"Where the hell are you going with this?"

"One of the items was a book titled *Catalog of Antique Looking Glasses in the Mirror House Collection*. It's over forty years old. There are a lot of black-and-white photos of old mirrors inside."

He thought about that. "Meredith must have taken it from the library at Mirror House. Wonder why she ripped it off?"

"I have no idea. She had no interest in antique looking glasses as far as I know. There was something else in the box, too. An envelope. It contains photocopies of some clippings of newspaper accounts of an old murder case."

A twinge of icy premonition drifted through him. "How old?"

"The murder occurred thirty years ago there in Wing Cove."

"Thirty years ago? Wait a second—are you talking about the Sebastian Eubanks murder?"

"Yes. Know anything about it?"

"Hell, yes. Not exactly a secret here in town. A local legend, as a matter of fact. Sebastian Eubanks was the son of Nathanial Eubanks, the man who established the original endowment for Eubanks College. The story goes that Nathanial was brilliant but very weird. Committed suicide. His son, Sebastian, was also very, very smart. A mathematician and major-league eccentric. He was shot dead one night at Mirror House some thirty years ago. The murder was never solved."

"That's it? That's all you know?"

"What else is there to know? It happened three decades ago and, as I said, they never caught the killer. It's not like there's anyone around who still cares about what happened. The Eubanks family line ended with Sebastian. You say Meredith had some clippings of the story?"

"Yes."

"Why the hell would she have been concerned about an old murder case?"

"I have no idea," Leonora said softly. "But Bethany Walker may have been concerned about it, too."

He went very still. "What's that supposed to mean?"

"The clippings were in an envelope that is imprinted with Bethany Walker's name and the address of an office in the Department of Mathematics at Eubanks College."

For a few seconds he just stared at the fog-bound cove, trying to make sense of that information.

"Meredith must have gotten hold of some of Bethany's professional stationery. I don't know how she managed that. We cleaned out Bethany's office. Deke burned all of the unused stationery that had her name and address on it."

"There was a short note from Meredith in the safe-deposit box. It says that she found the clippings together with the book in Mirror House. She makes it clear that she intended to send them to you and your brother once she was safely out of your reach in the Caribbean."

"She *found* them?"

"Apparently."

"Where?"

"I don't know. The note doesn't say. Just somewhere in Mirror House."

"Huh." He tapped one finger on the window edge, looking for some connections. He didn't see any right off. "All right, send them to me. I'll see if they mean anything to Deke. Let's get back to our other business."

"My finder's fee? Forget it. I'm not interested in your money, Mr. Walker."

"What does interest you, Miss Hutton?"

"Finding out who murdered Meredith."

For a split second he thought he hadn't heard her right.

"Who *murdered* her? What the hell is this? She died in a single-car traffic accident down there in L.A., remember?"

"I don't believe that anymore," Leonora said firmly. "Not after the rumors of her using drugs and not after finding these clippings in an envelope with Bethany Walker's name on it. Not after what you said about your brother concluding that Bethany was murdered and the drug rumors surrounding her death."

"Damn it—"

"Something is going on there in Wing Cove. I intend to find out what that something is."

"Fine. You want to play private eye? Be my guest. It's a free country. All I care about is the number of that off-shore account. Tell me what you want in exchange for that information and we can both get on with our lives."

"Yes, well, it's not quite that simple," she said carefully. "I'm afraid that what I want in exchange for this number is your help."

"My help? What do you expect me to do?"

"I need your cooperation and assistance, Mr. Walker. You know Wing Cove. I don't."

"Listen closely, Miss Hutton. The answer is not just no, it is hell, no. Got it?"

"I thought the number of this account in the Caribbean was important to you."

"Are you seriously trying to blackmail me?"

She cleared her throat again. "Well, yes, I suppose you could look at it that way. Now, shall we discuss the details?"

"What details?"

"Well, I'll need a cover story."

"A cover story. Right. Got any brilliant ideas, Mata Hari?"

"I believe you mentioned a library at Mirror House," Leonora said slowly.

"Forget it. Mirror House doesn't need a librarian. No one uses the old library. The only books in it are the ones Nathanial Eubanks collected years ago. They're all concerned with antique mirrors and looking glasses."

"Are the books cataloged?"

He summoned up a mental image of the musty library on the second floor of the mansion. He had only seen the place once when Deke had given him a quick tour. There was a small office on one side. Inside the office was an old-fashioned wooden card catalog with a lot of little drawers.

"I think so," he said.

"Cards or computer?"

"Cards. I told you, no one has touched that library in years."

"I think it's time the catalog was updated and put on-line, don't you?"

In spite of his irritation, he was starting to see some possibilities. Mirror House was one of the few real connections that existed between Bethany and Meredith. Meredith had found the book and the clippings somewhere in the mansion and for some reason she had been convinced that he and Deke would want to see them. They had to be important, although he could not envision how that was possible.

As much as he hated to admit it, Deke and Leonora might both have a point. One thing was certain, this situation wasn't going to go away quietly. He knew that now.

"I might be able to work something out," he said slowly.

"Excellent."

The not-so-subtle triumph in her voice made him set his teeth. She thought she had won.

"Before we take this any further," he said, "there's something you should—"

"I'll need a place to stay," she said.

He gave that two seconds' worth of thought. More possibilities.

"I recently picked up a fixer-upper with a view of the cove," he said. "It's solid and tight. It could work."

"Perfect."

"Before we call this a done deal," he said deliberately, "there's one stipulation."

"What is it?" she asked. Careless in victory.

"If you decide to come up here to play girl detective, you're going to have to do things my way."

"Good heavens, Mr. Walker. Why on earth would I agree to a clause that puts you in charge?"

"Because if you don't agree to it, I will come down there to Melba Creek and get the number of that offshore account out of you the hard way."

"You handed in your resignation?" Gloria put aside the yellow pad she had been using to make notes for her ho-

tel exposé and looked at her over the tops of her reading glasses. "Oh, my. Do you think that was wise?"

"No, but I didn't have much option."

Leonora picked up the two cups of toasty Hojicha green tea that she had just brewed in the tiny efficiency kitchen of Gloria's apartment. She carried the cups to the small table near the window and sat down across from her grandmother. There was a plate with four shortbread cookies in the center of the table. Gloria had made the cookies.

"Bristol wouldn't go for an extended personal leave unless I could give him a very good reason," Leonora said.

"Such as?"

"Giving birth."

"I see. Well, that would have been a bit difficult to manage on such short notice, I suppose."

"I didn't think he'd buy the concept of me playing Sherlock Holmes, either." Leonora helped herself to one of the rich, buttery cookies. "The good news is that he made it clear that I was welcome to reapply for my position when I'm finished with my personal affairs."

"That was very generous of him." Gloria sipped her tea. "You say Thomas Walker has agreed to help you?"

"He's not exactly enthusiastic about the deal, but he went for it."

"Hmm."

Leonora paused, the shortbread halfway to her mouth. "Hmm, what?"

"From what you've told me about your Mr. Walker, I have the feeling that he wouldn't have allowed himself to be blackmailed unless it suited his own agenda."

"He's not my Mr. Walker." She crunched down very hard on the flaky cookie and chewed grimly. "He was Meredith's Mr. Walker."

"Only for a very short period of time from the sound of it."

"None of Meredith's men lasted long."

"True. Nevertheless, the fact that he was willing to assist you with your cover story makes me wonder about his own motives."

Leonora shrugged. "I told you, his brother, Deke, apparently has a lot of questions about his wife's death last year. Thinks there's some connection to Meredith's accident. I have a hunch that Thomas sees my plan as an opportunity to get some answers for Deke."

"In other words, since you insist on getting involved, Thomas Walker has decided to make use of you."

"I think that about sums up the situation, yes."

Gloria smiled.

"Don't go there, Grandma."

"Do you know, dear, you get a certain gleam in your eye when you talk about your Mr. Walker."

"For the last time, he's not my Mr. Walker, and that look in my eye is extreme caution, not lust."

"With you, dear, I'm afraid those two things go together. One of these days you're going to have to take some chances. That's how it works, unfortunately."

"I took a chance, remember?"

"With Professor Delling? Nonsense. You didn't take any real risks with him. You just sort of dabbled your toe in the water. You never really took the plunge."

Leonora wrinkled her nose. "Even if I did happen to find Thomas Walker interesting, I can promise you that he definitely does not think very highly of me."

"Opinions can change."

"Something tells me that Thomas Walker doesn't change his mind very often."

She looked out the window at the gardens. The morning exercise class was just starting. Three rows of seniors clad in loose-fitting sweats faced a zesty-looking young woman in tight spandex. The instructor was blond. Just like Meredith.

"She had such a difficult life and now it's over too soon," Leonora said quietly. "Talk about being born under an unlucky star."

"She was a thief and a con artist, dear. She made a lot of her own bad luck."

"That's one of the things I love about you, Grandma. You have a way of putting stuff into perspective."

"Unfortunately, it's a talent that only comes with age."

Chapter Four

Leonora sat next to Thomas in Deke Walker's darkened living room and tried to conceal her dismay.

Thomas had told her that Deke was suffering from some kind of depression but she had not been prepared for the grooming issues. With his bushy beard, long, uncombed hair and rumpled clothes, Deke looked a little like a troll sitting there in the sickly glow of the computer.

There was a general air of gloom in the shadowy house. The fact that all of the blinds were pulled shut gave her the creeps.

Easy to see why local opinion held that Deke had gone off the deep end.

It was Wrench's casual acceptance of the situation that reassured her the most. The dog lay sprawled on the floor, nose between his big paws, and radiated a complete lack of concern for his surroundings.

She glanced at Thomas, seated beside her. He appeared

accustomed to the morbid atmosphere, she thought. But unlike Wrench, he was worried. Maybe with very good reason, she thought. Deke Walker did not look like a prime candidate for National Mental Health Month poster boy.

"I have a good feeling about you being here, Leonora," Deke said earnestly. "It's like you're a catalyst or something. I'm hoping that you might be able to help us stir things up a bit. Get us looking at the problem from a fresh angle."

"Show Deke the book and the clippings," Thomas said.

"Right." Leonora rummaged around in her satchel, found the book and the photocopies and put them on Deke's desk. "Meredith made it clear in her note that she wanted you and Thomas to see these."

Deke shoved his glasses higher on his nose and pulled the book and the clippings closer. He studied the envelope with Bethany's name and address on it for a long moment.

"Bethany must have made these photocopies and put them in this envelope," he said. "I don't think anyone else would have had access to her stationery, let alone used it."

"The question is why?" Thomas stretched out his legs and lounged deep in his chair. "She couldn't have had any reason to be concerned about a murder that took place thirty years ago."

"Maybe it aroused her professional curiosity," Leonora said. "The victim was a mathematician, after all."

"But hardly an eminent figure in the field." Deke shook his shaggy head. "He was just a junior member of the faculty who probably got the job because he was Eubanks's son and heir."

Leonora frowned. "Heir? I hadn't thought about the financial angle. Was there a lot of money involved? Did someone get rich after Sebastian Eubanks died?"

"Eubanks left no heirs," Thomas said. "His money went to the college endowment. That's a well-known bit of local history. I suppose it's just barely conceivable that one of the upstanding trustees murdered him in order to hurry things along, but I think that's a bit of a reach."

"And even if that did happen, why would it have interested Bethany?" Deke asked softly. "All she cared about was her work. I can't see her bothering to investigate the details of that old murder case, even if she had some suspicions."

"Say for the sake of argument that she had uncovered some new information on that old case," Thomas said. He steepled his fingers. "I'm sure she would have mentioned the facts to you, Deke."

"Sure." Deke scowled. "No logical reason why she wouldn't have said something."

Leonora looked at Deke. "I went through that catalog of the antique mirrors in the Mirror House collection but I didn't see any notes. The only odd thing is someone circled one of the illustrations in blue ink. Whoever did it must have been very old or very young or drunk. The line is quite uneven."

Deke opened the book. "What page?"

"Eighty-one."

He flipped pages to a point near the end of the catalog and paused. He stared at the picture for a long time, as though trying to read runes.

"The ink hasn't faded," he finally said. "The catalog was put together some forty years ago, but this picture must have been circled at some point in the recent past."

"Do you recognize the mirror?" Leonora asked.

She knew exactly what it looked like in the illustration. She had studied it a dozen times, trying to see whatever it was that might make it important.

The antique looking glass was an eight-sided, convex

mirror, typical of a style that her research showed had been popular in the early 1800s. The frame was fashioned of heavy silver worked in a design that featured a variety of mythical creatures. Griffins, dragons and sphinxes cavorted around the edges of the dark reflective surface. A phoenix was perched on top, wings raised.

Deke shook his head. "No. But I never paid much attention to those old mirrors in the mansion. I'm not into antiques."

"Neither was Bethany," Thomas said. "I can't see her marking one of those illustrations."

"I suppose it's possible that Meredith drew the circle around the picture," Leonora said hesitantly. "But why?"

Thomas's jaw hardened. "A lot of those old mirrors are very valuable. Maybe she planned to steal one or two on her way out the door."

Leonora shot him a disgusted glare. "That's ridiculous. Meredith wasn't into the antiques market." She paused and then exhaled slowly. "Besides, her attention was focused on that endowment fund money. She wasn't the type to let herself be distracted."

"I haven't heard that any of the mirrors are missing," Deke said absently.

"How would we know if Meredith or anyone else had ripped off a couple of looking glasses?" Thomas asked bluntly. "Every room and corridor in that old house is covered with antique mirrors. I doubt if anyone would notice if a half dozen disappeared. Especially if they were removed from some of the unused chambers upstairs on the third floor or the attic."

"True." Deke adjusted his glasses a little and slowly paged through the book. "We'd have to conduct a complete inventory to see if one of the mirrors has been stolen. That wouldn't be easy."

"It would also be a waste of time," Thomas said. "It

would take days, maybe weeks to organize and carry out a thorough inventory, always assuming we could talk the Alumni Council into it. And what would it prove if a couple of old mirrors did turn up missing? It's been forty years since that catalog was put together. The theft could have occurred at any time since it was published."

"Motive." Deke yanked his glasses off his nose and jabbed at the book with his forefinger. "As you just pointed out, some of those mirrors are very valuable."

"Take it easy," Thomas said. "We're talking about murder here. People don't get killed over old looking glasses."

"People get killed for all kinds of stupid reasons," Deke growled.

Leonora waited a beat.

"Like drugs," she said quietly.

Both men looked at her.

She spread her fingertips on the desk. "That's one of the connections between Meredith and Bethany, remember? Rumors of drug use."

"Bullshit," Deke said. "Bethany would never have used crap."

"Meredith didn't use it, either. I'd swear to that." She looked at Thomas and Deke in turn. "Do you have a source for those rumors you said circulated after Bethany and Meredith died?"

Thomas sank deeper into his chair. "Ed Stovall mentioned them. When I pinned him down about Bethany, demanding details, he said he'd heard the story from a kid he picked up for possession of pot. Stovall said the kid knew nothing solid. Just mentioned some gossip that was going around the local scene about a designer drug, a new hallucinogen that had appeared from time to time in the past couple of years."

"Hallucinogen?" Leonora repeated.

"Something the drug crowd has labeled S and M, apparently," Thomas said.

She frowned. "As in sadomasochism?"

"No. As in Smoke and Mirrors. Ed said that's what the kid called it. There was no way to confirm the talk."

"Because Bethany never used drugs," Deke said fiercely.

"Take it easy, Deke," Thomas said quietly. "No one's arguing that point. Not even Stovall."

"Ed Stovall is an idiot."

"I don't think so," Thomas said. "He's definitely anal-retentive, but that's probably a good thing in a cop."

"How, exactly," Leonora asked, "did Bethany kill herself?"

"She jumped off a bluff on Cliff Drive," Thomas said quietly.

Leonora studied her hands. "People have been known to think they can fly while under the influence of hallucinogenic drugs. A person might jump off a cliff or crash her car while under the influence."

"But we're all certain that neither Bethany or Meredith would have used heavy drugs, remember?" Thomas said. "And in this case, we've got the authorities on our side. They're not saying the deaths were drug-related."

Deke looked up from the catalog. "Doesn't mean some bastard couldn't have slipped some unique kind of poison into their food or a glass of orange juice. The routine tests done at the time of death wouldn't catch something as new and exotic as this S and M stuff, anyhow. It takes a lot of expensive, time-consuming testing to pick up that kind of crap."

"But why?" Thomas asked patiently. "Where's the motive?"

They all looked at the book again.

"We don't have a lot to work with here, do we?" Leonora asked finally.

"We know one thing for sure," Deke said. "We know that things don't add up. We've also got these clippings and this book. That's more than we had before you arrived in town, Leonora."

"But where do we go now?" she asked.

Thomas unsteepled his fingers.

Leonora and Deke both looked at him.

"What?" Leonora prompted. "Got an idea?"

"If you want to start somewhere, Deke," Thomas said deliberately, "I guess you could check out the murder of Sebastian Eubanks."

Leonora frowned. "Why?"

"What good would that do?" Deke demanded. "Eubanks was killed thirty years ago."

"I'm not saying it will get us anywhere," Thomas said. "But as Leonora just pointed out, we haven't got a lot to work with. One of the few facts we do have is that, for some reason, the Eubanks murder apparently interested Bethany enough to cause her to make copies of the newspaper stories concerning the case and later Meredith put them into a safe-deposit box for us. That's something. Not much, I agree, but something."

"You're right." Deke flattened his palm possessively on the photocopies. "I'll get on it right away. Doubt if there will be anything out there on the Net because the story is so old but the library has microfilm of the *Wing Cove Star* that goes back to the founding of the paper."

There had been a distinct change in Deke since she had first met him an hour ago, Leonora thought. There was a new crispness in the way he folded his spectacles and dropped them into his pocket. His facial expression was more alert, more alive. The moody, gloomy quality was gone. In its place was renewed determination. Deke was now a man with a mission.

She glanced at Thomas. Something in his face told her that he had mixed feelings about the transformation. She understood. Deke might very well take a turn for the worse, psychologically speaking, if their investigation went nowhere. False hope could be worse than no hope because it fed fantasies and nurtured delusions.

So be it, she thought. She was on Deke's side in this thing. She had come here to Wing Cove to find answers and the only way to get them was to follow every possible lead even if it led to a dead end.

"I told you that we needed a new point of reference if we were to have any chance of finding something that the investigator missed last year," Deke said to Thomas. "This book and the clippings may give it to us."

Leonora sat forward. "You hired a private investigator to look into Bethany's death?"

"Sure," Deke said. "But he got nowhere. All he came back with were the same rumors about drugs that Stovall gave us. I fired him after a month."

Wrench's bent ear twitched. He lifted his nose and aimed it at the front door. A second later, someone knocked forcefully, interrupting Leonora before she could ask any more questions.

"That will be Cassie." Deke shut the catalog of looking glasses and got to his feet with unexpected alacrity. "My yoga instructor. I'll let her in. Open those curtains, will you, Thomas? She's always complaining about how dark it is in here."

"No problem." Thomas rose from the big chair and yanked the curtains away from the nearest window with unmistakable zeal. "Can't say that I'm real fond of the décor, myself," he added in a low voice meant only for Leonora's ears.

Deke raked his fingers through his unkempt hair and beard and opened the front door.

Leonora turned and saw an amazon with short, curly red hair and a figure that could have been used as a model for the Statue of Liberty. Except that Lady Liberty was not dressed in sweats.

"Cassie, this is Leonora Hutton," Deke said. "She's a friend of Thomas's. Leonora, Cassie Murray."

"How do you do?" Leonora said.

"A pleasure." Cassie crossed the room with long, ground-swallowing strides. Her right hand was extended.

Leonora scrambled up out of her chair and braced herself.

Wrench hauled himself to his feet and wagged his tail. Cassie patted him on the head and then grasped Leonora's hand and pumped it enthusiastically a few times.

"Nice to see a new face around here." Cassie gave Leonora a brilliant smile. "I've been telling Deke for months that he needs to widen his circle of acquaintances and make some new friends. He spends his days in this cave, looking into the totally artificial light of a computer screen, and then wonders why his energy lines are obstructed."

Cassie had to be at least six feet tall, Leonora mused. She towered a good two inches over Deke and she wasn't wearing heels. There didn't appear to be anything wrong with her energy lines. She practically vibrated with vitality.

"Hello, Cassie." Thomas opened another set of curtains. "How's it going?"

"Fine, just fine. Here, let me give you a hand with those." Cassie went to the nearest window and snapped open the heavy drapes. "Can't do good yoga without some natural light. What do you think of Deke's beard, Leonora? I've been trying to convince him to shave."

Leonora glanced quickly at Deke. She could have sworn that he was blushing. But there was something else going on. He watched Cassie as if she were a gift he dared not open.

"Each to his own," Leonora said gently. She didn't think the beard did much for Deke, but she had no wish to add to his obvious embarrassment.

Cassie snapped the last set of drapes apart and then stood back to survey the results.

"Much better," she announced. "In yoga one must reach for the sun, not the darkness."

"It's foggy outside, Cassie," Deke said. "You can't see the sun."

"Doesn't matter. Natural light is the key. Fog is natural."

"Whatever you say." Deke shrugged. "You're the expert."

Thomas touched Leonora's arm, silently urging her toward the door.

"We were just about to leave," he said. He helped Leonora into her coat. "Right, Leonora?"

"Yes." Leonora hastily seized her satchel. "We'll let you two get on with your yoga lesson."

Wrench was already at the door. Thomas attached his leash. The three of them went outside into the fog-shrouded morning.

Thomas pulled the collar of his jacket up around his ears. He said nothing as they walked down the road toward the footpath.

It was cold. Leonora slipped on her gloves and tugged the hood of her coat up over her head.

"Think he's sleeping with Cassie?" Thomas asked abruptly.

The question startled her out of thoughts of old murder and old mirrors.

"Are you talking about your brother?" she asked.

"Yeah. Deke. Think he and Cassie are having an affair?"

She felt herself turn red. "Why on earth are you asking me? He's your brother, not mine. You know him better than I do."

"I'm worried. Deke has changed a lot in the past year. He's been a different man since Bethany died. Depressed. Morbid. Spending too much time on the Net."

"You think maybe an affair with his yoga instructor would help cheer him up, is that it?"

"Couldn't hurt." He warmed to his theme. "You saw Cassie. I think she'd be a good antidote for his obsession with Bethany's death and all those damned conspiracy theories he's been weaving for the past few months."

Leonora halted on the path and rounded on him. "Why do men always think that getting laid will fix everything?"

Thomas stopped. "I didn't say that getting laid would fix everything," he muttered. "I just thought it might, you know, lift his spirits. Take him out of himself for a while. He seems to like Cassie. At least, that's what it looks like to me. Those yoga lessons are the one thing he actually looks forward to every week. I was amazed when he signed up for a whole year's worth in advance."

"So in your considered opinion Deke should jump into bed with Cassie? You see sex as a form of therapy for his depression?"

Thomas raised one broad shoulder. "Worth a shot."

Outrage swept through her. "I don't know how Cassie feels about your theory but, speaking personally, I can tell you that I certainly would not hop into bed with a man who was just using me to work through some psychological issues."

Thomas blinked, obviously surprised by her anger. "Take it easy, I'm just saying that I think Cassie would be good for Deke."

"If you were in your brother's shoes would you want to go to bed with your yoga instructor merely to see if you could cheer yourself up for a while?"

He thought about that. "Depends on the yoga instructor."

"Good grief."

"It was just a thought."

"Really? How much *thinking* have you actually done about this bright idea of yours? Have you thought about Cassie, for instance? Have you considered her feelings? Maybe she wouldn't care to be used as a form of therapy any more than I would."

"I said forget it." He turned and started walking again. "I just wanted to see if you thought they might be having an affair. But it's obvious you're going to twist everything I say, so there's no point trying to talk rationally about it."

Leonora took a deep breath and told herself to get a grip. Thomas was right. She was definitely going over the top here. There was no reason to take this personally. They were discussing Deke and Cassie. Two people she barely knew.

It wasn't as if Thomas had suggested that she jump into bed with *him* for therapeutic purposes.

She hurried to catch up with him. "Look, I know you're concerned about Deke. I'm no expert, but I really don't think sex is going to fix what's wrong with your brother."

"I gotta tell you, he's scaring me."

Understanding dawned. "That's why you're going along with this plan to investigate Bethany's death, isn't it? You see it as a distraction for him."

"I'm not sure I'm doing him any favors. What if we don't come up with answers? He might sink even deeper into his depression."

She contemplated the fog for a while, thinking.

"Closure," she said eventually.

"What?"

"I think that's what this is all about for Deke. Not just answers, but some kind of closure."

Thomas halted on the path once more and searched her face. "What the hell are you talking about?"

"I'm no shrink but it wouldn't surprise me to learn that part of the reason Deke is obsessing on Bethany's death is because his grief is complicated by some other emotion."

"You think he feels guilty because he wasn't able to protect her?" Thomas shoved one hand into his pocket. "I thought about that. Any man would have problems dealing with the fact that he wasn't able to keep his woman safe. I've tried to talk to Deke about it. There was nothing he could have done. There was nothing anyone could have done."

"Maybe there's more to it. No marriage is perfect, and sudden death doesn't give anyone a chance to say good-bye or resolve outstanding issues. Who knows what was going on in Deke's and Bethany's relationship in the weeks and months before her death? Maybe they were having problems. Maybe they had argued that morning and Deke feels guilty because he never got a chance to say he was sorry."

"You think maybe some of those unresolved issues are haunting him?"

"Maybe. I don't know. I'm just saying that he probably needs closure and he has convinced himself that finding Bethany's killer will give it to him." She hesitated. "Who knows? Maybe I'm here for the same reason. Closure. I never got to say good-bye to Meredith, either."

"This is damn complicated, isn't it?"

"Life is complicated and sex does not make it less complicated. If anything, it only muddles things."

Thomas said nothing.

She glanced at him. "You don't believe me, do you?"

"Well, I've got to tell you that sex never seemed all that complicated to me."

"Which only goes to show."

He frowned. "What does it show?"

"That men and women view sex from entirely different perspectives."

"Damn. How the hell did we end up talking about sex?"

"You started it," she said. "You asked my opinion and I gave it to you. I don't think Deke can allow himself to be happy again as long as he's obsessing on the past. So in answer to your question, no, I don't think he is sleeping with Cassie Murray, and even if he is, I doubt that it would bring him peace or solve his problems."

"Then we need to get some answers," Thomas said.

Chapter Five

"*Please make yourself at home while you're working here at* Mirror House, Leonora." Roberta Brinks looked up from pouring coffee. "My staff and I will be very busy for the next several weeks, what with the annual alumni weekend coming up. I'm afraid there will be a lot of coming and going around here."

"Believe me, I understand the importance of alumni weekends," Leonora said in honest, heartfelt tones.

"A great nuisance." Roberta chuckled. "But where would we all be without our generous alumni, hmm? In any event, I think you'll find that you'll be quite undisturbed upstairs on the second floor. No one uses that part of the mansion very much. And the third floor is completely closed off. It's only used for storage these days."

"I appreciate the tour of the house," Leonora said. "It's quite amazing, really."

She dropped her heavy satchel on the floor, sat down in

one of two chairs that were positioned in front of the desk and watched Roberta pour coffee.

Roberta had introduced herself as the executive director of Mirror House. She was a handsome, robust woman of some sixty years who carried herself with an air of authority. Her hair, cut in a classic, patrician bob, had evidently once been very dark. It had turned a striking shade of silver. She wore a white silk blouse with a paisley scarf, a navy-blue skirt and a pair of pumps that matched the skirt.

"I must admit I'm curious about the architectural style of Mirror House," Leonora said. "I can't quite identify it."

Roberta made a face. "Technically speaking, I believe that it is considered a cross between Victorian and Gothic. It has been declared quite hideous by several self-respecting architects. But Nathanial Eubanks was very rich and very eccentric. Rich eccentrics who endow private colleges and thereby make it possible for generations of lucky professors to obtain tenure are allowed to build bizarre mansions."

"Ah, yes. The tenure thing."

"Indeed." Roberta winked. "And you must admit this place does have character."

Leonora privately thought that *character* was a polite architectural euphemism in this instance. Prior to her arrival in Wing Cove she had assumed that she'd had some idea of what to expect, but her first close-up view of the mansion this morning had sent a fluttery chill of genuine dread down her spine. She'd seen enough horror films over the years to recognize Mirror House for what it was: the sort of place where mad scientists engineered monsters in the basement.

Fortunately, she thought, she was an academic, a clear-headed librarian who did not go in for that sort of nonsense.

Nevertheless, there was no denying that Mirror House was a hulking, gray stone gargoyle of a mansion. Three stories tall and badly proportioned, it crouched amid the trees on the heavily wooded point that marked the southern entrance to Wing Cove. On a dreary day like today, with snaky tendrils of fog writhing and twisting ashore from the cold waters of the Sound, the mansion literally loomed in the mist. It could have served as inspiration for the artwork on the cover of a gothic novel.

The inside was worse than the outside, as far as she was concerned. The towering fir and cedar that hung over the mansion did an excellent job of cutting off what little natural daylight might have managed to seep through the narrow windows.

Roberta's office here on the first floor was the most cheerful room she had encountered in the course of the tour. It even seemed warmer than the rest of the house. The walls were crowded with photographs and framed letters from important alumni. A large potted palm rose from a colorful pot near the window, offering a bright, if utterly incongruous, tropical element to the décor. The sides of Roberta's computer were covered in sticky notes. Colored file folders and a truly impressive collection of pens were scattered across the surface of the desk.

The door of the office stood open, revealing a stretch of paneled hallway. From where she sat, Leonora could see some of the antique mirrors that lined the walls.

A young woman dressed in jeans and a sweater, her long honey-colored hair clamped in a ponytail, went past in the corridor.

"Excuse me, there's my student assistant." Roberta put down the pot. "I want you to meet her. She's here several hours a week."

Roberta hurried to the open door.

"Julie?" she called.

Julie came back to the doorway. She had a can of soda clutched in one long-nailed hand.

"Yes, Mrs. Brinks?"

"I want to introduce you to Leonora Hutton. She'll be working upstairs in the library for the next couple of months. Leonora, this is Julie Bromley."

Julie nodded politely. "Hi, Ms. Hutton."

"Nice to meet you, Julie," Leonora said.

Roberta turned back to Julie. "Don't forget to call the janitorial people this afternoon. They still haven't taken care of the carpets."

"I won't forget, Mrs. Brinks."

"Fine. That will be all for now, dear."

Julie disappeared. Roberta went back to pouring coffee.

"Sugar or cream?" she asked.

"Neither, thanks." She did not like coffee, but she had refrained from saying so when she noticed that Roberta had no tea bags to offer. She could certainly manage a few swallows for the sake of politeness.

"How long have you been executive director here?" she asked when Roberta handed her the mug.

"Long enough." Roberta went around behind her desk and sat down. "I'm retiring next month. Six weeks from today I'll be on a cruise ship bound for the Greek Isles."

"That sounds wonderful."

"I'm really very excited. Bought a whole new wardrobe for the trip." Roberta looked around the office. "But I must admit, it will feel strange to leave this place behind. When I stop and realize that this will be my last alumni weekend, I get a little teary-eyed."

"I understand." She tried a cautious sip of the coffee. It wasn't bad, if you liked coffee. She didn't. "Thanks again for the tour. I know how busy you must be."

"Not at all. I'm delighted that the library is going to be put online. I've said for years that it was a shame that those books were not widely accessible to scholars. There are some very rare and interesting volumes upstairs. I suspect some of them are worth a great deal of money. Nathanial Eubanks collected them in conjunction with the antique mirrors."

"What was his fascination with old mirrors, anyway? He seems to have obsessed on them, from what I can see. Every surface in this house is covered with them."

"Very sad, really. Insanity ran in the family. Some say Eubanks had a crazy notion that as long as he could see his reflection in a mirror, he would not go mad like the others in his line. Others say he was convinced that he could see his past lives in some of the mirrors. All we really know is that the family's bad genes caught up with him in the end. He committed suicide."

"I see."

It had been surprisingly easy to slip a librarian into Mirror House. Deke, as the head of the Bethany Walker Endowment Fund, had simply informed the Eubanks College administration that the fund was willing to pay to have a professional librarian put the Mirror House library online. In memory of Bethany Walker.

College administrators never said no to money, even if they privately thought it was going down a drain.

Leonora made it through half of the coffee before she excused herself.

"Mind if I finish this upstairs?" She held up the mug of coffee. "I really should get to work. I want to do a survey of the collection. Get my bearings, as it were. I'll return the cup later."

"Of course. Run along and don't worry about the cup." Roberta waved her off. "And please don't hesitate to let me know if there's anything I can do. My door is always open."

"Thanks."

Half-full mug in hand, Leonora went down the long hall toward the grand staircase. There were a handful of offices on this floor. Roberta and Julie occupied two of them. A third was dark. The sign on the door read *Eubanks College Alumni Fund Development*. It was the office that Meredith had used during her short stint as a fund-raiser. Roberta had mentioned her only briefly during the tour.

Miss Spooner left on very short notice. Something about being offered a position in California. Fund-raisers are in huge demand these days, you know. We haven't been able to replace her yet.

There was a lot of activity here on the first floor. The mansion's large public rooms were being readied for the major event of the upcoming alumni weekend, a formal reception. Leonora had to dodge members of the cleaning crew and a man on a tall ladder, who was replacing light-bulbs in a massive chandelier.

Mirror House was well-named. Nearly every wall was covered with mirrors and antique looking glasses. But strangely, the enormous quantity of reflective surfaces did little to brighten the place. The interior of the old mansion, decorated in the heavy Victorian style with a strong emphasis on red velvet and dark woods, seemed drenched in perpetual twilight.

It got worse at the top of the staircase. Leonora came to a halt and looked down the long, shadowed hall on the second floor. The library was four doors down on the left. The scrolled and gilded looking glasses on the walls glittered malevolently. Beckoning her into the gloom? Or warning her to stay out of the darkness?

An inexplicable and almost overwhelming urge to turn and run swept through her. She gripped the carved banister until the sensation eased.

After a few seconds, she made herself walk down the

corridor toward the library. She took refuge in the background research she had done before coming to Wing Cove. She knew there was a very logical reason why the mirrors and looking glasses that lined the walls were so dark and dim. They were all antiques, several of them dated from the late-eighteenth and early-nineteenth centuries.

Vintage looking glasses lacked the brilliant optical properties of modern, contemporary mirrors. Their reflective surfaces had not been very bright to begin with because of the limitations of the technology of the eras in which they had been crafted. The old mirrors had continued to darken with age due to impurities in the original glass and the tarnishing of the various metals used to back them.

Okay, the mirrors were old and dark. But why did she get the disturbing sensation that the antique looking glasses here in this hall seemed to literally suck up the light rather than reflect it?

Wrench looked up from his water bowl when Thomas emerged from his workroom.

"Six o'clock." Thomas went to the window and studied the view through the trees across the night-darkened cove. "Light's on at her place. She's home."

Wrench did not appear to be impressed by that observation. He did, however, gaze hopefully in the direction of the front door.

"You're right." Thomas turned away from the window and crossed the front room to collect his jacket, a small flashlight and the leash. "We both need a little exercise. What do you say we go see how our new tenant is doing? Could be she needs a little maintenance work."

Wrench needed no urging. He trotted happily out the front door and stood waiting patiently on the porch while Thomas locked up and attached the leash.

They went down the front steps and found the dark lane that led to the illuminated footpath.

Just a business conference, Thomas thought. He pulled up his collar against the damp night air. That's all he was going for here. He just wanted to see how her first day at Mirror House had gone. Find out if she thought she might actually learn something useful. Compare notes. See if she had any plumbing issues. He hadn't had much time to get the old cottage in shape for her. He had intended to start major remodeling work after the holidays.

There was only a light crowd on the footpath this evening. Thomas let Wrench forge a path for both of them through a flock of joggers. People tended to get out of Wrench's way. For some reason, no one seemed to see him as a reincarnated miniature poodle.

They reached the footbridge and, as usual, had it to themselves. Serious fitness buffs rarely deigned to take the shortcut across the cove.

Thomas could not take his eyes off the warm glow that emanated from Leonora's window. Images of bugs with very small brains drawn to hot lamps designed to fry them to a crisp danced in his head. He ignored them.

This was business.

It was a short walk, no more than fifteen minutes from his house to hers. Wrench gave him a curious look when they turned off the footpath to go along the lane that led to Leonora's front porch, but he did not object.

They came to a halt at her front door. Wrench sat and did his tongue-lolling thing. Thomas knocked. He promised himself that no matter what happened he would not do the tongue-lolling thing.

The door opened almost immediately. Leonora stood in the opening. She wore a deep-purple corduroy shirt that skimmed her curves and a pair of black trousers. Her night-dark hair was brushed straight back from her face and caught with a black cord at the nape of her neck.

"Hello," she said. Wary but polite.

"Evening," Thomas said. Damn. The woman looks good. Very good. No tongue-lolling, he reminded himself.

Wrench pushed his nose against Leonora's hand. She looked down at him and patted him gingerly on top of his head. He grinned.

She raised her eyes to Thomas. He wondered if she intended to pat him, too.

"Just thought I'd make sure you got settled in okay," he said when it became obvious that she was not going to scratch him behind the ears.

"Everything is fine."

He glanced around her, trying to get a look at the living room. "Furniture working out?"

"Yes. Some of the pieces are a little oversized for the space, but they'll do for my purposes."

He remembered how he had stood in the showroom at the furniture store and made his selections from the three basic rental packages that had been offered. In the end he had gone with the Traditional Rustic Comfort set-up because it had the largest bed and he liked a big bed, himself. What the hell had he been thinking? Not like she would ever invite him to join her in it.

Contemplating that big bed in her small bedroom was not helpful. Time to change the subject.

"Had dinner yet?" he asked.

"No. I was just about to fix something."

"Want to join me? There's a café in town that serves some good fish. Very casual. We can have a couple of drinks. Talk about our, uh, investigation."

She pondered that for a few seconds. Then she shrugged. "Okay, I guess that would be all right."

"Hey, thanks," he said. "I really appreciate the enthusiasm, you know? I was braced for outright rejection."

"Really?" She arched one brow. "Do you get rejected a lot?"

"It's a case of love me, love my dog. Not everyone takes to Wrench."

She looked down at Wrench. "You blame your dog when you get rejected?"

"He doesn't mind taking the heat and it saves a lot of wear and tear on my ego."

"A win-win situation."

"Yeah, that's how I look at it. Why don't you get your coat and we'll be on our way?"

"What about Wrench?"

"We'll go back across the bridge and leave him at my house."

She nodded, turned, opened the hall closet and removed a long, black, down-filled coat.

He helped her into it. The small task gave him an opportunity to examine the curve of her neck and get a whiff of her scent. He liked the elegant line of the first and figured the latter for a mix of lemon-infused soap and warm woman. No heavy perfume. He appreciated that. He was not a fan of strong fragrances.

They walked across the footbridge and along the lane to his house. Wrench gave him a pitiful look when he realized that he was about to get left behind.

"You know they won't let you in the café," Thomas reminded him. "You've tried sneaking in before and it didn't work."

"Management probably finds it hard to overlook a wolf coming through the front door," Leonora said dryly.

"I keep telling you not to judge by appearances." Thomas unsnapped the leash.

"Sure, right. A poodle in his former life."

"A miniature poodle. Pink, I think."

Wrench abandoned the pathetic look and wandered off in the direction of the kitchen and his food dish.

Leonora watched Thomas lock the door. "You're sure he doesn't bite?"

"I told you, he's a pacifist at heart. Totally harmless."

"What breed is he, anyway?"

"Beats me. Got him out of a shelter when he was a pup."

They went down the steps and took the footpath into the small town of Wing Cove. The tiny business district consisted of two bookstores, a hardware store, a post office, a handful of miscellaneous shops that catered primarily to students, a pub and some small restaurants.

Thomas ushered Leonora through the double doors and into the cozy warmth of his favorite café. A fire crackled on the stone hearth. Hardwood floors gleamed in the subdued light. Two college-aged waiters in white aprons and black trousers circulated among the small crowd.

He recognized several of the diners. They nodded to him when he and Leonora followed the hostess to a table in the corner. Polite nods. A little reticent. Cautious. He was the brother of that obsessed Deke Walker, after all.

When he pulled out a chair for Leonora he noticed Osmond Kern, silver-haired and vaguely regal-looking in the manner of the tenured aristocrats of the academic world, sitting at a nearby table. He was with the woman Ed Stovall had identified as Kern's daughter, Elissa.

Even from here it was easy to see that Osmond's movements had the careful, exaggerated quality that indicated he was attempting to compensate for too much alcohol. A half-finished martini sat on the table in front of him. It was obviously not the first of the evening.

Elissa was steeped in that grim tension that was unique

to those who were obliged to appear in public with relatives who drank too much and who might prove extremely embarrassing at any moment.

He sat down across from Leonora and opened his menu. "How did things go at Mirror House?"

"So far, so good, but I haven't got anything exciting to report. I'm settled into the office in the library. I was surprised by the book collection, though."

"How's that?"

"It really is quite extraordinary. I only did a quick survey but it looks like it contains a number of old and rare works. Everything from scholarly papers on ancient Greek bronze hand mirrors to technical treatises on the manufacture of looking glasses in seventeenth-century France and England. There's a good deal of material on the symbolism of mirrors in art and mythology, too. Humans have a long history of being fascinated with reflections."

He smiled. "Mirror, mirror on the wall?"

"To cite just one instance." She unfolded her napkin and placed it neatly on her lap. "There's a wealth of mythology in a lot of cultures that relates to mirrors and reflections. Remember the story of Narcissus?"

"Fell in love with his own reflection and pined away, right?"

"Yes. In addition to the myths and fairy tales that feature mirrors, there are all those old master painters such as Jan van Eyck and Rubens and Goya who used them for symbolic purposes in their art. Leonardo da Vinci studied mirrors."

"I've seen pictures of pages from his notebooks," Thomas said. "He kept them in something called 'mirror-writing,' didn't he? Left-handed and moving right to left."

"Yes. Mirrors were a big part of Aztec rituals and the ancient Egyptians were really into them, too."

Her enthusiasm amused him.

"Okay, I believe you," he said.

She made a face. "Didn't mean to bore you. It's just that the Mirror House collection is very unique. It really should be put online and made accessible."

He shrugged. "I've been told that a lot of the antique mirrors and looking glasses hanging on the walls are extremely valuable, too. But according to the terms of Nathanial Eubanks's will, neither they nor the books can be sold or donated to any other institution unless the house itself is demolished for some reason."

"Roberta Brinks, the director of Mirror House, told me that Nathanial Eubanks had a real thing about mirrors." Leonora made a face. "That second-floor hall is a little spooky."

"Some folks think that he drove himself crazy with those antique looking glasses." He studied the menu even though he had memorized it months ago. "Bethany was fascinated by them, too. She spent hours in the library, working on what she called her Mirror Theory."

"What was that?"

"Something to do with explaining mathematical relationships between positive and negative numbers. She hoped that ultimately her theories could be used to help physicists understand exactly what went on in the universe in the first few seconds after the big bang."

"Oh."

"Right. Oh." He held up one hand when she opened her mouth. "Don't ask me for any more details, I'm no mathematician." He lowered his voice. "That man sitting over there with his daughter could explain it better than anyone else in this room. If he wasn't sloshed to the gills, that is."

She glanced quickly around and then looked back at Thomas. "Who is he?"

"Dr. Osmond Kern. Believe me, if you're anybody at all

in mathematics, you'd recognize the name. Several years ago he won a prize and got his name into the textbooks. Came up with an algorithm that turned out to be very important in the computer world. Made a lot of money off it, too, I understand. He's on the faculty at Eubanks."

She smiled. "Tenured, I imagine."

"Oh, yeah."

One of the young waiters finally stopped at their table. Leonora ordered a glass of wine. Thomas ordered a beer. They both decided on broiled halibut.

Thomas was oddly pleased. Something in common at last, he thought. A fish.

"The thing that bothers me the most about our own conspiracy theory," Leonora said midway through the meal, "is that there don't seem to be many similarities between Bethany and Meredith. They were two very different women who came out of very different worlds."

"That's what makes this whole mess so damned frustrating." Thomas forked up a bite of halibut. "If Deke is right, there should be some obvious links between the two. But they weren't even working on the same things at Mirror House. Bethany was completely absorbed with her math theory. Meredith was focused on her scam."

"They both used computers," Leonora offered.

"For entirely different purposes." Thomas waved that aside. "Trust me, Deke checked out that angle. He crawled through every inch of Bethany's hard drive after she died. Ditto for all the stuff he downloaded from Meredith's computer. Nothing. Maybe now that you're here, he'll be able to make sense out of that book and those clippings Meredith left in the safe-deposit—"

A man's voice, angry and petulant, rose from a neighboring table.

"I want to go home, damn it. Now."

Thomas did not have to look around to identify the voice. Everyone in the café was being very careful not to look at the table next to the fireplace.

"Osmond Kern," he said very quietly.

"I feel sorry for his daughter. She looks mortified. Not to mention scared. She doesn't know how to handle the situation."

"Rumor has it Kern's drinking problem has been getting worse in recent months."

"The hell with you." Kern's voice rose another notch. "You sound just like your mother. Leave me alone, damn it."

He shoved his chair back and lurched to his feet.

"Dad, please, sit down." Elissa's voice was soft and hoarse with humiliation.

"Stay here if you want," Kern growled, slurring the words. "I'm leaving."

He swung around and nearly fell.

"Dad, wait." Elissa rose quickly. "I'll help you."

"Shut up and leave me alone."

The tension in the café was palpable as everyone studiously ignored the unfolding scene.

"I'll be right back," Thomas said quietly to Leonora.

She watched him with a troubled expression, but she said nothing.

He got to his feet and crossed the room to where Kern was swaying like a wounded bull trying to find the matador. He took the professor's arm and steered him toward the front door.

"Let me give you a hand, Dr. Kern."

"What?" Kern glared at him, confused and angry. "You're Deke Walker's brother, aren't you? Crazy bastard. Let go of my arm."

"Sure. Just as soon as we get outside."

He had Kern halfway across the room. The hostess rushed to open the front door and gave him a look of sincere gratitude.

Elissa grabbed her purse and hurried after them.

Kern was too befuddled to resist.

Outside on the sidewalk the cold night air seemed to have a calming effect. Kern subsided into a sulking silence. Elissa gave Thomas a shaky smile.

"Thank you," she said. "I'm very sorry about this. I'll take him home now."

"Can you handle him?" Thomas asked.

"Yes. When I get him home he'll fall asleep. In the morning we'll both pretend nothing happened."

She took Kern's arm and guided him toward a dark SUV parked at the curb. Kern muttered, but he allowed himself to be stuffed into the front seat.

Thomas waited until Elissa got behind the wheel, started the big vehicle and drove off down the street before he went back into the restaurant.

Leonora was waiting for him, an enigmatic expression in her vivid eyes.

"It was very kind of you to help her," she said when he sat down across from her.

"That's me, Mr. Fixit," he said.

"There's no need to brush it off that way. It was a genuinely nice thing that you did."

He looked at the door of the restaurant. "Kern was a colleague of Bethany's. She admired his accomplishments in the field of mathematics. Practically idolized him, according to Deke. She wouldn't have wanted to see him humiliate himself or his daughter in public."

"It's getting worse." Elissa got Osmond through the door of his bedroom. She was shaking now. Her heart was

pounding and her breathing was shallow. She could barely contain her rage and frustration. But she knew from previous experience that losing her temper would do no good. "You've got to stop the drinking, Dad. You're killing yourself."

"It's my own business." Osmond dropped down onto the bed and turned his head toward the wall. "If I want to kill myself, I will."

"Please, don't talk like that."

"Get out of here."

"I think you should talk to your doctor. Or maybe see a therapist."

"What do you know about any of this? Get out of here and leave me alone."

The helplessness threatened to swamp her in a sea of despair. There was no point talking to him anymore tonight.

She went out into the hall and quietly closed the bedroom door.

It had been a mistake to come back here. She knew that now. What had made her think that she could establish a relationship with the distant man who was her father? Osmond Kern was not interested in family bonds. He lived in a time warp. The singular, defining event of his life had occurred all those years ago when he had published the algorithm and established his reputation.

Nothing else had ever mattered to him, not even his daughter.

If she had any sense she would leave Wing Cove and go back to her life as a financial analyst in Phoenix.

Every time she started to pack, however, she thought of Ed. Strong, dependable, reliable Ed. She did not know if he would ever see her as anything more than a friend, but she could not stand the thought of leaving town until she knew the answer to that question.

She went slowly along the hall to the door of Osmond's study and stood looking into the room that seemed to contain the essence of her father.

The plaque he had received for his work in mathematics hung on the wall. His computer sat on his desk. The bookcase was crammed with volumes and notebooks.

There were few personal effects. No pictures of her or her mother. He had not kept any of the cards or letters that she had sent to him over the years.

She sat down in his chair and looked at the computer. She wondered how he had invested the money he had made from his work on the algorithm. He had certainly not asked her to help him with his finances, although she was very good at that kind of thing. She knew that she was not the mathematical genius that he was, but she had gotten some of his talent for numbers.

What had he done with the money?

Curiosity made her reach out and boot up the computer.

Chapter Six

Wrench greeted them at the door. He had a length of badly gnawed rope in his mouth. He dropped it at Leonora's feet and sat back proudly on his haunches.

"It's a very nice rope, Wrench." Gingerly she picked it up by one end, trying to avoid the section that had been soaked with dog slobber. "Thank you."

Pleased that his gift had been accepted, Wrench prowled back toward the living room.

Leonora followed. And stopped short when she realized that the entire space was infused with warmth and light and rich, vibrant color. Stunned, she halted in the center of the living room and turned slowly on her heel, examining every surface.

"This is incredible." She had her back to Thomas but she could feel him watching her. "Who did all the tile work?"

"I did. Went a little over the top but it's a small space. Didn't take long to cover it."

She crossed to the nearest wall and ran her fingertips lightly over the thickly applied yellow-gold plaster. Wrench padded after her and leaned heavily against her leg. She patted him again. He leaned a little more heavily. She looked up and saw a handsome crown molding defining the line where wall and ceiling met.

There was an uncanny depth to all the finishes in the room. The palette would have done credit to a Renaissance architect, she thought. The small house was a beautifully cut and polished gem.

"Did you do all of this work?" she asked.

Thomas shrugged. "It's a hobby. Part-time job. I buy fixer-uppers and remodel them."

"This is more than a hobby or a part-time job. This is art."

He smiled and went around the end of the counter.

"How can you bear to put it on the market?"

He shrugged. "I don't put my houses on the market. Not usually."

"You don't sell them?"

"They all sell. In their own good time. But I rarely have to go looking for buyers. The houses always seem to find their own owners. The right ones."

"Is this how you make your living?" She walked to the counter and sat down on a stool.

"Only a small part of it. In my real life I manage money."

"Whose money?"

"The money Deke and I made when he sold his software firm a few years ago. I had a big stake in it because I had provided the venture capital."

"I see." She waved a hand at the interior of the house. "Where did you learn to do this kind of work?"

"My father was a contractor. My mother was an artist. I got some weird combination of their genes, I guess."

Absently she traced the bold relief of the design in the tile work that wrapped the edge of the counter. "What happened to your parents?"

"They're doing fine. They split up when Deke and I were kids. It was one of those nasty divorces. You know, the kind where everyone argues about child support and visitation rights and each person tries to get even with the other. But things have settled down. Dad married his girlfriend. She's about twenty years younger. Mom joined an artists' commune. They both seem reasonably happy."

"But you and Deke got caught in the riptide."

"That's the way it goes, sometimes. Deke and I stuck together. We did okay. What about you?"

"My parents died when I was three. I don't remember them. All I have are some photos. My grandparents raised me. Now there's just me and Gloria. Gloria is my grandmother."

He put two brandies down on the counter, positioning the glasses on two napkins. Instead of coming around to her side of the barrier to take a stool he remained standing across from her.

He raised his glass. "Here's to Grandma."

She smiled. "I'll drink to that."

She took a tiny sip of the potent brandy and thought about how she hadn't intended to come back here with him tonight. After dinner he had said something about continuing their conversation someplace where they couldn't be overheard. She had agreed, thinking he intended to take her home to her place.

She had been struggling with the big question of whether she should make a truly bold move, maybe invite him in and offer him tea, when she had finally noticed that they were headed for his place, not hers.

The part of her that didn't take chances had immediately gone on red-alert status. She had shut down the alarms by reminding herself that there was nothing sexual about their relationship. This was a wary partnership at best, one she had more or less blackmailed him into.

Make that more, not less. It was a good bet that he didn't think too much of her, personally, let alone find her sexy and alluring. The number of that offshore account had endowed her with a lot of bargaining power. The fact that she had used that leverage without mercy had probably given him a rather jaundiced view of her character.

But somewhere along the line she had begun to revise her initial impression of him, she realized. He still made her think of a junkyard dog, but at least this dog was on her side. For the time being, at any rate.

Thomas took a swallow of brandy. "Mind if I ask you a personal question?"

"What is it?"

"How did you and Meredith become friends? I can't see a lot of similarities."

"She showed up when I was in college. Used her computer to fiddle with the dorm assignments. Ended up on my floor."

"Why did she go to the trouble?"

"It's a long story." She drew her finger around the rim of the brandy glass. "Meredith had a very unusual history. She never knew her father. Her mother was an intelligent, but deeply troubled woman who refused to get psychiatric help. At some point Meredith's mom went to a sperm bank and had herself impregnated by an anonymous donor who was selected for intelligence, good health and good looks."

"A sperm bank."

"Yes."

"Well, hell." Thomas rested his forearms on the counter, cradled the glass between his hands and shook his head, looking bemused. "A sperm bank."

"Uh huh."

They drank brandy in silence for a while.

"On the one hand, she hated her father, even though she never knew him."

"Probably *because* she never knew him."

Leonora looked up quickly. "Probably."

"Don't look so surprised. Guys have insights, too. Once in a while."

"I'll bear that in mind." She paused. "On the surface, Meredith was one of the most confident people I've ever met. But I think she had some major self-esteem problems. She was always making grim jokes about how she was the offspring of a man who cared so little about fathering her that he hadn't even bothered to meet her mother, let alone sleep with her. He was a man who literally hadn't given a damn about his own kid. Didn't even bother to find out if she had been born. Didn't want to know her name."

Thomas said nothing.

"Meredith said her mother assured her that she was the product of good genes that had been carefully chosen. But Meredith saw it differently. As far as she was concerned she was the product of some seriously flawed genes. She always said that a man who felt so little concern for his daughter had to be damaged goods, himself, in some really fundamental way. No commitment genes, or something."

"By definition," Thomas agreed.

"Maybe things would have been different if Meredith's mother had been more stable. Or if there had been other close relatives who could have stepped in and taken care of a little girl. But she wasn't and there weren't."

"Must have been rough."

"About as rough as it gets, I think. Meredith's mom wouldn't get professional help but apparently she had no qualms about self-medicating with a variety of drugs, legal and illegal. Eventually she managed to commit suicide with them. Meredith was seventeen years old when she walked into her mother's bedroom and found the body."

"Christ." Thomas was quiet for a moment, thinking. "That kind of addiction costs a lot of money."

"It also makes it difficult to hold a steady job or make house payments or eat regular meals. I guess Meredith and her mother moved around a lot. And there were a number of men who came and went in her mother's life."

"Figures," Thomas said.

"I think that the extreme insecurity of that time left its mark. Meredith was obsessed with money-making scams. Always talked about the big score. Everything she did was done with a view toward ensuring her own financial stability."

"How did she get into your life?"

"After her mother died, Meredith went looking for her father. There was no one else, you see. She had to find someone."

"Sure." Thomas nodded. "I'd have probably done the same in her shoes."

"Me, too." She fell silent for a moment, letting the sadness well up.

"What happened?" Thomas prompted.

"She hacked into the records of the sperm bank her mother had used. Got her father's name out of the supposedly anonymous files." Leonora hesitated. "She discovered that he had died many years earlier. Plane crash. So she went in search of her relatives on that side of the family."

Thomas set his glass down on the counter and looked at her. "Oh, man. Don't tell me—?"

Wrench came to sit by Leonora's stool. She rested her hand on his head. "Meredith found her half sister."

Thomas did not take his eyes off her face.

"That would be you?" he said quietly.

"Yes."

"Damn."

There was another silence. The fire crackled on the hearth.

"Goes to show," Thomas said after a while, "that the gene pool isn't destiny. You and Meredith are as different as night and day."

"That bothered her, you know. She asked me once why I thought we had turned out so differently."

"What did you tell her?"

"What could I say?" She raised one shoulder in a small shrug. "I lost my own parents, but I had my grandparents to take their place. There was no one to take care of Meredith. She learned the hard way how to fend for herself."

Thomas drank more brandy.

"Well," he said eventually, "that information does help to fill out a big chunk of the puzzle."

"What puzzle?"

"You," Thomas said. "I've been trying to figure you out from the beginning."

She liked the idea that he had been trying to figure her out. She had never considered herself the mysterious type.

She took off her glasses. The small action was designed to buy her a little time to contemplate his comment. Absently, she fiddled with the temple.

"I always thought of Meredith as the mystery woman in the family," she said.

"Nah, she was easy to understand compared to you. You, on the other hand, are a real enigma. At first, I assumed you were Meredith's accomplice. Thought you were after the money."

"I know."

"You shredded that theory when you made the deal to hand over the number of that offshore account in exchange for my help in finding out whether or not she was murdered."

"Did you come up with another theory?"

"I was damn sure Meredith wasn't the type who had close friends. Couldn't see any of her acquaintances giving up a good job and moving here to Wing Cove for a while just to get some answers about her death. Knew there had to be another reason why..." He broke off abruptly.

She arched one brow. "What?"

He looked at the eyeglasses in her hand, frowning intently. "That temple looks a little loose."

She followed his gaze. "Yes, I know. I've been meaning to find an optometrist and get it tightened. Haven't had a chance."

"You're going to lose that screw if you're not careful. Here, let me see those."

He reached across the counter and plucked the glasses from her fingers. Before she could ask him what he planned to do he opened a door next to the refrigerator and disappeared. A light came on in a small room.

She hopped down off the stool and went to stand in the doorway. She found herself gazing into a room filled with gleaming tools of all sizes and descriptions.

Thomas stood at a workbench, studying a box filled with very small screwdrivers.

"Thomas?"

"I think I've got one that will fit. Yeah, here we go."

He took a tiny screwdriver out of the box and went to work on her glasses.

When he was finished he handed them back to her. "How's that?"

She tested the temples. They were both snug.

She put on the glasses. And was oddly pleased.

"This is great," she said. "I'll have to get myself one of those itty-bitty screwdrivers. Then I wouldn't have to look up an optometrist every time I need to tighten a temple. Thanks."

"You're welcome."

She looked at him. "I'm here in Wing Cove for the same reason you are, Thomas."

"I know," he said. "A family thing. I've got that much figured out now."

"Yes."

He smiled faintly. "And here I've been thinking that you and I had nothing in common."

She'd been telling herself the same thing. Over and over again.

Thomas and Wrench walked her back across the foot-bridge a short time later. The fog had moved in, cloaking the cove. The low lamps that marked the jogging trail and the narrow bridge glowed weakly. The lights of the town at the tip of the wing were a blurry glow in the distance.

At her door, she said good night, locked up and then went to the window and pulled the curtain aside. She stood there, watching, until Thomas and Wrench disappeared into the mist.

There was something similar about the way both man and beast moved, she mused. An easy, fluid, deceptively unhurried quality that was the hallmark of natural-born hunters.

A couple of junkyard dogs, all right. She wasn't buying that line about Wrench being a reincarnated miniature poodle for a minute.

Chapter Seven

The ancient swivel chair squeaked when Leonora leaned back in it. She waited a couple of seconds to make sure it wasn't going to collapse under her weight. When she was sure it would hold, she stacked her ankles on the edge of the battered wooden desk and reached for the phone. She punched out a familiar number.

Gloria answered on the second ring, sounding slightly distracted.

"Hello?"

"It's me, Grandma. How was bridge last night?"

"I came in first."

"Of course you did. Someday you'll have to decide how you're going to invest all those quarters you've won during the past couple of years. You could probably afford to open up your own personal casino by now."

"I had good cards," Gloria said, brimming with false modesty. "It's about time you called. I've been worrying about you. Are you all right? What's going on up there in Washington?"

"I'm fine." Leonora glanced out the door of the tiny office. She checked the aisles between the floor-to-ceiling bookstacks to make sure she was alone. "Nothing to report yet but, as we in the detective business like to say, progress is being made."

"Forget the progress, get to the good stuff. How are you and your Mr. Walker getting along?"

"I keep telling you, he's not my Mr. Walker. For the record, Gloria, Thomas and I have both concluded that we don't have anything in common other than a mutual interest in finding out what happened to Meredith and his brother's wife, Bethany."

"Hmm."

"But if it makes you feel better, Thomas's dog likes me."

"Well, I suppose that's a start. Has Mr. Walker taken you to dinner?"

"Well, yes. Last night, as a matter of fact. But it was solely for the purpose of discussing our mutual problem."

"Did you go back to his place or your place?"

Leonora took the phone away from her ear, stared at it for a second and then put it back to her ear. "His place. But only for a few minutes. It was on the way. Sort of."

"Did he make a pass?"

"No." Leonora took her feet down off the desk and sat forward. "He tightened the screw in my glasses."

"Ah."

"It was amazing. He had one of those little tiny screwdrivers. You know, the kind that optometrists use."

"Imagine that. I do like a man who is handy with his tools. Such a useful talent."

It was impossible to argue in the face of such determined optimism. Leonora gave up, told Gloria to say hello to Herb and ended the call.

She sat back, steepled her fingers and brooded for a while.

It was a strange experience. She rarely brooded. She tried to get into it. It wasn't like she didn't have stuff to brood about. It just wasn't easy. Her thoughts kept going back to Thomas and his little jewel of a house.

A low, sighing groan snapped her out of the odd mood. The sound emanated from the other side of the wall behind the card catalog.

Startled, she swung around in the chair and stared at the old wooden catalog. A second groan and a squeak followed hard on the heels of the first. She could have sworn she also heard a muffled giggle.

The easy explanation was that the sounds were coming from people in the room next to the library. But she was certain that there was no one in that chamber. The door was closed and locked.

She left the office and hurried through the stacks to the door of the library. She was about to step out into the hall to see if anyone was about when she caught the dim flicker of movement in the old convex mirror that hung on the opposite wall directly across from where she stood.

The bulging curve of the heavily framed looking glass reflected the corridor for a distance of several feet on either side. The shifting of light in the dark glass was a reflection of the hall to her right. As she watched, a section of the corridor wall swung open.

Two figures slipped out into the hall. One of them paused to make certain that the hidden door swung shut. Then they both turned and disappeared in the direction of the main staircase at the far end of the passage. There was more muffled laughter and soft conversation.

Julie Bromley and her boyfriend, Travis Todd. Julie had introduced him to Leonora that morning.

She waited until the two students had vanished downstairs and then walked to where she had seen them emerge from the wall. A narrow seam in the paneling was the only evidence of a door.

She pushed gently. Nothing happened. She pushed a little harder. The invisible door swung inward with a creak of rusty hinges.

There was just enough light coming from the hall behind her to reveal a narrow flight of steps that curved around itself. It led to the closed floor above.

An old-fashioned set of servants' stairs, she thought. Julie and Travis were no doubt using a room on the third floor for a trysting spot.

Personally, she couldn't see how anyone could get into a romantic mood in this grim house but maybe that was her age showing.

She let the door swing shut and continued along the shadowy hall toward the main staircase. The dark mirrors glittered unpleasantly on the walls. She glanced at one as she went past. The frame was made of wood, heavily carved with crests and scrolls. The design and workmanship were typical of mirrors from the end of the seventeen hundreds, according to what she had read.

She saw her own image reflected dimly back at her in the old glass. There was something wrong with her reflection. She stopped and examined it more closely.

There were two reflections, she realized. The second was a ghostly duplicate of the first, slightly off-center. The result was an eerie doppelganger effect that made her shiver.

You can't sleep yet.

Where had that stray thought come from? It drifted through her mind, a ghostly whisper with no form or ob-

vious source. Her heart pounded. Her hands went cold.
Her breath felt tight in her lungs.

Stop it. Get a grip.

She quickly averted her gaze and hurried off down the
hall.

There was no reason to be unnerved by the double image, she told herself. It was simply the result of deficien-
cies in the early manufacturing process. The techniques
of mirror making had been closely guarded trade secrets
in the old days. The results produced had been less than
perfect by today's standards.

But she knew, deep down, what had sent the chill
through her. It was because, for just an instant, the second
reflection imposed over her own had looked a lot like
Meredith.

She went quickly down the stairs, relieved to be able to
descend into the hubbub of activity on the first floor.

She made her way through a pile of electrical equipment and a maze of folded tables and rushed out into the
parking lot. Outside, she was relieved to see that a crisp,
chilled sunlight had, temporarily at least, driven off the
fog. It also banished what was left of the strange panic
that had welled up inside her when she had looked into
the double-image mirror.

Chapter Eight

"You're new around here, aren't you? Welcome to Wing Cove."

At the sound of the unfamiliar male voice directly behind her, Leonora jumped. She dropped the package of frozen soybean pods back onto the stack, straightened and turned away from the supermarket's large, glass-walled freezer.

A strikingly good-looking man with aquiline features and riveting amber eyes stood in the aisle. His jet-black hair was combed straight back and tied in a ponytail at the nape of his neck.

Dressed in a black, ankle-length leather coat, black pants, a black turtleneck and black boots, he certainly stood out there in the grocery store aisle. She was willing to bet that all of the articles of clothing had designer labels inside.

"Sorry," he said, managing to look both amused and apologetic at the same time. "Didn't mean to startle you. My name is Alex Rhodes."

"Leonora Hutton," she said automatically.

She told herself she shouldn't stare into his unusual eyes. Then again, what else was a person supposed to do when talking directly to someone except look into his eyes? The alternative was to stare at his chest and that didn't seem like a socially correct option.

"You're the librarian they brought in to catalog that collection of old books out at Mirror House, aren't you?" Alex asked.

"How did you know?"

He smiled, displaying very white, near perfect teeth. "This is one very small town. Word gets around. I also hear that you had dinner with Thomas Walker the other evening."

She became aware of a cold draft chilling her backside. Hastily she closed the freezer door. "Looks like you've got my life story in a nutshell."

"Not all of it. Just the stuff that happened here in Wing Cove. Want to hear my story?"

She gave up trying to avoid his strange tiger-yellow eyes. Why bother to be polite? He wanted her to look at him. Probably would have been crushed if she had not found him fascinating.

His unabashed, darkly sensual style held a certain piquant charm. He knew how good he looked and he was accustomed to having people notice, especially women. He possessed a comfortable nonchalance that told her he was used to trading on his sexy appearance. A masculine version of Meredith, in that respect, she thought.

"Before I decide whether or not I want your life story," she said, "maybe you should tell me why, out of all the grocery stores in all the world, you walked into this one and chose me to honor with your tale."

His black brows rose. "Damn. The cautious type. I was afraid of that."

"It's an old habit I'm trying to break, but it kicks in once in a while in spite of all my good intentions."

"Ah, yes." He nodded with an air of grave wisdom. "I know all about old habits. You could say I'm something of an expert in the field."

"Really? How did that happen?"

"I'm in the business of breaking old habits." He drew a black-and-silver case out of his pocket, opened it and handed her one of the little white cards inside. "I'm a stress-reduction consultant. I specialize in helping people deal with the problems of modern life. That usually means getting rid of old habits. I do counseling and I sell a special nutritional formula designed to offset the metabolic effects of stress."

She glanced at the card. Alex's name and a phone number were the only things printed on it.

"Are you expensive?" she asked.

"Very. But the real money is in the nutritional supplement. You wouldn't believe how willing people are to take a spoonful of medicine rather than make genuine changes in their lives."

"Nice work if you can get it."

"You can say that again." He gave her a Cheshire cat smile. "And I've got it. Want to go back to my place and look at my stress-reduction videos?"

"Some other time, maybe."

He gave a theatrical sigh of deep regret. "All right, I get the point. You aren't going to let me sweep you off your feet and onto my couch."

"You actually have a couch?"

"Sure. Clients expect it. And it gives me a place to take a nap between appointments."

"I can see the logic. How long have you lived here in Wing Cove?"

"Opened up my practice about a year ago. I can give

you a list of references, if you like, but you probably can't afford me."

"Probably not."

"I occasionally do some pro bono work, however."

"Thanks, but in my family we have this thing against taking charity."

Alex Rhodes had been in Wing Cove while Meredith was here, she pondered. They would have met. Alex would have made certain of it. And Meredith would have found him entertaining, to say the least. More importantly, she would have considered him a prime source of information. A stress-reduction consultant who catered to the high-end market was bound to pick up a lot of interesting tidbits about his clients' private lives. Meredith had collected interesting tidbits that might prove profitable the way other folks collected antiques.

"No need to give me a list of references," she said, "and the only nutritional supplements I use are the chocolate-covered kind."

"Can I talk you into having a cup of coffee with me, instead? There's a place just down the street."

"I'm still looking for a reason."

"How about because I saw you from the far end of this grocery aisle and I was captivated by the vision of you bending over to reach into that freezer?"

"How about you try again?"

He laughed. "All right, I'll tell you the flat-out truth. As I mentioned earlier, this is one small town. Most of the women who are anywhere near my age are either married or clients of mine or students. I never date members of any one of those categories, so that seriously cuts down my social options in Wing Cove."

"I see."

"I'm a mature, intelligent, sensitive man, Ms. Hutton. I have needs."

"I'll bet you do."

"What I need," he said deliberately, "is a conversation with a sophisticated, interesting woman that does not revolve around a personal neurosis or a relationship issue that is impacting her ability to deal with stress or to have an orgasm. I need such a conversation very badly, Ms. Hutton. I do believe that I would sell my soul for such a conversation."

"Oh, well, in that case, let's have coffee."

She ordered tea, of course. Alex got an espresso. Of course. The little cup of extra strong, extra dark coffee went with the rest of the outfit.

They sat at a small, round table near the window. The crowd was a mix of academics, students and townsfolk. The walls were painted in warm hues of brown and ocher. The wood floor had been finished to look old and worn. A fire burned on a central, open hearth in the middle of the room.

The fog was back. Outside the window it was so thick it was difficult to make out the shops and galleries that lined the opposite side of the street.

"Mind if I ask you a question?" Alex said.

"Depends on the question."

"Hate to do this. But before I try to impress you with the breadth and depth of my intellect and sophistication, I feel the need to ask you to define your relationship with Thomas Walker."

She paused in the act of removing the tea bag from the cup. "My what?"

"I hear the two of you had dinner together last night. In this town that constitutes a relationship."

"I see." She set the wet bag down very carefully on the saucer. "We're just friends."

"That's it? Just friends?"

"Yes."

Alex pondered that for a moment and then shook his head. "I don't know. 'Friends' is a vague term, don't you think?"

"Is it?"

Alex lounged back in his chair, long, lean legs extended, and looked at her with his glowing gold eyes. "For instance, a few months back, Walker was *friends* for a while with another woman who worked up at Mirror House. Close friends. One might even say intimate friends."

Meredith.

She concentrated on taking a sip of tea. It wasn't bad tea. It wasn't good tea, either. It had the subtle but distinctive aftertaste that tea made from a bag always had. Not as dreadful as instant tea but not nearly as good as tea made from fine quality loose leaves in a proper pot.

Okay, stop stalling. You're supposed to be playing private detective here.

"I will tell you one thing," she said smoothly. "My relationship with Thomas Walker most definitely cannot be defined as intimate."

Alex nodded. "I just wanted to be sure. I dated Walker's other *friend* for a while after they stopped seeing each other. Not sure how he felt about that. Things can get a little too cozy in a small town like this."

"Nice to know you've got a personal code of conduct that applies to your social life."

"More like I'm just damned cautious. I don't need a rep for sleeping with the locals' wives and girlfriends."

"Bad for business?"

"Very bad."

"I can understand that." She had nothing to lose by being a little bolder, she decided. "My turn for a personal question. What happened to your relationship with Thomas Walker's other friend?"

"We didn't see each other for long. Between you and me, I think she may have had a problem with drugs. She left town a few weeks ago. I heard she was killed in a car crash."

She started to pick up her cup again but quickly changed her mind when she realized that her fingers were trembling. She put her hand back in her lap.

"This woman used drugs, you said?"

"Can't swear to it, you understand. She sure as hell never did them in front of me. But the rumors were all over the place after she died."

"Where would she get them in a small town like this?"

"Don't you read the papers? You can buy that junk anywhere these days. Besides, this is a college town. That makes it even easier."

"I see." So much for getting the name of the local drug kingpin. This detective work was hard.

"How did you meet Walker?" Alex asked.

"He's my landlord." She was pleased with the way that came out. Very casual. Very innocent. "I met him when I rented my cottage."

Alex looked briefly surprised, as if he hadn't considered that mundane possibility. Then he nodded. Thoughtful now. And maybe less intent. More relaxed.

"That's right," he said. "I think Meredith mentioned that he was into the home improvement scene in a big way. She said he had picked up a couple of the old summer cottages overlooking the cove and planned to remodel them."

"I have the cottage that hasn't been redone yet. But it's warm and dry and comfortable enough for the short time I'll be in town."

"How long do you expect your project at Mirror House to last?"

"I'm estimating that it won't take me more than a few months at most to put that collection online. The original cataloging was clearly done by a pro who devised a unique classification system for the books. It resembles the Library of Congress system to some degree but it's been greatly enhanced and expanded to allow for nuance and very fine distinctions in the subject—"

"Where's home?" he interrupted.

Apparently Alex was not terribly interested in the details of her professional work at Mirror House. Before she could decide whether or not to invent a false answer to that query, the door of the coffeehouse opened. She did not have to turn her head to know who had just entered. She was developing a sixth sense where Thomas Walker was concerned.

Alex did turn his head. He watched Thomas coming toward them. There was an almost imperceptible hardening of his spectacular eyes.

"You sure about the status of your relationship with Walker?" he asked. "He's just your landlord?"

"Yes."

Thomas arrived at the table. "Don't knock it, Rhodes. The relationship between landlord and tenant is damn near a sacred trust. Backed up by the full weight and authority of several centuries' worth of law, custom and tradition. Sort of like marriage."

Leonora gave him a warning look. Thomas did not appear to notice. He pulled out a chair, reversed it and straddled it. He rested his arms along the back and smiled at her.

"I was at the hardware store across the street. Thought I saw you come in here. Everything okay at the cottage?"

"Fine, thank you."

"Be sure to let me know if you need any maintenance work."

"I will."

She picked up her cup and took a sip of tea while she tried to figure out what was going on here. The testosterone levels were climbing fast. Had she unwittingly achieved that pinnacle of feminine accomplishment that occurred when one became the object of the rampaging lust of two men who were willing to fight for the honor of her favors?

Nah. Stuff like that never happened to her.

Alex glanced at his heavy gold watch and pushed back his chair. "Hate to leave, but I've got an appointment with a client. Can't be late. Nice to meet you, Leonora. You've got my card. Give me a call if you feel the need for some advice on how to handle stress."

"I'll do that," she said.

He winked. "One of these days I'd like to know what you planned to do with those frozen soybeans." He nodded at Thomas. "See you around, Walker."

"Sure," Thomas said.

Alex walked away toward the front door of the coffeehouse. He collected his long black coat from a rack, pulled it on and went outside.

Thomas watched through the window as Alex disappeared into the fog.

"Frozen soybeans?" he asked, his gaze never leaving the window.

"They make a wonderful, low-cal appetizer."

"I'll have to remember that. Think Wrench would like 'em?"

"I doubt it. Wrench doesn't strike me as the type who would have much interest in soybeans."

"Yeah, you're probably right about that." Thomas switched his attention back to her.

The ice in his gray eyes caught her off guard.

"Something wrong?" she asked.

"What did Rhodes want?"

She hesitated and then gave a small shrug. "He said that he longed to indulge in a stimulating conversation with a single female who was not a client, student or the wife or girlfriend of a potential client."

"Stimulating conversation, huh? Could have sworn he was coming on to you."

She sipped some more tea. "That, too, perhaps."

"Were you enjoying this stimulating conversation?"

"I will have you know," she said primly, "that I was playing detective."

"Is that so? Mind if I ask why you chose to practice your detecting skills on Rhodes?"

"There were a couple of very sound reasons. First, I found it quite interesting that he approached me out of the blue, so to speak. Just sort of materialized there in the frozen-foods aisle, if you will."

Thomas tapped one finger lightly against the wooden chair back. "Okay, I'll give you that. It is interesting. Any idea why he initiated the conversation?"

"My derriere was apparently displayed in an extremely provocative and enticing manner when I bent over to pick up the previously referenced package of soybeans in the freezer case." She took a sip of her tea. "Never had that happen before. I may have to start buying more soybeans."

"Doubt if the soybeans had much to do with it. Guys tend to notice things like women's derrieres. What was your other reason for letting him drag you in here for tea and stimulating conversation?"

"Very early on in our chat, he mentioned Meredith."

Thomas was silent for a beat.

"Is that right?" he said very softly.

"He brought up the subject all by himself without any prompting from me."

"Not real subtle, is he?"

"No. I got the feeling that he didn't have time to be subtle. He wanted answers and he wanted them quickly. He also volunteered the information that he and Meredith had dated for a while after you stopped seeing her."

"I could have told you that."

She picked up the teacup and looked at him over the rim. "But you didn't, did you?"

He shrugged. "Didn't think it was important."

"You may have been wrong about that."

He gave it a few seconds' thought. "I may, indeed, have been wrong. Damn. What's going on here? Where the hell does Alex Rhodes fit into this?"

"I don't know yet. But I can tell you this much, he was extremely concerned about the precise nature of our relationship."

"*Our* relationship?" Thomas frowned. "As in you and me?"

"Yes. You and me. I was in the process of assuring him that we were merely landlord and tenant when you arrived."

"Well, now."

"One could, of course, jump to the conclusion that Mr. Rhodes is a fine example of the upstanding, noble sort of male who does not wish to be known for seducing other men's girlfriends."

"In other words, he may have been swept off his feet there in the frozen-foods aisle and was merely doing the manly thing, making sure you were single and free, before he attempted to put his hands on your charming derriere."

"Always assuming that I would have allowed him to put his hands on my charming derriere, even if I happened to be single and free."

"Assuming that," Thomas said.

"Anything is possible in this crazy old world." She heaved a sigh. "But somehow, I don't think that it was instant and immediate lust that prompted him to buy me tea and attempt to interrogate me."

Thomas gave her an approving look. "Obviously you have a natural aptitude for this detecting business. Very clever of you not to be deceived by his sneaky tactics."

"Yeah, I'm smart all right. But I must admit I'm extremely curious about why he bothered to employ such wily tactics in the first place."

"Me, too. Think maybe he knows about the money Meredith skimmed off the endowment fund? Figures she stashed it somewhere before she died and now hopes maybe he can find it?"

"I hadn't thought about that." She wrinkled her nose. "A million and a half bucks could explain a lot of phony lust. But how would he have discovered her scam? She wasn't the type to confide in a man even if she was sleeping with him."

"I figured out that she was up to no good," Thomas reminded her softly. "With a computer and my brother's help."

"But you didn't become suspicious of her until she left town in a very sudden manner and you got a hunch that it might be a good idea to check out the endowment accounts. What would have made Alex question her disappearance?"

"Rhodes may have had his own reasons to suspect that Meredith was running a con."

"Why do you say that?"

"Got a feeling they might have had a few things in common," Thomas said evenly. "Meredith was a scam artist. As far as I'm concerned, that antistress formula Rhodes is selling puts him in the same professional category. Takes one to know one."

"You think Alex is a fraud?"

"Give me a break. The guy charges a fortune for that nutritional supplement he peddles."

"A great many people believe wholeheartedly in alternative medicine. And with good and valid reasons."

"Rhodes strike you as the holistic medicine type?"

She hesitated. "All right, let's say for the sake of argument that he guessed that Meredith was up to something. How would he know about the missing endowment money?"

Thomas shrugged. "Beats me. But we can't rule out the possibility that he's looking for it and thinks that you might be able to help him find it."

"In other words," she said neutrally, "Alex may have picked me up in the frozen-foods aisle for many of the same reasons that you cornered me in Meredith's apartment the other day. He knows that Meredith ripped off a million and a half bucks and he knows that she knew me so I might know where the money is."

Thomas looked irritated by that summary of events.

"The money may have brought us together," he said, "but it's not the reason we formed our partnership. If you will recall, you more or less blackmailed me into this arrangement."

"Oh, yes, that's right. I forgot."

"You've got a selective memory."

"My librarian training, no doubt." She paused. "You know, I'd say it's just barely possible that Meredith mentioned me to Alex, although not very likely. But I'd stake my last dime that she did not tell him about her scam or the money. She was very cautious with her secrets. I certainly never knew her to confide them to those of the male persuasion."

He considered that briefly. "Good point."

"Not to change the subject, but what did you do with Wrench?"

"He's tied up outside where he can ogle females of the four-footed variety."

She raised her brows. "You mean he's still capable of enjoying the opposite sex? I thought when you got a dog from a shelter they made you get the animal neutered."

"I never explained the details of the operation to Wrench. Figured it would depress him."

"Thoughtful of you to withhold the facts."

"He's my buddy. A guy does stuff like that for a pal. You ready to leave? I'll walk you back to the cottage."

"All right." She got to her feet.

He helped her into her coat. "By the way, while you were busy with your detective work, did you happen to notice Rhodes's eyes?"

"How could one fail to do so?"

"Weird, huh? I've never seen anyone with eyes like that."

She smiled. "Tinted contact lenses."

"...*And center yourself.*" Cassie assumed a half-lotus position, one ankle tucked into the crease between torso and thigh. "Ground yourself, clear your mind and allow yourself to sink into the stillness."

Deke followed instructions, folding himself into the final pose of the session. He tried to concentrate on clearing his mind but the process was, of course, a contradiction in terms. If you concentrated on something, after all, you were not exactly clearing your mind.

That was especially true when his concentration was focused almost entirely on the lush curves of Cassie's thighs.

The woman had outstanding thighs, full and ripe and elegantly curved. They were excellently showcased in her snug, black tights. But, then, everything about Cassie was outstanding. She was magnificent, in his opinion.

If he had any sense he would cancel these sessions. Doing yoga with her always made him hard. He was torturing himself.

"...Relax and find the nexus of your energy lines..."

He lived for these yoga lessons. They were the bright spot of his week. No need to search himself for the nexus of his energy lines. They were all fused into a stiff erection.

"...And release..."

Nothing he would like better, he thought, than a good release. If only...

Cassie studied him with a troubled expression. "This was not one of our better sessions," she said. "I got the feeling that you were unable to ground yourself today. Is something wrong?"

He told himself that he should keep his own counsel. She was his fitness instructor, not his best friend or his therapist. But he needed to talk to someone and she was a woman. Women sometimes saw things that eluded men.

"Do you think Thomas is sleeping with Leonora Hutton?" he asked.

"I beg your pardon?"

He had made a mistake. He knew that now. But it was too late to turn back.

"You saw them together the day before yesterday when you arrived for our Tuesday session. I just wondered if you got the impression that they might be involved in a relationship."

"Deke, I only saw them for five minutes. They were on their way out the door, remember? How could I possibly tell what kind of relationship they have?" She gave him a scorching glare and uncoiled to her feet. "Besides,

Thomas is your brother. You know him much better than
I do. What do you think?"

"I don't know. Thomas can be hard to read sometimes,
even for me. But it seemed to me that there was something different about the way he was with her. He
couldn't stop looking at her. And he seemed sort of restless. Like he wanted to get up and move around. Pace the
room, maybe. That's not like him. He's the most laid-
back guy I know, even when he's with a woman he happens to be, uh—"

"Even when he's with a woman with whom he's having an affair?" Cassie unzipped her gym bag and pulled
out her sweatpants. "Is that what you were trying to say?"

He'd been about to say that Thomas was always calm
and centered and at ease with himself even when he was
with a woman he happened to be screwing. But he did not
want to use the word *screw* around Cassie. It sounded a
little crude. She might find it offensive. Besides, she already seemed a little irritated for some reason.

"Just thought I'd ask your opinion," he muttered.

Cassie yanked her sweatpants on over her tights with
uncharacteristically quick, violent motions. "From what
you've told me, Thomas hasn't been exactly celibate
since his divorce. He dated that woman who worked up at
Mirror House for a while a few months ago. Why would
it be so strange if he was having another affair?"

"There's just something different about this situation."
He struggled to put his hazy impressions into words.
"Something different about Thomas."

Cassie bent at the waist to tie the laces of her running
shoes. "What?"

"Like I said, he seems very intense around Leonora.
There's a sort of energy between the two of them."

"Sexual attraction produces a great deal of energy between two people. It charges the air around them."

"But he wasn't flirting with her. It was almost as if he was annoyed with her. Or maybe with himself. But that doesn't feel right, either."

Cassie straightened abruptly. "Sexual energy is like any other kind of energy. If it is ignored or resisted, it can form a kind of friction that easily translates into irritation or even outright anger. The only way to deal with it is to acknowledge it and channel it in a healthy, natural manner. I recommend concentrating on breath awareness. Very helpful."

Deke winced. Cassie had that crisp, impatient tone in her voice that never failed to confuse and disturb him. It was as if she were lecturing a pupil who was being willfully slow.

"I never saw Thomas get this edgy around a woman," he said.

"He's probably on edge because they are not yet sleeping together." Cassie reached for her sweatshirt and pulled it on over her head. "My guess is that once they start an affair, assuming they do, a lot of the tension will be removed from their relationship."

"Think so?"

"Sex is an excellent means of reducing stress and elevating one's general sense of well-being." Her words were muffled by the enveloping folds of the shirt. "It can be very therapeutic."

"Therapeutic? You really think so?"

"Yes." Her head popped out of the neck hole. She avoided looking at him. "Under the appropriate circumstances, sex is a natural, wholesome way of revitalizing the lines of energy."

"Appropriate circumstances?"

"I'm referring to a situation in which both parties are unattached, mutually attracted and in good health."

Deke nodded. "Thomas is unattached and in good health and I think he's attracted to Leonora."

"What about you, Deke? You're unattached and in good health, too. It's been a year since you lost your wife. Don't you occasionally think about getting involved with a woman?"

"Me?" Shit. Had she noticed his erection? "Involved?"

She exhaled slowly. "I'm sorry. I shouldn't have said that. It's none of my business. I'm just your yoga instructor."

Deke said nothing.

She slung her gym bag over her shoulder and went to the door. "I'll see you on Friday. Meanwhile, work on that cobra pose. You're forcing it. You need to relax into it."

She opened the door and let herself out before he could formulate a response.

A familiar silence returned to the house. He had the feeling he hadn't handled things well, but for the life of him he couldn't see what he had done to make her mad. He'd just asked for her observations on Thomas and Leonora's relationship, for crying out loud. Somehow she'd twisted the conversation into a discussion of his lack of an active sex life.

He didn't need her to point out how barren his sex life was these days. He was all too well aware of that fact, especially when she was in the vicinity.

He went to the nearest window and pulled the curtains closed. He moved to the next window and repeated the action. He continued around the room until the shadows had returned.

When the familiar, comfortable gloom had pooled and deepened in the house he went to the desk and fired up the computer. He sat down and gazed into the glowing screen. He had planned to continue looking for anything he could find on the Eubanks murder, but for some reason he found himself thinking of the long-ago afternoon when he and Thomas had sat on the bed in Thomas's bedroom and listened to their parents hurl accusations at each other out in the kitchen.

He was nine at the time. Thomas was thirteen. Deke had wanted to cry. But Thomas wasn't crying, so he couldn't allow himself to give in to the tears.

"I think they're going to get a divorce, Deke. I heard Dad say something about seeing a lawyer."

"You mean like Jason's folks?"

"Yeah. Dad will probably move out. That's what usually happens, Mark told me."

"Dad's got a girlfriend, doesn't he?"

"That's what Mom says."

"Think Mom will get a boyfriend after Dad moves out?" Deke asked.

"Maybe."

"Jason says he only sees his dad once a week now. He doesn't like the woman his dad married. He says she's a bimbo. But he really hates the jerk his mother is dating. The guy sleeps in his mom's bedroom when he stays over and he hogs the remote."

They listened to the muffled yelling in the kitchen for a while. Deke hugged the pillow he was holding and fought the tears.

"I'll tell you one thing, Deke, I don't think I'll ever get married. But if I do, I'm sure not gonna have any kids. I'd never do this to my own kids."

"Me, either," Deke said.

"No matter what happens," Thomas said, "you and me, we stick together."

"Okay," Deke said.

Chapter Nine

"The formula is tailored to your body's needs," Alex said. "No two clients get the exact same version of the product. That is because no two people are exactly the same."

"I understand," Elissa said.

He opened a cupboard and selected one of the small blue bottles inside. "Also, the formula must be taken under supervision. Close monitoring is essential. That's why I insist that clients return at least once a week for their supplies."

She looked at the blue bottle in his hand. "What's in it?"

"Basically it's a complex mix of ingredients extracted from several species of seaweed." He closed the cupboard. "My research shows that most people lack the essential nutrients that are found only in the sea. Remember, our blood is very close to seawater, chemically speaking. Here on land we are often deprived of several substances that are common in the saltwater environments. As a result, we frequently function in a chronic state of chemically induced stress. Over the years, it takes a toll."

"I see."

"My therapy is based upon the principle of restoring the proper levels of certain nutrients and enzymes to the system. Once your body chemistry is back in balance, you will be able to deal with stress much more efficiently."

"That would be wonderful." Elissa gripped her purse. "I'm certainly not doing very well as it is."

Alex walked toward her, blue bottle in hand. "In my professional opinion, it is best to take a two-pronged approach to the problem. In addition to using my formula, I strongly recommend counseling."

Elissa stiffened. "I really don't want to talk about my personal life. I can't discuss it with anyone. I just made this appointment so that I could try your formula."

"Don't worry," he said soothingly. "I don't insist on the counseling. But it would be unethical of me not to mention the additional beneficial effects. I use a very unique therapeutic style. I call it mirroring. It's a form of past-life regression therapy. I've had amazing results with it."

He hadn't changed the basic scam much over the years but he routinely gave it a new name every time he set up shop. He was pleased with the term *mirroring*. He had invented it shortly after arriving in Wing Cove. This town and that architectural monstrosity, Mirror House, had proven to be downright inspirational in many respects. Mostly financial.

"I don't believe in past lives," Elissa said uneasily.

"Many people don't believe in them. Until they start to do the personal research, that is. Events and traumas in our previous lives often induce stress in this life, you see. By exploring your past lives and dealing with the tensions in them you can reduce your current stress levels."

"Maybe I'll try it. Someday. May I just have the formula for now, please?"

"Yes. But if you ever feel the need to go deeper, please contact me. I am a trained professional and you can trust me completely to keep anything said between us strictly confidential."

He gave her his reassuring smile, the one that always made the client trust him, and handed her the bottle. He didn't really care if she eventually opted for the mirroring treatments. Elissa Kern was too rigid and uptight for his taste. He had no interest in getting her into bed.

"I think you'll find that you will start to notice some of the beneficial effects almost immediately after the first dose," he said.

"I hope so."

"This feels very bizarre." Leonora raised the binoculars to her eyes and peered through the lenses. "I've never actually spied on anyone before."

Thomas kept his set of compact, high-powered binoculars trained on the front door of Alex Rhodes's rented house. The cottage was old and weather-beaten. It was located in an isolated stand of trees nearly a mile from the center of Wing Cove. Rhodes apparently liked his privacy.

"Obviously you've led a sheltered life," Thomas said.

"Obviously." She swiveled the binoculars. "I assume the big black SUV is Alex's?"

"Yeah. The guy has a thing for black."

"What about the little tan compact?"

"Probably belongs to his client," Thomas said.

"Recognize it?"

"No. Be interesting to see who gets into it, though."

"I wonder if we could get arrested for this," Leonora said.

"Watching Rhodes's house? Doubt it."

"If we do get picked up, I want you to remember that this was your idea."

"You were pretty eager to come along, as I recall."

"Okay, I'll admit that the way Alex approached me this afternoon was very suspicious. And I certainly didn't want you coming out here without me. But I don't see what we're going to learn by watching his clients come and go."

"You're bored, aren't you?"

"A little," she admitted. "I'm also cold. This fog is getting thicker by the minute."

"I warned you this might take some patience."

"I'm not the patient type."

Thomas adjusted the focus a hair. "I've noticed."

She paused a beat. "I take it you *are* the patient type?"

"I don't believe in rushing around unless there's a really good reason and, in my experience, there rarely is."

"Hmm."

She fell silent for a while but he could tell that she was fidgeting.

"It will be dark soon," she said eventually. "Might be hard to drive home if this fog gets any heavier. How long do you intend to stay out here?"

"Long as it takes."

She lowered the glasses. "You don't plan to stay out here all night, do you?"

"You're free to leave anytime," he said mildly. "It was your idea to come out here with me."

She groaned. "I'm whining, aren't I?"

"Yeah, but that's okay. You're good at it." He continued studying the view through the lenses. "I wonder why Rhodes has the shades down on all the windows."

"The shades?" She raised her binoculars again and aimed them at the house. "You're right. They are all down, aren't they? Well, your brother keeps his shades down, too."

"Yeah, but I think it's because he's depressed and he likes to spend a lot of time on his computer. Rhodes didn't look depressed to me and we know he's not on the computer because he's got a client in there. Which leaves one other likely possibility."

"What's that?"

He lowered the glasses. "Wouldn't surprise me if Rhodes was the kind of therapist who sleeps with his female clients."

"You don't think much of him, do you?" she said.

"'Never trust a guy who wears yellow contact lenses' is sort of a Walker family motto."

She thought about that. "Probably as good as any other family motto." She broke off suddenly. "There she is."

"Who?"

"Alex's client. She just came out the front door. She's headed for her car."

"A woman?" He snapped up the binoculars. Tendrils of fog lay heavily in the driveway but there was still enough light left for him to make out the stiff-shouldered, tawny-haired woman getting into the tan compact.

"Elissa Kern," he said. "Think he's screwing her?"

"As a highly trained academic librarian, I refuse to leap to conclusions without supporting evidence. But I must admit that scenario would certainly explain the covered windows."

"Damn. Poor Ed Stovall."

"The police chief? Why are you feeling sorry for him?"

"Because I got the impression he's lusting after Elissa in his own anal-retentive way."

"Oh." She lowered the glasses. "That would be sad, wouldn't it?"

"Yeah, but it's not our problem, luckily. We've got our own problems."

He watched Elissa's compact disappear into the fog. Then he switched the binoculars back to Alex.

Rhodes waited on the porch until Elissa's car was gone. Then he turned and went inside the house. Thomas was just about to suggest that it was time to call off the surveillance and start thinking about dinner when the front door opened again.

Rhodes came back out onto the porch, dressed in running clothes and a windbreaker. He locked his front door, went to the porch railing and did some stretches. When he was finished he loped down the steps and set off.

"No wonder he's in such excellent condition," Leonora murmured.

"A man his age ought to think twice about running. Hard on the knees."

"His knees don't seem to be giving him any trouble."

"Knees are tricky. You never know when they'll go out on you." Thomas dropped the small binoculars into the pocket of his jacket. "Wait here, I'll be right back."

She glanced at him with a startled frown. "Where are you going?"

"Long as I'm in the neighborhood and the neighbor in question isn't around, I thought I'd seize the moment."

"To do what?"

"Check out his house."

"What? You're going to break in?" Her voice rose on the last two words. "Are you crazy? What if Alex returns unexpectedly? He could have you arrested."

"He just left for a run. He'll probably be gone at least half an hour. Maybe longer. I'll only be inside for a few minutes."

"I don't think this is a good idea."

"Don't watch, if it bothers you." He started off through the trees.

"Oh, no, you don't." She hurried after him. "If you insist on doing this, I'm going in with you."

He heard her muffled footsteps on the damp ground and came to a halt, turning to confront her.

"No," he said.

"You can't stop me, Thomas." She halted. "We're partners, remember?"

The fierce stubbornness in her voice warned him that he wasn't going to be able to keep her from following him. He could always come back later when she wasn't around.

"All right, forget it. It's a bad idea, like you said." He reached for her arm. "Come on, let's get out of here."

"I know what you're thinking." She stepped hastily out of reach, spun around on her heel and started toward the cabin. "You plan to come back some other time and do your little breaking-and-entering routine without me, don't you?"

"Damn it, Leonora, wait." He caught up with her. "I agree with you. This is too risky."

"But that won't stop you, will it?"

He thought about picking her up and putting her over his shoulder. Somehow he didn't think she'd go along with that plan.

What the hell was a man supposed to do with a woman like this? He looked around. The oncoming night and the fog provided excellent cover. Chances were they were safe enough for the moment. If they went in and got out fast they should be okay.

"All right," he said. "We're here. Might as well do it."

She surveyed the windows. "How do we get inside?"

He reached inside his jacket, removed the small tool

kit he carried on his belt and opened it. He selected two of the gleaming picks.

"With these," he said. "Now you watch out for Rhodes."

"Good grief. You planned this, didn't you?"

"I never do anything without a plan. I'm sort of obsessive-compulsive that way."

He mounted the three steps to the back door and went to work.

It took less than thirty seconds to pop the lock.

"Wow," Leonora whispered. "Where did you learn to do that?"

"I'm into remodeling, remember? You install and repair enough locks over the years, you learn how they work."

He pulled on his gloves and opened the door cautiously. He found himself gazing into a small room. A trash can loomed in the shadows. A pair of dirty boots sat on the floor. The shelves that climbed one wall held the usual assortment of odds and ends you expected to see in a storage room: A flashlight. Some batteries. A garden hose. Kitchen supplies.

A bag of golf clubs stood propped in the corner.

Behind him Leonora came to stand in the doorway. She glanced back over her shoulder and then followed him into the storage room.

"Don't touch anything," he ordered.

"Don't worry, I've got gloves on, too, see?" She held up one sheathed hand.

"We don't want to disturb anything. No sense making him suspicious."

He eased the door closed with a gloved hand and went past her into a narrow hall that connected the bath and bedroom to the front room and kitchen. He halted to give his eyes time to adjust to the gloom.

"Watch your step," he said. "It really is dark in here with those shades down."

"What are we looking for?"

"How should I know?" He went down the hall toward the bedroom. "I've never done this before."

"But it was your idea. I thought you had a clear objective."

He ignored that to open a closet. An array of small vials and bottles were displayed on the shelves.

"Take a look at this," he said.

She came to stand beside him. "The ingredients of his nutritional supplement, probably."

He picked up one of the bottles. "Think he'd miss any?"

"Are you serious?" she asked sharply.

"I'll just take a little pinch from a couple of the bottles. Rhodes will never notice. Think of it as a random sample. Consumer quality-control testing."

"What are you going to put your samples into?"

He went back into the small storage room and helped himself to some plastic bags. "These should do the trick."

He opened three of the little vials and dumped a tiny amount of the contents of each into three bags. He sealed the bags and closed the cupboard.

"Let's see what else we can find." He led the way into the bedroom.

The small room looked surprisingly normal. A wooden dresser, bed and chair constituted the extent of the furnishings.

He opened the closet door and confronted a sea of black. An array of black shirts and black trousers and jeans hung on the rod. Several pairs of black boots and black loafers were neatly lined up on the floor. A cluster of black-on-black ties were draped over a tie rack.

"You notice there's a real touch of the theatrical about

this guy?" he said. "The phony yellow eyes, the black clothes. It's like Rhodes is acting a part. Kind of surprised to see he doesn't have any mirrors over the bed."

"Please." She gave him an enigmatic glance. "Are you so biased against Alex because he dated Meredith for a while after you split with her?"

"That has nothing to do with it."

It was the truth, as far as it went. But not the full story.

He had to admit that Alex Rhodes hadn't even been on his radar screen until this afternoon when he had stood on the sidewalk outside of Pitney's Hardware & Plumbing Supply watching the guy escort Leonora into the coffeehouse. At that point a deep and abiding distrust of the man had flashed through him.

But he didn't think Leonora would understand. Hell, he wasn't sure he understood his reaction himself, although he had a sneaking suspicion that he was way too old and much too jaded for this kind of elemental, hormone-driven stuff.

He closed the closet and opened the nightstand. "Well, now, what do you know?"

She looked at him across the width of the bed. "What's in there?"

"A large, industrial-size box of condoms. Which suggests that Rhodes may indeed be sleeping with some of his clients."

Judging from the fact that the box was half empty it was also a good bet that Rhodes's sex life was a lot more interesting than his own had been of late. But that was probably not a very professional thought for an amateur detective to be thinking.

Leonora came to stand beside him. "My goodness. He seems to have gone through quite a few of them. Maybe it's all that running."

He slammed the drawer shut. "I told you, running is bad for the knees."

"I know, but he probably doesn't use his knees for this sort of thing."

"If that's true, the man lacks imagination."

He opened a dresser and saw stacks of black T-shirts and black briefs. He closed the drawer and opened the next one.

Black socks.

"You know, it would be nice to turn up some banking or financial records but that's probably not real likely." He closed the last drawer and stood looking around the room. "Rhodes strikes me as the cautious type. Doubt if he'd leave anything useful lying around."

"Now what?"

"You take the bathroom. Check for prescriptions or anything that looks interesting." He went out into the hall. "I'll do the front room."

"Right." She disappeared around the corner.

He wandered into the shadowed living room. It appeared unremarkable at first glance. The sofa was covered in a subdued print. There was a circular braided rug on the floor. A laptop sat, closed, on a desk.

He looked longingly at the computer, but he didn't dare swipe it and, unlike Deke, he didn't have the skills to get past whatever personal security Rhodes used.

He turned his attention to the long, low table positioned on the rug instead.

There was something odd about it.

He went closer and saw that it was draped in black velvet. He could see that there was an object under the velvet.

The whisper of unease that drifted through him was as inexplicable and primordial as the feeling of sexual possessiveness he had experienced when he walked into the coffeehouse and found Rhodes trying to charm Leonora. Not quite civilized.

"Nothing unusual in the bathroom," Leonora said behind him. "Find anything out here?"

"Maybe."

"Black velvet?" She came quickly forward to join him. "*Without* a picture of Elvis painted on it. This doesn't look good, does it?"

"Looks damn weird, is how it looks."

He reached down, grasped a fistful of black velvet and lifted it away from the table.

A circular mirror, its reflective surface darkened with age and surrounded by an elaborately worked and heavily tarnished metal frame, glittered in the shadows.

The mirror was not a single, flat plate. It was composed, instead, of what appeared at first glance to be several concentric circles of glass bubbles. Each bubble produced a tiny, slightly distorted, independent reflection. The result was a myriad of miniature fun-house images that had a disturbing effect on the eye.

"Uh oh," Leonora said. "This is definitely strange."

"Couldn't have put it more pithily, myself. I've never seen anything like it."

"I have—in one of the books in the library at Mirror House."

She leaned down to take a closer look. There was just enough light left in the room to reveal a small image of her face reflected in each of the bubbles. Some of the reflections made her look larger. Others made her look minuscule. An eerie feeling swept through him. It was as if there were a hundred little Leonoras trapped inside the bubbles.

Without thinking, he reached out and pulled her upright and away from the mirror so that the distorted reflections disappeared.

She was startled by his sudden movement but she did not resist.

"What's wrong?" she asked.

"Nothing," he said, lying through his teeth. "I just want to check something out." He reached down to grasp the edge of the mirror and lifted it partway off the table. It was surprisingly heavy.

He looked at the faded number written on the back.

"It's from the Mirror House collection. There's an old inventory number on the reverse." He lowered the looking glass back down onto the table. "Rhodes must have stolen it."

Leonora watched him arrange the black velvet cloth over the mirror and table.

"Each one of those little bubbles is a tiny convex or concave mirror," she said. "I'm no expert, but I've been doing a lot of heavy research lately. My guess is that it dates from the early nineteenth century. According to what I've read, the technology required to produce that kind of unusual mirror plate wasn't widely available until the end of the eighteenth century. I suspect it's very valuable."

"Probably." He contemplated the black velvet that covered the mirror. "The question is, why did Rhodes take it and what the hell is he doing with it?"

Leonora gave a small shudder. "Playing games with his clients?"

He could feel the hair stirring on the nape of his neck. Adrenaline pumped through him. Time to get the hell out of Dodge.

"Come on." He grasped Leonora's arm and hauled her toward the back door. "We've seen enough. Let's get out of here."

She offered no protest. In fact, judging by her willingness to move quickly, he got the impression that she was as eager to leave as he was.

He heard the footsteps on the front porch just as he opened the back door.

Rhodes was back from his run.

He sensed rather than saw the flutter of fear that went through Leonora. He bundled her through the open door and motioned her to head for the fog-bound trees. She whirled and disappeared quickly, almost instantly, into the fog.

Now you see her, now you don't.

He suddenly understood why Rhodes had returned unexpectedly early from his run. The fog had grown much heavier while he and Leonora had been inside the cabin. When the last of the light vanished it would be impossible to see your hand in front of your face out here.

Rhodes's keys jangled in the lock.

Thomas heard the front door open just as he carefully shut the back door.

Bending low he made for the cover of fog and trees.

"Over here," Leonora whispered.

He saw movement in the shadows off to his left, reached out, groped and caught her hand. Together they plunged deeper into the damp mist. Darkness closed in around them, offering safety and a new kind of danger.

A short distance into the woods it became almost impossible to see where they were going. Getting lost or brained by a long hanging branch was not on his agenda. There were other risks inherent in this activity. In the damp, chilly muck they could wander around for hours and fall prey to hypothermia.

He drew Leonora to a halt. "Hold on. I need to get my bearings. We don't want to get too far from the cabin. It's our only solid reference point in this pea soup."

At that moment a dim glow appeared in the mist behind them.

"Thank you for turning on the porch light, Rhodes," he said softly. "Just what we needed."

He tightened his grip on Leonora's hand and moved toward the right. He kept the dim glow of the porch light at his shoulder as they made their way through the trees. The result was a path that described an arc with the cottage at its center.

A few minutes later they emerged onto the graveled drive that led to the road.

"Okay," he said. "Gravel has a nice crunch to it. Sort of like breakfast cereal. As long as we're crunching we're headed in the right direction."

"I've never seen fog this thick."

"They're saying in town that this is the worst spell of the stuff that anyone has seen in Wing Cove in years."

They struck pavement a short time later. The fog seemed somewhat lighter here on the road. The SUV was where it was supposed to be, parked out of sight behind an empty summerhouse.

He glanced at the run-down cottage with its drooping front steps and boarded-up windows.

"I almost bought this place instead of the one you're living in," he told Leonora as he opened the door on the passenger side. "It was a real steal. Glad I picked the other one, though."

"Me, too." She scrambled up onto the seat. "I'm not sure I'd want to be living this close to a guy who sells unidentifiable stuff out of unlabeled bottles."

"Location is everything in real estate."

The thought of her having old golden-eyes as her neighbor was more disturbing to him than Thomas wanted to admit, and not just because of the unidentified powder in the blue bottles.

He got behind the wheel and checked the road. He

could see the white line now. The fog had thinned out, at least for a while. They could make it back to Wing Cove.

There was a distinct chill in the vehicle. He shoved the key into the ignition and fired up the heater.

"That," he said, pulling out onto the pavement, "was a little close."

She folded her arms and gazed straight ahead through the windshield. "Well, what can you expect? We're still new at this detective business. I'm sure we'll get the hang of it sooner or later."

Chapter Ten

He brought the car to a halt in her driveway a short time later and switched off the engine. She was very conscious of him sitting there close beside her in the front seat. It was comforting, not to mention extremely reassuring, to have him nearby. There was something solid and substantial about Thomas. She was, she realized, reluctant to let him go.

"I can't believe we did that," she said.

"It was a different sort of outing for me, too." There was no inflection in his words. "When it comes to entertainment, I usually prefer to go down to the hardware store and look at screwdrivers."

"We could have been arrested."

"Doubt it."

She turned her head quickly to look at him. "If Alex had caught us inside his house he would have been perfectly within his rights to call the cops."

"Sure. But then he would have had to explain that

weird mirror, which he obviously swiped from Mirror House. And something tells me he wouldn't want Ed Stovall going through his cupboards and maybe taking a few samples, the way we did."

She caught her breath. "You don't really think Alex is selling drugs, do you?"

"Who knows what the hell that guy is selling? Even if it's just powdered sugar, he won't want the word to get out that he's a complete con. No, I don't think he'd have called the cops."

She exhaled slowly. "Nevertheless, in hindsight, it was probably not the brightest thing either of us has ever done."

"On a scale of one to ten, I'd give it a two."

"You've done dumber stuff?"

"Sure." He pondered that briefly. "I'd have to rate my marriage as a one. Definitely a dumb thing to do. But, then, I was a lot younger back then. Youth is always a good excuse. Doesn't work so well these days."

She nodded. "The only thing that I've ever done that was dumber than breaking into that house was get engaged to Professor Kyle Delling."

"What happened to the engagement?"

"I came home from work one afternoon and found him in my bed with Meredith."

Thomas winced. "Ouch."

"She set it up, of course. Called me at the library that day. Told me there was an emergency and that I had to come home immediately. Timed it so that when I walked through my front door, she and Kyle were between the sheets."

"Why did she do that? Sheer cruelty?"

"Not in her mind. She felt that she had done me a huge favor by showing me that Kyle was weak and couldn't be trusted." She rubbed her arms briskly. "But I'm not sure it was a fair test."

"Why do you say that?"

"I've never met the man who was able to resist Meredith." She summoned up a bright little smile and opened the door. "You know something? Either I got a little too cold running around out there in the fog or my nerves are acting up. Either way, I think I could use a medicinal glass of wine. Care for some of the same tonic?"

"Sure."

He already had the truck door open, the keys in his pocket.

Relief flooded through her. He wasn't going to leave her alone with her frazzled nerves just yet. They were partners, after all.

"The fog is getting bad again. You might as well stay for dinner." She tried to make the invitation sound offhand. "No sense risking your neck trying to drive until this stuff lifts a little."

"You've got a deal."

She waited for him to walk around the front of the car and join her. They went up the front steps together. It was dark now. She paused to sort keys in her palm with the aid of the porch light.

"Here we go." She let them into the front hall and switched on a lamp.

She caught a glimpse of herself in the mirror when she went to hang up her coat and suppressed a small groan. Not exactly a ravishing sight, she thought. Tendrils of hair had come free of the twist. Behind the lenses of her glasses her eyes had a stark, strained quality, and her cheeks looked hollow. The dark, cable-knit sweater she wore did nothing to brighten the reflection.

Thomas shrugged out of his jacket and came to stand behind her. Their eyes met in the mirror. Unlike her, he looked terrific, she thought. Hard and tough and totally in control. She had to fight an irresistible urge to turn and put her head down on his chest.

His hands closed over her shoulders. "Take it easy. You're just feeling the aftershock of the adrenaline. It'll fade."

"I know."

The weight of his hands was not having the calming, soothing effect he probably intended. Little sparks of excitement were snapping across her nerve endings. Energy hummed through her.

She suddenly wanted to do a lot more than just put her head down on his shoulder. She looked at his mouth in the mirror and wondered what it would be like to kiss him.

Wondered how his mouth would feel on other parts of her body.

Wondered how his big, competent hands would feel on her breasts.

Her thighs.

Wondered if he was thinking similar thoughts.

Adrenaline. This is all nerves and adrenaline. Get hold of yourself, woman.

"I'll pour the wine," she said quickly.

She rushed into the old-fashioned kitchen, opened the cupboard, grabbed a bottle of red and went feverishly to work with a corkscrew.

By the time she got back to the living room Thomas had the fire going.

She handed one of the glasses to him. When he took it from her, his knuckles lightly grazed hers. Another jolt of electricity sparked along her overstimulated nerve endings. She pulled away so fast she nearly dropped her glass.

"You okay?" Thomas asked, sounding concerned now.

"Just a little tense." She took a healthy swallow of

wine and looked around, searching for something mundane and normal. "Did you buy this place furnished?"

"No." He frowned. "I rented the furniture. What's the matter? You don't like it? There wasn't a lot of choice. The company had three basic packages. I had to pick one."

"It's fine. Just fine." She took another sip of wine. "Some of the pieces are rather large like I said. The bed barely fits." Oh, damn, what on earth had made her mention a bed? "But the sofa is great. Really."

"Yeah, the bed is kind of large, isn't it?" he said thoughtfully. "I noticed that when they delivered the furniture. Guess I was thinking of myself when I picked it out. I like my beds big."

She could not think of any reasonable rejoinder to that comment. She told herself the smartest thing she could do right now was keep her mouth shut.

They stood in front of the fire for a while.

She gazed into the leaping flames and forced herself to concentrate on more important things. Alex's tinted contact lenses and the strange mirror and the little vials in the cupboard came to mind.

"What in heaven's name is Alex doing out there?" she asked eventually, when she was sure that the subject of big beds had been forgotten.

"Hard to tell what kind of game he's playing. But he's in this right up to his yellow contacts, I'm sure of it."

She hesitated. "He said he moved here a little over a year ago. That means he was in Wing Cove when Bethany died."

Thomas thought about that. "As far as I know he and Bethany never even met. I'm damn sure she wasn't going to him for stress counseling and she wasn't taking any of that nutritional supplement he's selling. Deke would have been aware of it. Trust me. He looked after Bethany."

"Looked after her?"

"She was so lost in her work most of the time that she needed a guardian or a keeper more than she needed a husband."

"I know what you mean. I've met a couple of truly brilliant types who fit that description. They could give you a mathematical explanation for the origin of matter, but they couldn't match their socks."

Thomas nodded. "That was Bethany. Deke did everything for her when it came to the regular stuff of ordinary life. He kept track of her dental appointments, shopped for groceries, bought her new clothes when she needed them. Everything."

"Hmm. Think maybe that was a problem for Deke?"

"What do you mean?"

"Remember I told you that part of his depression might stem from some unresolved issues in his marriage?"

"So?"

"So, just speculating wildly here, but what if he married Bethany because the guardian job appealed to the knight-in-shining-armor side of his nature? What if, eventually, playing keeper all the time lost some of its allure? What if they were having trouble in the marriage and before they could work things out, she died?"

Thomas looked into the flames. "I liked Bethany, but I know I couldn't have been happy married to her. She never did anything for Deke as far as I could tell. I'm not sure how much she really cared for him, deep down. She was content to let him take care of her and admire her brilliance. I used to wonder if she really loved him or if she just found him convenient."

"Mind if I ask you what happened to your marriage?" she said softly.

"It ended."

The complete lack of inflection spoke volumes.

"Sorry," she said.

He swallowed more wine. "We were married for four years before she left me for my business partner."

"Aaargh."

"Yeah. That sums it up pretty accurately. Aaargh. But life goes on."

"Yes."

"You know, when my parents got divorced, I told myself I probably wouldn't ever get married. And if I did marry, I sure as hell wouldn't have any kids."

"Because you never wanted to take the risk of putting them through the trauma of divorce?" she asked.

"Yeah. Turns out I should have stuck with my initial decision not to marry. But at least there weren't any kids to get hurt when I did end up in a divorce court. I got singed, but no one else got badly burned. I learned my lesson."

Time to change the subject again, she thought. It was depressing to listen to him talk so coolly about how he never intended to remarry or become a father.

"Getting back to the problem of Alex Rhodes," she said very deliberately. "I think I've got an idea."

"What?"

"I could sign up for some stress counseling."

"Don't," Thomas said flatly, "even think about it."

"You're not being logical here, Thomas."

"Rhodes wasn't offering stress counseling. He wants to get you into bed."

"You don't know that."

"I know it."

"Thomas, be reasonable. We need a lead. Alex is a lead."

"Maybe, but you're not going to be the one to follow it."

Anger flared, startling her with its intensity. "Damn it, no one voted you the boss of this operation. I'm willing to discuss things with you, but in the end, we're equal partners. I make my own decisions."

"Listen up," he said, his voice low and rough. "The last woman who had a connection with me and who later went out with Alex Rhodes is dead. Remember?"

Icy fingers slithered down her spine. "Meredith."

"Yeah. Meredith. No offense, but we both know that she was a lot more capable of dealing with a guy like Rhodes than you will ever be."

For some reason, probably because she was already tense and on edge, that observation *did* offend her. A lot. The worst part was that she knew that he was right. Meredith had been much more qualified to handle dangerous men. She knew it, but she didn't like it and she was not going to admit it.

She whirled around and strode toward the kitchen. "I'll get dinner going. That fog will probably lift soon and I'm sure you'll want to get home to Wrench as soon as possible."

"Hell." He came after her, halting in the doorway of the kitchen. "You're mad, aren't you?"

"I really don't want to talk about it."

"And they say men are the ones who don't do a good job of communicating."

She jerked open the freezer drawer and removed the package of frozen soybeans. "There's no need to reduce this to the personal."

He was very still in the doorway. "In case you haven't noticed, this thing between us has already become personal. Real personal. At least on my side."

"No, I hadn't noticed."

He left the doorway without warning. Before she realized his intentions, he was only inches away, looming over her, enveloping her in an invisible force field.

"Thomas?"

He slammed his half-empty wineglass down on the counter beside her so hard she wondered that it didn't shatter. He caught her face between his hands. She could feel the work-roughened skin of his palms against her throat.

"This is what I mean by personal," he said into her mouth.

He kissed her before she could catch her breath. Her fully charged nerve endings exploded on contact. The resulting flash of lightning was so hot she was amazed it didn't fry the frozen soybeans she held in her left hand.

Definitely personal, she thought. More personal than anything she could remember experiencing in a very long time. Maybe in her entire life.

He pushed her back until the edge of the counter pressed against her spine. He moved one leg between hers. His mouth shifted, deepening the kiss. She was melting faster than the contents of the open freezer drawer.

All she cared about was heat. Lots of it. She lived for heat. She needed it. Craved it. She wanted to go up in flames. She had been so cold for so long she wasn't sure she would ever be able to get enough of the red-hot energy Thomas was generating.

She heard a soft *plop* and was vaguely aware that she had dropped the package of soybeans back into the freezer. She wrapped her arms around Thomas, seeking escape from the cold draft.

He muttered something unintelligible and kicked the freezer drawer shut with one booted foot. Then he put a strong, muscular arm around her lower back just above her hips and cradled her head in his other hand. His mouth slid down her throat. She shoved her fingers into his hair. She shivered, but not because she was still cold.

His hands shifted again, closing snugly around her waist. He gripped. Lifted. And then her feet were no longer touching the floor. She thought that he intended to carry her back out into the front room. Instead, he set her on the edge of the counter and moved between her thighs. His mouth never left her body.

He was making love to her right there in the kitchen. As if he just couldn't wait to get her to a bed. No one had ever been in this much of a hurry before. She had never been so eager, either. It was unbelievable. It was also almost unbearably erotic.

Recklessly, she tightened her thighs around him. He got his hands under her sweater. And then they were on her bare breasts. What had happened to her bra? Somehow he had gotten it unfastened without her even being aware of it.

The man really was very good with his hands. She couldn't wait to see what else he could do with them.

Her blood beat more heavily in her veins and the fire got hotter.

Without warning, it all came to a crashing halt.

Thomas went very still, as if he had hit a wall. Bemused, she opened her eyes and found him watching her with grim intensity.

"Do you," he said with grave precision, "happen to have anything handy that would be useful in a situation such as this?"

She blinked, trying to reorient herself. "Such as?"

"Condoms."

"Oh." Reality slammed through her. She felt herself flush. "No, I don't."

"Pills?"

"No." She was probably an embarrassing shade of pink by now. "I certainly didn't anticipate needing anything here in Wing Cove."

No need to tell him that she hadn't needed anything since her engagement had been abruptly terminated.

"I came prepared to pop a couple of locks today." He gave her a rueful, sexy smile and leaned his forehead against hers. "I didn't come prepared for this kind of excitement."

"Oh." She couldn't think of anything intelligent to say. She was badly rattled and she knew it.

He straightened and took a step back. "Well, as neither one of us appears to be what you'd call farsighted or visionary, I think we'd better concentrate on dinner, don't you?"

She managed to resist a terrible impulse to grab him by the collar and scream something idiotic along the lines of, *You can't stop now. I'm hot enough to thaw the contents of that freezer.*

Thankfully, common sense prevailed. Of course they had to call a halt. Good grief, what on earth was she thinking? This wasn't love or romance. This was lust. Triggered, no doubt, by the adrenaline overload they had both experienced this afternoon.

"Dinner. Yes. This is crazy." She took a deep breath and realized she was still sitting on the kitchen counter. "Not to mention extremely unsanitary."

"Maybe. But it does settle one burning hypothetical question."

She shoved several wild tendrils of hair behind her ears and hopped down from the counter.

...And nearly landed ignominiously on her rear when her knees threatened to dissolve. She had to grab the tiled edge to steady herself. This was mortifying. Absolutely mortifying.

She took a deep breath and pulled herself together with an act of will.

"What burning hypothetical question is that?" she asked.

"When I picked out that bed you're using, I definitely was thinking about myself."

Forget the steamed soybeans in their pods and the dazzling display of deceptively casual culinary skill with which she had planned to wow him tonight. She jerked open the refrigerator and reached inside for the plastic container filled with the remains of the potato salad she had made yesterday. She grabbed the leftover hummus and some lettuce, too.

"I wouldn't read too much into that little display of hormones on parade, if I were you." She slammed the refrigerator shut and put the containers on the counter. "We were both overstimulated from our big, scary adventure. Too much adrenaline, like you said earlier."

He watched her, a disturbing intensity in his gaze. "Blame it on the adrenaline if you want. But whatever it was, it wasn't fake. Right?"

She pretended she had not heard him while she washed her hands at the sink. The project provided her with the perfect excuse to keep her back to him.

"Leonora?"

"What? I'm trying to put a meal together, in case you hadn't noticed."

"You weren't faking it a few minutes ago, were you?"

"Oh, for goodness's sake." She picked up the knife and sawed violently at the loaf of crusty bread she had bought in town yesterday.

"Give me that much, at least," Thomas said. "My male ego is on the line here."

She glanced quickly over her shoulder. Sexy laughter gleamed in his eyes. He did not look like a man with a serious ego problem. She very much doubted that he needed her to assure him that her response had been genuine. She had been nothing if not blatant.

On the other hand, his wife had run off with his business partner. That kind of thing had to leave a mark.

"For the record," she said, "I'm a terrible actress. I don't fake anything well." Then she went back to work on the sandwiches.

"I wasn't faking anything, either," he said softly.

She thought about the feel of his heavily aroused body between her thighs.

"I noticed," she said.

By the time they sat down to eat at the table near the window, the atmosphere in the kitchen had subtly altered. The charged sensuality still shimmered in the invisible currents of air that swirled around her, but there was something else, too. She was aware of a cozy, comfortable, intimate warmth. It felt good to have Thomas sitting here across from her.

She suddenly regretted that she had fed him leftovers.

The fog lifted while they did the dishes. Thomas got his coat from the closet. She followed him outside, hugging herself against the chill of the clear, starry night.

He paused and looked past her into the hall of the small house. "I've got a lot of work to do in there. I'm going to replace the windows and redo the bathroom from the plumbing out. The flooring is good, though. Solid oak. Just needs to be refinished."

She followed his gaze. "Do you plan to stay on here in Wing Cove after this is all over?"

"Depends. I came here after Bethany died because I could see that Deke was in trouble. Figured I'd stick around until he came out of his depression. But I'm not tied to Wing Cove. I can do my work anywhere. Wrench isn't fussy, either. What about you? You tied to that job down in California?"

"Not anymore. I can go back if I want, but I'll see how I feel about it when the time comes." Hard to explain, even to herself, but this journey to Wing Cove felt like a turning point in her life. She couldn't make out the shape of the changes that were coming but she knew things would be different after this venture. "The only thing I'm tied to is a person. My grandmother. If I move, she'll move."

"Sure."

Thomas took a step closer and kissed her. He did not put his hands on her. She could have pulled back. But she didn't.

He ended the kiss.

"Didn't think it was just the adrenaline," he said, looking satisfied.

He went down the steps, got into the SUV and drove away into the night.

She went to bed and lay awake in the darkness for a long time, thinking about how it had been to have Thomas there that evening. This situation was already complicated enough as it was. It would be extremely reckless to add a torrid affair to the volatile brew.

She forced herself to refocus on the business that had brought her to Wing Cove. When that got her nowhere, she spent some time mulling over what she and Thomas had seen in Alex's cabin.

Eventually she slipped into a restless sleep.

...And plunged straight into a dark dream.

She walked down a long, shadowed hall lined with old, dark mirrors. Somewhere in this corridor the truth was trapped inside a looking glass. All she had to do was look into the right mirror and she would get the answers she had come here to find.

She stopped in front of an ornate, Rococo-style English looking glass and saw Meredith inside, looking out at her.

You can't sleep yet, Meredith said silently.

She whirled around and found Alex Rhodes watching her from inside the depths of a garish fun-house mirror. He gave her his sexy smile, inviting her to join him in some private joke. But the smile was all wrong. As she watched his features became twisted and distorted. His yellow eyes glowed.

She turned away and continued down the endless hall of mirrors, searching for the truth.

Chapter Eleven

They sat in the dark room with the glowing monitor and looked at the little plastic bags on Deke's desk. Wrench was flopped on his back on the floor, legs in the air. Thomas draped his arm over the edge of the chair and absently rubbed the dog's stomach.

"I can't get past a vision of the two of you breaking into Rhodes's house." Deke shook his head, looking amazed and maybe even a little amused. "I'd like to have been there to see you both hustling your rears out the back as he was coming in the front door."

"Trust me, you didn't miss anything."

"Black velvet and a weird mirror, huh? Guess it goes with those phony yellow eyes of his. Interesting."

"I don't know what he's up to, but he's in this thing deep," Thomas said. "He made the move on Leonora. Mentioned Meredith's name to her. Probably trying to see how she'd react. The only thing I can figure is that he knows about the million and a half bucks."

"That money is safely back in the endowment account, thanks to Leonora."

"Yeah, but Rhodes wouldn't have any way of knowing that, would he?"

Deke's amusement faded. "He was in town at the time Bethany died."

"I know. But I can't see any connection. Except the drug rumors."

Deke picked up one of the bags and looked closely at the blue-green powder in the corner. "If this stuff is some kind of illegal shit we probably should be careful about how we deal with it. Don't want to give Ed Stovall an excuse for arresting us."

"Can you get it tested quietly?"

"Sure. I know someone in the chemistry department. A grad student. He'll do it, for a price."

"We need to check out Rhodes, too."

"That," Deke said, "I will handle personally. I just hope I have more luck than I did with my other research."

"You didn't find anything new on the Eubanks murder?"

"Nothing more than what was reported in those clippings. Sebastian Eubanks, widely held to be a couple of bricks shy of a full load, was presumed to have been shot by a burglar he surprised in the mansion one night. No one was ever arrested. End of story."

Thomas gripped the arms of the chair. "Leonora is talking about playing lady spy. Mentioned signing up for some stress counseling from Rhodes. Said it would be a good way to get close to him. Maybe pick up more information."

Deke studied the bags. "Might work."

"I don't give a damn if it would work or not. She's not going to do it. Not if I have anything to say about it."

"The thing is, you don't have anything to say about it," Deke pointed out.

Thomas looked at him.

Deke held up a hand. "Remember what that therapist you dated for a while told you. You've got control issues."

"This isn't a control thing. It's common sense." Thomas shoved himself up out of the chair and walked to the nearest window. He yanked the curtains open. "I don't want her alone with that son of a bitch for five minutes. Rhodes is up to something. I can feel it. He may be dangerous."

Crystalline silence descended. It lasted only a few seconds but that was more than enough time for him to realize how much he had given away. Deke wasn't the only one taken by surprise.

"Sure, I understand," Deke said. "Can't be too careful around a guy with fake yellow eyes."

He thinks I'm jealous. Thomas tightened his grip on the curtain. *Hell, he's right.*

All he had been able to think about last night after leaving Leonora was how much he hadn't wanted to leave her. When he had gotten back to the house he'd spent a couple of hours in his workshop, drilling holes in some boards he planned to use for shelving. The effort to distract himself from memories of the superheated kiss in her kitchen had been spectacularly unsuccessful.

When he had awakened this morning he had taken Wrench up into the woods on the bluffs where the dog could run free of the leash. The two of them had prowled through the dripping trees for over an hour while Thomas had come to terms with the new reality in his life.

He wanted Leonora more than he had wanted anything else in a very long time.

With acceptance came the need for planning and action. So, okay, he had control issues. So what? He worked damn hard at staying in control. He'd practiced diligently since the nights when he'd been a kid trapped in a bedroom with Deke, listening to the noise of their parents quarrelling, both of them afraid to go to sleep because they might wake up and discover that their father had moved out.

He had gotten so good at the control thing that when he was confronted with situations he could not control physically, he could at least control his own emotional reaction to the events.

Take his divorce, for instance. In the end, he'd been more annoyed by the dissolution of a perfectly good business partnership than he had the ruination of his marriage. Which probably didn't say much for the marriage, but that was another matter.

The bottom line was that with Leonora he was, for the first time, conscious of feeling edgy and restless, not quite in full control. He needed to do something, anything.

Before coming here to Deke's house, he'd rearranged the drawer in the nightstand beside his bed. It hadn't been easy. He'd been forced to remove a flashlight, the remote, some electrical cables, a stack of financial magazines, a carton of tissues, three pens and a notebook to get at the box of condoms that had somehow worked its way to the rear of the drawer.

He had opened the box, removed two of the little packets and put them into his wallet. Then he had carefully placed the box back into the drawer. Right at the front, where he could find it again quickly. In the dark.

It wasn't much in the way of concrete action, but it was something.

A man had to think positive.

She heard the muffled squeak behind the paneled wall just as she pulled out the *C* tray in the old wooden catalog. The faint noise was followed by the low murmur of voices. Julie Bromley and her boyfriend, Travis, were doing their lunch hour disappearing act again, taking the concealed flight of servant's stairs to the third floor.

She gave them a few minutes to get where they were going, marking their progress by the creaks and groans of the hidden staircase. When the sounds ceased, she closed the catalog drawer, left the office and went to the door of the library to check the long, gloom-filled central hall.

The old looking glasses glimmered malevolently in the dim light. There was no sound of activity downstairs on the first floor of the mansion.

Satisfied that everyone was at lunch, she went to the narrow door set into the wooden paneling next to the library and pushed it open. She moved cautiously into the small space on the other side and let the panel swing shut behind her.

Julie's and Travis's voices filtered down from the floor above. Somewhere overhead another door opened and closed.

She removed the pencil-thin flashlight she had stashed in her pocket that morning and switched on the slim beam. The narrow ray revealed the twisted staircase that coiled around itself and disappeared into the shadows. The prints of Julie's and Travis's shoes were evident in the heavy coating of dust that covered the skinny treads. Judging from the heavy smudges in the thick grime it was obvious the pair made this hike to the forbidden third floor on a regular basis.

She started cautiously up the staircase. The treads were so narrow that her heels hung out over the edge of each step. How in the world had the servants of yesteryear, laden as they must have been with heavy silver platters and stacks of bedding, managed to navigate these treacherous steps? It was a wonder they had not fallen and broken their necks.

Halfway up the spiraling staircase one of the steps groaned loudly beneath her weight. That was the telltale sound she heard in the library when Julie and Travis made this trek, she thought.

At the top of the stairs she found another slender door inset in the wooden paneling.

She shut off the flashlight and pushed carefully against the panel. The door swung open on creaky hinges. She went through the opening and found herself in a cramped, unlit corridor that was much narrower than the hall on the floor below. In the old days this would have been the section of the house where the servants and less important guests had had their bedchambers. The only light came from the small windows at both ends of the passage.

There were no carpets up here, she noticed. The wooden floor had not been swept or polished in a very long time. It was easy to follow the footprints in the dust.

She went slowly down the hall. Rows of old mirrors hung on the walls, just as they did in every other section of the house. But unlike the well-kept looking glasses on the first two floors, these were all covered with a heavy accumulation of grime.

The metal frames were badly tarnished; the wooden ones were cracked in places. Corners were missing. The gilded finishes on the eagles and scrollwork were flaked and chipped.

There were hairline and spidery cracks in most of the reflective surfaces. In others, large shards of glass had fallen out, leaving jagged slivers of the original mirror in the frame. The layers of dirt on what was left of the glass were so thick that she could not see her own image in any of them as she went past.

Occasional blank spaces on the walls marked places where a mirror had been removed at some time in the

past. Presumably the most valuable and interesting looking glasses had been taken downstairs to add to the main
collection. The ones left up here were, for all intents and
purposes, in long-term storage. She wondered if the odd
mirror in Alex's house had been stolen from this floor.

In addition to the mirrors several pieces of old, heavy,
Victorian-style furniture had also been stashed up here. A
pair of long, wooden tables loomed in the shadows on either side of the hall. At the far end of the corridor she
could see a tall cabinet projecting out from the wall.

Halfway along the shadowed passage, the footsteps in
the dust came to a halt in front of a door.

Assorted muffled groans reverberated through the pan-
els. Obviously she had discovered Julie and Travis's secret retreat.

*"Oh, yeah, oh, yeah, oh, yeah, baby, that feels so
good."*

Travis's voice rose into a hoarse groan of undisguised
masculine satisfaction.

Leonora flushed. She felt like a voyeur standing out
here in the corridor, listening to Julie and Travis have sex.
Okay, maybe not exactly a voyeur. She couldn't actually
see anything, she reminded herself. Nevertheless, it was a
very uncomfortable feeling.

Embarrassed, she hurried off. There was no excuse to
hang around here. The small mystery was solved. The
pair's reasons for disappearing upstairs to this floor were
now obvious.

She might as well take the opportunity to have a quick
look around before she went downstairs.

Three-quarters of the way along the corridor she heard
a door open behind her. Panic sizzled through her. She
ducked behind the nearest large object, an antique cabinet, and held her breath.

"Your zipper," Julie said urgently. "Jeez, are you

crazy? Do it up. If Mrs. Brinks sees you like that, she'll probably fire me. We both know I can't afford to lose this job."

"Take it easy." A soft hissing sound announced that Travis had corrected the oversight. "There. All neat and tidy. Happy now?"

"This is serious, Travis." Julie's voice sharpened. "I mean it. If you get me fired we're both going to regret it."

"Don't worry, it's going to be okay. Ready?"

"Yes. Hurry."

Leonora heard the door to the servants' staircase squeak when it opened.

"What's the big rush?" Travis asked. "Brinks went into town for lunch, remember? She won't be back for at least an hour."

"There's something I need to do today if I get a chance."

"What?"

The door to the servants' staircase closed on Julie's muffled answer.

Silence settled.

Leonora waited a few seconds and then stepped out of the protective shadow of the cabinet. She went back along the passageway to the panel door and stepped into the tiny stairwell.

Going down the narrow staircase was more precarious than climbing it. She took her time, keeping the slender beam of the flashlight focused on the steps.

Halfway down, she saw the thin crack of slightly lighter shadow that marked the door that opened onto the second-floor hall.

She was about to continue on down when, out of the corner of her eye, she glimpsed a second line of less dense shadow in the wall to her left. The wall that separated the library office from the staircase.

That explained why she had heard Julie and Travis going up and down the servants' steps so clearly through the
wood. There was another door off the landing that had, at
one time, been used to service the library.

She continued down the steps, moving cautiously, not
just for reasons of safety but to avoid making noise. The
last thing she needed was for someone passing by in the
hall on the second floor to hear her and come to investigate the strange sounds emanating from the staircase. Ex-
planations would be awkward.

At the foot of the stairs, she paused to aim the flashlight at the second panel door. She summoned up an image of the layout of the little office. The card catalog was
positioned directly on the other side of this wall. Years
ago someone had evidently concluded that the servants'
stairs were no longer practical and that there was, therefore, no reason not to shove the heavy wooden catalog up
against that wall.

She was about to switch off the penlight and let herself
out into the hall when she caught the faint glint of gold. A
chill went through her. She lowered the beam of light to
the crack that marked the base of the narrow door that
had once opened into the library.

Approximately half an inch of what looked like the
trailing end of a bracelet or a necklace stuck out below
the edge of the wooden panel. It was almost invisible in
the shadows. If she hadn't noticed the second door and
aimed her flashlight in that direction, she would never
have seen it.

How could anyone lose an item of jewelry in such an
odd location? Perhaps it had been placed on top of the
card catalog years ago. It could have fallen off the back
and landed on the floor behind the catalog.

But in that case, how had a tiny section of it ended up
under the old servants' door?

Curiosity laced with an inexplicable sense of dread drew her toward the bit of gold. She stopped in front of the panel door, searching for a way to open it.

The sound of rustling movements on the other side of the wall made her go cold. Someone was in the library office.

. She listened to drawers being opened and closed in the desk. Whoever it was, he or she was moving quickly, as if afraid of being caught.

A moment later the rustling sounds ceased. The faint echo of footsteps hurrying away through the bookstacks announced that the intruder had departed.

She waited until she heard the footsteps go past the hall door before she went to it and opened it very carefully.

She stuck her head out in the corridor just in time to see Julie Bromley turn the corner and disappear down the main staircase.

She thought about that for a moment and then went back to the other servants' door.

With the card catalog hard against the wall on the opposite side, it was impossible to push the wooden panel inward toward the office. She had to pull it toward her.

She had almost decided to go into the library to find a ruler or some other object she could use to pry the door open when she noticed the small depression in the wooden panel. It was just the right size to allow her to set her fingers into it.

She tugged gently. The door groaned, reluctant to move on its aged and rusty hinges. But in the end she got it open.

She found herself looking at the solid wooden back of the tall card catalog. When she aimed the flashlight at the floor she saw the bracelet.

With trembling fingers she reached down to pick up the slender band of gold links. She didn't need to see the name inscribed on the small gold plaque to identify the bracelet. She recognized it immediately.

She tightened her fingers around the strand of gold and closed the panel. She went to the other door and let herself out of the dark stairwell into the hall.

A moment later she was back in the library office. She looked around, examining things closely. A few items were askew on the desk. Nothing obvious. She probably wouldn't have noticed the new position of the pen and the pad of paper if she hadn't been looking for trouble.

She pulled open the bottom drawer in the desk and removed her satchel. When she undid the clasp and looked inside she saw at once that the contents had been disturbed.

She took out her wallet, opened it and quickly counted the cash inside. It was all there. So were her credit cards.

But if Julie Bromley had not come in here to help herself to some easy money, why had she searched the office?

The restlessness drove him out of his workshop late that afternoon. Wrench looked up from his empty food dish.

"Want to go for a ride?" Thomas said.

Wrench trotted briskly toward the front door. Thomas picked up his keys, the binoculars and his jacket and they left.

Outside, Wrench bounded up into the passenger seat of the SUV and took up his usual position, riding shotgun. Thomas got behind the wheel and fired up the engine.

They drove to the abandoned cottage near Alex Rhodes's house, parked the SUV behind the old structure, got out and locked up.

Together they made their way through the wet trees to the vantage point Thomas had discovered yesterday with Leonora.

Wrench amused himself investigating scents and smells while Thomas settled down with the binoculars.

He wasn't sure what he expected to discover today. He had just needed to get out of the house for a while. Spying on Rhodes was as good a way to pass the time as any.

An hour later he was about ready to head back to the SUV with Wrench when a small, battered Ford drove into the front yard of the cottage.

A young woman dressed in jeans and a red leather jacket got out of the car. Her long hair was caught back in a ponytail.

"Not his usual kind of client," Thomas said to Wrench. "Judging by that old beater she's driving, I don't think she can afford his antistress formula. So what's she doing here?"

He heard her car in his driveway just as he was about to check the living room window for the twelfth time to see if the lights had come on in her cottage on the other side of the cove.

The realization that she had come here on her own volition sent a rush of pleasure through him. The uneasy sensation that had been worrying at him all day faded beneath the onslaught of anticipation.

"Okay. All right. This is good, Wrench. This is a very positive sign."

Wrench was already on his feet, heading toward his pile of personal possessions.

Thomas opened the front door. Leonora came up the steps looking tense, not like a woman who wished to engage in acts of wild sexual abandon. She clutched something in her hand.

"What's wrong?" he asked.

"I found this today." Leonora dropped a gold bracelet

into his palm as she went past him into the hall. "It belonged to Meredith."

Wrench appeared, a badly gnawed leather chew-toy in his mouth. He sat down on his haunches in front of Leonora and dropped the imitation bone at her feet.

She stooped, picked up the toy and patted Wrench on the head.

"Thank you, Wrench. It's lovely."

Wrench was satisfied with the response.

Leonora handed Thomas her jacket, went into the living room and stood at the window, arms folded tightly around herself.

He examined the bracelet. There was a small gold plaque inscribed with Meredith's name.

"I gave it to her when she graduated from college with a terrific grade average." Her mouth curved in a wry smile. "Of course, that was before I discovered that she had fiddled with the computer database in the college records office to adjust her final grades."

He studied the gold links coiled in his palm. "Where did you find it?"

"Behind the card catalog in the library office. There's a door there. It opens off a flight of servants' stairs. Do you know, I never saw Meredith without that bracelet after I gave it to her. She even had it on the day I found her in bed with Kyle."

Thomas looked up suddenly, his attention caught by the grimly resigned inflection of her voice. Leonora's face was angled away from him. She appeared to be fascinated by the view of the cove.

The light of the flames on the hearth gave her khaki-green silk sweater a soft sheen. The garment had a rolled neckline and long sleeves. It fit snugly across her elegantly sculpted shoulders and skimmed over her small, high breasts. The trousers she wore were also green, a hue that was several shades darker than the sweater. Her hair was caught up in its customary sleek knot.

He forced his attention back to the broken bracelet.

"I remember seeing it on her wrist," he said, not stopping to think.

Leonora looked at him over her shoulder. The icy irritation that glittered in her eyes made him tighten his fingers around the bracelet.

"What do you want me to do," he said, "pretend that I didn't have an affair with her?"

"Of course not." She turned back to the window. "What would be the point? I already know the truth. There are enough lies and half-truths floating around as it is."

Anger sparked, catching him off-guard. He crossed the room in three strides and came to a halt directly behind her. Close enough to catch her scent. He did not touch her.

"That's the real issue here, isn't it?" he said. "You want me as much as I want you but you can't handle the fact that I had a brief affair with Meredith."

"Let's stick to the problem at hand, okay?"

"Hell, no, it's not okay. There's something we need to get settled first. Correct me if I'm wrong, but I get the feeling that you see me as just another one of Meredith's dumb-as-a-rock conquests."

"That's not true."

"It is true and I don't appreciate your low opinion of my intelligence, maturity or self-control."

"I never said you weren't intelligent or mature or self-controlled."

"You didn't have to say it. You've made it clear in a thousand other ways. For the record, I'm not some nineteen-year-old, hormone-driven kid who follows his balls wherever they lead him."

"There's no need to get angry about this."

"Too late. I'm already angry. You know what? It really pisses me off that you assume I was powerless to resist Meredith. You think she was some kind of succubus? A siren who was totally irresistible to weak-minded men like me and your ex-fiancé?"

"I never said you were weak-minded."

"I'm not your ex-fiancé, either."

"I know that." She took a jerky step away and swung around to confront him. "You're not anything like Kyle. You're very different."

"Thanks for that much, at least." He closed the space between them. "While we're on the subject, I'd like to clarify a couple of other issues here. Meredith and I had a very short-lived relationship. You want to know who ended it?"

Leonora took another step back and came up against the window ledge. "I'm sure it was Meredith who ended it. She was always the one who ended things. There's no need to go into the details."

"Tough shit. We're already into the details." He planted one hand on the windowsill behind her head and leaned in close, wanting her to get the point. "I'm the one who called a halt to the relationship, if you can call it that. Want to know why?"

She blinked and then cleared her throat. "I'm sure you had your reasons."

"Damn right I had my reasons. I ended things with Meredith because I got bored. That's why."

"Bored? With Meredith?"

"Yeah. Bored. That overgrown, sexy cheerleader routine wears thin fast. At least it did with me. I knew it was time to call it off when I realized I was a whole lot more interested in finishing the tile work in the bathroom than I was in enduring another dinner with Meredith. You got any idea how hard it is to talk to a woman who is always watching you to see if you're responding to her?"

"Tile work, huh?" She pursed her lips. "I've never heard of any man getting *that* bored with Meredith."

"Meet one."

He took his hand off the window, straightened and turned away. He realized that he still held the gold bracelet. He tossed it lightly in her general direction and watched her snatch it out of the air with a quick, reflexive movement.

"I can't figure out why I'm bothering to explain myself to you," he said. "Probably a complete waste of time."

She looked at the bracelet in her palm. "I wouldn't say that."

"I would." He went to the counter, leaned back, crossed his arms and took a grip on his temper. "You're right. We've got more important things to discuss."

"Just one thing before we change the subject."

"Yeah? What would that one thing be?"

"You should know that I never thought of you as just another one of Meredith's casual conquests."

"Like hell you didn't."

"No. It's true. I knew from the first moment I met you that you weren't her usual type." She closed her hand around the bracelet. "I couldn't figure out why she had gotten involved with you in the first place. Later, when I found out about the money, I assumed she made a play for you because she thought you might be useful. It was the only thing that made any sense."

"If that's your not-so-subtle way of telling me that I'm not as sexy or interesting as her standard seduction targets, you can stop right there. Leave me with a few shreds of masculine pride."

Her quick laugh came out of nowhere, momentarily dazzling his senses. He was transfixed. Probably looked like some stupid deer caught in the headlights.

"I certainly wouldn't want to put any dents in your

ego," she responded. "Look, since we're setting the record straight, it's my turn to clarify a few issues. The reason I said you weren't Meredith's type is because she wasn't in the habit of spending a lot of time on men who would probably turn out to be difficult."

"You think I'm difficult?"

"In a word? Yes. What's more, Meredith would have sensed that straight off."

"You think?"

"The thing about Meredith was that she didn't go after men because she liked a challenge. She didn't even enjoy sex. She told me once that, at its best, she considered it a form of exercise. Sort of like jogging."

He hesitated, thinking of how things had been with Meredith. Not great.

"I wondered about that," he said finally. "Figured it was me."

"It wasn't you."

"Did she prefer women?"

"No. She didn't like *any* kind of sex. Remember me telling you about all the men who came and went in her mother's life?"

"Yes."

"One of them assaulted Meredith when she was ten."

"Shit."

"Yes. In some ways she never got past the trauma. Oh, sure, she knew she had a body that men found attractive and she took advantage of that fact. But she never learned to enjoy the experience."

"Explains a few things."

The room grew quiet except for the crackling of the fire.

"You really think I'm difficult?" he said eventually.

"Uh huh. Interesting, but definitely difficult."

She sank down onto the curved and padded arm of the

sofa. One leg swung gently. She dropped the bracelet on the coffee table and watched him intently.

He shoved his fingers through his hair. "You know, I'm not the only one here who could be labeled difficult."

To his surprise, she gave him a slow smile.

"I'll take that as a compliment," she said. "I'd rather be difficult than easy."

"There is nothing easy about you, Leonora Hutton."

"And nothing easy about you, Thomas Walker. Where does that leave us?"

He walked to where she sat and lifted her gently to her feet. She made no move to resist.

"They say two negatives make a positive." He put his hands on the curve of her shoulders. Testing. "Maybe two difficult people would find it easy to have an affair."

She slid her arms around his neck. "I doubt that it would be easy but it's bound to be interesting."

"Oh, yeah."

He covered her mouth with his own.

Chapter Twelve

Her response was immediate and electric in its intensity, just as it had been last night when he had kissed her in her kitchen. She gave a soft, husky little moan and tightened her arms around his neck. Energy exploded in the air around them.

The sense of urgency that swept through him made his blood pound. He had some vague goal of carrying her into the bedroom but it seemed too far away. He fell with her onto the sofa instead.

She ended up on top, her legs tangled with his, fingers splayed across his chest. He shoved one hand through her hair, pulling it free of the pins that had anchored the sleek knot. A curtain of dark silk tumbled over his fingers and brushed his jaw. He gripped her head with both hands and deepened the kiss until she opened her mouth for him.

There was a soft thud at the back of the house. Loud enough to break the spell. Leonora flinched.

"What was that?" she whispered urgently.

"Wrench," he muttered, pulling her close again. "Dog door."

Wrench had opted to discreetly disappear in the face of this display of uncontrollable human lust. Thomas did not blame him. If he hadn't been personally involved in this wildfire, he would have stepped outside for a while, too.

But he was involved. Completely and totally.

When he slid his hands down the length of Leonora's spine and up under the silk sweater, she shuddered against him. He felt the tremor go through her from head to toe. Her back was warm and elegantly contoured beneath his palms.

It took him a frustrating minute or two to unfasten the waistband of her trousers, lower the zipper and get his hand inside where he could feel her warm skin against his palm. When he finally succeeded, he stroked the firm, rounded curves of her buttocks and moved his fingers lower still. The crotch of her panties dampened at his touch.

He was afraid he might come then and there.

She stirred against him, lifting herself away in an effort to shift her position. He realized she was fumbling with his belt.

"No," he got out. "Not yet."

"I only want to touch you."

"Touch me and I'm doomed."

She raised her head and looked down at him. "Really?"

"Yeah. Really."

"Cool."

She went back to work on his belt buckle.

He closed his hand over hers and pulled it away from the vicinity of his groin. He guided it to his shoulder instead. Then he raised one knee and pressed it tightly against her hip, pinning her there where he could savor the soft weight of her against his erection.

She shifted urgently when he caressed her buttocks again.

"Thomas."

He pressed his fingers into the damp crotch of her panties.

"Thomas."

She twisted against him. He moved to maintain contact, rolling toward her. The sudden shift in their positions sent them tumbling over the edge of the sofa. He cushioned the fall with one arm. They landed on the rug, barely missing the coffee table.

She made a husky sound, half laugh, half moan, and wrapped herself tightly around him, burying her face against his shoulder.

He managed to get the green sweater up over her head. Slinging the garment out of the way, he went to work on the lacy, cream-colored bra. Usually he was good with hardware. But it seemed forever before the fastening came undone, releasing her breasts into his hands.

They were the most beautiful breasts he had ever seen. Sweetly shaped, the tips taut and tight. He bent his head and drew one nipple gently between his lips, letting her feel the edge of his teeth.

She stiffened beneath him. He heard her sharp intake of breath. She reached down between their bodies, fishing for his zipper. He caught her fingers and dragged them out of the danger zone.

"I told you, do that and it will be all over for me," he said. "I want to make this last."

She looked up at him, stark urgency blazing in her eyes. "Maybe you can wait. I can't."

"Who said anything about you having to wait?"

She looked bemused. "What?"

"Nothing I like to tackle better than a little home im-provement project."

He stripped off her trousers, slid between her legs and moved slowly down her body until he found her hot little button with his mouth.

"Thomas." Her hands clenched in his hair.

He parted her with his fingers and kissed her inti-mately, absorbing the heady scent and taste of her body. When she sucked in her breath, he eased a finger into her, working her gently, searching for the magic spot.

He knew when he found it.

She gave a soft, startled, half-strangled shriek, tighten-ing around him. Her climax flooded through her. He could feel the gentle contractions. He knew a rare sense of wonder and a kind of satisfaction that had nothing to do with a physical release.

She continued to shudder long after the little convul-sions had ended.

He raised his head, suddenly uneasy. She had her face buried in a velvet sofa pillow. Her shoulders were shaking.

His unease turned to alarm.

"Leonora?"

She pressed the pillow more tightly against her face.

"Leonora? Are you okay?" He levered himself up higher and gripped her quivering shoulder. "Damn it, are you crying? What's wrong? What did I do?"

"I'm...I'm not crying."

He could barely make out the words.

He yanked the pillow away from her face.

She was laughing. Her eyes were brilliant with delight.

"I've never been able...I've always assumed that I had a few things in common with Meredith when it came to sex," she whispered. "I just found out for the first time that I don't."

A long time later she stretched against him, then propped herself on his bare chest. In the shadows she looked quite smug. Very pleased with herself.

"I may nominate you for Handyman of the Year," she said.

"Thanks. Want me to show you what else I can do with a set of tools?"

"Oh my, yes." Her hand closed over his erection. "I can't think of anything else I'd rather do than play with your tools."

When he got inside her again he confirmed his initial conclusions. Everything fit perfectly.

Like she'd been made for him.

She could hear rain on the roof. She opened her eyes and found herself gazing at the pattern on the rug less than five inches away. Thomas was no longer sprawled alongside but she was warm, even though she was quite naked. She realized that he had put a blanket over her.

He had also stoked the fire. It burned brightly, casting a golden glow over the carpet and sofa. She heard a cupboard door close in the kitchen. It was followed by the sound of the refrigerator being opened. A moment later silverware jangled.

"You awake in there?" Thomas called over the top of the counter that divided the two rooms.

"Yep."

"Hungry?"

"Yep."

"You're in luck. I'm prepared to feed you."

"I'm not sure I can move."

"I managed it. So can you."

She sat up cautiously, holding the blanket close around her shoulders, and performed a quick, personal assessment of her various working parts.

There was some tenderness in places and a bit of stiffness here and there. Only to be expected when you made love on the floor, she thought. She'd never tried that before.

Correction. They hadn't made love on the floor. They'd had sex on the floor. Proper terminology was important, she reminded herself. But she refused to dwell on semantics tonight. She felt good. Relaxed. Satisfied beyond her wildest dreams.

She realized that Thomas was watching her with unconcealed amusement from the other side of the counter. He had put on his trousers and shirt, but he hadn't bothered to button the latter.

"Want some help?" he asked.

"I do believe I can get up all by myself." She adjusted the blanket around her shoulders and managed to stand. She gave him a triumphant smile. "See?"

"Congratulations."

"Thanks. Which way is the bathroom?"

He folded his arms on the counter and angled his chin toward the hall behind her. "Thataway."

"Mind if I take a shower?"

"Help yourself."

She shuffled down the short hall, opened the first door she found, groped for a switch and flipped it on. The lights came on, revealing floor-to-ceiling walls covered in gleaming blue-and-white tiles set in an intricate pattern.

She turned on the water in the shower and let it run until the small room was filled with steam. When she was convinced that it was hot enough, she dropped the blanket, shoved aside the curtain and got beneath the spray.

She stood there thinking about what had happened out there in the living room.

Just good sex. It was important to keep things filed under the proper subject heading. Thomas had made his feelings on the subject of marriage and children very clear.

Make that subject heading *great sex*.

She suddenly understood how Alice had felt when she found herself on the other side of the looking glass. The world appeared very different now that she had experienced serious passion at the hands of Thomas Walker.

She had no idea how much time had gone by until the bathroom door opened and closed, yanking her out of her deep thoughts.

Thomas pulled back the curtain. Steam roiled around him. His gaze traveled leisurely from her head to her toes. "You okay?"

She scowled at him through the billowing vapor. "Of course. Why wouldn't I be okay?"

"Just wondered. You've been in here quite a while."

"Oh. Sorry." Hastily she turned off the taps.

"I brought you a robe. Probably a little on the large side but it's clean. Deke gave it to me one year for Christmas. I've never worn it."

"Thanks."

He held out an oversized towel. She took it from him and wrapped it completely around her body. She cast about for something witty and sophisticated to say, the sort of comment a modern woman of the world made when she found herself showering in a man's bathroom after hot sex.

"Nice tile work," she mumbled.

"Thanks." He gave the wall behind her a brief, critical look. "I thought it came out well. You sure you're okay?"

"Just ducky."

He nodded, looking somewhat dubious. "I'll go see how dinner is doing."

She waited until he was gone. Then she turned to look at herself in the mirror over the sink, hoping she didn't look beet red and straggly haired from the hot water.

She could not make out her reflection clearly. It was lost in the mist of steam that covered the glass.

But as she gazed at the enigmatic mirror, some possibilities materialized.

Fifteen minutes later, feeling almost normal, she swathed herself in the thick, man-sized robe and ventured out of the bathroom.

And stopped cold at the entrance to the main room when she heard the low rumble of masculine voices.

"What the hell was it doing behind the old card catalog?" Deke asked.

He was sitting on one of the counter stools, his back toward her. There was a bottle of beer in front of him. He had one hand stuck inside a box of crackers. Wrench was sitting on the floor next to the stool, watching the progress of the crackers, clearly ready to move in the event one happened to fall.

"Damned if I know," Thomas said.

He lounged against the counter on the kitchen side. There was a second bottle of beer in front of him. His blatantly relaxed, sexually satisfied air made her feel warm all over again.

She took a firm hold on her scattered emotions and went forward.

"Under the circumstances, I think we have to assume that Meredith must have done some exploring while she was working up at Mirror House," she said briskly. Trying for cool. "I was doing just that, myself, when I found the bracelet."

Thomas looked at her, his smile intimate and knowing. "Here comes our intrepid heroine. At long last."

Deke swiveled on his stool and saw her. It was impossible to tell what he was thinking, but she thought she could guess. He would have to have been dim in the extreme not to figure out what had happened here. Deke was definitely not dim.

"Evening, Leonora," he said. He kept his curiosity politely confined to his eyes, leaving it out of his tone. "Sorry to barge in like this. I walked over to talk to Thomas about a few things I pulled off the Net today. Didn't know you were here."

She glanced toward the fireplace and saw that her clothes were neatly folded on the chair, bra and panties tucked discreetly out of sight. But that didn't make the situation look any less risqué. It was obvious that she had stripped naked for some purpose and it wasn't as if there were a large number of logical reasons why a woman would do that in a man's living room.

Well, the damage was done. Nothing for it now but to act worldly. Self-possessed. Like she did this kind of thing all the time.

She managed a smile.

"Hello, Deke. We were just about to have dinner."

"I know. Thomas invited me to stay. But I don't want to intrude."

"Nonsense." She walked forward, conscious of the overlong robe trailing on the floor behind her, and perched on a stool next to him. "Of course you're welcome to stay. The three of us have a lot to talk about."

Wrench looked at her with melting eyes. She reached

into the box, removed a cracker and fed it to him. He promptly abandoned his position near Deke's stool and moved to sit beside her.

She smiled at him. "Make that the four of us."

Wrench leaned closer and touched her leg with his nose. She gave him another cracker.

"That's outright bribery," Thomas said. He set a glass of red wine in front of her.

"No, it's not. I'm repaying him for all the gifts he's given me."

Thomas rested his elbows on the counter, the beer framed between his big hands. "I was just telling Deke about your little adventure this afternoon. But I don't know all the details myself. If you will recall, we were interrupted before you told me how you found that old door off the servants' stairs."

Interrupted was as good a word as any, she decided.

She cleared her throat. "I followed Roberta Brinks's student assistant, Julie Bromley, and her boyfriend, Travis, up to the third floor today."

"Thought that floor was closed to the public," Deke said.

"It is." Leonora munched a cracker. "Nothing like labeling something forbidden to make it absolutely fascinating to a couple of nineteen-year-olds. Meredith must have found the staircase at some point also. It's in the wall on the other side of the library office."

Deke's brows bunched together. "Think she went exploring out of sheer curiosity?"

"It wouldn't surprise me. Certainly within character for her to do that kind of thing. If she found that staircase she would have climbed it just to see where it led. She wouldn't have been able to resist. It's quite possible that when she came back down she noticed the second door, just as I did."

"And opened it?" Deke asked.

She recalled the bracelet sticking out from beneath the door and nodded. "I think so, yes. She didn't work in the library so she might not have known that the card catalog had been shoved up against the wall on the other side. The bracelet must have snagged on something. A nail or a splinter, perhaps."

"Bethany spent a lot of time in the library," Deke said quietly.

She looked at him and then at Thomas. She thought about the possibilities that had occurred to her when she looked in the steamy mirror a few minutes ago.

"Did you take a good look around the library after Bethany's death?"

Deke's lips disappeared into a thin line. "No. I went through her office desk and her files with a fine-tooth comb and I took her laptop apart. I always figured that if Bethany had left any clues behind they would show up on her computer. But I didn't search the library. Never saw any reason to do so."

"It occurred to me," Leonora said carefully, "that the reason Meredith lost her bracelet was because she saw something when she opened that servant's door. Something that maybe had slipped off the top of the card catalog and gotten wedged between it and the wall." She waggled her fingers. "I can see how, if she pushed her hand between the catalog and the wall to retrieve the object, the bracelet could have snagged and snapped. Maybe she didn't even notice at the time."

Deke sat unmoving, his hand locked around the beer bottle.

"Oh, shit," he whispered. "The envelope? You think maybe she found that envelope stuffed with the Eubanks murder clippings behind the card catalog?"

"Maybe the book, too," Leonora said. "The catalog of

antique mirrors in the mansion's collection. Maybe they were both there."

There was a short silence while they all contemplated those simple facts. Leonora took a sip of wine. Deke and Thomas both drank some beer.

"The night Bethany died, everyone assumed she had been in her office on campus," Deke said. "She often worked there until very late. Sometimes stayed there all night, working. But what if she was at Mirror House that evening?"

"The place would have been locked up at night," Thomas reminded him.

Deke brushed that aside. "Bethany had a key. They gave her one because she liked to go to the library at odd hours."

Thomas drew the bracelet toward him across the counter. "Okay, say she was there that night. Why would she have hidden the clippings and that book?"

Deke's hand clenched around the bottle. "Because the killer had followed her. Maybe he cornered her in the library."

There was another brief silence.

"This is all wild speculation," Leonora said after a while.

"Not entirely." Thomas looked at the bracelet. "Whatever else we can say, we know that Meredith opened that door behind the card catalog."

"What made you decide to go exploring today?" Deke asked.

"I was playing detective," Leonora said. "I've noticed that Julie and Travis have a habit of disappearing together at lunchtime. I followed them today. They're using one of the empty rooms on the third floor as a, uh, trysting spot."

Thomas cocked a brow. "Trysting?"

"I believe that would be the correct technical term for it, yes," she murmured.

He whistled softly. "I do admire you academic types," he said. "Must be nice to have such a wide-ranging command of the English language."

She glared. "What would you call it if a couple of healthy young people disappeared at lunchtime for the purpose of having sex?"

"A nooner," Thomas said.

Deke grinned fleetingly. "Gotta love the English language. Such nuance. Such subtlety."

Leonora blinked, startled by the flash of humor. Deke's amused smile brought home the family resemblance between him and Thomas as nothing else could have done. The grin was gone in the next moment but not before it gave her a whole new insight into the real Deke.

"Something else happened today," she said. "I'm not sure what it means, but given that we are all trying to weave a conspiracy theory, it may be important. Then again, it might mean absolutely nothing."

"What's that?" Thomas asked.

"I have reason to think that one member of our trysting couple went through my satchel. Julie, to be precise."

Thomas and Deke both looked at her.

"She was in the library office while I was in the stairwell on the other side of the wall. I could hear her opening drawers. When I went back into the office I checked my things. It was obvious she had gone through them."

"She take any money?" Thomas asked. "Credit cards?"

Leonora shook her head. "Nothing was missing as far as I could tell. But it made me recall something she said to Travis when the two of them left their little hideaway upstairs."

"What was that?" Deke asked.

"I think she told him that they had to hurry because there was something she had to do today if she got a chance."

"Well, hell," Thomas said softly. He took a sip of beer and put down the bottle. "Well, hell."

She looked at him. "Now what?"

"This Julie Bromley. She have a ponytail? Wear a red leather jacket?"

"How did you know?" Leonora asked.

"Because I saw her this afternoon. Visiting Alex Rhodes. I told Wrench I didn't think she was a client."

"Oh, wow," Leonora said. "Julie and Alex Rhodes. I don't like the sound of that."

"Neither do I," Thomas said.

"Funny you should mention Rhodes," Deke said dryly. "This is probably as good a time as any to tell you why I came calling this evening. I learned a few things about our friendly neighborhood antistress counselor."

"You have our undivided attention," Thomas said.

"A few years ago Rhodes was ABD at a small college in the Midwest," Deke began.

"ABD?" Thomas said.

"All But Dissertation," Leonora explained. "A Ph.D. candidate who hasn't quite finished all the requirements."

"Got it. Go on, Deke."

"Rhodes was working as a graduate teaching assistant in the department of chemistry. His contract was, as they say, not renewed."

"Meaning he was fired?" Thomas said.

"More or less." Deke made a face. "From what I could find out online, Rhodes was let go because he had a hobby of seducing his female students."

"Why am I not surprised?" Thomas said.

"One of the sweet young things was the daughter of a very wealthy alumnus who had given a lot of money to the school. Said alumnus was furious when he discovered that his precious offspring had been fooling around after hours in the chemistry lab with Rhodes. He insisted that the college dump Rhodes."

"I don't blame him," Leonora said.

"After he got kicked out, Rhodes seems to have moved around a lot. He got some one-year contracts in the chemistry departments of various small colleges. Never lasted very long anywhere, though. Apparently he continued to engage in his hobby of seducing the wrong students. There were complaints."

"I'll bet there were," Leonora said.

"Here's the really interesting part." Deke sat forward on the stool, radiating controlled excitement. "There were rumors that Rhodes used that stuff they call the date-rape drug, and maybe other junk in the course of his seductions."

"And now he's here in Wing Cove," Leonora whispered. "Selling his antistress formula."

Thomas looked at Deke. "Any luck with those lab tests on that powder?"

"Not yet," Deke said. "But I'm expecting to hear from my friend soon."

"What do we do if the results show that Alex Rhodes is selling hard drugs labeled as antistress formula?" Leonora asked.

"That's easy," Thomas said. "If we get that lucky, we take everything to Ed Stovall and dump it into his lap. No way he can ignore that kind of problem."

Deke took a swallow of beer. "But you don't think we'll get that lucky, do you?"

"Nothing else about this mess has been simple," Thomas reminded him.

Two hours later Thomas and Wrench stood on Leonora's front porch. Leonora had her key in her hand. They had driven back to her place in her car. They would walk home across the footbridge.

Thomas had suggested that she might want to spend the night at his house. She had declined. He hadn't pushed. It was okay, he told himself. He could play the waiting game.

"Don't get me wrong," she said, inserting her key into the lock. "I've got no problem with the theory that Rhodes is up to no good. But I don't see him as a killer. He's more the slick, con artist type." She sighed. "You know, like Meredith."

"I'd agree with you," Thomas said. "Except that there are drugs involved. And where drugs are in the mix, all bets are off. People in the drug business get killed. Just ask any cop."

"We don't know for sure yet about the drugs. All we've got are rumors."

"You see enough smoke, you start to wonder if maybe there's a fire." He shoved his hands into the pockets of his jacket. "You know what I'd really like to find out? I'd like to find out where Alex Rhodes was on the night Bethany jumped off that bluff on Cliff Drive and the night Meredith crashed her car in L.A."

She got the door open and turned to face him. "That may not be possible."

"In the meantime," he continued, "I think we should lean on Julie Bromley a little."

She thought about that and nodded. "Might work. She's only nineteen years old. Doesn't strike me as a hardened criminal. If we confronted her with the fact that we know she searched my satchel and that we also know she's connected to Alex Rhodes, she would probably fall apart pretty fast. But I doubt if she'll be able to tell us very much."

"It's worth a shot. I'll dig up her address tonight. We can

catch her tomorrow morning before she leaves for classes."

"All right." Leonora gave Wrench a good-night pat and prepared to close the door. "Not like we've got a lot of other leads."

Thomas realized she was about to close the door. He put one foot over the threshold, making that action impossible. "One more thing."

"What?"

"You going to just pretend tonight never happened?"

"I beg your pardon?"

"After seeing you in my bathrobe this evening, Deke is going to think that we're sleeping together. I was sort of under the same impression, myself."

"So?"

"So, I'd like a little clarification," he said. "Are we involved in some kind of relationship here, or was this evening just a one-night stand?"

She gave him her dazzling smile, the one that made him feel like he was standing in a dark tunnel watching the light of an oncoming train coming toward him.

"For the record," she said, "I *never* engage in one-night stands."

He suddenly felt a lot better than he had a moment ago. "Is that a fact?"

"It is, indeed."

"Correct me if I'm mistaken, but by process of elimination, it would appear that if our encounter earlier tonight was not a one-night stand, then what we have here is some kind of relationship."

"I do admire a man who can connect the dots," she said. "Good night, Thomas."

The relief morphed into a totally irrational euphoria. He leaned forward and kissed her without removing his hands from the pockets of his jacket. Just to see what she would do.

She kissed him back. Without putting her arms around him.

He took his foot off the threshold. She closed the door in his face. Gently.

"Let's go home, Wrench."

They went down the steps together. A movement in the window made Thomas glance back over his shoulder. Leonora stood there, holding the curtain aside, watching them leave. She was silhouetted against the warm lamp-light of the living room. He took one hand out of his pocket and lifted it in a small wave. She waved back.

He was whistling by the time he and Wrench got to the footbridge.

Chapter Thirteen

*Leonora opened the door of her cottage very early the fol-*lowing morning and was confronted by watery sunshine. It made a pleasant change from the fog, she decided.

She pulled the hood of her jacket up over her head, tugged on a pair of gloves and went briskly down the steps. When she reached the jogging path, she turned left, the direction that would take her toward the footbridge, the shortcut to Thomas's house.

Pure intellectual curiosity, she thought. She just wanted to see if he was an early riser like herself. Find out if they had that much in common, at least.

Not that having a lot of interests in common was a guarantee of a sound and lasting relationship, as she had discovered the hard way with Kyle.

She walked briskly, wondering what Thomas would be wearing if he did happen to be up at this hour. Maybe he wouldn't be out of the shower yet. She indulged herself in a harmless little fantasy that involved Thomas answering the door wearing his robe. With nothing at all on underneath.

They could discuss strategy for the confrontation with Julie Bromley. Or maybe some other topic equally pertinent to their investigation.

Or maybe he would invite her to go back to bed with him.

She walked a little faster.

The rhythmic thud of running shoes coming up behind her broke into her pleasant daydream. She heard heavy breathing and moved to the side.

A moment later Cassie, impressive physique sheathed in a halter top, tights and a pair of running shorts, pulled up alongside. Perspiration beaded her brow and soaked her running bra. Her red curls were held back off her forehead by a terry-cloth sweatband.

She saw Leonora. Surprise flickered across her face. She slowed to a walk and smiled.

"Hello," she said. "Didn't see you until I almost ran over you."

"Good morning." Leonora kept moving. "Don't let me stop you."

"No, no, this is fine. I was almost finished, anyway." Cassie wiped her brow on the back of her arm. "Actually, this is good timing, at least for me. I wanted to talk to you. I was thinking of dropping by your cottage this afternoon. Mind if we keep moving while I cool down?"

Leonora had to lengthen her strides to keep up with her. "I appreciate the thought, but I don't really have time to take yoga lessons."

"I wasn't planning to sell you any." Cassie's mouth twisted in a wry grimace. She breathed deeply. "I wish it were that simple. I'm afraid this is a little more personal."

"Ah. Deke and Thomas."

Cassie gave her a quick, searching look and then she

drew another long breath and planted her hands on her hips. "Yes. Deke and Thomas. Especially Deke. I won't beat around the bush. You've met him. Talked to him. What do you think?"

"I think he's having some problems getting past the death of his wife. Probably could use some grief counseling."

"I suggested that. So did Thomas. Deke won't do it. He doesn't think it will help."

"He needs closure."

Cassie sighed. "His job, as he saw it, was to take care of Bethany. In the end, he feels he failed."

"No one can take complete responsibility for another person's life, health or happiness. It isn't possible."

"I know. But for some reason Deke is obsessing on Bethany's death. His guilt and depression have caused him to weave all sorts of bizarre theories."

"I'm no psychologist," Leonora said. "But from what I've heard about Bethany, I would say that she was fragile. Evidently she had trouble coping with real life or maybe she just wasn't interested in it. She preferred to retreat to the realm of mathematics as often as possible. Deke said she sometimes spent days and nights in her office and long, long hours at Mirror House."

Cassie snorted inelegantly. "I never met her, you understand, but I'd say that calling her fragile is a polite euphemism for selfish. I think she must have used her brilliance as an excuse to become extremely self-centered."

"I've known one or two people whose IQs were literally off the charts. True genius can be a burden. It can make a person feel very isolated."

"I understand," Cassie said. "I'm sure that it's difficult for anyone who is extraordinarily gifted to deal with the demands and routines of ordinary life."

"Easy to see why such a person might feel more at

home in a parallel universe where logic and mathematics
hold sway and order prevails. It's also easy to see how
others might want to protect such a delicate flower."

"I suppose so," Cassie agreed. She sounded grim and
morose.

"Maybe for Bethany, that other universe was where
she felt at home," Leonora continued, getting into her
theory now, thinking of the ramifications. "To one of
those rare high IQ types, *this* world probably seems like a
strange, unpredictable, illogical place."

"Yes." Cassie's jaw twitched. "I'm sure you're right.
Bethany probably did feel as if she was different from
everyone else."

"Because she *was* different. Who knows? Maybe she
really did need to be protected from the demands of daily
life. But one person can't do that for another. Not for
long, at any rate. The task would be frustrating, thankless
and, in the end, futile. A man who tried to do it for a
woman would inevitably come to the conclusion that he
had failed."

Cassie came to a halt on the path and turned to face
her. "Exactly."

Leonora halted, too. "A man who feels he screwed up
big-time as a knight in shining armor would probably be
extremely reluctant to risk getting involved in another
relationship."

"Damn. It's hopeless, isn't it? He'll never look at me as
long as he's obsessed with finding out what happened to
Bethany."

"I'm not so sure it's a lost cause."

"What do you mean?"

"I don't think Deke is as depressed as everyone believes. I do think that he's on a mission to find out what
happened to Bethany. Clearly he needs some answers. In

that sense, you could say he's obsessed. But I have a feeling that kind of single-mindedness is a family trait."

"You think so?"

"I can see Thomas doing the same thing under similar
circumstances. Heck, when you think about it, he *is* doing
the same thing because he's committed to helping Deke."

"What this boils down to is that all I can do is stand
back and wait until Deke gets the answers he needs. But
what if he never finds those answers?"

"I don't see why you have to be passive in this. Maybe
you should take some steps to get Deke's attention."

"How?"

"I'm not exactly an expert." Leonora smiled. "But I
know one I can call for advice."

A short time later, she went up the steps of Thomas's cottage and knocked on the front door. It opened almost at
once.

Wrench bounded out, an old yellow tennis ball in his
mouth. He placed it at her feet and sat down proudly, prepared to have his gift appreciated.

"Thank you, Wrench." She bent to pick up the tennis
ball. "It's lovely."

Wrench looked pleased. She tugged gently on his
bent ear.

"Don't know where the hell he got that," Thomas said.
"I've never played tennis in my life."

She straightened when she saw him looming in the
hallway. His hair was damp from the shower. His bare
shoulders seemed to stretch from wall to wall. He had a
towel wrapped around his waist.

Just a towel. It rode low on his hips and left a great deal
of him exposed.

And here she had been fantasizing about a bathrobe. Obviously she lacked imagination.

"Come on in. I was about to make some breakfast." Thomas gave her a slow, sexy smile. "What brings you calling at this hour?"

"I was out for my morning walk. Thought I'd see if you were an early riser."

"I am, as a matter of fact. Goes with having a dog." He stepped back to allow her inside. "I just got out of the shower."

She looked down at the towel he had wrapped around his waist. "I noticed."

"I was hoping you would." He grinned and pulled her into his arms. "I don't generally answer my door draped only in a towel, you know."

She flattened her palms on his chest and wiggled her fingers in the crisp curling hair that covered him there. "You went to all this trouble just for me? I'm very flattered."

"Would you like to come back to my bedroom and help me finish getting dressed?"

"If you feel you need help selecting your attire, I would be only too happy to assist. I have a good sense of color and style."

"This must be my lucky day." He scooped her up in his arms and started down the hall. "Thing is, I'll have to take off the towel before I can put on any clothes."

"Of course you will."

"You know," Thomas said a long time later, "if you're going to make a habit of walking past my house every morning just in time for breakfast, maybe you should think about spending the nights here. Be a lot more efficient."

She watched him ladle the steaming oatmeal he had

just finished preparing into two bowls. "I like to walk in the mornings. Good exercise."

He wondered if he had been a little too subtle. He didn't do subtle well. He decided to try again, keeping it light but a bit more to the point.

"If it's exercise you're after, I would be happy to provide you with the type we just had in the bedroom on a daily basis," he said.

"It did get my heart rate up a bit. But I'm not sure sex is a substitute for aerobic walking."

Maybe he was still erring on the subtle side.

"Okay, I've got another idea." He put the bowls of oatmeal on the counter and opened the container of brown sugar. "How about I spend the nights at your place and then we both walk back here for breakfast every morning? Think that would work?"

She opened the refrigerator and took out the carton of milk, keeping her back to him. "Sounds a lot like moving in together."

"You're not ready for that, I take it?"

She closed the refrigerator and turned around. Her expression was very serious. "I don't think we should rush things, Thomas. They're already moving fast enough."

"Right. Wouldn't want to move too fast." Probably trip and fall flat on his face.

He sat down by the counter. Leonora slid onto the stool beside him and picked up a spoon.

"Maybe we should talk about how we're going to handle Julie Bromley," she said.

Okay. No one had to hit him over the head with a two-by-four to drive home a point. She wanted to change the subject. Right now.

"How about the good cop, bad cop routine?" he suggested.

"I don't know. Neither of us are cops." She wrinkled

her nose. "Besides, everyone who watches television knows that trick. Hard to believe that sort of elementary psychological manipulation would work in real life."

"Are you telling me that you actually doubt the truth of what you see on television?"

"Well—"

"Besides, our goal isn't to manipulate Julie Bromley with clever psychology."

"No?" She raised her brows. "What is our goal?"

"To scare her into telling us the truth."

"Oh, right. Got it."

"I didn't steal anything," Julie shrieked. "I swear it. I just looked at some of your stuff, Miss Hutton, that's all, honest."

Thomas winced and glanced uneasily at the wall that divided Julie's apartment from the one next door. The off-campus building had been constructed as student housing and it was obvious that no one had worried much about sound insulation.

Julie's small studio apartment was crammed with the clutter of student life. There were several oversized cushions and a single chair. The bed was unmade. A half-full bag of potato chips was propped against the computer. Textbooks and a couple of notebooks were scattered across the desk. The closet door was open. Thomas could see several pairs of shoes and boots tumbled on the floor. A red leather jacket hung over the back of a chair.

Julie had looked startled to find them in the hall outside her apartment, but she had allowed them inside without protest. She had been drinking a can of cola and had tentatively offered her visitors some. The idea of drinking pop at that hour of the morning sent a shudder through

Thomas, but he had declined politely. Each to his or her own source of caffeine, he thought.

Leonora had explained in a very firm voice that they needed to speak with her about an important matter. Julie had backed down in the face of an authoritative adult.

Her initial nervousness had turned to outright alarm when Leonora had confronted her with the information that she had been seen sneaking out of the library office. Panic had set in immediately. After a weak stab at denial, she had plunged straight into mitigating circumstances.

Leonora had been right. Julie wasn't what anyone would call a hardened criminal.

"I realize you didn't take anything." Leonora sat in the chair at the desk. "But I want to know why you searched my satchel. I'm sure you can understand my concern."

"I was just curious, that's all," Julie said sullenly.

"About what?" Leonora asked.

Julie twisted restlessly on her chair. "I dunno."

Thomas decided it was time for him to play his part. He had been standing silently at the window, letting Leonora handle the interrogation, waiting for his cue.

He faced the girl. "What did you tell Alex Rhodes about the results of your search?"

Julie froze, a terrified rabbit confronting a predator. Being the bad cop wasn't as much fun as the television shows made it appear, Thomas thought. Especially when the victim was only nineteen years old.

But her reaction told him that he had hit the nail on the head. He had to keep going forward or risk giving her time to recover and think up a story.

"I saw you at Rhodes's place yesterday afternoon," he said. "That would have been after you went through Miss Hutton's things. You were obviously reporting back to him."

"I didn't…I didn't—" Julie's face crumpled. Tears slid down her cheeks. "I don't know what you're talking about."

"Look," Thomas said. "We don't give a damn if you're sleeping with him. Speaking as an official adult, I've got to tell you that I think it's a mistake, but—"

Julie clamped both hands into fists and shot to her feet. Her face flushed with outrage. "I'm not sleeping with Mr. Rhodes. Who told you I was? It's a lie."

"Rhodes has a thing for attractive students. But that's your problem, not ours."

"I am not sleeping with him, damn it," Julie stormed. "He's old. Why would I want to go to bed with a guy who's almost forty? I love Travis. We're going to get married as soon as we graduate."

"Sure," Thomas said.

It occurred to him that he was damn close to forty himself and getting older by the minute. He wondered if he looked old to Leonora.

"It's the truth!" Julie was shouting now.

"That's enough, Thomas." Leonora rose from her chair, plucked some tissues from the box on the desk and crossed the small space to where Julie stood trembling. "I think Julie is telling us the truth."

She put the tissues in Julie's hand and gently eased her back down into the cushion.

"It is the truth," Julie sobbed into the tissue. "I swear I'm not letting that old dude screw me. Jeez. I can't even imagine getting into bed with someone his age. It's disgusting."

"Take it easy," Leonora said gently. "We know you've been to see Alex Rhodes and we know you searched my satchel. We think there's a link between those two facts and we're trying to figure out what it is, that's all. We're a little worried, you see."

"I'm not sleeping with Mr. Rhodes," Julie mumbled dejectedly into the tissue. "I'm working for him."

Thomas stilled. Leonora must have sensed that he was about to pounce. She shook her head silently in warning. He hesitated and then reluctantly subsided.

Annoyed at having his prey snatched out from under his paw, he turned back to the window.

"It's all right, Julie," Leonora murmured behind him. "We understand. It was a job. That's different."

Thomas kept quiet. He turned around again, in time to watch Leonora pat Julie in a comforting, almost maternal manner. Not just playing good cop, he realized. There was genuine empathy in her stance and the way she touched the younger woman.

"We need the money," Julie whispered in a broken voice.

"You and Travis?" Leonora pressed.

"Travis's grades haven't been so good lately. His dad's threatening to cut off his tuition and expenses. Travis can't make enough with his part-time job as a gardener to cover his rent and fees and stuff."

"So Rhodes offered you some extra cash for going through Miss Hutton's things, is that it?" Thomas asked.

His voice must have been a little rougher than he had intended. Julie flinched visibly. Leonora gave him another repressive glare.

"He said he just wanted to know if Miss Hutton was a legitimate librarian."

"There's such a thing as an illegitimate librarian?" Thomas asked.

"He said he was concerned because at the last campus where he worked he remembered hearing about a phony librarian who used fake credentials to get into the rare book archives and steal some really valuable old books. He said the description fit Miss Hutton. But he told me that he didn't want to get her in trouble unless she really was a phony."

"He sent you to get a look at my identification?" Leonora asked.

Julie sniffed. "He just wanted to get your social security number or a credit card number so he could check it out on his computer to make sure you were who you said you were."

"Just doing his civic duty, is that it?" Thomas said.

"I told you," Julie muttered. "He didn't want to get Miss Hutton in trouble unless she was a real phony."

"A real phony." Leonora handed Julie a fresh tissue. "An interesting turn of phrase."

Thomas looked at Julie. "Did you give Miss Hutton's social security number to Rhodes?"

"No. I couldn't find it." Julie blew her nose into the new tissue.

Thomas exhaled slowly. Maybe this wasn't going to turn out so badly.

"So I gave him her driver's license number instead," Julie concluded.

"Shit," Thomas said.

Leonora frowned.

Julie jerked violently.

"Anything else?" Thomas asked.

Julie swallowed. "Well, I also found a couple of credit cards, so I gave him those numbers, too."

"Shit," Thomas said again. "Little Miss Helpful."

"I thought I was helping Mr. Rhodes catch a book thief," Julie added. "I thought I was doing the right thing."

"Good to know that folks like you and Alex Rhodes are out there making the world safe for scholarly research." Thomas leaned back against the edge of the window and folded his arms. "All right, Julie, pay attention. Here's what you are going to do. You will not have any more contact with Rhodes. Is that clear?"

Dismay widened her eyes. "But he still owes me another fifty bucks. He promised to give me two hundred altogether and I only got one hundred and fifty so far."

"The thing is, if you try to collect your money, some people might not understand that you were just holding down a part-time job. The cops, for instance, might get the wrong impression."

"Cops?" Julie looked horrified. "What wrong impression?"

"They might be excused for thinking that you were aiding and abetting an identity thief."

"But I didn't steal anything."

"Julie, you're pushing the envelope with the naïve innocent act. Everyone knows that identity theft is big business and a serious crime. A social security number unlocks all the doors and, given a driver's license and a credit card or two, it's not that hard to get it."

"But I told you, Mr. Rhodes was just making sure that Miss Hutton was for real."

"Is that right?" Thomas asked. "And what makes you think that Alex Rhodes is for real?"

Julie stared at him, obviously staggered by the implications of that question.

"You mean that Mr. Rhodes is...you mean that he may be a criminal? But he's like a doctor or a shrink or something."

Her voice had risen to such a shrill pitch Thomas was surprised that the window behind him did not shatter.

"I don't know yet who or what Alex Rhodes is," he said. "But I think it's safe to assume that any man who would hire a nineteen-year-old student to go through someone's personal effects in search of identification data is probably not a very nice guy."

Julie started to weep again.

Leonora touched her shoulder. "Calm down. Mr. Walker and I will handle this from here on in. But in the meantime, I think he's right. It's probably best if you don't have any more contact with Alex Rhodes."

Julie looked up at her with wet, doleful eyes. "But what about my fifty dollars?"

"I'll tell you what." Leonora reached down to unclasp her satchel. She took out her wallet. "I'll give you the fifty dollars that Rhodes owes you."

"Uh, Leonora," Thomas said.

She paid no attention. Instead she opened the wallet, took out some cash and handed the bills to Julie.

"Thanks." Julie took the cash with alacrity, counted it swiftly and stuffed it into the pocket of her jeans. "Don't worry, I won't go to see Mr. Rhodes again."

"We appreciate your assistance in this matter," Leonora said.

"Sure." Julie hurried to open the door. "Well, I'd better get going. I've got a ten o'clock English Lit class."

Thomas followed Leonora to the door. "With any luck," he said casually, "this will be the end of it for you."

Julie frowned. "What do you mean, with any luck?"

"In the end, we might be forced to bring in the police." He moved out into the hall and turned to smile at her. "You never can tell."

Julie threw him another traumatized look and shut the door.

Leonora glared at him. "There was no need to add that last bit about the cops. She'd told us what we wanted to know."

"She conned you out of that money."

"Big deal. It was worth fifty bucks to find out that Alex Rhodes was doing research on me, wasn't it?"

"That's beside the point. I didn't like the way she did

it. What I told her about the cops may be the truth," he said. "The more we get into this thing, the more I think we will eventually have to take it to the authorities."

"Fine by me." Leonora clutched her satchel in her left hand and fell into step beside him. "When?"

"I don't know. We don't have enough yet. Ed Stovall has made it pretty clear he can't justify reopening the investigation into Bethany's death unless we bring him something solid in the way of evidence. Not after what he went through with Deke when Bethany died. He thinks my brother is a nutcase."

She searched his face. "You're starting to believe that we may actually be investigating a couple of murders, aren't you?"

He rubbed the back of his neck, trying to ease the nagging sensation that something big and nasty and endowed with a lot of teeth was bearing down on him.

"I'm still not ready to buy into a murder conspiracy theory," he said. "But I've got to admit that I'm coming to the conclusion that Rhodes is a serious problem."

Chapter Fourteen

"I'm calling because a friend of mine needs some professional advice and Herb is the only advice columnist I know," Leonora said on the other end of the line. "I'd go online and email him in care of 'Ask Henrietta,' but I know he's busy and he might not notice my question right away."

"He's swamped, all right." Gloria settled into her armchair and propped her feet on the small hassock. She surveyed her ankles closely. By the time she had gotten home from the shopping expedition to the mall, they had been swollen. She knew from experience that if she kept them elevated for a while they would slim down. "Don't tell Herb, but between you and me, 'Ask Henrietta' is the most popular column in the *Gazette*. More questions coming in every day. Herb's talking about getting an assistant."

"I was afraid of that. This is sort of an emergency. I thought maybe you could go down the hall, get the answers we need and then call me back right away."

"We?" Gloria repeated cautiously.

"I mean, the answers my friend needs," Leonora amended quickly. "Here's the deal. The guy lost his wife about a year ago. He hasn't gotten involved with anyone else since her death. I think maybe the marriage had some problems and he's got some unresolved issues. The point is, my friend wants to get his attention. Make him focus on her, if you see what I mean."

"I understand, dear." Gloria cradled the phone between her shoulder and ear, picked up a pen and a pad of paper and started to make notes. "Does this man have children?"

"No."

"Hobbies?"

"Well, he's really into computers."

"I see." She wrote down *nerd*. "Anything else Herb should know about him?"

"I can't think of anything. Call me back as soon as you can after you talk to Herb, okay?"

"All right, dear, I'll see what I can do."

"Oh, and, Gloria?"

"Yes, dear?"

"While you're asking Herb about my friend's problem could you ask him one other quick little question?"

"What's that, dear?"

"Ask him—" Leonora broke off and cleared her throat cautiously. "Ask him if he thinks there's any possibility of a long-term, committed relationship between a divorced man who likes to work with his tools and who doesn't plan to ever marry again and is afraid to have kids, and a . . . a woman who is from a somewhat different background."

"How different?"

"Well, she's more academically inclined, I guess you could say. And she does think she might like to get married. And have kids. Assuming the right man comes along."

Gloria was proud of herself. She didn't miss a beat. "No problem, dear. I'll get back to you as soon as I talk to Herb."

"Thanks."

"Everything else going all right up there?"

"Yes, I think we're actually making some progress. Thomas is talking about taking the information we have to the cops. I have to say, it would be a great relief to turn everything over to the authorities."

Gloria frowned. "Does that mean you think Meredith and this other woman, Bethany Walker, really were murdered?"

"I'm afraid it's possible, yes. Drugs may be involved. We still don't know exactly what's going on here."

"Dear heaven." She thought about that for a few seconds and then tightened her grip on the phone. "Leonora?"

"Yes?"

"Listen, dear, you're not in any personal danger there in Wing Cove, are you?"

"Good grief, no. Don't worry about that, Grandma. I'm fine. Honest."

"You're quite certain?"

"Absolutely certain."

"Very well. I'll go talk to Herb and then call you back."

"Thanks. Bye for now."

"Good-bye, dear."

Gloria ended the call and sat studying her notes for a long moment. A man who likes to work with tools...a woman who is from a somewhat different background...

She tossed the notebook aside, grabbed the walker that stood next to the chair and hauled herself to her feet.

She paused in the bathroom long enough to apply a

coat of bright-red lipstick and then she headed toward the door of her apartment.

To hell with her swollen ankles. She would worry about elevating them later.

She made the trek to Herb's apartment in excellent time. He opened the door in short order.

"If you're here to chew me out because my column is running too long, forget it," he said. "Not my fault half the subscribers want advice from 'Ask Henrietta.'"

"I'm not here about the column, Herb, this is personal. I think Leonora is falling in love. We need help. Fast."

"Huh." He stood back. "Come on in. I'll see what I can do."

She maneuvered the walker into the apartment, turned around and sat down on the attached seat. "She called on the pretext of getting advice for a friend. But toward the end of the conversation she threw in the zinger about the man she's interested in herself. At least, I think she's talking about herself."

Herb sat down in the chair in front of the computer and put on his reading glasses. "Give me what you've got."

She ran through her notes very quickly.

Herb thought for a while. "This is easy."

"Easy?"

"Well, I'm sure Leonora and her friend will make it a lot more difficult than it needs to be on accounta when you're that age, this kind of thing is always more complicated. But we'll see what we can do. Get her on the phone."

Gloria took her cell phone out of her pocket and punched in Leonora's number.

Leonora answered on the first ring.

"Gloria?"

"Yes, dear. I'm here in Herb's apartment. He's ready with his advice."

"Great. I've got a pen and some paper. Fire away."

Gloria looked expectantly at Herb.

"Feed 'em," Herb said.

Gloria frowned at him.

"What did he say?" Leonora asked.

"Hang on a second, dear." She looked up. "What did you say, Herb?"

"I said, tell Leonora and her friend to cook up a real nice meal for those two men they're after. Way to a man's heart is through his stomach. Always has been, always will be."

Gloria spoke into the phone. "Herb says to cook a nice meal for the gentlemen in question."

"Cook for them?" Leonora sounded skeptical. "Isn't that a little old-fashioned?"

Gloria held the phone away from her face. "Leonora says that sounds old-fashioned."

"Look, you came to an expert for advice," Herb said. "I'm giving it to you."

"Take it easy, I was just double-checking." She went back to the phone. "Herb says the old adage about the way to a man's heart being through his stomach is still valid."

"Well, all right. Any advice on the meal?"

Gloria held the phone away again. "Any advice on what to serve, Herb?"

"Lasagna would be nice." Herb leaned back in his chair and got a wistful expression on his face. "With lots of cheese. And maybe a nice green salad made with romaine lettuce and some of those little crouton things. Some red wine. Good bread. And don't forget dessert. Dessert is real important."

"Are you getting this down, dear?" Gloria asked.

"I got the part about the lasagna, salad, bread and red wine. What about dessert?"

Gloria looked inquiringly at Herb. "What's best for dessert?"

"Pie," Herb said. "A big slice of hot apple pie with homemade crust. The flaky kind, not that ready-made cardboard crap they sell in the supermarkets. And a big dollop of vanilla ice cream on top."

"I can tell someone is pining for the days when he didn't have to worry about his cholesterol medication." Gloria chuckled. She went back to the phone. "Did you hear that, dear? Apple pie and ice cream."

"I heard." Leonora paused and lowered her voice. "What did he say about my other question? You know, the one concerning the man who likes to work with tools and is afraid of marriage and having a family?"

"Hang on, dear." Gloria looked at Herb. "What about the chances of an academically inclined woman finding true love with a man who likes to work with tools and is afraid of marriage?"

"Don't see any problem there." Herb looked wise and all-knowing. "Been my experience that a man who's good with his tools can handle just about anything that comes along in life."

"That sounded very cryptic," Leonora said on the other end. "What's it supposed to mean?"

Gloria scowled at Herb. "What's that mean? That stuff about a man who's good with tools being able to handle things?"

"Never mind," Herb said enigmatically. "Tell her to concentrate on finding some good recipes for lasagna and apple pie."

"That's it from this end," Gloria said. "Good luck, dear."

"Wait," Leonora said. "One more thing. Say this person from an academic background, say she had already served one meal to this man who's good with tools."

"Yes, dear?"

"Say that what she fed him was leftovers," Leonora said grimly. "Would that be a problem? Has she already shot herself in the foot?"

Gloria put her hand over the mouthpiece and looked at Herb. "She wants to know if she has already shot herself in the foot because she served this tool man a meal made up of leftovers."

"What kind of leftovers?" Herb asked.

Gloria took her hand off the mouthpiece. "What kind of leftovers?"

"Potato salad and some sandwiches." Leonora hesitated. "The potato salad was made from your recipe, Grandma."

Gloria looked at Herb. "My potato salad and some sandwiches."

"No problem with your potato salad," Herb said. "Tell her she's still in the running."

Gloria cleared her throat. "Herb says your *friend* who served the leftovers is still in the running, thanks to my potato salad."

"Oh, good. Thank Herb for us, Gloria."

"I will, dear." Gloria ended the call and dropped the cell phone into her pocket. She beamed at Herb. "I appreciate this, Herb."

"If I get her married off for you, you're gonna owe me, Gloria."

"I'll cook you a nice lasagna-and-apple-pie dinner."

"Forget the lasagna and apple pie. You know what I want."

She sighed. "Your name on the column."

"You got that right. We got a deal?"

"Deal," Gloria said.

They were standing on Deke's back porch looking out at the cove. Wrench was investigating some bushes at the foot of the steps. Technically speaking it was twilight but it was hard to tell for sure, Thomas thought. The fog had come in again, blurring the line between day and night. The wispy stuff had thinned a little during the afternoon but it had never entirely dissipated. Now, in the face of the oncoming darkness, it was once again growing dense.

In fact, he decided, the fog this evening was downright eerie. With a little imagination you could almost convince yourself that it was some kind of otherworldly vapor. It seemed to rise up from the cove, weakening the barrier between the real world and the one on the other side of the looking glass.

Down below on the jogging path, occasional shadowy silhouettes appeared and disappeared in the mist. Each was heralded by the distant, hollow echo of shoes hitting pavement. You could tell whether the next figure to materialize briefly would be a runner, a jogger or a walker based on the rhythm of the footfalls.

"So, Rhodes was checking up on her?" Deke asked.

"Either that or he was planning to steal her identity but it seems a little unlikely that he'd choose her for a target."

"Yeah. He was checking her out," Deke said softly. "Just like we checked him out. What the hell is going on here?"

"Wish I had an answer to that one."

"She's stirring things up, isn't she?"

"Who? Leonora?" Thomas exhaled deeply. "I think you can say that, yes."

"I had a feeling she would. Like I said, she's a catalyst."

"You were right."

A brisk, martial-sounding *thud-thud-thud* preceded a sturdy aerobic walker who appeared briefly and then vanished in the mist.

"She seemed right at home at your place last night," Deke offered very casually. "Using your shower and all."

"Uh huh."

"Cassie mentioned that she passed Leonora on the jogging path early this morning. Said it looked like she was on the way to your house. For breakfast maybe."

"We're both early risers."

Deke nodded. "Something else you two have in common."

"Something else?" Thomas glanced at him and then went back to watching the ghostly joggers. "You've noticed other things Leonora and I have in common?"

"Sure."

Thomas hesitated but curiosity got the better of him. "Such as?"

"Hard to explain. Maybe it's the way you two do things."

"The way we do things?"

"Yeah, you know." Deke moved one hand a little, searching for the words. "Once you've made up your mind to do something, you just keep at it until it's done. You make a commitment, you keep it, even when you've got some doubts. Look at how you've stuck by me this past year. I know you've wondered, deep down, if I was looney-tunes."

"Hey, so what if you are a wack-job? You're still my brother."

"And the Walker brothers stick together, right?"

"Right." Thomas wrapped both hands around the railing. "If it's any consolation, I don't have any doubts about your mental health. Not anymore. When it comes to your conspiracy theories, you've made a believer out of me."

"I think I've got Leonora to thank for that," Deke answered. "My point is that she is a lot like you in some respects. Look how she put her life on hold to come here to find out what happened to her half sister. That's the kind of thing you would have done. Hell, it's exactly what you did."

Thomas shrugged. "You'd have done it for me."

"Sure."

They both looked out at the cove for a while. The fog coalesced into an impenetrable veil. The *thud-thud-thud* on the path announced a covey of joggers. They materialized in the mist, three middle-aged men who should have known better. Thomas wondered if any of them had started to notice some problems in his knees. Just a matter of time when you got close to forty.

"I hear we're invited to Leonora's house for dinner tonight," he said after a while.

"Cassie called about an hour ago. She said she and Leonora are going to cook for us."

"Be a good chance for all of us to put our heads together and discuss strategy."

Deke's face became impassive. "Cassie thinks I'm obsessing."

"You are. So what? It's what we Walker boys do."

"Might be a little embarrassing talking about some of this stuff in front of her," Deke said.

"Nah. Look at it this way, after six months of doing yoga with you she knows as much about this mess as the rest of us. Maybe she can give us a different perspective, the way Leonora is doing."

"I never thought about it that way." Deke hesitated. "I just don't want her to conclude that I'm a total space cadet, you know? Things are awkward enough between us as it is."

"Give her a chance, Deke. Also, you could look on the bright side."

"What's the bright side?"

"Worst-case scenario is that, even if Cassie decides you're a total nut case, we get a home-cooked meal and the company of two very nice ladies tonight."

"There is that," Deke said.

Maybe Leonora really was some sort of catalyst, Thomas thought. A lot of things around here were starting to show signs of movement and change.

He and Wrench walked back to the house along the jogging path. The late afternoon rush hour was in full swing. Runners, bikers, walkers and people with dogs crowded the trail. Twice he almost got run down by a jogger. Life in the fast lane was dangerous.

The phone was ringing when he and Wrench let themselves into the hall. He closed the door and picked up the cordless extension.

"This is Walker."

"Thomas?" Leonora said.

"I'll be there in about half an hour." He glanced at his watch. "I need to shower and change."

"No rush. Cassie and I are still fussing with the last-minute stuff. I called to ask if you would mind bringing your tools?"

A rush of red-hot anticipation warmed his blood. "Don't worry. I never go anywhere without my tools."

There was a short, startled pause on the other end of the line.

Leonora giggled.

"Actually, I was referring to your *other* tools," she said. "The kind you keep in your workshop. I've got a leaky faucet in the bath that has gotten so loud it's keeping me awake at night."

"Oh, those tools. Sure, I'll bring some of them, too."

Half an hour later, freshly showered and dressed in a

button-down shirt and chinos, he went into the workshop. He selected a wrench and some other odds and ends he figured he might need to fix a leaky faucet.

When he emerged, Wrench was waiting for him at the front door, leash in his mouth.

"Sorry, pal, not this time."

Wrench looked pathetic.

Thomas crouched in front of him and rubbed his ears. "Here's the situation. There's a possibility that I might get asked to spend the night at her place. I don't think I've got a chance in hell if you're there with me. It's one thing to ask a man to stay over. It's another thing altogether to invite him and his dog to spend the night. See what I mean?"

Wrench remained unconvinced.

Thomas gave him one last pat, rose and went out the door. The wrench was heavy in the pocket of his jacket.

"Care for some hors d'oeuvres, Deke?" Cassie said.

She offered him the bowl of steamed and salted soybean pods. He eyed them closely and then took a small handful.

"These are interesting," he said. "Tricky looking, but interesting."

"You'll get the hang of it after a while," Leonora assured him. "Watch me."

She put the end of one of the salted pods into her mouth, held on to the other end with her fingers and winkled out the soybeans with her front teeth. She dropped the empty pod into a small bowl.

Deke tried the same process. There was a loud sucking sound.

"Got 'em," he announced. He tossed the empty pod into the bowl.

"If you can do it, so can I," Thomas said.

He put the tip of a soybean pod into his mouth and scraped lightly with his front teeth. When he was finished he held up the empty pod in triumph.

Everyone laughed and reached for more.

Leonora exchanged a look with Cassie. So far, so good. The evening was off to a promising start.

Thomas sniffed the aromas emanating from the kitchen. "Smells good. What's for dinner?"

"Spinach and feta cheese lasagna," Leonora said. "Cassie made an apple pie for dessert."

"Lasagna?" Thomas got a dreamy expression. "Oh, man. I really, really like lasagna."

"I can't even recall the last time I had homemade apple pie," Deke said. "It's my favorite." He looked at Cassie. "Didn't know you could cook."

"You never asked," she said sweetly.

He blushed furiously, reached for his beer and changed the topic. "Good news, bad news from the grad student who ran the tests on that sample of Rhodes's nutritional supplement."

"What's the good news?" Thomas asked.

"It's just colored sugar and cornstarch."

Leonora raised her brows. "And the bad news?"

"It's just colored sugar and cornstarch."

Thomas grunted. "In other words, we're not going to get him for selling drugs."

"Not this easily, at any rate," Deke said. "He's a phony but I don't think you can say he's doing anything that's dangerous or illegal with that nutritional supplement he's selling."

Leonora looked at him. "Anything new on the old Eubanks murder?"

He swallowed more beer and slowly lowered the bottle. "Like I told Thomas, nothing that would explain

Bethany's interest in the case. According to the old records, it was just one more interrupted burglary in progress."

Thomas picked up another soybean pod and put it between his teeth. "Eubanks was in the math department. Bethany was a mathematician. Are you sure there's no connection?"

Deke shook his head. "Not that I can see."

"You know, she was your wife, but I knew her, too," Thomas said. "If you ask me, there's only one reason why Bethany might have taken an interest in an old murder case. And that's because it somehow impacted her own work in mathematics."

Deke stiffened. "You make it sound like she didn't care about people."

Thomas shrugged. "I'm not sure she did. Not in the way you care about them. Oh, she liked to have people take care of her so that she could focus on her work, but she didn't go out of her way to help anyone else. You know that, Deke."

There was a short, strained silence. Leonora met Cassie's anxious eyes. She knew they were both wondering if Deke would explode into a furious defense of his dead wife.

End of dinner party.

But to her amazement, Deke just scowled.

"She wasn't cruel or mean or unkind," he said, sounding stubborn but not angry.

"No." Thomas leaned back in his chair and regarded his brother. "She wasn't any of those things. She was simply self-absorbed. Most of the time she was off in her own world, doing her own thing. All she wanted was to be left alone with her work."

"She was brilliant." Deke took another swallow of beer. "A genius. Geniuses are different."

He didn't offer anything else in defense of his dead wife.

Cassie seized the bowl of soybeans. "Have some more?"

"Thanks," Leonora said quickly. "I'd love another one."

There was a small flurry of action as Cassie shoved the bowl in front of everyone, one by one. Deke and Thomas were both equally willing to be distracted. They helped themselves to more of the green pods.

Leonora released the breath she had been holding. "All right, it looks like the Eubanks connection is a dead end for now. We'll have to concentrate on another angle."

"I'm not so sure about that," Cassie said slowly.

They all turned to look at her as if she had just announced that she could fly.

"What do you mean?" Deke asked in surprise.

"If you really want to find out if there's anything more to the Eubanks murder than what was in the papers," Cassie said quietly. "I have a suggestion."

"Go on," Thomas said.

Cassie sat forward. "On Tuesdays I teach a yoga class for seniors at the Cove View Retirement Community. One of the members of that class, a woman named Margaret Lewis, used to be the chief secretary in the Department of Mathematics at Eubanks. She worked at the college for over forty years. She would have been there at the time Sebastian Eubanks was murdered."

"Oh, my," Leonora whispered. "The department secretary from thirty years ago is still alive?"

"And kicking," Cassie added. "One of my best students."

Deke stared at Cassie. "Holy shit. The department secretary."

Thomas looked bemused. "I get the feeling I'm missing something here. So one of the math department secretaries is still around. So what?"

They all turned toward him.

"What's wrong?" He looked down at the front of his shirt. "Did I drop a soybean pod or something?"

"Thomas," Leonora said with exasperation, "we are talking about a *department secretary*. Don't you understand? There is no one on a college staff who is more wired into what is going on behind the scenes. Only the good lord above would be a better source of gossip. And he's not talking."

"Leonora is right," Deke said enthusiastically. "You've got to trust us on this one, Thomas."

"If you say so."

Cassie chuckled. "There are a lot of old jokes about the hierarchy of the academic world, Thomas. The general theme of all of them is that while the dean, department chair, professor, associate professor, assistant professor and instructor all have their place and a certain measure of authority, it's really the department secretary who runs the show."

"Okay, okay, I get the point." Thomas contemplated them each in turn. "You think it might be worth talking to this Margaret Lewis, is that it?"

"Oh, yeah," Deke said. "If there was anything unusual going on at the time of the Eubanks murder, the department secretary would have known about it."

Leonora got up and went into the kitchen to check on the lasagna. "If this Margaret Lewis can't recall anything more about the events surrounding the Eubanks murder than what was in the newspaper clippings, we can rest assured that there was nothing more going on at the time."

Thomas concentrated on reassembling the bathroom faucet. Out of long habit he had arranged the various small components one by one on the counter in the order in which he had removed them. The theory was that all he had to do now to complete the leak repair was put the faucet back together in reverse order. It was a good theory and sometimes it actually worked. But plumbing was an art, not a science. It did not always respond to logic. In that, it had a lot in common with whatever was going on between Leonora and himself.

"I thought things went well," Leonora said from the doorway behind him. "Deke and Cassie were getting along great by the end of the evening."

He thought about how close together Deke and Cassie had been walking when they had gone down the steps to the footpath a short while earlier. They hadn't been holding hands, but there had been a sense of intimacy that seemed new in their relationship.

"May have been the apple pie," he said. He picked up a screwdriver. "Deke loves the stuff. Especially with ice cream. The lasagna was terrific, too, by the way."

"Glad you enjoyed it."

"Haven't had homemade lasagna that good in years." He jiggled the lever delicately a bit to reseat it. "Mostly I buy the frozen kind when I get a hankering for it."

She folded her arms and propped one shoulder against the door jamb. "I have to tell you, I got a little worried there when you mentioned that Bethany wasn't exactly the nurturing type. I wasn't sure how Deke would react."

"Neither was I," he admitted. "But sometimes I get fed up listening to him talk about her as if she was a saint."

"I also got the feeling that his rush to defend her memory tonight came more from habit than unresolved grief."

"He's changing. Moving forward, I think." He went down on one knee, reached into the open cabinet and turned on the valves that controlled the water supply. "I just hope that he doesn't slide backward again if we don't get some final answers."

"I don't think that will happen. He's starting to focus on Cassie. That's a big step."

"Yeah." He got back to his feet and turned on the faucet. There was some sputtering and coughing, but the old pipes were sturdy. After a moment water flowed steadily. "You really think this old math department secretary will be able to tell us anything useful?"

"Who knows? Worth a try."

"If you say so." He shut off the water.

They both gazed steadily at the faucet for a time. No drips.

"My," Leonora said in tones of near-reverent awe. "You are good. You are *extraordinary*."

"What can I say? It's a gift."

She smiled at him in the mirror. "I believe it."

He looked at her reflected image. There was a graceful, seductive curve to her body as she lounged there in the doorway behind him. Her eyes were warm and deep and mysterious.

"Got anything else that needs adjusting?" he asked.

"Now that you mention it, I believe I do have another home improvement project that could benefit from an expert application of your tools."

He twirled the gleaming adjustable wrench with the practiced skill of an Old West gunfighter. "Lead me to it."

"This way."

She turned and drew him down the hall into the shadows of the bedroom.

An hour and a half later he went out onto her front porch and inhaled the chilled, damp night. Another wave of fog had crept up off the dark waters of the Sound, shrouding the footpath. The low lamps spaced at intervals along the route glowed dimly.

He looked at Leonora, who stood on the threshold. She was draped in a thick robe, her hair loose and tumbled around her face. She was squinting ever so slightly. She had left her glasses on the nightstand.

"Good night." She kissed him on the mouth.

"Night."

He kissed her back, not lightly, the way she had kissed him. He wanted to leave an impression. Give her something to think about when she got back into the warm, mussed bed that he had just vacated.

"Good party?" the stranger asked.

Brett Conway staggered to a halt and tried to focus. The guy had freaked him out, materializing out of the fog and the darkness like that. He hadn't heard anyone else on the footpath.

The stranger looked weird. He was dressed in black and he had a ski mask on over his face. It was cold, Brett thought, but not that cold.

"Party was okay," Brett muttered.

It had been a good party. Plenty of booze and some pot. But none of the girls had shown any interest in him. Just as well. He was feeling a little sick. Wouldn't take much to make him hurl straight into the cove.

"You don't look so good," the stranger said.

"Too much beer. I'll be okay."

"I've got something that will make you feel a lot better in a hurry." The stranger held out his gloved hand, palm up. "Try it. You'll like it."

Brett looked at the little package. "What is it?"

"Smoke and Mirrors."

A thrill shot through him. He forgot about his uneasy stomach. "No shit? The real thing?"

"The real thing."

"Heard the rumors. But no one I know has been able to get any."

"Be the first on your block."

Wariness returned. "How much? I haven't got more than twenty or thirty bucks on me."

"Free."

Now he knew there was a catch. "I don't believe it."

"Well, there is one little favor I'd like you to do for me," the stranger said.

"What favor?"

"Swallow this and then we'll discuss it."

Brett hesitated. But it was just too easy. He could already hear himself telling his friends about this tomorrow. *You'll never believe it. Met a guy on the footpath last night. Gave me S and M. The real stuff. For free.*

He swallowed the powder. It tasted bitter.

"About that favor," the stranger said.

"What?" Brett squinted through the fog, trying to get a better look at the stranger's eyes. Something weird about those eyes.

"You're going to kill a monster for me."

"You're crazy, man." Brett chuckled. He was feeling better already. Kind of excited. "No monsters around here."

"You're wrong. There's one coming along the path right now. He'll be on the footbridge in a few minutes." The stranger handed him a long object that was weighted at the end. "Take this. You'll need it."

Brett looked down at the golf club the stranger had put in his hand. "Huh?"

Something was really wrong here. He wanted to ask

some more questions. But the hallucinations started in
and he saw the monster in the fog.

Some of the heavy satisfaction that had come over
Thomas after the truly memorable sex started to fade. In
its place he felt the familiar stirring sensation. Maybe that
deliberately provocative good-night kiss hadn't been
such a good idea. He was going to be the one who spent
the night thinking deeply unsettling thoughts.

The sound of a jogger's footfalls behind him warned
him that there were still a few diehards out ruining their
knees, even at this late hour. He moved to the edge of the
path, giving the runner plenty of room.

The echo of the pounding steps got louder. A moment
later a young man galloped past. A nearby lamp gleamed
briefly on his running shoes and lower legs. The rest of
his body was in darkness.

Thomas wondered if he should warn the kid that if he
kept up the running his knees would probably be shot by
the time he was forty. He decided not to mention it. Why
give the competition an edge? Things were tough enough
at forty. Besides, young guys didn't want to hear about
bad knees. They planned on living forever and being in
great shape the whole time.

The young man vanished into the night. The sound of
his footfalls faded into nothingness. Silence flowed back,
swirling together with the fog.

He reached the footbridge and started across. From
here he could see his own porch light in the trees on the
hillside. Wrench would be waiting up for him. Nice to
know your dog was always there for you.

Footfalls sounded behind him. Another jogger, one
who had decided to cheat and take the shortcut to the
other side of the cove. The *thud-thud*s were heavier, not

quite in sync, as if the guy was struggling to keep the rhythm going. Maybe his knees hurt.

Thomas became aware of the runner's heavy breathing. He could hear audible gulps of air. As he listened, the pattern of the footfalls altered. They were more closely spaced. Picking up speed.

Closing the distance.

Don't look back. Something may be gaining on you.

The *thuds* were coming very swiftly now. The runner was really sucking air, preparing for an even greater burst of speed. Working himself up for a major push. This guy sounded as if he was calling on all of his resources to make it past an invisible finish line.

The runner was almost upon him.

The hell with it. The only thing worse than looking nervous was looking like a victim.

Thomas stopped, turned and stepped back toward the rail, giving the runner plenty of room. He kept his right hand in the pocket of his jacket. His fingers tightened around the handle of the wrench.

A dark shadow exploded out of the fog. There was something wrong with his posture. Both arms were raised in an unnatural manner. He clutched a long object.

The runner grunted, an incoherent cry, and swung the object downward the way a butcher swings a cleaver.

Thomas yanked the wrench out of his pocket. He raised it, simultaneously shifting sideways along the railing.

The runner's club struck the wrench instead of Thomas's head. The jarring impact sent shudders through the wooden span beneath Thomas's feet.

The runner, propelled by his own momentum, kept going for a few paces before pulling up abruptly. He spun around, sucked in more air and started back toward his target at full speed.

The broad head at the end of the long object in the man's hand glinted briefly in the low light.

A golf club.

Even as he identified the assault weapon, Thomas threw himself forward, wrench raised again to block the club. The move was reflexive. He did not have much choice in the matter of tactics. Ducking back out of the way was not on his list of available options. He would end up trapped against the guardrail.

Wrench and club shaft collided a second time. More shock waves jolted through Thomas and the footbridge. The attacker howled and reeled back against the rail.

The club flew from his hand and spun away into the darkness below the bridge.

Thomas grabbed the opportunity and moved in fast. He drove one shoulder into the other man's midsection, taking both of them down. They hit the wooden planks and rolled, coming up hard against a post. Thomas lost his grip on the wrench. It clattered on the boards.

He wasted no time trying to find his tool. He was too busy dealing with the man beneath him. His assailant had gone from murderous rage to what seemed to be sheer panic.

The runner punched and thrashed wildly, screaming in fear.

"Let me go. *No. No.* Don't touch me. *Let me go.*"

His fist connected with the side of Thomas's face, then slammed into his ribs. The blows were frantic and wild.

Cold fury flashed through Thomas, adding more raw chemicals to the potent brew swirling through his bloodstream.

He struck back, his hand chopping into the soft flesh of an abdomen. He heard the runner's gasp of pain.

"Don't hurt me. Don't hurt me."

The runner flailed, but he was clearly weakening rapidly.

"Please, please, please. Don't hurt me. Don't hurt me."

The runner put his hands up, as if to shield his head.

Thomas realized the guy was sobbing hysterically.

"Please, don't hurt me."

Thomas got warily to his feet and reached for his cell phone.

He was in luck. It was still in his pocket and it had survived the fight. A tribute to modern technology.

He stood with Ed Stovall in the lobby of the Wing Cove Community Hospital. Ed was in full uniform, crisp and pressed. You'd never know he'd been awakened from a sound sleep to answer the 911 call.

"Juiced up and high as a bird on some kind of crap." Ed snapped his notebook shut and stuck it into his pocket. "Probably that new hallucinogen. S and M. The doc in the E.R. said the kid's on one very bad drug trip. Seeing things that aren't there. Keeps screaming about the monster on the footbridge."

"That would be me," Thomas said.

"Apparently he decided you were a fiend in human form. He was convinced that he had to destroy you. Guess the idea was to toss you over the rail into the cove."

"Might have worked. Especially if that golf club had connected with my head first."

"The medics said I probably won't be able to get any more out of him until tomorrow at the earliest. Assuming he even remembers what happened."

"Got an ID?"

"His name's Brett Conway. He's a junior at Eubanks. He went out drinking with some friends earlier this evening. They ended up at a private party. He left on his own. Told his buddies that he was going to walk back to his apartment. That's the last anyone saw of him until he decided to go after you."

"What about the golf club?" Thomas said.

"Eubanks fields a golf team. Brett Conway is on it."

"What happens now?" Thomas asked.

Ed looked grim. "Now I get to call Conway's parents and tell them their boy has gotten into trouble with drugs."

"Don't envy you," Thomas said.

"Yeah, I really hate this part of the job."

Someone was leaning on her doorbell. She glanced blearily at the clock. Three A.M. Not good.

A chill went through Leonora. It was her own fault that she was here alone. Thomas had made it clear earlier that he would have been quite happy to spend the night. But she had not invited him to do so. She had told herself that she needed to maintain some emotional distance in this relationship. Things were precarious enough as it was.

She pushed aside the covers and groped for her glasses on the nightstand. She found them, got them on and then rose and pulled on her robe.

She went down the hall and looked across the darkened living room to the door.

The bell continued to chime relentlessly.

She tied the bathrobe more securely around her waist, picked up her cell phone so that she could dial 911 instantly if necessary, and made her way through the shadow-drenched living room to the door.

She flipped on the porch light and peered through the peephole. Relief swept through her when she saw Thomas on the doorstep.

Then she saw the dark stains on his shirt.

"Oh, my God." She wrenched open the door. "*Thomas.* Is that blood on your shirt?"

He looked down, face twisting with irritation. "Bastard. Cut my lip. This was a new shirt."

"What happened? Are you all right?" Stupid question. He was very clearly not all right.

"Accident on the footbridge." He took his finger off the bell button. "Can I come in and clean up?"

"An accident?" She stepped back hurriedly. "Yes, of course. Come in. Maybe I should take you to the emergency room."

"Just left the E.R. I'm okay."

"You were at the hospital? Thomas, for heaven's sake, what happened?"

"Long story. But don't worry. Nothing's broken."

He came through the doorway, moving stiffly, and stopped in the hall. She finally got a good look at him in the overhead light. There was a bad scrape high on his left cheek, his knuckles were raw and his hair was badly mussed. His jacket, trousers and shirt were stained with mud and blood; his shirttails hung loose.

She closed the door very carefully, locked it and turned around.

"Thomas, what happened to you?"

"Ran into a jogger." He caught sight of himself in the hall mirror and winced. "Damn. Coming here was a mistake. Didn't realize I looked this bad. I should have had Ed drop me at my place."

"Tell me about this accident."

"On the footbridge."

"You said you went to the emergency room but you certainly don't look like you've seen a doctor."

"They were busy with the other guy. I didn't let them clean me up. Figured I could do that here."

"You're not making any sense, Thomas."

"Like I said, it's a long story."

"You can tell it to me while we get you patched up."

He did not argue.

She stepped around him, leading the way back through the living room and down the short hall.

She sat him down on the edge of the white tub and then she turned on the water in the sink. She saw him watching her in the mirrored door of the medicine cabinet. His eyes were colder than the waters of the cove.

"Are you sure you don't need a doctor?" she asked.

"I'm sure."

She opened the cabinet and took down some alcohol, cotton swabs and a tube of antibiotic ointment.

"You always travel with a fully equipped medicine cabinet?" he asked.

"As a matter of fact, I do. I keep the basics handy, at any rate. My grandmother taught me that. She believes in being prepared. Take off your jacket and shirt." She faced him. "I need to see the full extent of the damage."

"It's not that bad." He started to shrug out of his jacket, halted briefly to draw a slow breath and then peeled it off with a stony, stoic expression.

"You're in a lot of pain, aren't you?" She took the jacket from him and hung it on the hook behind the door. Something clanked against the wood panel, distracting her. "What is that?"

"The wrench I brought with me to fix your leaky faucet." Methodically, he undid the buttons of his shirt.

When he got it off she was relieved to see that things did not look too bad. "Can you take a deep breath?"

He tried it cautiously, feeling his ribs with his fingers. "Yeah. No sharp pain. Relax, Leonora, I'm okay. Just a little bruised."

She moistened a ball of cotton with alcohol and went to work on his scraped cheek.

"All right," she said, "let's have it. What exactly happened out there?"

"Some kid high on dope tried to brain me with a golf club and throw me into the cove. He missed. That's the end of the story, as far as Ed Stovall is concerned."

For an instant she didn't think she had heard him correctly. She lifted the cotton ball away from his cheek.

"What?" She had a hard time getting the word out. Her tongue felt thick. "The kid tried to kill you?"

"They think he was on that S and M stuff we've been hearing about. He's still seeing monsters in the E.R. Apparently he thought I was one."

The floor of the bathroom fell away beneath her feet, leaving her hanging, weightless, in midair in some other universe. The world on the other side of the mirror, she thought.

"You're serious, aren't you?" she whispered.

"I'm sure as hell not in what you might call a jocular mood."

She took a grip on her plummeting stomach and moved back to get a better look at him. "He used a golf club?"

"Ed said the kid's on the Eubanks team. Ouch."

"Sorry." She applied the cotton ball a little less forcefully. "I know what you're thinking."

"I'm thinking about that bag of golf clubs we saw in Alex Rhodes's back room."

"I knew it. Did you mention the clubs to Ed Stovall?"

"No point. He's satisfied with his version of events and it's not like I've got any evidence to contradict him. My only hope is that when the kid comes off his drug trip he'll be able to tell Ed where he got the crap that made him see monsters. But I'm not holding my breath. The E.R. folks said he might not remember anything about the experience. They said that judging from the few cases they've handled, the drug is very unpredictable and that goes double when it's mixed with alcohol."

"Oh, my God, Thomas. Do you think Alex got the boy high and deliberately sent him out to murder you?"

"Maybe not. Maybe he just wanted to send a warning." Thomas gingerly touched his right shoulder with his left hand. "Make it clear that it would be best if I stayed out of his private business."

She turned away to drop the bloody cotton ball in the trash. "How could he possibly know?"

"About our interest in him? Julie Bromley. Wouldn't be surprised if he found out about our little chat with her this morning. Probably made him nervous."

She stared at him in the mirror, unable to look away. "You have to talk to Ed Stovall."

"I wish like hell it was that easy. Trust me, at this point it would be a complete waste of time."

"Maybe if I went with you to talk to him?"

"No offense, but that won't help." Thomas's mouth twisted grimly. "He'll assume you're backing me up because you're sleeping with me."

She cleared her throat. "I see. He'll think that I'm blinded by passion, is that it?"

Thomas started to get to his feet. "Ed will look for any excuse to dismiss my story, because he'll figure I'm still working on a conspiracy theory with Deke."

"Sit still." She picked up the tube of antibiotic ointment. "I haven't finished with you yet."

When she had done what she could for his bruises, she steered him into the kitchen. Some of the feral quality had finally faded from his eyes but he still looked much too dangerous.

She sat him down at the table and gave him some of the over-the-counter anti-inflammatory tablets she kept handy for occasional stress headaches.

She poured a glass of milk and put it down in front of him to accompany the painkillers.

He looked at the milk. "Got whiskey?"

She smiled slightly. "No. Sorry."

"How about that cognac you served with the apple pie?"

"Right." She opened a cupboard, took down the bottle and poured a hefty measure into a glass.

He took it from her. "Thanks."

She watched him down the tablets and half the contents of the glass in a single swallow.

"Thomas, what on earth are we going to do?"

"Don't know yet. I need to do some thinking."

"What about Alex Rhodes?"

Thomas contemplated that for a long moment.

"He'll probably assume that I suspect he was the one behind the assault tonight, but he'll also know there's not much I can do about it. He's well aware of the local situation. He knows that everyone, including the chief of police, thinks that Deke is obsessed with his murder conspiracy, and that any move I make will be viewed as aiding and abetting my brother's delusions."

"We can't just ignore the fact that he may have tried to have you killed tonight."

"I think it might pay to let him worry for a while," Thomas said. "He's bound to be sweating a little by now, wondering what move I'll make. Wouldn't hurt if he gets a bit nervous. Nervous people make mistakes. Meanwhile, we'll have our chat with Margaret Lewis tomorrow and see what comes of that. We need a strategy."

"Strategy?"

"A plan, you know? I'd really like to have one of those. I always feel better when I'm working from a blueprint."

She frowned. "Thomas, I don't think—"

"Mind if I spend the night here?"

Not long ago she had been half-wishing that she had invited him to sleep in her bed tonight, thinking of all the reasons why that would not have been a good idea. Now the very direct question left her flustered.

"That's real smooth, Walker," she said. "Whatever happened to subtlety and romance?"

"I'm not feeling subtle or romantic right at the moment. If you don't want me to sleep here, we can go back to my place."

His businesslike tone gave her pause.

She cleared her throat. "I get the impression that this request to spend the night is not about finding a convenient venue for hot, sizzling sex. Why am I being asked to make this choice?"

He looked at her. "If I'm right in concluding that Rhodes tried to scare me off or maybe even get rid of me tonight, we have to assume that he had his reasons."

"So?"

"He's got to know by now that you and I are both involved in this thing. Doesn't take a rocket scientist to figure out that if Rhodes thinks I'm a threat, he probably figures you for one, too."

"A threat." She breathed out slowly. "I do believe I see where you're going with this."

"We have to assume that if he has reasons for wanting me out of the way, he probably isn't feeling real charitable toward you, either."

"In spite of the view of my derriere he got that day in the supermarket?"

"Your derriere is incomparable, but I'm not sure that

we can count on its wonders, splendid as they are, to stop
Rhodes from doing something unpleasant." Thomas
paused. "Guy like Rhodes isn't capable of fully appreci-
ating your derriere, you see."

"Just one disillusionment after another. But I take your
point. We should probably stick together for a while.
Watch each other's backs."

"Be a good idea."

"You can stay here tonight."

"Thanks. Sorry about the lack of subtlety and romance."

She lounged back against the counter. "They say that a
good relationship should be founded on something more
substantial than subtlety and romance because those
qualities never last long."

"I've heard that," Thomas said.

"Lucky for us we've got something more solid and
substantial than subtlety and romance to work with
here."

"Yeah? What's that?"

"Your tools."

When she came out of the bathroom in her robe she discovered that he had already eased himself into the large
bed. Maybe it was her imagination, but it seemed to her
that he took up most of the available space. He leaned
back against the pale sheets, his hands linked behind his
head, and watched her turn out the light.

"Meant to correct a mistaken impression you had earlier," he said when she slipped in beside him.

She touched his chest lightly, wondering how much he
hurt and where. "What mistaken impression was that?"

"When I asked you if I could spend the night here?"

"Umm hmm?"

"That request was, indeed, based primarily on my concerns for your safety. But there was an ulterior motive, as well."

"And that ulterior motive would be?"

"I was also seeking a convenient venue for hot, sizzling sex."

"Really? In that case, it's certainly a pity that you got all beat up tonight."

"I don't think that will be too much of a problem. Just promise me you'll be gentle."

The hot, sizzling, very gentle sex, the anti-inflammatories and the knowledge that Leonora was in the same bed combined to put him to sleep for a while.

Unfortunately, he dreamed.

. . . He stood at the sink in Leonora's bathroom, trying to shave. But it was hard to see what he was doing because the mirror was covered in steam.

He picked up a towel and wiped the mist off the reflective surface.

He could see a face in the glass now, but it wasn't his own. Alex Rhodes looked out at him, malevolent golden eyes gleaming with dark, taunting amusement.

Chapter Fifteen

Shaving the next morning, even without having to look at Rhodes's phony yellow eyes in the bathroom mirror, turned out not to be an option. He did not have his razor.

Thomas turned off the shower, wrapped a towel around his waist and leaned over the white porcelain sink. He examined the dark stubble on his jaw in the steam-clouded mirror. Not a pretty sight.

But there wasn't a lot he could do about it, he thought. Leonora probably wouldn't appreciate him borrowing her little pink plastic disposable razor. It was just one more thing to jot down on the list of vital necessities that he intended to pick up at his place sometime today. The list was growing longer by the moment. It now included, in order of importance, condoms, toothbrush, razor, fresh shirt, underwear and a pair of socks.

Damn. It would take a small duffel bag to hold it all.

And then there was the matter of Wrench.

He had a vision of himself packing a bag every

evening and setting out with Wrench to make the trek to
Leonora's house. A pain in the ass. Be a hell of a lot more
convenient if Leonora moved in with him. But he had a
hunch she might not go for that pragmatic plan. It meant
that she would be the one who had to pack up every night
and women always seemed to have more stuff.

Might not be a good idea for him to get too accustomed to having her around the house, anyway. She
would probably head back to her own world the minute
her adventures here in Wonderland were concluded.

Great. Now he was actively working to make himself
depressed.

He viewed his reflection. No getting around the fact
that he looked like a train wreck. There was a lot of ugly
purpling on his ribs. The beard stubble didn't hide the
crust that had formed over the scrape on his cheek. The
area under his left eye was badly discolored and would
probably get worse as the day wore on. His hands, especially the knuckles, were pretty roughed up, too.

He turned away from the mirror, picked up his shirt
and winced when he caught a whiff. Not real fresh. He
had done some serious sweating in it last night during the
scuffle on the footbridge. Maybe better to go without this
morning.

He finished toweling himself dry, pulled on his
trousers and ran his fingers through his hair. Satisfied that
was the best he could do under the circumstances, he
opened the door and went out into the hall. He needed
coffee and some more anti-inflammatories. Food would
be nice after that. He was hungry. Hot, sizzling sex with
Leonora seemed to have that effect on him.

The sound of a man's voice emanating from the direction of the kitchen made him forget about both the caffeine and the painkillers.

"This is insanity, Leo. You must be delusional if you've

managed to convince yourself that Meredith was murdered and that you can find the killer. You need serious psychiatric help."

"Maybe, but I don't think my HMO would cover it," Leonora said mildly. "Would you like some coffee?"

Thomas crossed the living room in a few long strides and halted in the kitchen doorway. He took in the scene in one swift glance.

Leonora was at the counter, pouring coffee for her guest. She had made a pot of tea for herself.

He couldn't help but notice that, unlike him, she looked terrific this morning. She was dressed in easy-fitting black trousers, a long, scarlet sweater and a pair of fluffy slippers. Her hair was clipped back in the familiar French twist.

An intense-looking man with curly brown hair and sharp features occupied one of the two chairs at the table. He wore an unpressed blue oxford cloth shirt, a pair of khaki trousers and loafers. A well-worn corduroy jacket with suede elbow patches was draped over the back of the chair.

An expensive leather book bag that looked a lot like a purse, but was probably intended to serve as a briefcase, stood against the wall next to him.

The guy might as well have worn a sign on his forehead with the words *I'm going for tenure* stenciled on it, Thomas decided.

Leonora looked toward the door. "There you are, Thomas." She gave him a quick visual examination, her eyes clouding with concern. "How do you feel?"

"I'll live, thanks."

She did not appear entirely convinced, but she did not argue the point. "Meet a, uh, former colleague. Kyle Delling. You may have heard me mention his name once or twice."

The ex-fiancé. Just what he needed. Another man in the vicinity who had also gotten tangled up with Meredith. He wondered if Leonora was looking at the two of them here in her kitchen and mentally filing them both under the same subject heading: *Meredith's discards*.

Kyle stared at him, nonplussed. Maybe it was the shock of seeing a strange man coming out of his ex-fiancée's bathroom without a shirt, Thomas thought. It struck him that if he was Leonora's ex-anything, he'd have a real tough time in Kyle's place. The thought of her with another man now, after what they'd shared these past few days, would be very difficult to handle.

That realization hit him harder than any of the punches he had taken from Brett Conway last night. Leonora did not fit into the same category as the other women he had known during the years since his divorce. He was not going to be able to stay in the safe zone this time. When this was over he was going to go down hard.

Oh, man, this was serious.

Kyle's mouth opened. The small action broke into Thomas's morbid thoughts. He wondered if the professor was going to take a swing at him. He hoped so. Be nice to have an excuse to work off some of this new stress. Nothing like a little exercise to elevate a man's mood.

Belatedly he recalled that Leonora had said that her ex was a very modern kind of guy. So maybe Kyle wasn't staring at him with that weird expression because he was jealous. Maybe it was the bruised ribs, black eye and scraped knuckles that were failing to make a great first impression.

Kyle finally managed to get his jaw back in place. "Who the hell are you?"

Leonora blew on her tea and answered for him.

"This is Thomas Walker. He's a friend." She put a little extra emphasis on the last word.

Thomas nodded once. "Delling." Who said he couldn't be a modern guy?

Kyle appeared deeply troubled by the fact that Thomas had proven himself capable of human speech.

Thomas spotted the little bottle on the counter. He left the doorway and went to help himself to the tablets.

"Probably shouldn't take those on an empty stomach," Leonora warned.

She put down her tea, plucked a slice of toast out of the toaster and buttered it with quick, economical motions. When it was ready she handed it to him.

He took a large bite out of the toast and swallowed a couple of pills with the glass of juice she gave him. He made a halfhearted attempt to think of something civil to say to Kyle. When nothing leaped to mind, he abandoned the effort in favor of another bite of toast.

"Cassie called while you were in the shower," Leonora said. "Margaret Lewis has agreed to see us this morning. Cassie and Deke said they'd pick us up around ten o'clock."

"Sounds good." He glanced at his watch. It was seven-thirty. "That'll give me plenty of time to go back to my place, check in with Wrench and change into some fresh clothes."

"What happened to you?" Kyle blurted, obviously unable to contain his curiosity for another second. "Run into a brick wall?"

"Accident on the footbridge that runs across the cove." Thomas polished off the last of the toast. "Dangerous places, footbridges."

Kyle looked dubious. "Looks like you were in a fight or something."

"Or something." He swallowed some coffee. "Sorry to eat and run, but I've got things to do and places to go. Better be on my way. See you at ten, Leonora."

"Right." She put her cup down.

He went to where she stood at the counter and kissed her. A bit more forcefully than necessary.

She didn't resist, but when he raised his mouth from hers he could tell from the ironic gleam in her eyes that she knew damn well that it had been one of those dumb, staking-a-claim kisses men used to mark their women in front of other males.

He felt very immature until he noticed that Kyle was openly gaping, clearly appalled. That made him feel a lot better. In an immature sort of way.

"See you around," he said to Kyle.

Delling looked blank.

Thomas walked out of the kitchen and got his jacket out of the closet.

Leonora followed him to the front door. She did not speak until they were out on the porch.

"That was not real subtle or romantic," she said.

"I like to think that our relationship has progressed beyond the superficial."

"Progressed my left toe. What was with the macho show-off bit back there in the kitchen?"

"I have no idea what you're talking about. Only an extremely immature person would engage in macho show-off behavior." The cold air hit his raw face, stinging initially and then turning everything nicely numb. "What's with the ex-fiancé in the kitchen bit, anyway? Is he here to try to patch things up?"

"No. He's after something much more important than the repair of an ephemeral and transitory personal relationship."

"Yeah? Like what?"

"Tenure."

"Ah." He nodded. "I've hung with enough academics during the past year to know that tenure is some sort of

Holy Grail for that crowd. What makes Delling think you can help him get it?"

"One of my best friends is the chair of the department that is going to make the decision concerning whether or not Kyle gets moved onto the tenure track in the English department. She's very loyal to me, and she took great offense on my behalf last year when word got around that Kyle had jumped into bed with Meredith."

Thomas grinned. It hurt but it was worth it. "Revenge is sweet, ain't it?"

"Only an extremely immature person would dabble in something so ignoble as revenge."

"Like I said. Sweet." He nodded again, satisfied. "Good to know we both have a streak of immaturity. One more thing we have in common."

He went down the steps and headed for the footpath. He resisted a sudden, inexplicable urge to whistle. He was much too beat up and sore to whistle.

He opened his own front door a short time later. Wrench was waiting in the hall, looking reproachful in the way only a dog could.

"Okay, okay, you were right. I should have taken you with me last night."

They went through the routine greeting ritual, but Thomas got the impression that his dog was disappointed that Leonora had not come with him.

"I'll make it up to you," Thomas promised.

"What's with the Incredible Hulk?" Kyle asked when she walked back into the kitchen. "Not exactly your type. Playing Lady Chatterley out here in the provinces?"

"I'm going through an immature phase."

Kyle frowned. "Those bruises looked bad. Must have been a hell of a fall he took on that footbridge. Is he just clumsy or what?"

Leonora poured herself another cup of tea. "Actually, Thomas got those bruises in a fight last night. Some kid high on drugs attacked him. The boy is in the hospital."

"Shit." Kyle blinked a few times. "Is this a joke?"

"I haven't felt the inclination to share a joke with you since the day I found you in bed with Meredith."

Kyle's jaw went rigid. "You're still obsessed with that one insignificant incident, aren't you? You've got to get past it, Leonora. For your own sake. It's time to move on."

"But I have moved on, Kyle. I doubt if I could have appreciated a man like Thomas if I hadn't gone through a relationship with you, first. I suppose I owe you for that."

"Sarcasm is not a constructive mode of communication."

She thought about it. "You know what? I wasn't being sarcastic. What I just said was the pure, unadulterated truth."

The Wing Cove Retirement Community apartment complex was composed of three handsome redbrick buildings constructed in a three-story triangle.

"You sure Wrench will be all right here in the car?" Leonora asked, turning around in the front seat.

Thomas looked at Wrench, who was in the back of the SUV, his head hung over the rear seat where Deke and Cassie sat.

"It was his choice to come," he said.

"He'll be fine," Deke assured her. "We'll leave the window open."

"He won't be out here alone for long." Cassie unfastened her seat belt. "Margaret has an art class later this morning."

They entered the apartment community through a pleasantly furnished lobby. There was a large bouquet of fresh flowers on a round table. Thomas glanced at the list of the day's activities on the chalk board: *Aqua aerobics, current events lecture, art class, museum tour sign-up.* A Cary Grant film was scheduled for the evening.

A polite, polished receptionist verified that they were expected, and then gave them directions to Margaret Lewis's residence.

It wasn't easy squeezing all four of them into her tiny, one-bedroom apartment. Everything, including Margaret, seemed to be in miniature. Thomas felt like a giant in the little mauve and leaf-green room.

He lowered himself cautiously onto one of the dainty, undersized chairs, half afraid that it would shatter under his weight. Deke, he noticed, was just as careful. His brother was perched gingerly on the little sofa.

There was a small writing desk in one corner. A laptop sat on it, the lid neatly closed. The walls of the doll-sized apartment were covered with framed photographs, many of them photos of Margaret Lewis posed with various academics. Probably the deans, department chairs and other notables who had been associated with the Eubanks College Department of Mathematics during the time Margaret had reigned as secretary, he decided.

A large calendar hung on one wall. Thomas noticed that every square was filled in for the current month. He checked out a few of the entries. Bridge. Yoga. Bridge. Aqua Aerobics. Bridge. Current Affairs. Bridge. Dr. Appt. Bridge. Museum Tour. Bridge.

Margaret Lewis was a cheerful, self-possessed woman with dark-brown skin and a crown of tight, silver curls.

She used a cane and looked trim and fit in a mauve polyester pantsuit that matched her décor.

Thomas glanced at a photo of a young black man standing on the steps of an imposing building. He was smiling at the camera.

"My son," Margaret said proudly. "He's on the faculty at the University of Washington."

She lowered herself into a flower-print chair and nodded pleasantly at each of them as Cassie completed the introductions. When the formalities were concluded, she peered at Thomas with lively interest in her dark eyes.

"What happened to you?" she asked. "Get into a fight?"

"Accident on the footbridge," he said. "Jogger ran me down."

She made a tut-tutting sound. "Never understood the craze for running and jogging. Absolute nonsense. Hard on the knees. Knees wear out, you know."

He nodded. "I've heard that."

"Arthritis sets in fast. Eighty percent of the people down there in the pool doing water aerobics this morning have artificial knees. Why do you think I'm using this cane? Just had my second knee replacement."

"I hear you," Thomas said.

She rewarded him with another smile. "So nice when a young man has the sense to take sound advice."

So nice to be called a young man, Thomas thought.

Margaret Lewis switched her attention to Deke. "Oh, dear, are members of the faculty wearing beards at Eubanks these days?"

Cassie hid a quick grin.

Deke flushed a dull red. "I'm on sabbatical."

"I see. Well, take some advice from an old department secretary. If you want to get anywhere at Eubanks, you'd better shave off that beard. They're a conservative lot there. At least they were in my day."

"I'll think about it," Deke muttered.

"Doesn't do anything for you, anyway," Margaret said. "Makes you look years older than you are. Have some cookies."

Thomas needed no urging. Neither did Deke. They both reached for cookies. Margaret looked pleased.

Cassie contented herself with coffee. So did Leonora but Thomas noticed that she took only a couple of polite sips from the delicate china cup that sat on the table in front of her chair.

Cassie cleared her throat. "It was very kind of you to agree to talk to us about the Eubanks murder, Margaret. As I told you on the phone, we're interested in it because two people we know who died recently seemed to have been interested in it."

"We're starting to wonder if there's a connection," Leonora said. "We've read the old newspaper accounts but we can't see anything obvious."

"The Eubanks murder." Margaret snorted gently. "You certainly won't find much in the papers. The Eubanks College trustees exert a great deal of influence in Wing Cove these days, but it's nothing compared to the power they wielded thirty years ago. They literally ran the town at that time. They could get a police chief fired or force a mayor to resign. They wanted the murder of Sebastian Eubanks kept quiet and that's exactly what happened."

"There must have been a lot of gossip at the time," Deke offered tentatively.

"Of course there was gossip." Margaret wrinkled her nose. "The wildest rumors you ever heard circulated for weeks. The official verdict, however, was that Eubanks had surprised a burglar in the old mansion that night.

That is the version of events the administration wished to have prevail. So, naturally, it prevailed."

"What can you tell us about Sebastian Eubanks and his death?" Leonora asked.

"Well, now, where to begin?" Margaret hooked her cane over the edge of her chair and settled back against the flowered cushions. "Sebastian Eubanks was something of an eccentric, to say the least. And getting more so by the day. Took after his father, I'm afraid. He had become quite reclusive and odd at the end. Downright paranoid."

Thomas sat forward, resting his arms on his thighs. "Odd in what way?"

"He had stopped seeing his friends. Never left the mansion. That sort of thing. Word was, he had become obsessed with his work. He really was a very brilliant man, you know. Quite probably a genius, in my opinion. But we'll never know because he died before he could make any significant contributions to the field of mathematics."

"What were the wild rumors that circulated after his death?" Deke asked.

"Well, now," Margaret said very deliberately, "we were all warned by the dean himself that we must not breathe a word about the gossip. Bad for the college's image and so forth. Eubanks was even more conservative all those years ago than it is now."

Thomas exchanged glances with Leonora, Deke and Cassie. He turned back to Margaret.

"It's been thirty years," he said. "Can you tell us the gossip?"

Margaret chuckled. "I'm retired, remember? I can do anything I please these days. Besides, the dean who issued the warning died ten years ago. I never did care much for him."

Cassie smiled. "Don't keep us in suspense, Margaret."

"At the time," Margaret said, lowering her voice to a confidential level, "several people in the department and in the administration were convinced that Sebastian Eubanks was murdered by his lover, not a burglar."

They all stared at her.

"There was no mention of a lover in the newspaper accounts," Deke said.

"Probably because the lover was a man," Margaret said. "A very charming, rather good-looking instructor named Andrew Grayson in the computer science department. Grayson was forced to resign, naturally. The administration applied a great deal of pressure. I have always suspected that the trustees took steps to make certain that he never got back on the tenure-track at any other college."

Leonora leaned forward and folded her arms on her knees. "Why did the administration work so hard to keep that theory quiet?"

"The silly fools were terrified of a wealthy alumnus who was, at the time, a major donor. He was preparing to endow a chair in the political sciences department and build a new wing for the library. He was rabidly antigay."

"I get it," Leonora said. "The administration was afraid that if this donor discovered that Sebastian Eubanks had been involved in an affair with another man, he would pull his funding and take it elsewhere."

"In a nutshell, yes." Margaret hesitated. "I heard that the police chief did question Andrew. Supposedly he had an alibi for the time of the murder. But most of those in the know remained convinced that he had killed Eubanks in what amounted to a lovers' quarrel."

"What happened to Andrew Grayson?" Deke asked.

"I have no idea. He packed up and left very quietly and was never seen in Wing Cove again." Margaret looked pensive. "I've thought about him from time to time over the years. He was so very smart. His departure was a great loss to the college."

"Do you believe that he murdered Eubanks?" Thomas asked.

"Absolutely not," Margaret replied. "I didn't believe it then and I don't believe it now."

"Why not?" Cassie asked.

"Because I knew for a fact that Andrew Grayson had ended his relationship with Eubanks almost a month before the murder. I also know that it was Andrew's decision, and that he made it because Sebastian Eubanks's behavior had grown so extremely bizarre."

Deke took out a pad of paper he had brought with him and started to make some notes.

They left half an hour later. On her way to the door Leonora paused at the dainty little desk where the computer sat.

"I see you're online," she said to Margaret.

"Yes, indeed." Margaret's eyes brightened. "Can't imagine life without my email account."

"Do you, by any chance, subscribe to *Gloria's Gazette*?" Leonora asked.

"Wouldn't miss it for the world. How did you know about the *Gazette*?"

"My grandmother is the publisher and editor," she said proudly.

"You don't say. Please tell her for me that I look forward to every edition. My favorite column is 'Ask Henrietta.'"

"I'll tell her," Leonora said.

Thomas got behind the wheel. Leonora sat beside him. Deke and Cassie slid into the back. Wrench rested his head on the rear seat. All four doors closed. Belts were buckled.

"Okay." Thomas started the engine. "I admit it, I'm impressed. If all academic department secretaries are like Margaret Lewis, they are a force to be reckoned with."

"Every college and university in the nation would fall apart without them," Leonora said.

"Now what?" Cassie asked.

"That's easy." Thomas put the SUV in gear and drove out of the parking lot. "Now we see if we can track down Andrew Grayson."

"No problem." Deke reached into the pocket of his jacket and pulled out a wireless palm-sized computer. "If he's alive, I'll find him. Heck, I'll find him even if he's dead."

Thomas drove in silence. Thinking. Everyone else seemed to be doing the same thing.

A few minutes later Deke looked up from the tiny screen. "Got him. Or at least a current address."

Leonora turned in the seat. "So fast?"

Thomas glanced in the rearview mirror. "You're sure it's our Andrew Grayson?"

"Age fits." Deke worked on the computer for a few more minutes. "He's retired now. Got his social security number from the college records. It all matches. Says right here that he was employed at Eubanks for two and a half years. Yep, he was there at the time Eubanks was murdered."

"He's our guy." Urgency moved through Thomas. "What's he been doing for the past thirty years?"

"Figuring out what Grayson has been up to for the past three decades will take some time," Deke said. "But I can tell you one thing, he sure as hell isn't trying to hide. And judging by the address I've got here I'd say that whatever happened to his academic career at the time of the murder, it didn't ruin his life."

"Where's he living?" Cassie asked.

Deke looked down at his screen. "Mercer Island. It's in the middle of Lake Washington, between Seattle and Bellevue."

"Expensive neighborhood," Thomas said. "You're right. He must have done okay for himself."

Leonora put one arm on the back of the seat. "I vote we talk to Andrew Grayson. As soon as possible. Probably better to do it in person. We can be in Seattle in less than two hours."

Thomas flicked a quick glance at his watch. "It's a waste of time and energy to have all four of us move in lockstep like this. We need to get more efficient. I suggest that Leonora and I drive into the city to see Grayson. Deke, now that we've got some new leads, I think the best thing you can do is concentrate on digging up whatever else you can find online that concerns Grayson and Eubanks."

"Right," Deke said. "Cassie's got classes to teach this afternoon so she can't go with you either."

"That settles it." Thomas slowed for the turn that would take him to Deke's house. "You and Cassie stay here. Leonora and I will head for Seattle. We'll call you as soon as we've talked to Grayson."

Chapter Sixteen

Cassie halted in the short, shadowed hall. Deke closed the door slowly and tried to find words for what she had done.

"Thanks." That sounded pretty lame. He tried again. "If you hadn't come up with Margaret Lewis's name, we wouldn't have any of this new information."

"I hope it helps."

"I don't know where this is going, but at least we're no longer completely stalled."

She made no move to take off her coat. Instead, she glanced at her watch. "It's nearly noon. I'd better be on my way. Busy class schedule at the studio this afternoon. I want to get a bite to eat first."

She was going to leave. He didn't want her to go. Not yet. He wanted to talk to her. Discuss what they had learned from Margaret Lewis. Tell her how he planned to pursue his online search. Hell, he didn't care if they made inane conversation about the weather. He just wanted her to hang around for a while.

He groped for inspiration. And found it when he saw the half-finished loaf of bread on the counter.

"I've got to get to work, too," he said. "But we both need some lunch." He tried to sound casual. "I'm going to make a sandwich. Just as easy to make two."

She looked hesitant. Then she shrugged. "All right."

Panic assailed him, rendering him briefly speechless. She had accepted the offer of food. He prayed fervently that he had something on hand he could use to make a sandwich, any kind of sandwich. He vaguely recalled some cheese in the refrigerator. The bread was a little old but maybe it would be okay if he toasted it.

"Great," he said weakly.

Intent on heading for the kitchen, he moved past her. He stopped at the entrance to the living room. The day was gray and misty outside, but the living room was as dark as the interior of a cave. Was this how the place looked to her every time she came here to give him a yoga session? It was damned depressing.

"I'll open the curtains," he said. He changed course and headed for the nearest window.

She gave him a brilliant smile. "Good idea."

He went from one window to the next, parting the curtains to let in the gray daylight. When he surveyed his handiwork he concluded that the room was still a little gloomy. He switched on a couple of lights before he went into the kitchen.

He found the cheese on the middle shelf of the refrigerator and examined it closely. There was no obvious sign of mold. Relieved, he turned his attention to the half-finished loaf of bread. No green stuff on it, either. Definitely his lucky day.

Cassie made coffee while he constructed the sandwiches. It felt good to have her here in the kitchen with him. He wondered how she felt about it.

"Not exactly lasagna and apple pie," he said when he put the plate containing the toasted cheese sandwich in front of her a short time later. "I need to do some grocery shopping."

"It looks great." She sat down across from him and picked up half of her sandwich. "I'm hungry."

He watched her eat the food he had prepared, fascinated. Why hadn't he ever thought to invite her to stay for lunch?

She paused in mid-chew and gave him an inquiring look. "Something wrong?"

"No." Embarrassed, he picked up his own sandwich and bit into it.

They ate in silence for a while. Rain dripped steadily from the porch roof outside the kitchen window.

"There's something I have to ask you, Deke," she said eventually.

"Sure." He swallowed. "What?"

"When this business is over, do you think you'll be able to let go of Bethany's memory? Or is she going to haunt you all of your life?"

He went very still.

"I need to know," she said quietly. "It's important."

He closed his eyes for a few seconds while he worked to find order in the chaos of his thoughts.

When he opened his eyes he found Cassie watching him very steadily.

"It's been all jumbled up for a long time," he said, stringing the words together carefully, trying to get it right, for his own sake as well as hers. "Three days before Bethany was killed, I told her that I wanted a divorce."

"I see." She ate some more of her sandwich.

"I felt a lot of guilt at the time. I knew she needed me

to take care of her. But I needed something from her, too. After three years of marriage, I knew she couldn't give it to me."

"What did you need from her?"

"I wanted a wife." He raised his shoulders and lowered them. "Someone who slept with me, not in her office. Someone who occasionally remembered that I was a man, not a butler or a personal secretary. I wanted kids. She said they would interfere with her work."

"I get the point. How did she take it when you told her you wanted out of the marriage?"

"I'm not sure she even heard me that day, to tell you the truth. She had been completely wrapped up in her Mirror Theory for several weeks. Totally focused on her work. She said we would have to talk about it later because she was very, very busy. She didn't come home for the next two nights. The third night, Ed Stovall showed up at my door to tell me that she had driven her car to Cliff Drive and jumped off the bluff."

"I hate to ask, but are you certain there wasn't another man?"

He shook his head. "Positive. If you had met her, you would understand. Bethany lived only for her work. She wouldn't have had any interest in an affair."

Cassie slowly lowered the last portion of her sandwich. "That made your sense of guilt a whole lot worse, didn't it?"

"Yes." He groped for a few more words. "It would have been easier for me if I thought she was involved with someone else. I would have felt justified in filing for a divorce. As it was, I just felt bad because I knew she depended on me to take care of everything."

"Now you feel that you have to do this one last thing for her, is that it?"

"Yes."

"It's okay, you know," Cassie said gently. "If anything terrible and mysterious ever happened to me, I'd like to know that someone cared enough to go after the truth."

He took a deep breath, released it slowly. "I would care."

That didn't sound right.

"A lot," he added.

That didn't sound right, either.

"Hell, I can't even stand to think about something bad happening to you, Cassie."

"Good," she said. "Because I can't stand to think about anything terrible happening to you, either."

It wasn't exactly a declaration of love, he decided. But it would do. For now.

Thomas brought the SUV to a halt in the driveway of Andrew Grayson's home. Leonora examined it through the window.

The large house occupied a pricey stretch of waterfront property. Lush, green gardens framed an airy, modern structure that was oriented toward the view of the lake and the office towers of downtown Seattle on the other side. Two very expensive-looking vehicles of European extraction were parked outside the garage at the edge of the broad drive.

"Deke was right," she said. "Whatever happened after the murder of Sebastian Eubanks, Andrew Grayson doesn't seem to have suffered too much financially."

"Judging from his attitude on the phone when I called him a while ago, he isn't shy about discussing it, either."

They got out of the SUV and walked toward the entrance. The double front doors were lacquered in a rich, gleaming red. They opened just as Thomas reached out to ring the bell.

A silver-haired man with patrician features stood in the opening. He wore a cream-colored shirt and hand-tailored trousers. Intelligent curiosity lit his eyes. There was also a measure of caution in his gaze.

"Miss Hutton and Mr. Walker? I'm Andrew Grayson. Please come in."

"Thank you," Leonora said.

Thomas held out his hand. "Call me Thomas."

Andrew took the hand Thomas offered. His grip was firm and confident. He studied Thomas's black eye.

"Mind if I ask?" he said.

"No, but it will be easier to explain in context."

Andrew nodded. "This way, please."

Thomas followed behind Leonora as Andrew led the way through a wide, two-story-atrium center hall.

The hall opened onto an expansive great room. The floor-to-ceiling windows captured the sweeping, panoramic view of the lake. A green lawn rolled down a gentle incline to the water's edge. A sleek yacht was tied up at the private dock.

A man who looked to be about the same age as Andrew, but with more weight and far less hair, was working on the dock. Thomas watched him hoist a coil of rope and disappear inside the large craft.

"My partner, Ben Matthis," Andrew said. He motioned toward a pair of black lacquered chairs upholstered in tan leather. "Please sit down."

Leonora turned away from the window and sat down beside Thomas.

"Thanks for agreeing to see us on such short notice," Thomas said.

Andrew lowered himself to the cushions of a black leather sofa and leaned back into the corner with negligent ease. "I must admit, you said just enough on the phone to make me curious. I went online while I waited for you and I found nothing in the reports of the deaths of the two women you mentioned to connect them to the murder of Sebastian Eubanks."

Thomas glanced at Leonora and then clasped his hands loosely between his knees.

"We're not sure there is a connection," he said. "But we do know that, shortly before she died, Bethany Walker was interested in the details of the Eubanks murder. The second woman, Meredith Spooner, found some clippings of the murder that Bethany had apparently tried to hide. A short time later, she, too, was dead. Both women spent a lot of time at Mirror House before their deaths and both women were rumored to have been using drugs."

"We don't believe that last part," Leonora said. "We're very sure that neither Bethany nor Meredith was into the drug scene."

"That's all you've got?" Andrew asked.

"There's more." Thomas gestured toward his shiner. "Some guy in a ski mask tried to throw me off the footbridge last night. He was high on drugs at the time. The chief of police says the kid probably won't remember much about the assault."

"But you don't think it was a random act of violence, is that it?"

"No," Thomas said. "I think a con man named Alex Rhodes is involved in this thing. He doesn't want us digging any deeper."

Andrew looked thoughtful. "The fact that you found me means you've already dug very deep. The college trustees went to great lengths to keep my connection to Eubanks a dark secret after I was asked to resign."

"We had a little help from Margaret Lewis," Leonora said.

Andrew's expression first showed surprise and then

quiet amusement. "Ah, yes. The department secretary. That explains everything. I'm delighted to hear that she's still alive. An amazingly competent individual, Mrs. Lewis."

"What can you tell us about the murder?" Thomas asked.

"About the murder? Nothing." Andrew moved one hand, palm up. "Except to say that I didn't do it. And I don't know anything about this Alex Rhodes person you mentioned. But I can tell you a few things about Sebastian Eubanks, if you like."

"Margaret said that Eubanks had turned very eccentric towards the end," Leonora said.

Andrew snorted softly. "He was a math geek. He was born eccentric. You had to remind him to change his underwear on a regular basis. But it's true that, in those last months of his life, he got very strange. He was more than just consumed with his work. He became obsessed."

"Obsessed is a heavy word," Thomas said.

"It's appropriate in this case," Andrew said. "To be honest, at the time I thought he had lost his grip on reality. He was a genius, you know. Few realized it because he didn't live long enough to prove himself. But I was close to him for several months and I was able to observe his incredible mind at work. Astonishing, really. Absolutely astonishing."

"He wouldn't have been the first genius to get lost in his own brilliance," Leonora said quietly.

"True. It was the paranoia that drove us apart, though, not his brilliance. But after he was killed I decided that maybe he'd been right to be paranoid."

"You don't buy the interrupted burglary story?" Thomas asked.

"I did at the time." Andrew propped his left ankle on his right knee. "I knew I wasn't the one who had killed him and there didn't seem to be any other logical suspects. But I've done a lot of thinking over the years. I've arrived at some private conclusions. Pure conjecture and wild speculation, of course. I have not one shred of proof."

"We're here to listen to pure conjecture and wild speculation," Leonora said. "We're used to it. That's about all we've had to go on so far."

"I can see that," Andrew said. "But I warn you that you won't get anywhere trying to prove my theory."

"Why do you think Eubanks was murdered?" Thomas asked.

"For the oldest reason in the academic world."

Thomas frowned. "Someone caught him in bed with the wrong person?"

"No." Andrew said. "Someone wanted to steal Sebastian's work and publish it as his own."

"Good heavens," Leonora whispered. "Publish or perish? Literally?"

"The academic world is very Darwinian," Andrew said. "But, then, you know that, don't you? According to the online check I did before you arrived, you work in an academic library. Piercy College, I believe?"

"Yes." She pushed her glasses up on her nose. "And I'll be the first to admit that things can get a little rough in the academy. But I can't say that I've ever heard of anyone murdering someone else in order to publish a paper."

"Any cop will tell you that some people will commit murder for virtually any reason," Andrew said. "But in this case there was far more than the publication of one minor paper in some obscure academic journal that only a couple of dozen people would have read at the time and which would have long since been forgotten."

He stopped talking for a moment. Thomas kept quiet. So did Leonora.

"I was one of two people on campus at the time who had some knowledge of the nature of Sebastian's work," Andrew continued. "In the course of our relationship, he talked to me a bit about his theories. He couldn't help himself. He needed to discuss them with someone and I was there." He moved his hand again, this time in a dismissing gesture. "Also, to be blunt, he knew full well that I wouldn't have been capable of stealing his concepts and publishing them as my own."

"Why not?" Thomas asked.

"I was in the computer science department. Exactly where I belonged. I'm more of an engineer than a mathematician. My mind doesn't work the same way that Sebastian's did. I freely admit that I wouldn't have been able to fake my way through a peer review article in his branch of mathematics even if I'd had unlimited access to his notes and papers. Which I did not."

"But someone else did?" Leonora asked softly.

Andrew looked past her, through the windows, toward the sleek yacht berthed at the dock below the garden.

"As I said, there was far more than the publication of a minor paper in mathematics at stake. There was fame and fortune to be had. Not to mention a reputation that would survive for generations in academic circles."

"Go on," Thomas said.

"There was an extremely ambitious assistant professor in the department of mathematics at Eubanks who was capable of comprehending the full implications of Sebastian's work. They had been friends and colleagues for a time, but they quarreled. Sebastian never trusted him after that."

Thomas watched him. "What are you saying?"

"I've done a lot of soul-searching over the years," Andrew said. "I've often wondered what might have happened if I had taken Sebastian's fears more seriously.

Perhaps I might have been able to do something. But to this day, I honestly don't know what that something would have been."

"I don't see how you could have done anything," Leonora said. "You couldn't possibly have guessed that someone might murder him in order to steal his work."

"No." Andrew sighed. "It simply never occurred to me at the time that Osmond Kern would kill for the privilege of getting his name in the textbooks."

Chapter Seventeen

Andrew stood in the doorway to say good-bye. "Sebastian's murder was a real turning point in my life. I took a long, hard look at my future and decided that I wasn't cut out for higher ed, even assuming I could get another teaching position. So I took a job with a local software startup instead. Ben worked there, too. We did okay when the company went public."

Thomas gave the big house an amused glance. "Yeah, I can see that."

"What are you going to do with the information I gave you?" Andrew asked.

Leonora exchanged glances with Thomas, who shrugged.

"We don't know yet," Thomas said. "We're still trying to fit pieces of a puzzle together."

"If anything comes of your investigation, I'd like to know about it."

"We'll keep you in the loop," Thomas promised.

Andrew nodded. "I'd appreciate that. Sebastian was a very difficult man. Exasperating. Brilliant. Eccentric. No social skills to speak of. But for a time he and I were more than friends. He deserved to have his name attached to that damned algorithm. I'd like to see him get his rightful place in the textbooks."

Leonora started to respond, but she stopped when she noticed the large car rolling toward them down the long drive. A woman was at the wheel. There were two children in the back seat.

"My niece's twins," Andrew said. "Their son of a bitch of a father filed for divorce last year. Married his girlfriend. Doesn't have much time for his daughters now. The girls started having a lot of trouble in school. You know how it goes."

"Yeah." Thomas thought about how his grades had gone south after his parents' divorce. "I know how it goes."

"The family decided that Katie and Clara needed quality time with a reliable male role model so they won't grow up thinking all men are undependable, untrustworthy scum like their dad. The upshot is that I get them a couple of times a week." Andrew smiled. "What the hell, I'm male and I'm reliable. I'm also retired so I've got plenty of time."

The car stopped a short distance away. The woman behind the wheel waved at Andrew. He returned the greeting. The rear doors popped open and two small girls erupted from the interior of the vehicle.

"Uncle Andrew."

"Uncle Andrew."

"I've been working with them on their studies." Andrew grinned proudly. "They're both doing fine now."

"Pretty cool," Leonora said.

"I could have used an uncle like you when I was a kid," Thomas said.

• • •

The short day was rapidly drawing to a close by the time they reached the Wing Cove exit. The mist that had dampened the windshield for the past twenty miles became a hard, driving rain with little warning. Thomas adjusted the wipers and eased into the right lane of Interstate 5.

He and Leonora had talked for a long time after leaving Andrew Grayson's Mercer Island home. But their reasoning was starting to get circular.

"You've got to admit that some of the pieces do fit together," Leonora said. "We've been looking for links and we've got some. Say that Bethany came to suspect, in the course of her own work in mathematics, that Sebastian Eubanks had actually developed the algorithm. Say she concluded that Osmond Kern had stolen it and published it as his own. What if she had confronted him with her suspicions?"

He kept his attention on his driving. "You think Kern murdered her to keep her from revealing the truth?"

"Why not? If he killed Eubanks thirty years ago to get the algorithm, why wouldn't he kill again to keep his secret?"

"Then what? You think Meredith stumbled onto the same truth so he killed her, too? Why would she have cared about a thirty-year-old discovery in mathematics?"

"That algorithm made Kern wealthy. Maybe she tried to blackmail him."

"Huh." Thomas slowed a little to compensate for the heavy rain and the gathering darkness. "Okay, I can see her trying a little blackmail and getting killed for her trouble. But that still doesn't explain Alex Rhodes's connection to this thing. Or the rumors of drugs."

Leonora fell silent.

They were on Cliff Drive now. Thomas slowed some

more to compensate for the poor visibility. Down below the bluffs the cold, deep waters of the Sound swirled in the darkness.

Lights glared suddenly in the rearview mirror. A car, coming up fast from behind. The lights disappeared when Thomas went into the next curve.

"You know, Rhodes has been in town for about a year," Thomas said. "Who knows what information he might have picked up from one of his clients? Margaret Lewis and Andrew Grayson can't be the only two people who had some suspicions about the Eubanks murder."

"Are you thinking that Alex figured out that Kern murdered Eubanks?" She considered that. "If he did, he might be blackmailing Kern. Maybe he killed Bethany and Meredith when they got too close to the truth to protect his investment."

"There's a certain logic to that scenario."

The lights hit the mirror again, this time with dazzling intensity. He adjusted the glass to deflect the undimmed glare. It didn't do much good. The big vehicle was closing the distance.

He was getting that weird, hair-lifting-on-the-back-of-his-neck feeling again. He wondered if he was starting to get paranoid.

"What a mess," Leonora said. "We'll never be able to prove anything."

"I don't know about that." He checked the mirror again. The car behind him was definitely closer. "Might be some possibilities. Blackmail payments are nothing more than simple financial transactions when you get right down to it. And money always leaves a trail."

"But how would we find it?"

"Remember that laptop we saw on Rhodes's desk the day we did our little B and E job at his place? Deke might be able to coax something useful out of that sucker."

"You're going to go back inside Alex's house?" Alarm sharpened her voice. "Thomas, no. My instincts tell me that is not a good idea. Not now. This is getting much too dangerous. We need to talk to Ed Stovall—"

Lights struck the side mirror. Thomas stopped listening to Leonora.

The vehicle that had been closing the distance from behind was pulling out to pass.

"Shit," Thomas said softly.

Leonora broke off abruptly and whipped around in her seat. "Oh, my God. No one but a drunk or a homicidal maniac would attempt to pass here, especially in this rain."

"Personally," Thomas said, "I'm going with homicidal maniac."

She looked at him. "What?"

He did not respond. They were heading into the very short stretch of straight pavement that ran along the highest point of Cliff Drive.

If it was going to happen, it would happen here, he thought.

The lights in the rearview mirror were as bright as the noonday sun. He did not look at them, but out of the corner of his eye he could detect the bulk of the vehicle coming up on his left.

"Check your seat belt. Make sure it's tight."

He did not wait to see if Leonora obeyed. Time had run out. He hit the brakes, feeling for that magical place between a controlled stop and a disastrous skid that would send them over the side.

The dark vehicle on the left swerved violently toward the SUV's fender, a metal shark swooping out of the night seeking a single, fatal bite.

The sudden deceleration of its prey caught it by surprise. The snapping jaws missed by a heartbeat. It swerved. For an instant Thomas thought the vehicle might go through the guardrail. It fishtailed wildly. But at the last possible instant the driver managed to recover control.

Thomas caught a glimpse of a black SUV. He watched the taillights disappear around the next curve.

For a few time-warped seconds that felt like an eternity, neither he nor Leonora said a word. They both looked straight ahead to the point where the other car had vanished.

Eventually Leonora turned to him.

"Is this the place?" she whispered.

"Yes." He accelerated deliberately. "This is the place where Bethany jumped."

Two hours later, Thomas sat in the front seat with Deke. They were parked in the trees behind the abandoned cottage, not far from Alex Rhodes's place. It had stopped raining, but the clouds hung low, an invisible weight pressing down from the night sky.

They had cruised past Rhodes's house a few minutes ago. There was no vehicle in the drive. The lights were off. It looked like Rhodes was out for the evening.

"Probably having a couple of drinks at the pub in town," Deke said. "Maybe getting sloshed. That near miss must have freaked him out. From what you told me, it sounds like he almost went over the edge when you did the sudden slowdown thing. Maybe he's thinking about how close he came to getting killed instead of killing you."

"I hope the bastard is having some shaky moments," Thomas said.

"You're sure it was Rhodes? There are an awful lot of dark SUVs and four-by-fours in this town."

"Can't be absolutely positive, but you've got to admit that the list of potential suspects is pretty damn short."

"Could have been Osmond Kern," Deke said. "He owns a dark-blue SUV, I think. And if Andrew Grayson is right, he's capable of murder."

"Maybe. But my money's on Rhodes."

"That's because you're pissed at him for the way he came on to Leonora and maybe arranged for you to get beaten up last night."

"Okay, so I'm a little biased." He opened the door. "Ready? Let's get this done and done fast, just like we promised Leonora and Cassie. We go in. You download whatever you can get off that laptop and we get out."

"And if I can't get through his personal security?"

"We take the whole damn laptop. Hell with it. Let him go whining to Ed Stovall about a stolen computer."

"Right." Deke got out on his side and zipped his jacket. "This should be interesting."

They started into the trees, heading toward the dark house at the end of the lane.

Leonora sat in the booth across from Cassie, a cup of very weak tea in front of her. The young man behind the bar had done his best, but there wasn't much anyone could do with a poor-quality tea bag and water that hadn't even been brought to the boiling point. Not that it mattered, she thought glumly. She couldn't concentrate well enough to taste anything right now. All she could do was worry about Thomas and Deke.

The Wings of Fire Pub and Restaurant was crowded with a mix of students, faculty and townsfolk, seeking warmth and companionship on a damp, chilly night. On-stage a small group of musicians crafted mellow jazz.

Cassie picked up her bottle of designer water and poured the contents into a glass that was filled with ice. "I'm not sure how I feel about being packed off here to wait while our men go charging into the wilderness to do manly stuff."

"I know how you feel. But you've got to admit, Thomas had a point when he said that it would be ridiculous for all four of us to tromp through the woods to Rhodes's house. Of all of us, he and Deke are the ones who have the best shot at accomplishing something useful tonight. Thomas knows about money stuff and Deke knows computers."

"I'm not arguing the logic of the decision. I'm just not real happy about it, that's all." Cassie helped herself to a pretzel from the small dish that sat on the table. She chewed for a while and then swallowed and leaned forward. "Do you really think it was Rhodes who tried to run you and Thomas off that road tonight?"

Leonora shuddered. "Rhodes or Kern. It had to be one of them. My money's on Rhodes. I think Kern is too far gone into the bottle to be able to drive that skillfully."

Cassie's face tightened with anxiety. "This is so very weird. I hope we're not all experiencing some form of mass hallucination here."

"Is there really such a thing as mass hallucination?"

"Sure. Happens all the time. Plenty of incidents of it recorded throughout history."

"Terrific." Leonora sipped tea. "Something else to worry about."

Neither of them spoke for a while. The music seemed to grow louder. So did the crowd.

"One good thing is coming out of all this," Cassie said with a determinedly upbeat air. "Deke is changing. He talked to me about his relationship with Bethany for the first time."

Leonora patted her arm. "That's good."

"He's been twisted up with guilt because three days before she died, he had asked her for a divorce."

"I got it. So when the verdict of suicide came down, he really took it hard."

"Yes. He didn't believe it. More to the point, he couldn't *allow* himself to believe it because that would have meant he might have been the one responsible for triggering the act."

"Nasty stuff."

Cassie nodded. "It's been eating him up inside. But he's moving past it now. Thanks to you."

"I had nothing to do with it. And neither did you or Thomas. Deke is saving himself. When it comes to this kind of thing we can all hold out helping hands to each other, doctors can supply some very helpful medications, but in the end, each of us has to have the will to swim to shore on our own. No one can carry another person. Not for long, at any rate."

Cassie made a face. "That's a very Darwinian view of life, isn't it?"

"As the evolutionary biology types are so fond of pointing out, all of us are descended from folks who did whatever they had to do in order to survive." Leonora paused. "Funny that you would use that phrase, though."

"Darwinian?"

"Yes. Andrew Grayson used it this afternoon to describe life in the academy."

"Well, you've got to admit that *Darwinian* is certainly one word for academic politics."

"True, but until I talked to Grayson this afternoon, I never took the law of publish or perish quite so literally."

"We still don't know for sure that Kern committed murder." Cassie broke off abruptly when a shadow fell across the table.

Leonora followed her gaze.

"Leo," Kyle said with a hearty enthusiasm that rang painfully false. "I've been looking for you. Where have you been? I called your house several times, but you never answered the phone."

"I've been busy all day, Kyle."

"That so?" He grinned pointedly at Cassie. "Going to introduce me to your friend?"

"This is Kyle Delling," Leonora said. "He's in the English Department at Piercy. Kyle, this is Cassie Murray. She has a yoga studio here in Wing Cove."

"A pleasure." Taking the introduction for an invitation, Kyle slid into the booth. He slipped an arm around Leonora's shoulders in a cozy, familiar manner. "Just to put you in the picture, Cassie, Leo and I are more than good friends. We used to be engaged."

"I see." Cassie looked at Leonora. "Has he met Thomas?"

"He met Thomas." She smiled very sweetly at Kyle. "You remember Thomas, don't you, Kyle? That man in my kitchen this morning? The one who looked like he'd been in a fight?" She glanced at her watch. "He should be here any minute."

Kyle tensed and then promptly removed his arm from her shoulders. He shot to his feet and gave both women a brilliant smile.

"What's everyone drinking?" he asked. "I'm buying this round."

"Tea," Leonora murmured. "Thank you."

"Water." Cassie held up the bottle so that he could read the label.

"Got it. Be right back." Kyle plunged into the crowd.

Cassie looked at Leonora.

"Your ex-fiancé?"

"Yep."

"I've got an ex-husband," Cassie said thoughtfully. "In my experience, exes of any kind don't tend to hang around unless they're after something."

"He's after something," Leonora said.

"You?"

"No. He's seeking a more durable relationship than the one we had."

"That would be?"

"Tenure."

He was sweating. Again.

It had been a near thing on Cliff Drive this evening. He was still jittery from the close call. He paced the front room, thinking about how he had almost lost control and plunged through the guardrail.

Had Walker gotten a good look at the SUV? Didn't matter. It was black, just like a hundred other SUVs in town. Luckily, he had remembered to tape the license plate.

He'd parked the vehicle in the trees out back just in case. He didn't want Walker to drive past tonight, see it in plain view and maybe start to wonder. Out of sight, out of mind. Maybe.

The jumpy feeling was really getting to him.

He glanced at the Rolex. His new client would be here at any minute. He tried to focus on that. She was spectacular. Blond. Great tits. Reminded him a little of Meredith.

No, don't think about Meredith. Everything had started to go wrong after Meredith.

Think about the new client.

He crossed the room and pulled the black velvet away from the mirror. Had to set the stage.

This past-lives regression-therapy stuff worked like magic. Once a client was convinced that she had had an affair with a dashing highwayman or a medieval warrior in a previous life, it was only a short step to convincing her that the best way to get rid of stress in this life was to relive the previous sexual experience. With a trained stress counselor, of course.

He needed the sex tonight. It would relax him. Get rid of some of the tension left over from the screwup on Cliff Drive. Tomorrow he would worry about finding another way to get rid of Thomas Walker. The SOB was proving hard to kill.

Maybe it was a sign. He'd had enough experience to know when it was time to bail out of an operation. Maybe he had pushed his luck far enough in Wing Cove. Murder wasn't his forte, anyway. He had never tried it until now and it was obvious he didn't have a talent for the business. He was a con man, not a killer.

That thought steadied him. It was time to get out. The scam and the drugs had been profitable, but nothing lasted forever.

The phone rang. He did not pick it up.

Whoever was on the other end hung up without leaving a message. Probably a cold call.

He looked down at the old, weird, bubbled mirror and saw dozens of miniature, distorted images of himself. No two were alike. None was the real Alex Rhodes.

The mirror reflected the truth, he thought suddenly. There was no real Alex Rhodes.

An icy shudder went through him. He had been living a lie for so many years now, he no longer knew who he really was. The truth was, he could never recall a time when he had had a clear sense of himself. It was ironic. He could make others see whatever he wanted them to see, but he couldn't see himself.

Shit. He was getting weird. Must be the stress from the incident on Cliff Drive.

He looked at the Rolex again. Where the hell was she? He needed the sex. Needed it badly. Needed those few, fleeting moments when he felt almost real. Almost human. Sex was his drug of choice.

A knock sounded on the door.

She was here.

Relief poured through him. He summoned up the magic smile, the one that said *trust me,* and went into the hall to open the door.

"I cancelled your appointment for this evening," the killer said.

"This doesn't look so good," Thomas said. "He's not supposed to be here."

He had called Rhodes's number on his cell phone a few minutes ago, checking to be sure that he was still out for the evening. There had been no answer.

Now they stood in the woods at the edge of the little clearing and studied the back of the small house. So much for the big plan to get inside and grab whatever was on Rhodes's hard drive.

From where he stood, Thomas could just make out the weak, pulsing glow of firelight behind the crack of a curtain. No other lights were on inside as far as he could see.

"Wonder if he's busy seducing a client in there?" Deke said.

"Where's the client's car? Hell, where's his SUV, for that matter?"

"Beats me. Hidden in the trees? Maybe the client is married and he doesn't want anyone to know she's here."

"What now? Go away and come back another night?"

Thomas did not move. "You know, I'd really like to find out if he's with someone and who that someone is."

"How do you plan to do that?"

"How about if I just walk up to the front door and knock?"

Deke looked at him. "Are you serious?"

"Why not?"

"This may be the SOB who nearly ran you off the road tonight."

"So? He's not going to try anything on his own front step. An accident on Cliff Drive is one thing. A body on the front porch is a little harder to explain."

"Even harder to explain two bodies," Deke said flatly. "I'm coming with you."

They moved out of the trees. Thomas felt exposed in the small clearing. Deke must have had the same sensation. Without discussion, they both headed for the deeper shadows beneath the eaves of the house.

There was no light coming from behind the curtains that covered the kitchen window, but when they passed it Thomas heard sounds of activity inside. Someone was opening and closing cupboard doors with furious abandon.

Thomas wondered if Rhodes had lost electrical power and was hunting for a flashlight. Guy like that probably didn't keep his emergency equipment in a convenient location.

He climbed the shadowed steps with Deke.

The front door stood ajar. The pulsing firelight flickering inside the opening reminded Thomas of a human heart beating.

A chill went through him. Something was very wrong.

"Oh, shit," Deke whispered. "I don't like this."

"Rhodes!" Thomas shouted through the partially open door. "You in there?"

There was an instant of frozen silence. And then the sound of footsteps running heavily toward the rear of the house. Thomas heard the muffled sound of the back door opening.

Thomas took two long strides to the edge of the porch and looked around the corner of the house. He was just in time to see a dark figure silhouetted at the edge of the clearing.

The figure paused, raised one arm.

Thomas pulled back quickly, out of the line of fire. The shot crashed beneath the eaves of the house. Wood splintered in a porch post.

And then there was only silence.

"He's gone," Thomas said. "So much for finding out who Rhodes was entertaining tonight."

"Thomas?"

The odd note in Deke's voice made him turn swiftly.

"What is it?"

Deke gazed intently through the crack in the doorway. "We've got a problem."

Thomas walked back to the door and pushed it open wider. From the threshold he could see through the small front hall into the firelit living room.

A figure dressed head-to-toe in black lay crumpled on the cushions in front of the low table.

Thomas slowly led the way inside and came to a halt beside the body. Blood soaked the braided rug behind Rhodes's head. There was more blood on the front of the black silk shirt.

"Dead," Deke said.

The antique looking glass was uncovered. Thomas could see the reflections of a hundred miniature fires blazing in the multitude of tiny convex and concave mirrors on its surface.

Small glimpses of hell.

The room was a scene of chaos and destruction. Cushions had been ripped, exposing the innards. Drawers and cupboards stood open, the contents scattered on the floor.

Thomas reached into his pocket for his cell phone.

"Whoever did this was searching the place and we interrupted him," Deke said.

"They always tell you not to do that." Thomas punched the emergency number on his cell phone.

"Now we know why. Good way to get killed."

In the distance a heavy engine roared to life.

The 911 operator came on the line. Thomas filled her in on the facts.

"Yeah, sure," he said, losing his patience with the endless litany of questions. "We'll stick around until Stovall gets here. Not like we've got anything better to do. Tell him to watch for a small truck or an SUV on his way here. The guy who did this is driving something big."

He ended the call.

The rising wind howled in the trees.

Chapter Eighteen

The drive in front of the little rental house was illuminated by the glaring lights of three police vehicles and Wing Cove's two ambulances. The crowd included medical personnel from the hospital, Ed Stovall together with all of the members of his small force, the mayor and a reporter from the *Wing Cove Star*.

Murder was big news in a small town.

"Been keeping a close eye on Rhodes for quite a while," Ed Stovall said. "Had a hunch he was dealing. He's got a background in chemistry and this S and M stuff is definitely something that got cooked up in a lab."

He stood ramrod stiff next to the gleaming front fender of his white SUV. Thomas figured it was mechanically impossible for Stovall to lounge casually against anything, even his own vehicle. The robotic construction of his compact frame probably did not allow for those options.

"Elissa volunteered to go undercover for me," Ed said. "A very brave woman. Insisted on doing her duty as a citizen. She got me a sample of some of that nutritional supplement Rhodes sold. I had it tested. Turned out to be flavored sugar crystals and cornstarch. Couldn't arrest him for peddling snake oil. But I was still sure there was something else going on with him. You ever notice those weird eyes?"

"Tinted contacts," Thomas said.

"I know. Creepy, if you ask me."

"I think Rhodes was trying to project a dramatic image," Thomas said.

"I would have nailed him eventually. Unfortunately, someone else got to him first."

Thomas watched two men load the gurney bearing Alex Rhodes's body into the back of an aid car.

Deke scowled. "You really think this was a drug deal gone bad, Ed?"

He was furious and he was making little effort to conceal that fact. Thomas did not blame him. The conversation was not going well. As usual, Ed was not interested in their theories. He had already jumped to his own conclusions regarding the murder.

"It all fits," Ed said, stubborn as ever.

"Okay," Thomas said evenly, "say he was dealing drugs. Even if that was the case, what makes you so sure Rhodes got removed by his competition?"

Ed squared his cap. "Drug trade's a rough business. Folks involved in it get killed pretty regularly."

"Any idea why the killer would take the time to tear the place apart after shooting Rhodes?"

"Sure. He was looking for Rhodes's supply and maybe some cash or valuables. Those bastards are all opportunists. Scavenger sharks." Ed shook his head. "Only good news is that whoever did this is probably halfway back to Seattle. With any luck he's someone else's problem now."

Deke made a disgusted sound. "Think so?"

Ed exhaled heavily. "I'm going to need written statements from both of you in the morning. Want my advice?"

"Not particularly," Deke said.

Ed ignored him. "Stick to the facts tomorrow. Don't drag your personal conspiracy theories concerning Mrs. Walker's death into this thing."

"Why not?" Deke squinted against the glare of the SUV's lights. "Because it might raise some awkward questions about your investigation?"

"No," Ed said quietly. "Because it will raise some awkward questions about the state of your mental health."

"You think I give a shit about your opinion of my mental health, Stovall?"

Thomas winced. "Take it easy, Deke."

Ed swung around abruptly to face both of them. "You two want to hear a really awkward question? Try this one: What the hell were you doing here tonight?"

"I told you," Thomas said, "we came here to confront Rhodes about that near miss out on Cliff Drive. I wanted to hear his excuses."

"You really think he tried to kill you?"

"Yeah, Ed. I really do think he tried to kill me and Leonora Hutton."

"You've got nothing to back that up. Hell, you didn't even file a complaint."

"Didn't figure you'd pay any attention to another complaint from one of the Walker brothers," Thomas said.

Ed's mouth tightened. The line of his jaw was rigid. "Should have filed a complaint."

"What good would that have done," Deke shot back, "given your views of the situation?"

"The death of your wife has nothing to do with this," Ed said. But he said it in a surprisingly quiet voice. "It's my job to deal with the facts and the facts are that this thing has all the hallmarks of a drug killing."

Deke looked at Thomas. "Anal-retentive, like you said."

"Take it easy," Thomas said. "We need to get back to Leonora and Cassie. They'll be worrying."

Deke combed his fingers through his beard. "You're right. Talking to Stovall is always a waste of time. Let's get out of here."

He turned on his heel and started toward the road, heading back to the old house where they had left the SUV.

Thomas moved to follow.

"Wait," Stovall said in a low voice. "One thing before you two take off."

Thomas stopped and turned. Deke reluctantly did the same.

"What?" Thomas said.

"I've been doing some thinking."

"That's gotta hurt," Deke said.

Ed ignored the barb. "Rhodes came to town a year ago. He was here when Bethany Walker died. If I can prove that he was in the drug business, and I don't think that will be tough, I'll take another look at Bethany Walker's suicide. See if Rhodes might have had a hand in it. I'll also contact the California authorities and request a copy of the report that was filed on Meredith Spooner's accident. See if there's any connection that might have been overlooked on that end."

Deke looked at him.

"That's all I can do," Ed said.

"Appreciate it, Ed," Thomas said.

Ed nodded. "No promises."

"That I can believe," Deke grumbled.

•   •   •

Leonora spotted Thomas and Deke first. Relief cascaded through her.

"They're here." She slid toward the end of the booth and got to her feet.

"About time." Cassie put the half-finished bottle of water down on the table and followed her.

Thomas and Deke forged a path through the crowd. Nobody dawdled in their way, Leonora noticed. When they got closer she understood why everyone was giving both men a wide berth. There was cold steel in both pairs of Walker eyes.

She could feel the chill all the way across the room.

"Something happened," she said to Cassie.

Cassie looked at Deke. "Dear God."

They both went forward, pushing past Kyle, who was returning from the bar with a tray containing a bottle of designer water and a fresh pot of tea.

"Hey," he said as they went unceremoniously past him on either side. "Where are you two going?"

They ignored him. Leonora reached Thomas first. She went straight into his arms.

"What happened?" she said against his jacket. "Are you all right?"

"I'm fine." He hugged her close. "We're both okay."

Cassie put her hand on Deke's shoulder. "What went wrong?"

"Long story," Deke said. He gave her a crooked smile. "Don't I get a welcome hug, too?"

With a small, choked cry, Cassie put her arms around his waist and pressed her face against his shoulder.

"We both need a beer," Thomas said. With one arm around Leonora's waist, he led the way toward the booth.

His expression chilled further when he saw Kyle. "What the hell is he doing here?"

"Never mind Kyle." Leonora grabbed his arm and urged him into the booth. "Sit down."

Thomas obediently lowered himself onto the bench. She got in beside him. Deke and Cassie sat down on the other side. Kyle stood, tray in hand, looking slightly confused.

"I'll have a beer. Whatever's on draft," Thomas said to Kyle.

"Same for me," Deke said.

Kyle opened his mouth, closed it. With a small sigh, he turned and started back toward the bar.

Leonora looked at Thomas. "All right, let's have it."

"Rhodes is dead," he said.

Cassie stared at him, speechless.

Leonora felt as if the air had been sucked out of her lungs.

"Dead?" Her voice rose. "He's *dead*? Are you sure?"

"Real sure," Thomas said.

"Not—?" Leonora let the words hang, unspoken, in midair.

"Not us," Deke assured her dryly. "Someone else got there first. Shot him twice."

"*Who?*" Leonora demanded.

"Didn't get a good look at him," Thomas said, "but our guess is—"

"What do you mean, you didn't get a *good* look?" Leonora shot up and planted both palms on the table. "You *saw* the killer? He was there when you arrived?"

"He didn't hang around long," Deke said. "Only fired one shot in our direction before he split."

"Oh, my God," Cassie whispered. "Oh, my God."

Leonora sat down again. Hard. She had a feeling her mouth was hanging open in an unattractive fashion, but she couldn't summon up the will to close it. She propped her elbows on the table and dropped her face into her hands.

"Stovall is convinced it was a drug killing and much as I hate to admit it, it's just barely possible," Thomas said. "But we may get something out of it. Because of the rumors of drugs being involved in Bethany's and Meredith's deaths, Stovall has promised to take another look at both files. See if there's any link to Rhodes."

Leonora raised her head. "You're right. That's progress."

Thomas folded his arms on the table and lowered his voice. "Still doesn't give us any connection to the Eubanks murder thirty years ago, though."

"I've been working on a new conspiracy theory," Deke said. "What if first Bethany and then Meredith figured out Kern had committed that murder all those years ago? What if, fearing exposure and the loss of his reputation from Bethany and maybe blackmail in Meredith's case, he decided to get rid of both women and wanted some help?"

"I see where you're going here," Leonora whispered. "Maybe Kern suspected that Alex Rhodes was selling drugs. Bought some S and M from him and used it to poison Bethany first and, six months later, Meredith. It would have been easy to stage a suicide and a car accident if they were in the grip of severe hallucinogens."

Thomas looked at Deke. "If you and Leonora are right, you see where it leads?"

Deke nodded. "Right back to Osmond Kern. Maybe that was who we surprised in Rhodes's house tonight. Maybe Kern knew that we were getting close. He had to get rid of Rhodes because Alex, as the dealer who had sold him the S and M, was the one person who could link him to the two deaths."

"If you're right," Thomas said, "Elissa might be in danger."

Cassie's eyes widened. "From her own father?"

"I don't think Osmond Kern is what any self-respecting psychologist would term a nurturing parent." Thomas reached for his cell phone. "I'll give Stovall a call. He'll probably tell me I'm as crazy as Deke, but I'm pretty sure he's got a personal interest in Elissa Kern. He cares about her. He'll want to be sure she's safe."

Ed was standing in Osmond Kern's darkened study, gazing at the text on the glowing computer screen when he took the call.

"Stovall here."

"This is Walker. Thomas Walker. I know you don't want to listen to any more conspiracy theories tonight, but if the Walker brothers and their associates are right about this one, Elissa may be in grave danger."

"Not anymore."

"Hear me out, Ed. There's a chance that Osmond Kern shot Alex Rhodes tonight to cover up a murder that was committed thirty years ago."

"You know something, Walker? You're good at this detective stuff. Maybe you should consider a career in law enforcement."

There was a beat of silence. Ed could hear the sounds of a crowd and easy jazz. The Walkers were in the Wings of Fire Pub. He wouldn't mind being there right now himself. He didn't drink much normally, but he could have used a shot of something strong right at that moment.

"Am I missing something here?" Thomas asked finally.

"I'll make sure Elissa is safe tonight, but I don't think there's anything more for any of us to worry about."

"What makes you so damn sure she's safe, Ed? I know you really like the idea that the shooter is on his way out of town but are you willing to bet Elissa's life on it?"

"The shooter isn't on his way out of town," Ed said. He could feel the weariness all the way to his bones but he wouldn't give in to it. There was no way he would get any sleep tonight. "I don't know where Kern is yet, but I expect to find him soon."

"Kern?" Thomas paused a beat, as if he was quickly reevaluating the situation. "Are you saying you believe that Kern was the killer? How did you put it together?"

"I didn't. Not until Elissa called me a few minutes ago to tell me that her father had disappeared. He left a suicide note." Ed gazed down at the words on the screen. "He wrote it on his computer. Elissa found it when she got home from the concert tonight."

"Suicide," Thomas repeated neutrally.

"Suicide?" a woman said on the other end of the line, her voice muffled against the noisy backdrop of the pub. *"What is it? What's going on?"*

Probably Leonora Hutton, Ed thought. Sitting next to Walker, listening in on the conversation.

"Kern and his boat are both missing," Ed said. "Looks like he took it out tonight after he returned from Rhodes's house."

"Any sign of the gun?"

"Right here in the study next to the computer." He hesitated, pondering procedure, and then thought, the hell with it. The Walkers had been through a lot this past year. They were entitled. "I won't give you all the details of the note, but between you and me, it looks like the whole thing went down pretty much as you and your brother figured. Starting way back with Eubanks."

"What about Bethany and Meredith?" Thomas asked.

"It's all here. Bethany Walker threatened to expose him

as a fraud. So he slipped her some drugs and pushed her off that bluff. Six months later Meredith figured out what had happened and tried to blackmail him. He arranged to meet with her in California. Said he wanted to make a deal. A one-time payment and her promise to disappear. They met for dinner in a neutral location. A restaurant."

"He slipped the drugs into her food and then set up the accident?"

"Yes. He hoped that would be the end of it. He assumed that everyone involved would continue to write off the Walker brothers' wild theories. But things just got more complicated. Leonora Hutton arrived on the scene. And the next thing he knows Alex Rhodes tries to blackmail him."

"You're sure about that?" Thomas said swiftly.

"He mentions it in his note. Also, Elissa tells me that she went through some of Kern's financial records recently and found indications of some transactions that she can't identify. She's almost positive they're the blackmail payments."

"Why did Kern fall apart after murdering Rhodes?"

Ed studied the screen. "Tonight he almost got caught in the act of murder. It was too close. He nearly botched it and he knew it. He says he realizes that it's just a matter of time before it all comes crashing down on him. Says he can't face the humiliation of having his colleagues and peers discover that he's been living a lie for the past thirty years."

"How about having folks find out that he killed three people in addition to Sebastian Eubanks? That give him any problem?"

"The way I read this note," Ed said, conscious of Elissa listening to every word, "I'd say the murders were the least of his concerns. It was his fear of having the truth about the algorithm come out that drove him over the edge tonight."

"How's Elissa doing?"

He glanced at her with concern. She stood quietly, her arms folded tightly around her midsection. In the glow of the screen he could see tears glistening on her face.

"It's been a tough night," Ed said. "But she's holding up okay. She's a strong lady." Elissa gave him a faint, brave little smile. "I've got to go, Walker. In addition to dealing with Rhodes's murder, I've got to get a search organized to find Kern. I'll talk to you tomorrow."

He ended the call.

Elissa walked toward him. "Thank you for being so kind tonight, Ed. I don't think I would have been able to deal with all of this if it hadn't been for you."

He put his arms around her and held her close for as long as he dared. About sixty seconds.

Reluctantly he released her. He pressed her hand and picked up his hat.

"Work to do," he said.

"I understand. Do what you have to do." She stepped away from him, her eyes full of admiration. "You have your responsibilities to fulfill, and I know you take your duties seriously. It's part of what makes you such a fine man, Ed."

He realized he was blushing. Grateful for the low light in the study, he turned quickly away and strode toward the door.

Not every woman understood the demands of his job. Elissa would make a first-rate cop's wife, he thought. But he couldn't allow himself to dwell on the possibilities the future held until he had found her father's body and answered all the outstanding questions.

First things first. That was how you got the job done.

Chapter Nineteen

She went home with Thomas. He acted as if it was the most natural thing in the world to do but that wasn't what made her uneasy. What worried her was that it *did* feel natural. Wrench apparently agreed with the consensus of opinion. He was waiting at the door with a rubber ball that squeaked when he squeezed it.

It was all very comfortable. Maybe too comfortable, she thought. Of course, she could have pointed out to Thomas that, with Alex dead and with Osmond Kern missing and presumed drowned, there was no longer any danger and therefore no logical excuse for spending the night together. But she said nothing.

The truth was, there was no place she would rather have been. Not tonight. She went into Thomas's arms with a glorious sense of rightness. He held her close and made love to her with a thoroughness that left her exhausted and satisfied. She had expected to battle a bad case of insomnia, given the excitement of the night. Instead, she sank into a dreamless sleep.

The next morning the three of them took the footpath into town to get coffee and tea and the latest gossip. The clouds hung low enough to cut off the tops of the trees and the air was cold. The early morning herd of runners and joggers stampeded past as they strolled in the slow lane.

She and Thomas went over the details of the murders and speculated on how long it would take for the authorities to find Osmond Kern's body. They discussed some of the loose threads that still dangled and wondered if they would ever get all of the answers. Probably not, Leonora thought.

"I wonder how much Meredith really knew and what she planned to do with the information," Thomas said. He had one hand in the pocket of his jacket. He held Wrench's leash in the other.

"My guess is, she knew enough to try to blackmail Kern. That's the only way to explain her death." Leonora watched Wrench investigate an empty latte cup. "But she obviously wasn't careful about how she handled the matter."

"Blackmail is dangerous work."

"Yes, but she would have known that. I wonder why she didn't do it anonymously."

"Maybe she did try to hide her identity. She went down to California, remember? But Kern must have figured out that she was the one behind the extortion."

"I still don't see how Meredith could have figured it all out using just those clippings Bethany left behind."

Thomas glanced at her. "Don't forget she had that affair with Alex Rhodes."

"Good point. Meredith, being Meredith, would have learned anything Alex Rhodes knew and he obviously knew about Kern."

They stopped at the coffeehouse, left Wrench attached to a bicycle stand and went inside to get some caffeine to ward off the chill. The room was crowded. The atmosphere hummed with conversation. Leonora stood at the counter with Thomas and listened to snippets of gossip.

"...Heard they found Kern's boat late last night. It washed ashore. The throttle was still set in the open position, but the fuel tank was empty. They think he jumped somewhere..."

"...Couldn't survive more than twenty minutes at most in that water....Hypothermia sets in fast, especially at this time of year..."

"...Who'd have figured it? I went to one of his lectures last quarter. Weird to think about him standing up there talking about his algorithm like everything was perfectly normal. I mean, the guy had killed a couple of people at that point. Two more to go..."

Leonora caught Thomas's attention. He paid for the coffee and tea and some warm scones to go with the beverages. They went back outside.

Julie and Travis stood on the sidewalk, a cautious distance from Wrench.

"Hi, Miss Hutton. Mr. Walker. This is Travis."

"Hello, Travis." Thomas nodded.

"Good morning," Leonora replied.

Julie watched Wrench warily. "We thought this was your dog. We've seen you out walking him on the footpath. He looks mean. Does he bite?"

Wrench paid no attention to the insult. He got to his feet, never taking his eyes off the paper bag in Leonora's hand. Focused.

Leonora opened the bag, broke off a corner of a scone and fed it to him.

"Wrench wouldn't harm an ant," Thomas said. "I assume you both heard the news?"

"About Rhodes getting shot?" Julie shuddered. "You were right. He was dealing drugs. I never knew, honest. I just wanted to tell you that."

Thomas nodded again and peeled the lid off his coffee cup.

"I heard you were there last night, Mr. Walker." Travis regarded Thomas with unconcealed awe. "They're saying that you and your brother went to Rhodes's house just as Professor Kern was leaving. You could have been killed."

"News gets around fast here." Thomas drank some coffee. "Any word on whether or not they've found Kern?"

"No," Travis said. "Heard they found his boat, though. Everyone says he jumped because he couldn't stand having folks find out that he was a phony."

"They're also saying that he murdered Professor Walker last year." Julie bit her lip. "And that lady who worked at Mirror House for a while. Meredith something."

"Her name was Meredith Spooner," Leonora said quietly.

"Yeah, her, too." Julie shivered again. "It is so freaky, when you think about it. He keeps his big secret all those years and then it all starts to fall apart, so he starts killing people to keep them quiet."

"Freaky, all right," Leonora said.

Travis moved closer to Julie and put his arm around her shoulders in a protective way. "What really gets me is that Julie did some odd jobs for Rhodes recently. What if she'd gone there last night to pick up her money? She could have been there when Professor Kern arrived."

Leonora gave Julie a pointed look. "Always a good idea to know exactly who you're working for."

Julie flushed and said nothing. Travis patted her shoulder.

Thomas untied Wrench. They headed across the street to join the crowds on the footpath.

"I'd better go home," Leonora said. "I want to call Gloria. Let her know what's been happening."

Halfway back to her cottage they saw the small crowd of joggers and runners gathered on the footbridge. Everyone was looking down into the deep waters of the cove.

Ed Stovall's SUV was parked across the path. An ambulance and another police vehicle were stationed nearby. Two medics were unloading a gurney.

Thomas studied the scene.

"What do you want to bet that they just found Kern's body?" he said.

Deke showed up on Thomas's doorstep late that afternoon. Thomas gave him a beer and opened one for himself. They sat in the recliners in the living room and talked.

"Stovall came to see me," Deke said. "Don't think the guy's had any sleep for the past twenty-four hours. He looked exhausted. But he said he felt we had a right to be kept informed."

"One thing you can say about Stovall. Man's got a sense of duty." Thomas swallowed some beer. "I like that in a public servant. Did he have anything more than what we already know?"

"Not much. They found some stuff they think might be drugs when they searched Rhodes's house."

"No surprise there."

"No." Deke drank some beer. "Stovall says they sent a sample to a lab for analysis, but he told me off the record that he's sure it will turn out to be that hallucinogenic crap that's been floating around since last year. He also said they're going to do an autopsy, but that it looks like Kern wrote his note, had a few drinks, got into the boat and set the throttle on full. Then he just went overboard. The cold water did the rest."

"Wouldn't be the first person to commit suicide that way."

They drank more beer. The silence between them felt good, Thomas thought. Familiar. Comfortable. Things were getting back to normal.

"I asked Cassie to go to the alumni weekend reception at Mirror House on Saturday night," Deke said after a while.

The news, delivered as it was, without any sort of pre-amble or warning, caught Thomas by surprise. "What did she say?"

"She said okay."

"Okay. Great." Thomas smiled.

"What about you?"

"Me?"

Deke settled deeper into the recliner and turned the damp bottle between his palms. "I was thinking maybe you could ask Leonora to go with you."

That stopped him cold. "I'm not a member of Mirror House. Neither is Leonora."

"No, but I am. I can take you both as my guests."

"I don't know how long Leonora plans to stay here now that she's got her answers. She may be gone by Saturday."

Deke's brows rose behind the rims of his glasses. He looked amused. "Have you tried asking her if she's think-ing of leaving anytime soon?"

"No."

"Is there a problem here? Why can't you ask her a sim-ple question?"

"Maybe I don't want to know the answer," Thomas said.

"Huh."

They drank more beer.

"Got an idea for you," Deke said after a while.

"Yeah?"

"Tell her that you'd like her to stay through Saturday

and attend the reception with you because it would make Cassie feel more comfortable."

"You think that would work?"

"Sure. Leonora seems to like the idea of matching me with Cassie. I think she'd stay a couple of extra days and go to the reception if you convinced her that it would help push my relationship with Cassie forward."

"Devious."

"Yeah," Deke said proudly. "I thought so."

Thomas contemplated the possibilities for a while. "All right, I'll try it."

"Excellent." Deke paused. "By the way, you can tell Leonora that the position we created for her at Mirror House is for real. I've decided she's right. That collection is valuable and should be cataloged and made available online. The Bethany Walker Endowment will continue to fund the job."

"I'll mention that to her."

Deke looked at the tips of his running shoes. "You know, it's been a while since I went out on a date."

"Don't worry. It's one of those things you don't forget how to do."

"Sort of like boolean algebra, huh?"

Thomas's mouth curved. "Sort of. Want a little advice?"

"What's that?"

"Lose the beard."

Deke looked startled. Then he grinned ruefully. "You don't think it's a fashion statement?"

"It's Cassie's opinion that counts here and I've always had the impression she didn't care for the beard."

Deke ran his fingers through his beard, thinking. "Neither did Margaret Lewis."

"There you go," Thomas said. "That settles it. According to you and Leonora and Cassie, department secretaries rule."

• • •

He waited until Deke left before he picked up the phone and called Leonora. She answered on the first ring.

"You want to help further the cause of promoting an intimate relationship between Deke and Cassie?" he asked.

"They seemed to be doing quite well on their own."

"Deke wants to take her to the reception on Saturday. He suggested that maybe she'd feel more comfortable if all four of us went together. But I've got a feeling he's the one who's a little nervous about getting back into the dating scene."

"Let me get this straight, you're asking me to go to the reception with you because you think your brother needs us to give him some moral support?"

"You're not buying this, are you?"

"Deke and Cassie are both adults and their main problems seem to be out of the way. They can manage a date on their own."

He went to stand at the window. Night was closing in fast. He could not see the new assault wave of fog that was rolling in off the water, but it seemed to him that he could sense its weight.

"Let me rephrase that question," he said. "Would you care to attend the reception at Mirror House on Saturday evening?"

"With you?"

"Yes, ma'am. With me."

"Oh, yes," she said softly. "Yes, I would like that very much."

The window reflected his own happy image staring back at him.

"Something else," he said. "Deke told me to tell you that he agrees with you about the importance of that library. He says the Bethany Walker Endowment will continue to fund the task of getting the collection online and he'd be pleased if you would agree to continue on in the position of librarian until the job is finished."

Leonora was quiet for a moment.

"I'll think about it," she said at last. "It would probably take me a few months."

"Yeah." He could do a lot with a few months.

Leonora said nothing.

"Of course," Thomas said, "I could always move to Melba Creek."

"Thomas—"

"I'm pushing this a little too hard, aren't I?" Thomas said.

"We both need to go carefully here."

"Right. Carefully. Measure twice, cut once. An old bit of tool wisdom."

Leonora surprised him with a laugh. "I wasn't planning on cutting anything."

"I can't tell you how reassuring it is to hear you say that."

"While we're thinking about things, why don't you come over here for dinner? Bring Wrench."

"I'll do that. And my tools, of course."

"Planning to give me another demonstration of your astonishing skill?"

"Wait'll you see what I can do with a drill press."

Thomas took his time making love to her that night. Probably the craftsman in him, she thought at one point. He was concerned with the smallest details. Who would have guessed that she would be so sensitive right *there*.

"Thomas."

"Squeeze a little harder."

"*Thomas*."

"That's it. Like that. Getting tighter. I can really feel those little muscles now."

"Thomas."

"No, you can't move any other part of your body, remember? Just this one little spot. We're working with a precision tool here."

"Damn you, Thomas." Frustrated beyond belief, she came up off the bed in a convulsive movement.

He laughed softly when she came down on top of him.

A moment later when the fiercely intense climax swept through both of them, he stopped laughing.

A long time later he pulled her close, tucking her securely against his body.

She fell asleep, warm and relaxed and feeling safe. Her last waking thought was that she would not have the dream tonight. She had her answers. Meredith could rest in peace.

. . . She was back in the endless hall of mirrors, fleeing the unseen menace. She must not gaze directly into any of the dark looking glasses. It would be fatal to make eye contact with any of the ghosts trapped inside the mirrors. She would be sucked instantly into the world on the other side.

Her pursuer drew closer. She heard laughter.

Don't stop.

She stopped.

Don't turn around.

She had to turn around. She had to know the face of her pursuer.

But something went wrong. To her horror she found herself staring straight into a terrifyingly familiar nine-sided convex mirror. The silver monsters carved on the frame writhed, mouths gaping, claws extended.

*Meredith's distorted face stared out at her from
the dark glass.*

"...You can't sleep yet..."

"Leonora. *Leonora.*" Thomas's voice shattered the
dream just as surely as if he had picked up a hammer and
smashed the silver-framed looking glass.

She came awake, her heart pounding, her nightgown
clinging damply to her body.

"It's all right," Thomas said. He held her tightly pinned
against his chest, one hand in her tangled hair. "You're
okay. Just a dream."

She gulped air and clung to him, taking comfort from
his strength and the heat of his body.

"That damned dream again," she whispered after a
while. Frustration and a strange anger burned in her. "I
thought there wouldn't be any more. I thought it was
over."

"Easy, easy. It is over." He stroked his fingers slowly
through her hair. "What's the dream about?"

"I'm in a long hall full of dark mirrors. Someone is
chasing me. I know I shouldn't look into any of the mirrors, but I do. I see Meredith's face looking out at me.
She's telling me that I can't sleep."

"Well, I guess we know where the symbolism for that
dream came from, don't we? Right out of Mirror House.
Try not to worry about it, honey. You've been through a
lot lately. Might take a while for your unconscious mind
to let go of the images."

He continued to run his fingers soothingly through her
hair. She loved the feel of his hands on her, she thought.
There was strength and sureness in his touch. Competence and cleverness. Power and passion.

Slowly she relaxed.

When she fell asleep this time, she did not dream.

Chapter Twenty

The following morning she sat at a table in the Mirror House library, computer at hand, a stack of books beside her, and thought about staying on in Wing Cove.

Putting the Mirror House collection online would be an interesting job and she knew Gloria would be delighted to fly up to Washington for a visit while she was here. Her grandmother would no doubt insist on it, in fact. She wouldn't be able to resist the chance to meet Thomas.

But those weren't the reasons she was giving serious consideration to Deke's offer.

It was time to face the truth: What she felt for Thomas was far more than a passing attraction. She was in love. Willing to take risks for it. But it was no good unless he was willing to take risks with her.

The realization had come softly somewhere in the night, but she knew that the knowledge had been with her for a while. She had tried to stay focused on the questions that had brought her to Wing Cove. But looking back she could see quite clearly that the intuitive part of her had been aware from the very beginning that something important was happening between her and Thomas. Something that made it seem worthwhile to take some chances.

It was probably foolhardy in the extreme to hang around now that she had her answers. A smart woman would go back to Melba Creek and pick up the threads of her life.

She opened one of the old books, a small, leatherbound volume written in the waning years of the seventeenth century, and examined the title page.

On the Proper Method of Trapping a Demon in a Magik Mirror. The author had chosen to remain anonymous, no doubt for social and political reasons. But in a lengthy introduction he assured the reader that he... *was a student of the occult sciences and one who is most excellently qualified to provide instruction in this most dangerous and powerful art.*

She wondered if the author of the little book had made a lot of money selling his method for trapping demons in mirrors. She thought about Alex Rhodes and his antistress formula and his mirroring therapy. No matter what the era, there was never a shortage of charlatans and frauds. Never a lack of people willing to plunk down their money for a magic fix, either.

Another line of text caught her eye.

...Beware, images in the magik mirror must be examined closely and interpreted wisely and with great caution for nothing is as it seems in that other world...

She heard Thomas's footsteps in the hallway just outside the door. A sense of great certainty swept through her. Unlike visions in a mirror, Thomas was exactly what he appeared to be, real and solid.

He materialized in the opening, a jacket hooked over his shoulder.

"Ready for lunch?" he asked.

She sat back in her chair and drank in the sight of him.

He came to a halt in front of the table where she was working and gave her a quizzical smile.

"Something wrong?" he asked.

"No." She closed the little book very carefully. "Nothing's wrong. Tell Deke I'll finish the job."

He stilled. "You're going to stick around for a while?"

"Yes. This is a very interesting and important collection. It has historical significance and should be made available to scholars."

"What about me?" Thomas watched her very steadily. "Do I have historical significance, too?"

"Yes, indeed," she parried. "But I wasn't planning to make you available to any other scholars."

Thomas gave her his slow smile. "Going to keep me just for yourself?"

"In my own private collection."

"Okay by me. So long as I'm the only guy in your private collection."

"You will be," she said.

More footsteps echoed in the hall. Kyle appeared in the doorway.

"What's with all these creepy old mirrors?" he asked.

"The original owner of the house collected them," she said. "What are you doing here, Kyle?"

He flicked a glance at Thomas. "Came to see if you wanted to join me for lunch."

"Thanks, but I'm busy."

"You heard the lady." Thomas took her arm and started toward the door. "See you around, Delling."

"Leo, wait." Kyle grabbed Leonora's free hand. "I've got to talk to you."

"Some other time." Thomas did not break his stride.

Kyle ignored him. He kept his grip on her wrist. "Listen to me, time is running out. I can't hang around here much longer. I've got to get back to my classes."

Both men tugged on opposite arms.

"I've always had this fantasy," Leonora murmured.

Thomas halted and turned around. "Let go of her, Delling."

Something in his expression must have rattled Kyle. Leonora found her hand suddenly free. But Kyle's desperation was apparent and made her pause.

"Leo—"

"It's all right, Kyle," she said quietly. "I'll call Helena this afternoon."

It took a few seconds for comprehension to sink in.

"You mean it?" Kyle asked.

"Yes. No promises regarding the final results, though. The decision is made by her committee, and I can't predict what she'll do. But I'll make the call."

"Thanks." Exuberant relief lit Kyle's eyes. "I knew you'd come through for me, honey."

Before she realized his intentions, he grabbed her by the shoulders and aimed an enthusiastic kiss at her mouth.

She started to turn her head so that she would take the caress on the cheek, but at the same instant Thomas used his grip on her arm to draw her out of Kyle's path.

Kyle wound up kissing air. He was too euphoric to notice.

"This calls for a celebration." He opened his hands in an expansive gesture. "Let me take both of you to lunch."

"Forget it," Thomas said.

He whisked Leonora out of the library.

"So much for my fantasy," she said.

"What fantasy?"

"Two men, dueling over my honor."

"Hey, you want me to go back and beat the crap out of him in your honor? No problem."

"Never mind," she said. "You're worth two of Kyle Delling. Make that a dozen."

He grinned, obviously pleased. He reminded her a bit of Wrench when she accepted one of his doggy gifts.

"Think so?" Thomas said.

Roberta passed them on the stairs before Leonora could answer. She gave them a slightly harried smile.

"There you are, Leonora," she said. "A very nice man came to my office asking for you a moment ago. I sent him up here. Did he find you?"

"He found me," Leonora said.

"Good, good."

"Preparations for the reception under control?" Thomas asked.

"I'm a wreck. It's complete chaos down there. The news about the Rhodes murder and Professor Kern's suicide has distracted everyone, including me, I must admit."

"I'm sure the affair will go off right on schedule," Leonora soothed.

Roberta chuckled. "Easy for you to say. You two off to lunch?"

"Yes," Leonora said. "The pub. Want us to bring you anything?"

"Very kind of you to offer, but no, thanks. I brought a sack lunch with me today. I knew that I wouldn't have time to leave." She continued on up the stairs. "I'll see you later."

Leonora walked beside Thomas through the busy confusion that gripped the first floor of the mansion. Neither of them spoke until they went out onto the terrace.

"You're really going to make that phone call to your friend, Helena?" Thomas asked neutrally.

"Yes."

"Whatever happened to sweet revenge?"

She thought about that as they went down the stone

steps to the parking lot. What *had* happened to sweet revenge? She wondered silently.

"I found something tastier," she said.

Shortly before four o'clock that afternoon, Thomas wandered into his favorite store in Wing Cove, Pitney's Hardware & Plumbing Supply. It was one of the oldest stores in town and one of the few that hadn't been gentrified to appeal to the tastes of the college community.

He found what he was looking for three-quarters of the way down one of the long aisles.

The elegant, compact household tool kit included an array of screwdrivers, including a Phillips head, a gleaming crescent wrench, a small hammer and a set of pliers. The tools were attractively boxed in a black plastic storage case.

He removed the hammer and hefted it in one hand, feeling for balance and weight.

A figure darkened the far end of the aisle. Thomas lowered the hammer and suppressed a groan when he saw Kyle coming toward him.

"Thought I saw you come in here, Walker," Kyle said. "I was having coffee across the street. Glad I caught you."

"I was sort of hoping you'd be on your way out of town by now, Delling."

"Don't worry, I'll be leaving soon. But I wanted to talk to you first." Kyle came to a halt in the middle of the aisle. "It's about Leo."

Thomas did not move. "I don't really want to discuss her. Especially with you."

"She's a nice person," Kyle said, looking serious and profound. "A genuinely nice person."

"Translated, that means that you came here knowing

that you could talk her into making that phone call to her friend for you."

"Well, sure." Kyle raised one shoulder in an easy, unconcerned shrug. "She was bound to do it eventually. I know her, you see. She wouldn't sabotage someone else's career by refusing to make a simple phone call."

"You got what you wanted. You can leave now."

Kyle looked amused. "You're in a hurry to get rid of me, aren't you?"

"Yeah."

"Take it easy, I'm on my way. But before I go I thought I'd give you a little advice about Leo. Don't make the same mistake I did."

"Don't worry, I won't."

"She's a little old-fashioned in some ways. Probably because she was raised by her grandparents. Some things she just can't handle."

"Like finding her fiancé in bed with her sister? Gosh, Delling. Think she overreacted?"

"It was a one-time thing." Kyle grimaced. "You sound as uptight as Leonora. Trust me, if you'd ever met Meredith, you'd know why I ended up in bed with her that day. She came on to me, not the other way around."

"I knew Meredith. We dated for a while."

Kyle looked momentarily confused. Then understanding dawned. "You screwed Meredith? No shit."

Thomas did not respond.

"This is not good," Kyle said. "Not good at all. Does Leo know?"

"She knows."

Kyle went back to looking bewildered. "I don't get it. Why the hell is she still seeing you if she knows that you and Meredith had a fling?"

"I dated Meredith before I met Leonora. You screwed around with Meredith while you were *engaged* to

Leonora. Can you grasp the basic distinction here, Delling?"

Kyle's gaze dropped briefly to the hammer. "No offense, but I don't need a lecture on semantics from a guy who knows how to use large and dangerous tools."

"I'm not delivering a lecture," Thomas said patiently. "I'm insulting your honor and integrity."

"I get the point. If you're looking for a fight, forget it. My doctorate is in English Lit. In my field, we prefer to settle our arguments in print."

"There you go, spoiling my whole afternoon."

Kyle sighed. "If you knew Meredith, you know why I screwed around and ended up shooting myself in the foot."

"No," Thomas said. "I don't understand why you risked losing Leonora for a fling with a woman who was cold as ice."

"Meredith? Cold?" Kyle looked startled. Then he chuckled. "Don't know how she was with you but with me she was one hot little firecracker."

"You bought into her act, huh? And here I thought you Ph.D. types were supposed to be smarter than the average single-celled animal."

"What act?" Kyle demanded.

"Meredith didn't like men."

"Didn't like men? You're out of your mind."

Thomas shrugged. "Ask Leonora. Meredith was sexually assaulted when she was a kid. Turned her off sex for life. She didn't like or trust men. Used her body to get what she wanted, but once she had obtained her objective, she ended the relationship."

"I don't believe that. Why the hell did she seduce me if she wasn't interested?"

"You really don't have a clue about what that one afternoon in Leonora's bed was all about, do you?" Thomas said. "It was designed to destroy your relationship with Leonora. Meredith didn't want her sister to marry you, so she seduced you to prove that you couldn't be trusted."

"That's bullshit."

"Hey, it worked, didn't it? Meredith knew Leonora well enough to know that cheating was the one thing her sister wouldn't forgive."

"That's pure bullshit."

"Use your head, Delling. Why do you think Meredith made sure it happened in Leonora's bed? Who do you think called Leonora a half hour before the big seduction scene to make sure she would walk in the door at the right moment?"

Kyle looked shocked. "Meredith called Leonora? So, *that's* why she came home early."

"You never figured that part out, huh?"

"Now just a damned minute here, you're twisting this."

"Tell me something," Thomas said. "Did Meredith ever make another play for you after you and Leonora broke up?"

Kyle's mouth compressed. "The situation was compli-cated. I doubt if you'd understand."

"Sure, I understand. You tried to call Meredith after-ward and she didn't give you the time of day, did she?"

Kyle reddened. "She had some issues. She and Leo were half sisters, after all."

"Meredith didn't have issues. Meredith had agendas. Once she had finished with you, she moved on."

Kyle looked as if he wanted to argue the point. But he must have reconsidered.

"Leo told you all this?" he asked.

"Yeah."

"She knew that her bitch of a sister set me up?"

"Sure."

"I don't get it." Kyle spread his hands. "If Leo knows that it wasn't my fault, why didn't she give me a second chance? It's not like her to just walk away from a relationship after putting so much into it."

"She may be willing to work hard at a relationship, but that doesn't mean she doesn't have certain standards. You failed to meet those standards, Delling."

Kyle's face worked. "*Failed?* That's hardly the appropriate word."

"It's the perfect word, when you get right down to it."

"I've never failed at anything in my life. I've aced everything, from my SATs to my comps. I've got a dozen peer-review papers in print. Who are you to tell me I *failed*?"

Thomas put the hammer aside and selected a gleaming screwdriver. "Think of yourself as one of these. You're bright and shiny, but you're made out of some weak alloy instead of good-quality steel. You won't stand up to extended use. Nothing for it but to chuck you into the discard pile."

Kyle turned livid. His hands clenched at his sides. "Leonora didn't *discard* me, you son of a bitch."

"You're the English Lit man here. I'd think you'd want to use the correct word. But suit yourself. The point is, she did what any smart person does with a poorly made tool that isn't up to the job. She junked it."

"Shut up," Kyle said through his teeth. "Just shut the fuck up. You know nothing about Leonora. From what I can see you've got zip-all in common with her."

"Because I don't have a couple of advanced degrees?"

"Get real, Walker." Kyle snorted softly. "You're hardly her type. She might enjoy the macho tool man routine for a while, but it won't last long."

"If you knew Leonora as well as you think you do,"

Thomas said softly, "you'd have realized that the fastest way to lose her was to prove to her that she couldn't trust you."

"Hell, that romp with Meredith wasn't about trust, it was about sex. It was just a simple fuck."

"Leonora didn't see it that way, did she, Delling?"

"If there was anyone she couldn't trust, it was her bitch of a half sister, not me."

"Unfortunately, Meredith had an advantage over you. One she knew going in and one she exploited all the way."

"What?" Kyle demanded. "What advantage did she have?"

"She was family."

Kyle stared, speechless.

"Leonora could ditch a guy who cheated on her," Thomas explained patiently, "but she couldn't ditch a sister. You know what they say, you can choose your friends, but you're stuck with family."

Kyle managed to get his sagging jaw back in place. "What makes you think you know how Leo's mind works?"

Thomas thought about Leonora setting out to find the answers surrounding the death of a half sister who had caused her nothing but trouble. He thought about how he and Deke had stood side-by-side all these years.

"When it comes to the important stuff," he said softly, "Leonora and I understand each other just fine."

Kyle's features clenched into an outraged mask. For a moment Thomas thought he might take a swing. The possibility raised his spirits.

But to his disappointment, Kyle subsided with a resigned sigh.

"Look," Kyle said, "believe it or not, I didn't come in here to get into an argument. I just wanted to tell you to treat Leo with respect, okay? She's not like Meredith. She's one of the good people in this world."

"I know."

Kyle hesitated. Then he nodded. "Maybe you do, at that. Looking back, I wish I had handled things differently. I think Leonora and I could have had something special together."

"But you'll get over her, right?"

"Oh, sure. Life goes on."

He'd said those very same, very casual words himself, Thomas thought. When he had told Leonora about his divorce. But he knew now that he wouldn't be saying them if he lost her.

"You know, Delling, I really hope you get that tenure-track position."

Kyle didn't bother to conceal his surprise. "Thanks. Mind if I ask why you give a damn?"

"Because I don't want you coming back into Leonora's life looking for more career assistance." Thomas snapped the lid of the tool case shut. "Understood?"

Kyle made a face. "Understood. Good luck with Leonora, by the way. I don't think you stand a snowball's chance in hell of marrying her, but good luck anyway."

"I don't plan to leave it to luck."

Kyle started to turn around. He paused. "By the way, that gray monster tied up outside. The one that looks like he works in a junkyard. Is he yours?"

"Wrench? Yeah, he's with me. Why?"

"Just wondered. Never seen a dog like that. What breed?"

"Beats me. I never asked."

"Does he bite?"

"He'd rip out your throat as soon as look at you."

"Huh."

"But only if I tell him to do it," Thomas added softly.

Kyle turned and walked off down the aisle.

Thomas waited until the bell over the glass door at the front of the store tinkled to announce Delling's departure before he carried the elegant little tool kit to the counter.

Gus Pitney, founder and proprietor of Pitney's Hardware & Plumbing Supply, looked up from his newspaper and peered over the rims of his reading glasses.

Gus's face reminded Thomas of the store, old and filled with lots of interesting stuff.

"Thought for a while you two were going to have a knock-down–drag-out right there in aisle three," Gus said.

"Nah. Guys like that don't get into fights." Thomas put the tool kit on the grimy glass counter. "They publish articles in peer-review journals, instead."

"That so?"

"Yep." Thomas reached for his wallet. "I'll take this."

Pitney squinted at the tool kit. "What the hell d'ya want with that? It's a real basic kit. You probably got several of everything that's in there."

"It's a gift." Thomas removed a credit card from his wallet. "Mind gift wrapping it?"

"Gift wrap? This place look like an outpost of Nordstrom's to you?" Gus reached under the counter and came up with a brown paper bag. "This is what we call gift wrapping here at Pitney's."

"Fine." Thomas made a mental note to pick up some fancy wrapping paper at the card shop across the street.

Gus went to work ringing up the sale on an ancient cash register. "None of my business, of course, but what was that all about back there in aisle three a few minutes ago?"

"Professor Delling and I were just having a friendly discussion on the subject of how important it is to have the right tool to do the job."

"Huh." Gus shoved the kit into the paper sack. "Best tool in the world is worthless unless the man using it knows what he's doing."

"I'm with you there," Thomas agreed.

Cassie came out of her bedroom, dressed in a bathrobe. Her red curls were wrapped in a towel. She held two dresses on hangers, one in each hand.

"Which dress?" she asked.

Leonora leaned back in the chair, stretched out her legs, steepled her fingers and surveyed the two offerings. The dress on the left was a short, sexy, black number. The tags were still pinned to the neckline. The dress on the right was a demure crepe sheath in beige.

"I like the black one," she said.

Cassie studied it, unconvinced. "I don't know. Might be a bit too much for a first date."

"It's not the first date. Dinner at my house was the first date. And then there were all those yoga lessons."

"I know, but I don't want to shock Deke. Call your grandmother."

"You don't think we can make this decision on our own?"

"I don't want to take any chances. Tell your grandmother we need advice from Henrietta."

"For heaven's sake, Cassie—"

"Call her. I want to have an expert opinion."

"Okay, okay." Leonora picked up the phone. "But I may not be able to get hold of her. This is one of her bridge days. And I think she has swim aerobics, too."

Cassie just stood there, hangers in hand, and looked stubborn.

Luckily Gloria answered on the second ring.

•   •   •

"Leo, dear, you just caught me on my way out the door."
Gloria draped her pool towel over the handlebars of the
walker and switched the phone to her other ear. "I'm on
my way to swim class. Everything all right?"

"My friend Cassie needs more dating advice. She's going to a semiformal reception. She's got a drop-dead,
sexy black dress and a simple but elegant beige thing
with long sleeves and a knee-length hem. She wants to
know which one Henrietta would suggest."

"I see. Your friend, you say?"

"Right. Listen, as long as you're asking for some advice for Cassie, would you mind asking Henrietta a question for another friend of mine, too?"

"This other friend is also attending the fancy reception?"

"Yes."

Resolve shot through Gloria. "Give me a minute to get
down the hall. I'll call you back from Herb's."

"I'm at Cassie's house. Let me give you the number."

"Hang on."

Gloria scribbled the number on the pad beside the
phone, hung up, tightened the sash of her pool robe and
headed for the door with her walker.

Herb answered when she pounded loudly on his front
door.

"What's up?" He frowned. "You look like you're on
your way down to the pool."

"Forget the pool. I've got more questions from my
granddaughter and her friend. I think this is getting serious, Herb."

He glanced at his watch. "I've got a computer class in
fifteen minutes."

"This is more important." She maneuvered the walker
through the door. "Out of my way, Herb."

"Hold your horses." Herb stood back to allow her into the apartment. He closed the door behind her.

She stopped, turned and sat down on the seat of the walker. She punched in the number Leonora had given her.

"Okay, shoot," she said when Leonora came on the line. "We're ready on this end."

"As I said, Cassie is trying to choose between a short, sexy black dress and a little beige number," Leonora said.

Gloria looked at Herb. "A short, sexy black dress or beige for the first friend?"

"That's easy," Herb said. "The sexy black dress."

"The black one," Gloria relayed.

Cassie came on the line. "Ask Herb if wearing a sexy black dress will conflict with my image as a nurturing female. I assume that was what we were going for with the lasagna and apple pie bit."

Gloria looked at Herb. "She's worried about messing up the nurturing image."

"Time and place for everything," Herb said. "Tell her to go with the black dress. No self-respecting man knows what the hell to do with beige."

"Right." Gloria spoke into the phone. "Did you hear that, Cassie? Herb says no self-respecting man knows what to do with beige."

"All right," Cassie said. "I'll wear the black one. Thank Herb for me."

Leonora came back on the line, sounding a little tense. "Tell Herb that the only dress my other friend has with her is a dark-green number with long sleeves and a cowl neckline. Does she need to go shopping?"

Gloria relayed the question to Herb.

"Tell her to go with the green," Herb said. "It'll be good with her eyes."

"Herb says green," Gloria said.

"Got it. Thanks, Gloria. And thank Herb, too."

"I will, dear."

Gloria ended the call, satisfaction bubbling through her. She looked at Herb.

"It's working," she said. "First dinner, and now a fancy reception. This Thomas Walker is definitely serious."

"I'm serious, too," Herb said. "When Henrietta's name comes off that column, I want my photo to go up with my byline."

"Columnists. You're all prima donnas."

Chapter Twenty-one

Leonora stood at the window and watched Thomas walk up the path to her front door. He didn't look like a junk-yard dog this evening, she thought. He looked exactly as she'd known he'd look in a suit and tie. Like a well-dressed mob boss.

The sleek, dark jacket he wore did nothing to conceal the feral quality. It only served to underscore the power in his shoulders. He looked exciting and dangerous. She was very certain that she had never seen anything so scrumptious in her entire life.

He carried a package wrapped in red foil in one hand. He saw her standing at the window and smiled. A storm of butterflies exploded in her stomach.

She was in love.

There were not a lot of moments in life like this one, she realized. Moments such as this; when awareness and anticipation and the sheer thrill of being alive all came to-gether in an intoxicating brew that made the heart sing and the pulse beat fast; such moments were to be savored and appreciated.

You'd think she was a teenager greeting her date for the prom. But she was no high-school senior and Thomas was definitely not a boy. He was a man in every sense of the word and that knowledge filled her with deep, feminine joy.

She opened the door. "You look fabulous."

He appeared slightly startled and then amused by the compliment.

"Amazing what a suit will do for a man," he said.

She shook her head a single time and stepped back. "What's amazing is what you do to that suit."

"Thanks." His gaze moved slowly, deliberately down the length of her green dress, all the way to her strappy high heels and then climbed back up to her mouth. "But you're the one who looks good enough to eat. Maybe later?"

She blushed. "If you're still hungry."

"I will be."

He handed her the foiled package.

"For me?" She took the gift from his hand. "Thank you."

"Decided I'd take a lesson from my dog. He's always giving you things."

She tested the weight of the gift. Much too heavy to be lingerie, jewelry or note paper, she decided. Curiosity consumed her. She ripped into the red foil.

To her surprise, the paper did not come off as easily as expected. The unusual gray sealing tape held the edges of the foil securely in place.

She pried at the tape with her fingernails. "I don't think I've ever seen a package wrapped quite like this."

"I did it myself. Got the paper at the card shop."

She plucked harder at the sealing tape. "Is that where you got this super-sticky tape, too?"

"No. I had that at home."

"I don't think I've ever seen anything quite like it."

"Duct tape," Thomas said.

"Ah. That explains it." She finally got rid of the last of the red foil and the duct tape. She looked down at the black plastic case in her hands. "It's lovely."

"Open it."

She unsnapped the catch and raised the lid. A row of graduated screwdrivers and a variety of other small tools, each neatly nestled in a specially molded plastic slot, gleamed in all their stainless steel glory.

"They're beautiful." She did not take her eyes off the handsome tools. "Absolutely gorgeous. I've never seen such a lovely set of tools."

Thomas was pleased. "You really like them?"

"I love them. No one ever gave me anything like this before. They're perfect."

"Yeah, well, it's a pretty basic set, but I think it will handle most of the routine jobs. The smallest screwdriver should work on your glasses."

She closed the lid of the tool kit, latched it carefully and set it down on the coffee table. She straightened and kissed Thomas lightly on the mouth.

"Thank you," she said softly. "I wish I had a gift for you."

"You're all the present I want. But I'll wait until later to unwrap you."

"Thomas, there's something I have to tell you."

He paused, a little wary now. "What's that?"

"I think you would make an excellent father."

He just stared at her.

She took his hand and led him to the door.

•   •   •

Some time later Leonora found herself standing alone in the relative calm of a small alcove on the edge of the dance floor. She was waiting for Thomas to return from the buffet table with some food.

The transformation of Mirror House was complete. There was no sign of the organized chaos that had reigned on the ground floor during the past few days. In its place was a glittering scene that could have come straight out of the Gilded Age. The handsome reception rooms were filled with elegantly dressed alumni, members of the faculty and their guests. The heavy wooden furnishings, together with the red velvet draperies and carpets, glowed richly in the light of the chandeliers. The walls of mirrors reflected the crowd in a series of dazzling, endlessly repeating images that seemed to stretch into infinity.

Roberta, clad in a gray silk suit and adorned with a single row of pearls, came to a halt beside Leonora and surveyed her production with evident satisfaction.

"I was a little worried for a while that the events of the last few days would put a damper on tonight," she confided. "But that doesn't seem to be the case. Everyone appears to be having a good time."

"You'd certainly never guess that one of Eubanks College's most esteemed faculty members had murdered several people and then committed suicide."

"In fairness, many of these people are out-of-town alumni," Roberta reminded her. "Most of them never knew Professor Kern, except, perhaps, as an instructor they had at one time. And very few of them were acquainted with his victims."

"That's true, I suppose."

"I saw Ed Stovall yesterday," Roberta continued. "He

told me that they found a stash of illegal drugs in Rhodes's cottage and some unusual chemicals. They think he was concocting the stuff right there in his kitchen. Can you believe it?"

"Unfortunately, yes."

Roberta watched the crowd. "The world is a much different place these days. Sometimes I look back on my own college years and I can't believe how life has changed."

"I'll tell you one thing," Leonora said. "Your successor is going to find you a very hard act to follow."

Roberta glanced around the glowing rooms with a wistful air. "I'll miss it, you know."

"Running Mirror House? Look on the bright side. Just think, no more dealing with crotchety professors. No more having to train new student assistants every quarter. No more soothing difficult alumni who threaten to cut off funds for the endowment if they don't get their way."

"All true. Still, it's going to seem strange to wake up in the morning next month and realize that I no longer have to come in to the office every day."

"I have a hunch that when you wake up that first morning on that beautiful cruise ship bound for all those exotic ports of call, you'll forget about the office routine very quickly."

Roberta chuckled. "You're right. And there's another big plus. In my position as retired executive director of Mirror House, I'll be able to attend the annual alumni reception next year without having to do any of the work ahead of time."

"That will be something to look forward to."

Roberta looked at Deke and Cassie, who stood a short distance away, talking to a small knot of people.

"One good thing has come out of all the terrible events of the past few days," she said. "Deke Walker appears to be a new man."

Leonora followed her gaze. Deke had his arm around

Cassie's waist in an intimate, casually possessive manner. Cassie's magnificent figure was displayed to advantage in the black dress. Her face was alight with happiness.

At that moment Deke laughed at something someone in the group had said. Leonora thought back to the first time she had met him, his face grim and haggard in the light thrown off by his computer screen. The transformation in him was even more breathtaking than the one that had occurred in Mirror House.

"Yes," she said. "He does look like a new man."

"It was getting rid of that dreadful beard that makes the difference," Roberta said. "He should have done it long ago."

Leonora caught Cassie's eye at that instant. She smiled. "I don't think it was the beard."

Deke looked at Cassie standing in the doorway. She was silhouetted against the seductive glow of the lamp she had left burning in the living room. It occurred to him that he had never seen the inside of her house.

"Thank you for a wonderful evening," Cassie said.

"This is the first time I can honestly say that I actually enjoyed one of those damn alumni receptions." He hesitated. "We'll, uh, have to do it again sometime."

"Next year," she said a little too brightly. "Same time, same place. I'll mark my calendar."

"I was thinking of maybe dinner this coming Saturday."

"Oh."

He waited but she did not say anything else.

"Can I take that as an affirmative response?" he asked eventually.

"Oh. Oh, yes. Yes, that would be great. I'll look forward to it."

"Is there something wrong here?" Deke asked. "I'm getting mixed signals."

"No, really, I'd love to go out with you on Saturday night."

He reached up to stroke his beard in a gesture that had become a habit. When he touched bare skin he winced. He dropped his hand.

"You've been very patient with me, Cassie. Very kind. I feel like I've been living in another world for a while. But I'm back."

"I'm so glad," she whispered.

"I'm okay," he plowed on. "I don't need any more acts of charity. Do you understand what I'm trying to say? I don't want you to go out with me just because you feel sorry for me."

"I do want to have dinner with you, Deke, it's just—" She trailed off.

Panic hit him. He struggled, trying to figure out how to handle the situation. The problem was, he hadn't had a lot of experience with this kind of thing. Too long out of the dating game, he thought. Not that he'd ever played the game that well in the first place.

Inspiration struck. He looked at her, squinting a little against the glow of the light behind her. "Maybe I could come in for a while so that we can talk about this over coffee?"

"Come in?"

"Is that an invitation or a question?"

She went very still. "Deke, there's something I need to tell you."

Damn. It had all been charity. She wasn't really interested in him as a man. She had just felt sorry for a client. He steeled himself. He could handle the truth, he thought. What he couldn't take was false hope and kindness disguised as passion.

"Say it," he demanded. "Just say it and get it over with. I won't shatter into a million pieces."

"I know that," she said. "Only a very strong man could have weathered all of the rumors and gossip concerning the state of your mind these past few months. Only a strong man could have stuck to his guns when everyone was telling him that he was obsessive and crazy."

"Not everyone said I was obsessive and crazy. You and Thomas never said it. At least, not to my face."

"What I'm trying to get across here is that I didn't go out with you tonight because I felt sorry for you, and I didn't agree to go out on Saturday because I felt like doing you a favor. I want you to know the truth before you come in for coffee."

"What truth?"

"Deke, you have been the target of a carefully calculated seduction."

Maybe he had flipped out, after all.

"Huh?" he said.

"Remember the dinner with Leonora and Thomas? The one I helped cook?"

"Yes," he said, cautious now.

"That was part of the strategy. And tonight, this black dress?"

"I really, really like the dress."

"More strategy. Leonora consulted her grandmother, who checked with Herb, who writes an advice column."

"I see."

"Herb chose the lasagna and the apple pie and this dress."

"I'll have to remember to thank Herb. Can I ask why I was targeted for this strategy of seduction?"

"Why? You have to ask me why? Isn't it obvious? You were targeted because *I'm in love with you*." She flung her arms wide. "I have been for the past six months. But you never noticed and I was afraid you never would, and your beard was getting longer and longer and it all looked hopeless. That's why."

The damp night air was suddenly as effervescent as champagne. Deke laughed.

"I think," he said, "that this may be the happiest night of my life."

She blinked once or twice. "You're sure?"

"I love you," he said. "I think I must have fallen in love with you somewhere in the middle of that first yoga lesson."

"Really?"

"Why do you think I signed up for a full year in advance?"

"Oh." Her expression softened. Her full mouth curved into a welcoming smile.

"Are you going to invite me in for coffee now?" he asked.

She stood back and held the door open for him.

A long time later, he settled beside her in the warm, shadowed bed, replete and content beyond measure. He reached for Cassie. She came to him, damp and happy, folded her arms on his chest.

"That was incredible," she said.

"It was, wasn't it?" He stroked the full curve of her hip. "Always knew those damn yoga lessons would be good for something someday."

Leonora kicked off her high heels the moment she walked into Thomas's house. Wrench brought her a mangled leather bone, which she admired while Thomas hung up their coats and got the fire going.

When he had a blaze crackling he went around the end of the counter, poured two brandies and took them into the living room.

She savored the sight of him as he lowered himself onto the sofa beside her. He had removed the jacket of his suit. The collar of the white dress shirt was open, the sleeves rolled up on his muscular forearms. His tie hung loose around his neck. He propped his feet, clad in black dress socks, next to her nylon-sheathed toes on the coffee table.

They sipped brandy in a comfortable silence.

"What do you think?" Leonora said eventually. "Are they in bed together yet?"

Thomas checked his watch. "It's been nearly forty minutes since we left them both at her place. I'd say, un-equivocally and without a doubt, yes. They're in bed."

"Unequivocally?"

"It's a fancy word meaning, for sure."

"I know what it means, I just wondered how you could be so certain that Deke and Cassie are in bed."

"Something about the way they were looking at each other during that last dance, I think."

"Mesmerized by each other."

"Yeah." He sipped brandy and lowered the glass. "Mesmerized."

She rested her head against the high cushion behind her and looked at his feet stacked one on top of the other on the low table. They looked very large next to her own. She felt a little mesmerized herself, she thought. She closed her eyes.

"I owe you," Thomas said after a while. "For a lot of things. For coming here to Wing Cove. For working with Deke and me to get the answers we all needed. For help-ing Cassie seduce Deke. For—"

"Don't say it." She did not open her eyes.

"Don't say what?" he asked.

"Don't say that you owe me for sleeping with you or I will never, ever forgive you."

"I wasn't going to say that."

She opened her eyes and saw that he was gazing thoughtfully at her toes.

"What were you going to say?" she asked.

"I believe that I was about to thank you for agreeing to stay on here in Wing Cove for a while."

"Oh, that."

"Yeah, that." He took another swallow of brandy. "I need to ask you something."

"Ummm?"

"What you said earlier tonight. About me being a good father. You really think so?"

"Yes." She waited. When he said nothing more, she risked a quick glance at his hard profile. "Why?"

"Just wondered what made you say it."

"You know how to make a commitment and stick with it. That's the most important element of fatherhood, as far as I'm concerned."

"You don't think maybe I'm a little old for fatherhood?"

"No."

He took the brandy glass out of her hand and set it beside his own on the table. He eased her down onto the sofa and lowered himself gently along the length of her. He was warm and heavy and unmistakably aroused.

She caught the trailing ends of his tie in her hands. "I love you, Thomas."

"I fell in love with you the first time I saw you."

"Impossible." She wrinkled her nose. "You thought I was a liar and a thief."

"Didn't change the situation." He framed her face between his hands. "Just made me worry about things for a while."

He kissed her, long and deep.

They were sitting in her living room looking out into the gardens. She had poured a shot of the fancy orange-flavored liqueur Leonora had given her on Mother's Day for both of them. The television was still on but she had turned down the sound an hour ago.

She and Herb had both seen the late-night movie when it first aired forty years earlier. It was a romantic comedy. They knew how it ended. Neither of them had lived lives that had even remotely resembled the Hollywood version, but that was okay.

The older you got, Gloria figured, the more you understood that reality and fiction didn't have to match up. They were mirror images, not exact duplicates. They each had a place. Both were important. But they were not the same. A smart person didn't try to make one into the other. That way lay disaster.

She checked her ankles and was pleased. They were hardly swollen at all tonight. In fact, they looked pretty good, if she did say so herself.

She glanced at Herb. He looked pretty good tonight, too. Relaxed. A little younger, maybe. More energetic, at any rate. She was feeling rather lively herself.

"What do you think?" she said. "Are they in bed yet?"

Herb checked his watch. "Damn well better be. If they aren't, you can't hold me responsible. An advice columnist can only do so much. After that, it's up to the advisees to take action."

She thought about the humming excitement she had

heard in Leonora's voice that afternoon when they had discussed what her *friends* would wear to the reception.

"I think she's in love, Herb. For real this time. Not trying to fake it the way she did with Kyle Delling just because it looks right on the surface."

Herb raised his glass in a small salute. "To love."

They both drank to that.

Herb checked his watch again. "Speaking of getting to bed, we'd better get a move on. I took that little blue pill forty minutes ago. The effects don't last forever you know."

"Nothing lasts forever, Herb. That's why you've got to reach out and grab life when it comes along."

"I know. What do you say we go grab us a little right now?"

She smiled. "You're a real smooth talker, Herb."

She put down her glass and pushed herself up out of the chair.

She didn't use the walker. Herb took her arm to steady her.

Together they walked into the shadowed bedroom.

"About our deal," Herb said sometime later.

She chuckled. "Relax, you've finally managed to sleep your way to the top, Herb. Your name and photo go on the column tomorrow."

Chapter Twenty-two

The phone in the librarian's office warbled at a quarter past three on Monday afternoon. It was the first time it had rung all day. Leonora started at the unexpected sound. She did not like the unpleasant jolt of adrenaline.

She had told herself that the strange, nervy sensation was a direct result of the stress she had been under in the past few days and the fact that she'd had the mirror dream again last night. But now she wondered if it had something to do with the eerie gloom that had descended on Mirror House this afternoon.

She and Roberta were the only ones here. In the wake of the activity that had prevailed downstairs for the past few days, the brooding silence that welled up from the first floor had a hollow quality as if it came from a distant place that was not of this world.

The phone rang a second time. Leonora closed the little treatise on the use of mirrors as symbols in art that she had been examining and got to her feet. She went into the small office and scooped up the receiver.

"Hello?"

"Awfully quiet around here today, isn't it?" Roberta said.

Leonora relaxed a little. "Downright spooky."

"It's always this way the Monday after alumni weekend. I just made some coffee. Thought I'd take a short break. Care to join me?"

The thought of drinking Roberta's coffee made her cringe, but she needed something to help her shake off this edgy feeling.

"Thanks. I'll be right down."

She hung up the phone and walked quickly out into the shadows of the hall. When she started down the main staircase, the somber gloom from the ground floor seemed to rise up to meet her in a relentless tide. Mirror House was a different world today. The glitz and glamour that had prevailed on Saturday night had vanished. The time-warped quality was back.

The sensation of impending dread grew stronger as she made her way down the stairs. She was conscious of having to push herself to go down the last few steps.

This was crazy. What was wrong with her? Maybe she was coming down with something.

She needed that cup of coffee, she thought. She craved the company of another human being even more than the stimulant.

The glow of the computer screen glinted off the lenses of Deke's glasses. His fingers moved over the keys with the virtuosity of a wizard crafting sorcery.

"Okay, I'm in," he muttered. He did not look up from the screen. "I've got Kern's banking records. Now what?"

Thomas turned away from the window and walked back to the desk. He looked over Deke's shoulder.

"Now we search for some kind of pattern," he said. "Whatever Elissa Kern found that made her think her father was making blackmail payments to Rhodes."

"I still don't get the point of this search. Stovall told us that Kern was being blackmailed by Rhodes. It's old news. Kern and Rhodes are both dead."

"I'm just trying to tie up some loose ends."

"What loose ends?" Deke sounded exasperated. "It's finished."

"Did I give you a hard time when you were acting like an obsessive nutcase because you wanted answers about Bethany?"

"Yes, you did, as a matter of fact. I seem to recall a lot of lectures on the subject of letting go of the past and getting on with my life. And then there were all those hints that I should talk to a shrink."

"So now I'm the obsessive nutcase. Humor me, okay?"

"Whatever you say." Deke went back to work on the keyboard. "But I gotta tell you, I had planned to spend today in bed working on my yoga exercises."

Roberta was standing behind her desk, stacking framed photographs in one of the three cartons arrayed in front of her. When she saw Leonora in the doorway she looked up with a relieved smile.

I'm not the only one who has a case of the creeps today, Leonora thought. The oppressive atmosphere had affected Roberta, too.

"Oh, good, you're here," Roberta said. "Please sit down." She put aside the photograph she had been about to stuff into the carton with evident relief, and crossed the room to the table that held the coffee things. She picked up the pot. "Thanks for joining me."

"I'm glad you called me downstairs. I wasn't getting much done, anyway. This place feels even stranger than usual today."

"I agree. And I'm used to Mirror House." Roberta poured the coffee into two cups. "Maybe it wasn't such a good idea to come in and pack up my office today. So many years and so many memories. But it has to be done. I just wanted to get it over with, I suppose."

"I can understand how strange it must feel to leave an office you had occupied for a long time." Leonora sat down in one of the padded leather chairs and glanced at the stack of framed photographs on the desk. "Almost as bad as packing up a house where one had lived for several years."

"I'll let you in on a small secret." Roberta set down the pot. "This office has felt more like home to me over the years than my own house. That was true even when my husband was alive, I'm afraid. Cream or sugar?"

"Neither, thanks."

"Oh, that's right. I forgot. You drink yours black." Roberta picked up the two cups and carried them back to the desk. She put one in front of Leonora and then sat down across from her.

Leonora took a tiny swallow of the coffee. The bitter brew tasted more burnt than it had the last time, but who was she to judge? She hated coffee. She could manage half a cup at least.

Roberta was not a small woman. Her chair groaned beneath her weight when she sat back in it. She drank her coffee with a reflective air. "Maybe we should both go home early today," she said. "There's really nothing that can't wait until tomorrow."

"That might not be such a bad idea," Leonora said. She looked at the cartons on the desk. "Where are you going to hang all those photos?"

Roberta regarded the pictures, head slightly tipped to one side. "I'm not sure yet. I think the kitchen wall would be a good place for them. But it won't be the same. Nothing will ever be the same. Even when you think you've prepared for change, it always seems to come as a shock, doesn't it?"

Leonora thought about how her own world had changed in the past few days. "Yes. But some shocks are good for the system."

"You may be right." Roberta sipped some of her own coffee and studied one of the photographs with a pensive expression. "It's too bad that George didn't live long enough to go on this cruise. He would have loved it."

"George?"

"My late husband. He was a tenured professor in chemistry here at Eubanks." The lines deepened around Roberta's mouth. "He was the stereotypical absent-minded academic. Lived for his work. If he'd had his way he would never have left his lab. He died there, you know. I often think that he would have wanted it that way. Sometimes I wonder—"

The sound of footsteps in the hall interrupted her. She looked up sharply. Leonora jumped, too. They had both assumed they were alone together in the mansion.

"Probably one of the student assistants." Roberta put down her cup and pushed herself up out of the chair. "I made it clear that no one was expected to come in today. But you know students. You have to tell them everything at least three times before they bother to remember it. Excuse me. I'll be right back."

She circled the desk and went out into the hall, pulling the door closed behind her.

Her muffled voice was just barely audible through the panel.

"Julie, what are you doing here? I told you that none of the students were supposed to come in today..."

Alone in the office Leonora looked down at her unfinished coffee. She had wanted the warmth and the caffeine, but the taste was so bad it wasn't worth the effort of trying to drink it. She did not think that she could manage another sip of the dreadful stuff. But she did not want to be rude.

She contemplated the potted plant in the corner for a few seconds and made her decision. The palm looked healthy enough to withstand a dose of caffeine.

A wave of dizziness crashed through her when she got to her feet. Alarmed, she grabbed the edge of the desk. She wondered if she was about to faint. But that was ridiculous. She had never fainted in her life.

The disorienting sensation passed. When the room steadied around her she walked slowly and carefully to the palm and dumped the remainder of the coffee into the pot. It vanished into the dark soil.

When she turned around, the room wavered a little at the edges. The angles straightened in the next instant, but she did not find that reassuring. Something was wrong with her. She was ill.

She had to get home. Maybe call a doctor. No, that wouldn't work. She didn't know any doctors here in Wing Cove. She would call Thomas.

Yes. That was the answer. Call Thomas. He would take her to a doctor.

First things first. She needed her car keys. They were in her satchel. The satchel was in the library.

Okay. That was easy. Go upstairs to the library and get the satchel.

Step One, go through the door.

What was it about that door, anyway? Then she remembered what Roberta had said that first day when she had given her a tour of Mirror House.

My door is always open.

But Roberta's door was closed now. She noticed that an antique mirror hung on the back.

It was an eight-sided, convex mirror framed in heavily worked, badly tarnished silver. Dragons, griffins and sphinxes cavorted and writhed at the edges of the dark glass. A phoenix decorated the top.

Late eighteenth century, probably, Leonora thought. She was becoming a real expert, thanks to all the time she had spent in the library upstairs.

She had seen this mirror illustrated in some book. She just couldn't quite remember the title.

The room wobbled a bit.

She moved unsteadily to the desk and leaned on it, waiting for the dizziness to pass.

When the world was stable again she found herself gazing into the old mirror.

And quite suddenly, through the growing fog that was creeping through her mind, she remembered where she had seen a picture of this particular mirror.

Page eighty-one of the *Catalog of Antique Looking Glasses in the Mirror House Collection.*

It occurred to her that when Roberta was seated at her desk with her door closed the old looking glass would reflect her image.

The face of a killer.

That was the message that Bethany, hallucinating wildly from the effects of the drugs, had tried to leave behind when she had circled the drawing in the catalog.

The room blurred again.

Drugged. She had been drugged. Just like Bethany. Just like Meredith.

She breathed deeply. The lines and angles of the room steadied again. She walked very carefully around the desk. With luck Julie would still be here. She would ask her to drive her home. Roberta would not be able to stop both of them.

She did not look into the depths of the convex mirror when she reached the door. She was afraid of what she would see. She got the door open and went out into the hall.

There was no sign of Julie or Roberta, but she heard voices somewhere in the distance, coming from the front hall. Too far away. She could not understand what was being said.

But there was no mistaking the faint sound of the mansion's front door closing.

Julie was gone. Despair threatened to freeze her right where she stood. It would be so much simpler to just sit down here in the hall and close her eyes.

You can't sleep yet.

Of course she couldn't just sit down and go to sleep. What was wrong with her? She had to get out of here. She had only swallowed a few sips of that drugged coffee, not the whole cup. She could do this.

Think.

Okay. There would be no help from Julie. That meant she had to get herself out of here.

Keys. She needed the keys to her car.

She pushed through the panic and started down the corridor toward the main staircase.

Footsteps echoed in the distance. Roberta was returning to her office.

Hurry. Need to hurry. The library. Keys in the library.

She was on the staircase now. One foot in front of the other.

The risers were uneven. Some steps were too high.

Others were too low. She gripped the banister with both hands and used it the way a mountain climber used ropes to haul herself up the face of a steep cliff.

"Leonora?" Roberta's voice came from downstairs. "Where are you? I see you finished all of the coffee. You must be feeling quite woozy by now."

Time was running out. Roberta was searching for her.

She made it to the top of the staircase, but she had to stop for a few seconds to get her bearings. The hall of dark mirrors had become a wormhole, a twisting path into another universe. Panic injected a dose of adrenaline into her bloodstream.

Forget the wormhole. Don't think about the world on the other side of the mirror. You're not going there. You're just here to get your car keys.

"It's all right, Leonora. I'll take you home."

The killer was on the staircase now.

She staggered forward along the shifting hall. A reflection flickered in one of the dark looking glasses on her left. Her own face? Or one of the trapped ghosts laughing at her?

No such thing as a ghost in a mirror. You're a trained librarian. You don't believe in ghosts. And you didn't drink all of the damned coffee. Keep moving. You stop, you die.

Resolutely she kept her eyes on the floor, counting doorways, not looking in any of the mirrors. The library was the fourth door on the left. She remembered that very clearly.

"I'm sure the hallucinations are very bad by now, Leonora." Roberta spoke from the top of the staircase. "I gave you a very large dose and the drug acts very swiftly. My husband invented it shortly before he died, you know."

Don't listen. Count doors.

"Dear George. He was really quite brilliant. But he never saw the full potential of his creation. I did, of course. I had to get rid of him. But first, I made him write down the formula. Quite simple, really, when you have the correct ingredients. Why, you can whip it up in your own kitchen."

She tried to tune out Roberta's voice. She had to concentrate on counting doorways.

Number two.

Number three.

Desperation turned her stomach to ice. The library was too far away. She would never make it before Roberta caught up with her.

She staggered past the third door. It was getting harder and harder to avoid looking into the mirrors. And she was getting tired. So tired.

An image glittered briefly in the gilded looking glass on the right. Unable to resist, she looked into its depths. She could not make out the reflection in the dark glass, but she heard words in her head. Words from a dream.

You can't sleep yet.

Car keys.

What good would it do to get her keys? She could never get past Roberta. She might as well just sit down here in the corridor and wait for the end.

No. She couldn't do that. She had a date for dinner with Thomas.

The thought sent another surge of adrenaline through her, knocking back some of the drug's effects.

"The drug can be made in various strengths. The weaker versions create amazing hallucinations and cause a person to be quite suggestible. Stronger versions also produce hallucinations, but not for long. One gets very drowsy, very quickly."

Keep going. Keep moving.

"I gave you the strong dose, of course. The same dose that I gave to Bethany Walker and Meredith Spooner."

She put one hand on the wall and turned her head. Roberta was coming toward her through the shadows. She had something in her hand.

A gun.

"You killed Rhodes," Leonora whispered. The words were thick and cumbersome in her mouth. "You were the one Thomas and Deke saw running away that night."

"Ah, yes, Mr. Rhodes. Such a handsome man. He was the one who came up with a name for my hallucinogen. Smoke and Mirrors. I thought it was very creative. He said a good name was essential for proper marketing. Mirror House gave him the idea, I believe."

"How did he ... how did he know about you? And the drug?"

"He figured out that I was mixing up the drugs the night I pushed Bethany off that bluff."

"How did he know that you killed her?"

"I was a trifle careless, I must admit. Alex was out running rather late in the evening. He passed by Mirror House just as I was getting Bethany into her car. He knew something was wrong. He followed me. Watched me push her off the cliff. The next day I very carefully planted the rumors of Bethany's drug use. And Alex put it all together."

"He tried to blackmail you?"

"No, no, dear. He offered to form a partnership. I was the manufacturer and supplier. He was the middleman who actually sold the product. He'd had experience in that line, you see, and I had none. Most of his transactions were with out-of-town clients, of course. Wing Cove is such a small community. He feared that if he sold too much locally, others would soon figure out that he was the source. But he couldn't resist experimenting with it from time to time, especially on some of his female clients."

"Why...why did you kill him if the partnership worked?"

"It was a lucrative arrangement for both of us, but when everything started to fall apart I knew I had to tidy up before I left town. Mr. Rhodes knew too much about me. I couldn't let him live, now could I?"

"Why...why did you kill Meredith Spooner?"

"Because for some reason that I was never able to determine, she grew extremely curious about the circumstances of Sebastian Eubanks's death." Roberta frowned. "She somehow managed to link it with Bethany's suicide. I simply don't understand how she put it all together. But that is neither here nor there now, is it?"

"Why did you feed that drug to me? You were in the clear after you shot Alex. No one was even suspicious of you."

Roberta's hand tightened around the gun. "I really couldn't leave town without punishing you, Leonora. I blame you for stirring things up here in Wing Cove. You very nearly ruined everything. You must pay for causing me so much trouble."

"Why are you okay?" Leonora whispered. "You drank the coffee, too. I saw you drink it."

Roberta chuckled. "The drug wasn't in the coffee. It comes in the form of a powder, you see. I merely sprinkled a little in the bottom of your cup before I poured. It dissolves instantly."

There were other questions she needed to ask, but she couldn't do it now. Time to prioritize. The first job was to survive. She had that dinner date with Thomas tonight. Couldn't be late.

For a very important date.

Oh, damn. She was losing it fast here. Get a grip.

She realized she was sliding down the wall. Fear lanced through her. She closed her eyes, summoned all of her will and straightened. She had to plant both palms on the wall to hold herself upright.

When she opened her eyes she found herself gazing into another dark looking glass. It was framed in gilded wood.

You can't sleep yet.

She reached out with both hands. Gripped the old mirror and lifted it off its hook. It was heavy.

"Oh, my, whatever do you want with that?" Roberta said. "Put it down. We must be on our way."

She held on to the mirror, never looking away from the nearly opaque reflective surface. "Where are we going?"

"Why, to your car, of course."

"So that I can fall asleep at the wheel the way...the way Meredith did?"

"Sleep is what you want most now, isn't it?"

"I can't sleep yet."

"Put the mirror down, Leonora."

She ignored the order. Staring into the mirror as though transfixed by her own image, she turned and staggered into the library.

Roberta would not shoot her here unless she felt she had no choice, she thought. Blood in the library would be hard to explain.

"The hallucinations must be very, very bad." Roberta came to stand in the doorway. "Don't you want to sleep now, Leonora? You should be very sleepy. Perhaps I didn't get the mix quite right this time. It is unpredictable and I was in something of a hurry when I made up this batch. What with getting rid of Osmond Kern and Mr. Rhodes and handling all the details of the alumni reception, things have been quite hectic around here lately."

"Kern. How did you manage his suicide?"

"Oh, that was no trouble at all. He was already quite drunk when I phoned him and told him that something important had come up and that he had to meet me at the boathouse. When I gave him some coffee to drink, he didn't hesitate at all. Probably thought it would sober him up. But the effects of the drug are intensified with alcohol. I got him into the boat, took him out a ways into the Sound and pushed him overboard. Then I went back to shore and set the boat free."

"Thomas will know. If you kill me, he'll find you."

"By the time the authorities have finished investigating your accident, I will be long gone, Leonora. A new name, a new identity, a new life. I have been planning it for several months. It is all in place."

"No."

Leonora dashed the heavy mirror against the metal upright of the nearest bookcase. The old glass fractured and shattered, breaking into a dozen tinkling, screaming shards. The jagged pieces of mirror bounced and skittered on the floor at her feet.

"Now, see what you've done." Roberta chuckled. "Seven years' bad luck, I'm afraid. But the good news is that you won't live long enough to worry about it."

Leonora crouched slowly, cautiously, one hand clutching the edge of a bookshelf to keep herself from toppling forward.

"Oh, good, it's finally hitting you," Roberta said. "Come along now. On your feet. Don't worry, you'll be able to sleep soon enough."

Leonora said nothing. She was too busy staring at the glittering shards that littered the floor.

"We've wasted enough time." Roberta came toward her down the aisle formed by the bookcases. "You and I must take a little trip. Get up, Leonora. Do you hear me? Get up right now."

She stayed crouched near the floor, looking at the fragmented images of herself in the shards. The bits and pieces of her reflections gave a whole new meaning to the words *pull yourself together*, she thought.

She started to giggle.

"Stop it." Roberta transferred the gun to her left hand, reached down, grasped Leonora's upper arm. She was a large, strongly built woman. She did not expect to encounter any resistance from her drugged victim.

Leonora made no effort to resist. She summoned all the strength and willpower that she had left and lurched to her feet.

Simultaneously she clawed at Roberta's face with her right hand.

Roberta saw the long, jagged piece of broken mirror clutched in Leonora's fingers. She shrieked in reflexive fear and fell back, putting up both arms in an instinctive move to protect her eyes.

Leonora raked her glass claw downward, not caring what part of Roberta's anatomy she struck. The shard bit into flesh.

A keening scream reverberated in the library.

Blood spouted. Not all of it was Roberta's. Leonora felt the sting of glass slicing through the skin of her palm.

The gun fell from Roberta's fingers. She shrieked again.

Leonora raised her bloody hand and tried another slashing swing. She missed this time because Roberta was reeling back down the aisle, her arms still raised to defend her face.

Leonora dropped the shard and grabbed the gun with both hands. She swung around. The aisle of books looped and dipped like a roller coaster. She stumbled toward the far end.

She knew now that she could not get to her keys, let

alone try to drive a car. But if she could get as far as the concealed flight of steps that led to the third floor she might be able to barricade herself inside the narrow passage until help arrived. The entrance was just around the corner out in the hall. All she had to do was stay awake.

A dark figure blotted out the light in the doorway.

"Leonora," Thomas said.

A glorious sense of relief flooded through her. She lurched into his outstretched arms.

"Knew you'd come," she whispered.

She was vaguely aware of Deke in the hallway. Claws clicked on the wooden flooring. Wrench.

Behind her, Roberta screamed in raw rage. Leonora managed to turn her head.

Roberta rushed toward the door, a huge chunk of mirror clutched in her hands.

"Shit," Deke said, "she's gone crazy. Get out of her way."

"Wrench." Thomas pulled Leonora out of the doorway, back into the hall, and motioned with the flat of his hand.

Wrench flashed through the opening, utterly silent, a sleek, fast predator doing what came naturally.

Inside the library, Roberta screamed.

There was no place to run. Leonora heard a crash. Books tumbled from the shelves. A body hit the floor hard.

She raised her head from Thomas's shoulder and looked into the library. Roberta sprawled on her back in one of the aisles, sobbing in fear, her bleeding arm thrown across her face. Wrench stood guard over her, the wolf in his genes etched in every line of his taut body.

"I thought you said he was a reincarnated miniature poodle," Leonora whispered.

"Must have been a poodle with attitude," Thomas said. "Hell, you're bleeding."

She wanted to smile, but she was so tired. He picked her up in his arms. It felt wonderful.

When he swung around to carry her toward the staircase she caught a glimpse of a reflection in the strange mirror that produced the double images.

For just an instant she thought she saw a familiar face, not her own, smiling at her from the other side of the antique looking glass.

> *You can go to sleep now, he'll be there when you wake up.*
> *We're going to name our first daughter after you.*
> *I know. Thanks. Good-bye, sister.*
> *Good-bye, Meredith.*

The hallucination in the mirror vanished.

Chapter Twenty-three

The next day they gathered together in Thomas's living room. A cheerful fire blazed. The hearth tiles glowed in all their splendor. Deke and Cassie sat side by side on the sofa. Their knees touched.

Leonora lounged in one of the recliners, feet stretched out toward the flames. She had bandages on her palms and she still felt wan and washed out, but the stuff they had given her in the emergency room had gotten rid of most of the drug in her system. She was feeling much better, all things considered.

Thomas occupied the other recliner. Wrench napped on the floor.

Ed Stovall sat very straight in an armchair. He did not take out his notebook. This was supposed to be a private conversation, he had explained. Off the record.

"I'm no shrink, but I think it's safe to say that Roberta Brinks must have started out warped and then got down-right nutzoid over the years," Thomas said. "Just your ordinary, garden-variety sociopath. The kind of freak no one even notices until after she's murdered a few folks."

"You still haven't explained how you and Deke realized I might be in major trouble yesterday afternoon," Leonora said.

"Thomas wanted to run down a few loose details," Deke replied. He rested one hand on Cassie's knee.

"I just wanted to know for sure who was blackmailing whom." Thomas steepled his fingers. "When Deke got into Rhodes's bank records he discovered that a couple of large transactions had been made during the past year. They were credited to a numbered account in an offshore bank. At first we assumed they were the profits Rhodes had made from blackmailing Osmond Kern."

"But just to be on the safe side, Thomas had me check Kern's bank records, too," Deke continued. "He wanted to make sure the amount of the blackmail payments matched."

Cassie frowned. "I take it they didn't?"

"No," Thomas said. "In fact, we found no large transactions at all in Kern's account. But we discovered a lot of smaller payments going into that same offshore account. They transferred like clockwork on the first of every month."

"We followed a hunch and went upstream in Kern's bank records," Deke said. "Those payments stretched back for years. The offshore account number didn't appear until three years ago, though. Before that the money went into a bank in California. The account was in the name of a trust, but we were able to get a social security number off some tax records."

"Roberta Brinks?" Leonora asked.

"Yep." Thomas put a hand on top of Wrench's head. "Osmond Kern paid blackmail, all right. For nearly thirty years."

"But to Roberta Brinks, not Alex Rhodes," Cassie concluded.

"Rhodes's two large payments into Roberta's offshore account this year had nothing to do with blackmail. They were to cover the cost of the two shipments of drugs that he bought from her," Ed said.

"But as soon as we saw the thirty years' worth of payments to Roberta Brinks," Thomas said, "we knew the situation was a lot more complicated than everyone assumed."

Leonora rested her head against the backs of the cushions. "Because it was clear that Osmond Kern had been paying blackmail to Roberta since shortly after the death of Sebastian Eubanks. And there was only one logical reason why he would do such a thing."

Ed nodded his head once. "Roberta Brinks knew that he had murdered Eubanks and that he had stolen the algorithm."

Roberta had babbled freely when Ed Stovall had arrived at Mirror House to take charge.

Thirty years ago she had been a grad student in the English department. She had struggled hard to put herself through school. In addition to teaching classes, she had taken on a part-time job working for Sebastian Eubanks.

"He was so paranoid at that point that he wouldn't allow any math or science majors into the mansion," Deke said. "But he figured an English Lit major wouldn't understand any of his work even if she did see some of it."

"Always a mistake to underestimate the liberal arts crowd," Leonora said.

Deke nodded. "You can say that again."

"Roberta was there the night Kern came to see Eubanks," Leonora said. "Kern didn't see her, but she witnessed the quarrel and the shooting."

"What did they fight over?" Cassie asked.

Ed looked at her. "As Andrew Grayson said, Kern knew enough about Eubanks's work to recognize its potential. He claimed that, because he and Eubanks had collaborated for a while, he had a right to have his name attached to the algorithm. He demanded that it be published under both of their names. Eubanks didn't want to publish at all. He had convinced himself that the algorithm was only the first step to more important work. He pulled out a gun. There was a struggle. Eubanks died. Afterward, Kern was stunned and confused. Roberta took charge. She told him she would take care of everything."

"And that's just what she did," Thomas said. "She got him out of the mansion and drove him home. The next day she went to see him in his office. He was still badly shaken. Panicky. She pointed out that there was no reason not to publish the algorithm under his own name. It would make him rich and famous. Secure his academic reputation forever."

"And Kern went for it," Deke said grimly. "But when the paper was accepted for publication, Roberta paid him another visit. This time she laid out the terms of the deal. She would protect him and his reputation as long as he paid blackmail. She protected herself by putting an incriminating account of Eubanks's death and copies of his early notes on the development of the algorithm in a safe-deposit box."

Cassie nodded. "In other words, if anything happened to her, Kern would also go down in flames."

Thomas scratched Wrench's ears. "In the end, the college administration was so eager to keep things quiet that neither Kern nor Roberta were even questioned. Things went smoothly for nearly thirty years. Kern got rich and famous. Roberta dropped out of the graduate program and married a chemist."

Leonora sighed. "Another ABD type gone bad."

Ed frowned. "ABD?"

"All But Dissertation," Leonora explained. "A little academic joke." .

Ed did not smile.

Thomas cleared his throat. "Roberta decided to forego a career in English Lit in favor of running Mirror House and organizing alumni events. Meanwhile she built up her private retirement fund with Kern's blackmail payments."

"And then she struck it rich a second time when her husband developed a hallucinogenic drug a few years ago," Leonora said. "Ever the opportunist, she saw the possibilities immediately. But she knew nothing about dealing illegal drugs. She was lucky she wasn't caught running her little experiments on some of the students."

"Meanwhile Bethany was deep into her work on her Mirror Theory," Deke said. "In the course of her research she came across notes that convinced her that Eubanks had done the early work on the algorithm, not Kern. She confronted Kern, demanding an explanation. Kern panicked. As soon as Bethany left his office, he called Roberta."

"Who understood immediately that Bethany's work might expose Kern and thereby ruin her retirement plan," Thomas said. "So she invited Bethany into her office, served her some of the drugged coffee and then arranged the so-called suicide."

"But in those last moments before the drug overwhelmed her," Deke said, "Bethany managed to leave behind some clues to her killer's identity. She must have been hallucinating wildly, but there were mirrors all around her and she had been thinking in metaphorical and mathematical terms about mirrors for several months. She was no doubt beyond being able to write anything legible. So she picked up the catalog of antique mirrors and circled the picture of the looking glass that reflected her killer. Then she hid it together with the clippings behind the catalog in the library."

"Alex Rhodes witnessed Bethany's so-called suicide," Ed said. "He figured out that Roberta Brinks was the source of the drugs and he formed the partnership with her."

"All went well for a while," Deke said. "Because no one was paying any attention to the crazy Walker brothers and their demands for another investigation."

"I wouldn't say that," Cassie offered thoughtfully. "The fact that you were pushing for answers was what inspired Roberta to start those rumors of Bethany's drug use. She thought it would serve as a simple, believable answer that would put to rest any murder theories."

"But I didn't buy it," Deke said.

"No," Leonora said. "That must have made her nervous. Then, six months later, Meredith arrived on the scene to start her endowment scam. She got involved with Thomas for a while and in the process learned that Deke had major questions about the circumstances surrounding Bethany's so-called suicide."

"Meredith and I weren't *involved*," Thomas said evenly. "We had a few casual dates, that's all."

"Meredith and Thomas stopped seeing each other after a few casual dates," Leonora said smoothly, "and Meredith went on with her project to rip off the endowment fund. She had a few *casual dates* with Alex Rhodes, probably because she figured he would be a good source of local information. She found out he was dealing drugs and stopped seeing him."

"At some point she found the catalog and the envelope full of newspaper clippings," Thomas said. "She guessed that Deke and I would want to see them. But she didn't want to jeopardize her own scheme, which was nearly completed. So she put the clippings and the book into a safe-deposit box."

"And then she made her fatal mistake," Deke said. "She had worked with Roberta Brinks for six months. Long enough to know that Roberta had been around at the time of the Eubanks murder. So she tried to pump her for information. As soon as she started asking questions, she was doomed."

"Roberta pretended she didn't know anything about the murder except the old gossip, but she got very nervous," Leonora said. "First, Bethany had become suspicious and now, only a few months later, another woman was probing into the past. She waited until Meredith had left Wing Cove. Then, one day, she contacted her via email saying she had learned something very interesting about the old Eubanks murder."

"She met Meredith in Los Angeles. Had dinner with her, fed her the drugs and then arranged the accident," Leonora said. "When the news of the funeral reached Wing Cove, she learned that Deke was trying to weave new conspiracy theories."

Ed nodded soberly. "So she started the second round of rumors, hoping to deflect any serious murder investigation."

"In the end, it was the fact that none of us believed the rumors that ruined her scheme," Thomas said.

They all sat in silence for a while, letting the details settle into place.

Eventually, Ed pushed himself up from the chair. "Appreciate the conversation, folks. I'll be on my way. Got a lot of paperwork waiting for me."

Thomas got up to see him to the door. He took Ed's jacket out of the closet.

Ed studied the tile work in the hall with an approving

eye while he zipped up his jacket. "First time I've seen this place since you bought it, Walker. You did a real fine job with the remodeling."

"Thanks," Thomas said.

"Let me know if you decide to sell," Ed said. "Elissa Kern and I will be getting married in the spring. We're looking for a place. Elissa doesn't want to live in her father's old house and my apartment is too small."

"I'll keep that in mind, Ed."

Ed went out onto the porch. Thomas closed the door and went back into the front room. Leonora looked at him. He spread his hands and smiled.

"I told you my houses always find the right owners," he said.

"What about us?" she asked. "Where are we going to live?"

"I don't know yet." He looked around. "But it won't be here. At least not for long."

"Why not? I love this place."

He grinned. "It's not big enough. We need more room. For the kids."

Chapter Twenty-four

A week later Leonora sat in front of the fire with Thomas and Wrench. There was a bowl of freshly made popcorn on the table. Wrench was eating most of the popcorn.

"Something I wanted to give you before we pick up your grandmother and Herb at the airport tomorrow," Thomas said. He handed her a small box.

She studied it closely. "Very tiny tools?"

"Not exactly."

She fed Wrench the last of the popcorn, wiped her hands on a napkin and opened the box.

A ring sparkled against dark velvet.

Happiness shimmered through her. "The answer is yes."

He grinned. "I haven't asked the question yet."

"Doesn't matter. The answer is still yes."

"I like a woman who knows her own mind."

"I've never been so sure of anything in my life."

"Neither have I," he said.

He kissed her.

The thing about Thomas Walker, she thought, was that you never had to worry about illusions or false reflections in a mirror. Thomas was for real.

And so was his love.

*Turn the page for a sneak preview of
Jayne Ann Krentz's new novel,*

LIGHT IN SHADOW

Coming soon from G. P. Putnam's Sons

The walls screamed at her.

"Oh, damn," Zoe Luce whispered. She halted in the doorway of the empty bedroom and stared at the white walls. *Not now. Not today. Not this time. I really need this job.*

The walls sobbed. Terror pulsed through layers of Sheetrock and the fresh coat of stark white paint that covered it. The silent shrieks ricocheted off the floor and ceiling.

She put her fingers to her temples in a purely instinctive, utterly useless gesture. She squeezed her eyes shut, bracing herself against the ragged bolts of icy lightning that were shooting through her and pooling into a glacial pond somewhere in the vicinity of her stomach.

Davis Mason had followed her so closely down the hall that he was only a pace behind her when she came to a sudden stop. He bumped awkwardly against her.

"Oops, sorry." He caught his balance. "I wasn't paying attention."

"My fault." With what she hoped was an unobtrusive movement, she eased out of the doorway and back into the hall. Things were much better out here. She could cope. She gave Davis what she hoped was a bright, assured smile. It wasn't easy, what with the muffled cries still leaking out of the bedroom.

She wanted out of this house. Fast. Whatever had happened in the bedroom had been bad.

"Hey." Davis touched her shoulder lightly. "Are you all right, Zoe?"

She gave him another shaky smile. It was relatively easy to smile at Davis. He had elegant lines and clean styling with just the right touch of roguish flair. If he'd been a car, he would have been a sleek, European roadster. Judging by the spacious home, the hand-tailored shirt and trousers and the onyx-and-diamond ring he wore, he was also wealthy. In short, she thought sadly, until that moment, she had considered him the ideal client.

Everything had changed now, of course.

"Yes, I'm fine." She did a little on-the-spot deep breathing using the techniques she had learned in her self-defense class. Summoning up her teacher's instructions, she sought the calm, stable center that was supposed to be somewhere deep inside her. Unfortunately she had not yet mastered that part of the program. All she could feel was a bad case of the jitters coming on.

"What's wrong?" Davis was looking seriously concerned now.

"Just the start of a headache," Zoe said. "I often get one when I forget to eat breakfast."

The lies came so easily these days. But, then, she'd had a lot of practice. Too bad she wasn't yet clever enough to convince herself, she thought. A little self-delusion would be very welcome right now.

Davis watched her intently for a few seconds and then he relaxed. "Missed your morning shot of caffeine?"

"And food. It's a blood-sugar thing. I should know better." Feeling an urgent need to change the topic of conversation, she looked back into the bedroom and blurted out the first thing that came into her mind. "What happened to the bed?"

"The bed?"

They both looked at the large, empty stretch of uncovered section of hardwood floor between two massive, Mission-style bedside tables.

Zoe swallowed uneasily. "The rest of the residence is fully furnished," she said. "I couldn't help but notice that there's no bed in here."

"She took it," Davis said grimly.

"Your ex-wife?"

He sighed. "She loved that damned bed. Spent months shopping for it. I swear, it meant more to her than I did. When she left, it was about the only thing she insisted on taking with her in addition to her personal stuff."

"I see."

"You know how it is in a divorce. Sometimes the biggest fights are over the smallest, dumbest things."

Whatever else it had been, Zoe thought, the missing bed had not been small.

"I understand."

Davis searched her face. "Headache getting worse?"

"It'll be all right once I've had lunch and a cup of coffee," she assured him.

"Tell you what. You've seen the rest of the house. I'm sure you've got the general picture. Why don't we take a break and get something to eat at the club? It will give us a chance to talk over your initial impressions."

The thought of eating made her stomach churn. She knew from experience that she would not be able to keep any food down until the chills stopped. That could take a while. This had been a really bad experience and it had caught her totally off guard.

It was her own fault. She knew better than to enter a room so recklessly. But she had been caught up in her plans for the interior, completely focused, and the rest of the spacious residence had seemed so new, so *clean*. She simply had not been expecting trouble and, as often happened, she had paid the price.

"I'd love to join you for lunch but I'm afraid I'll have to take a rain check." She made a show of glancing at her watch. "I've got another appointment this afternoon and I need to prepare for it."

Davis looked hesitant. "If you're sure—"

"I'm afraid so." She tried to inject a note of apology into her tone. "I really do have to run, and you're right, I've seen all I need to see for now." *And sensed far more than I ever wanted to know, thank you very much.* "I've got the floor plan you gave me earlier. I'll make some copies and do some sketches that will give you an idea of what I have in mind."

"I'd appreciate the drawings." Davis glanced into the bedroom and shook his head somewhat ruefully. "I'll admit I'm not what you'd call a visual person. It's easier for me to grasp the concept when I can see a picture."

"It's always easier when you can look at a drawing. Hang on while I check my calendar."

She reached into her voluminous tote, one of six similar bags in different colors that she owned. Each functioned as a combination briefcase and purse. She had chosen the chartreuse-green one today because she liked the way it contrasted with her deep-violet pantsuit.

Groping in the vast depths, she pushed aside the small

camera, a sketchbook, measuring tape, a clear plastic box containing an array of colored pens and felt markers, a folder of fabric samples and the large, antique brass door-knob attached to the ring that held the keys to her apartment.

The appointment calendar was at the bottom. She hauled it up to the surface and flipped it open.

"I'll get some ideas down on paper," she said briskly, "and I'll try to have some preliminary layouts ready for you by the end of the week. What do you say we meet in my office Friday morning?"

"Friday?" Davis was clearly disappointed. "That's a week off. Do we have to wait that long? I'd like to get started as soon as possible. The truth is, this house has been damn depressing since my wife walked out."

Yeah, I'll bet it has, she thought.

"I understand," she said aloud, trying to sound sympathetic. It wasn't easy, given the fact that the fine hairs on the nape of her neck were still tingling and there were goose bumps on her arms beneath the sleeves of her light-weight jacket.

"I'm trying hard not to be bitter," Davis said. "But the divorce is costing me a bundle. Got a feeling I'll be getting bills from the lawyers for a long time."

All the available evidence indicated that Davis Mason had come out of the divorce in excellent shape, financially. From what she could see, he possessed a very expensive residence—the interiors of which he was prepared to pay her handsomely to have redesigned—as well as a membership in a pricey country club. But she did not raise those points aloud.

She was rapidly learning to be diplomatic with the newly divorced, having discovered that they constituted a hot market niche for interior designers such as herself. People emerging from shattered marriages frequently yearned to redo their living spaces as a form of therapy to help them get past the negative emotional fallout caused by the breakup.

She flipped through the pages of her calendar pretending to study her schedule. Abruptly she snapped the leather-bound volume closed with a decisive air. "I'm afraid I'm booked solid. Friday is the only day I can give you the time this project deserves. Will two o'clock work for you?"

"Looks like I don't have much choice." Davis was not pleased. He was used to getting what he wanted. "Friday it is. Didn't mean to sound so impatient. It's just that I'm very anxious to get moving on the project."

"Of course. Once you've made the decision to redesign a personal living space, there's a natural urge to rush into the job." She spoke quickly, trying to inject a professional, businesslike quality into her voice. "But redoing an entire residence is a major undertaking and mistakes at this stage can be extremely costly."

"Yeah, I found that out the hard way." He took one more look at the bedroom. "I got as far as repainting this room and realized I needed expert help. I didn't think I could go wrong just putting a coat of white paint on the walls but as soon as I finished I realized it didn't look right. I wanted to make it seem light and airy in here and instead—" He shrugged and let the sentence trail off with a *who knew* expression.

And instead, the bedroom had all the cozy ambience of an autopsy room or an embalming chamber, Zoe concluded silently. No amount of the bright Arizona sunlight dancing on the surface of the sapphire pool outside could counteract that effect. Some of the unpleasant sensation was attributable to the stark white paint but she knew that the real problem had been treated by whatever it was that had happened in this bedroom. Some things could not be covered with a coat of paint.

She also knew that Mr. Ideal Client was not consciously aware of the emotions trapped in the walls. To her everlasting regret, she had never encountered anyone else who picked up on that kind of stuff the way she did: as pure, raw energy. But she had seen enough instances of others reacting in subtle, unconscious ways to the atmosphere of a particular room to be convinced that a lot of people responded to a space on some deep, psychic level.

She had also learned the hard way to keep her inner knowledge to herself.

"You chose a stark, bright white." She took another step back, putting more distance between herself and the bedroom doorway. "I know it seems like pure white should be simple and straightforward but it is actually very difficult to work with because it reflects so much glare, especially here in the desert. It also tends to create very cold shadows when you add furnishings. Ultimately that makes for a lack of harmony and tranquility. You were right to stop painting after you finished this room."

"Knew it wasn't the right direction." Davis made a casual gesture that invited her to go ahead of him down the hall. "I have to tell you, Zoe, when I decided I needed a professional designer, I didn't really put much stock in this feng shui thing that you do."

"A lot of people have doubts about it until they experience the result."

"I knew it was trendy and all. The women at the club are really into it. When Helen Weymouth gave me your name, she went on and on about how you had completely transformed her home after she got her divorce. She said she'd been on the brink of putting it up for sale because of all the bad memories. She credits you with changing the whole atmosphere of the place."

"The Weymouth project was an interesting one." Not much farther to the front door. A couple more minutes and she would be out of here. "Mrs. Weymouth gave me a free hand."

"She advised me to do the same thing. A few months ago, after Jennifer left, I would have said that all this business of arranging the furniture to regulate the flow of negative and positive energy was way too far-out for me. But the longer I live here alone with everything just the way it was when she was here, the more I'm convinced that there may be something to your design theories."

"I don't practice one particular school of feng shui." To her horror she realized she was talking much too fast. *Act normal. You know how to do this.* "I use elements of several different approaches combined with organizational principles from other classic design traditions such as Vastu."

"What's that?"

"An ancient Hindu science that sets out principles for architecture and design. I also incorporate what I consider the most useful elements from contemporary theories of harmony and proportion. My style is really quite eclectic."

Actually, I pretty much make it up as I go along, she added silently. But clients did not like to hear that.

She walked swiftly toward the front of the house, desperate to escape into the fresh air. Now that she had been sensitized by the experience in the bedroom, she was picking up wispy tendrils of dark, unwholesome emotions from other walls in the residence. She had to get out of this place fast.

She reached the terra-cotta foyer at last. Davis was right

behind her. He opened the front door and she escaped into the reassuring warmth of the early November day.

"Are you sure you're feeling well enough to drive back to your office?" Davis asked.

Act normal.

"I've got an energy bar in the car." Another lie. Was she getting good at this or what?

"All right. Well, take care. And I'll see you on Friday."

"Right. Friday."

She gave him what she hoped was a bright, professional-looking smile, tightened her grip on the chartreuse tote and went briskly toward her car. She tried not to appear as if she was rushing away from the screaming house.

She breathed a sigh of relief when she reached the vehicle. Yanking open the door, she tossed the tote onto the passenger seat, slid behind the wheel, put on her dark glasses and fired up the engine, all in what felt like a single motion.

Her hands were still trembling. Aftershocks from the surge of adrenaline, she surmised. This wasn't the first time. She could handle it.

But she had to grip the wheel very tightly in order to steer her way out of the exclusive community. To her left was the long stretch of impossibly green fairway that served as the approach to the sixteenth hole of the Desert View Country Club. Elegant homes similar to the Mason residence were scattered artfully around the golf course.

Beyond the vivid green links stretched the rugged expanse of the Sonoran desert and low, rolling mountain foothills. The golf club community and the adjoining town of Whispering Springs were a little more than an hour's drive from Phoenix, close enough to catch some of the spillover from the tourist trade but far enough out to avoid the traffic and congestion of the city.

The harsh, dry landscape had seemed a strange and alien place to her when she had moved here a year ago but somewhere along the line her new environment had begun to feel familiar, even comfortable. She had discovered an unexpected beauty in the desert, with its spectacular sunrises and sunsets and the astounding depths of light and shadow. She had always been drawn to contrasts and there was nothing subtle about this place.

The decision to move to Whispering Springs had been a good one, she mused, but maybe she should reconsider the career move she had made at the same time. Interior design had seemed like a natural, logical way to go. After all, she had a background in the fine arts, a good, trained eye and she certainly knew how to get the feel of a living space. Best of all, she hadn't needed any additional degrees or qualifications in order to set herself up in business legally. But today's encounter was enough to give her some second thoughts.

A uniformed guard came out of a small building located at the gated entrance. The emblem on his snappy khaki jacket declared him to be an employee of Radnor Security Systems. He greeted her politely, wished her a good day and went back inside his air-conditioned sanctuary to make a note on his log.

Security was tight here in this carefully planned enclave of wealth and status but someone in the Mason residence had not benefited from it.

She waited until she was clear of the gates and on her way back toward the downtown section of Whispering Springs before she picked up her phone. She punched in the only number that she had coded into her speed dial.

Arcadia Ames answered on the third ring, giving the name of her gift shop in her low, throaty voice. "Gallery Euphoria."

Arcadia sold unique, expensive gifts to an upscale clientele but Zoe was pretty sure her friend could have sold sand here in the desert with that voice.

Arcadia was her best friend; make that her *only* friend. She had once had other friends, Zoe thought. But that was a long time ago; back when she had had a real life and had not been living in the shadows.

"It's me," Zoe said.

"What's wrong? Something happen with Mr. Ideal Client?"

"You could say that."

"He decided not to hire you after all? That idiot. But don't worry, there will be other good clients like him. The divorce rate doesn't seem to be going down very much."

"Unfortunately, Mason didn't change his mind," Zoe said evenly. "I wish he had."

"Did the creep make a pass at you?"

"He was a perfect gentleman."

"He must be rich because everybody who lives in Desert View is, by definition, a high-roller," Arcadia said patiently. "So what went wrong?"

"I think Mr. Ideal Client may have murdered his wife."

JAYNE ANN KRENTZ

LIGHT
in
SHADOW

PUTNAM

JAYNE ANN KRENTZ

Lost & Found

JOVE

PENGUIN PUTNAM INC.
Online

Your Internet gateway to a virtual environment with
hundreds of entertaining and enlightening books
from Penguin Putnam Inc.

*While you're there, get the latest buzz on
the best authors and books around—*

Tom Clancy, Patricia Cornwell, W.E.B. Griffin,
Nora Roberts, William Gibson, Robin Cook,
Brian Jacques, Catherine Coulter, Stephen King,
Ken Follett, Terry McMillan, and many more!

**Penguin Putnam Online is located at
http://www.penguinputnam.com**

PENGUIN PUTNAM NEWS

Every month you'll get an inside look at our upcoming books and new features on our site. This is an
ongoing effort to provide you with the most
up-to-date information about
our books and authors.

**Subscribe to Penguin Putnam News at
http://www.penguinputnam.com/newsletters**